D0394806

REIGN

OF

SERPENTS

**Books by Eleanor Herman
available from Harlequin TEEN**

Blood of Gods and Royals series

(in reading order)

Voice of Gods (ebook novella)
Legacy of Kings
Empire of Dust
Queen of Ashes (ebook novella)
Reign of Serpents

ELEANOR HERMAN

REIGN
OF
SERPENTS

HARLEQUIN®TEEN

ISBN-13: 978-0-373-21233-0

Reign of Serpents

Printed in U.S.A.

www.HarlequinTEEN.com

To my dear cousin, Emily Heddleson, for bringing me here.
Always remember, mermaids are real!

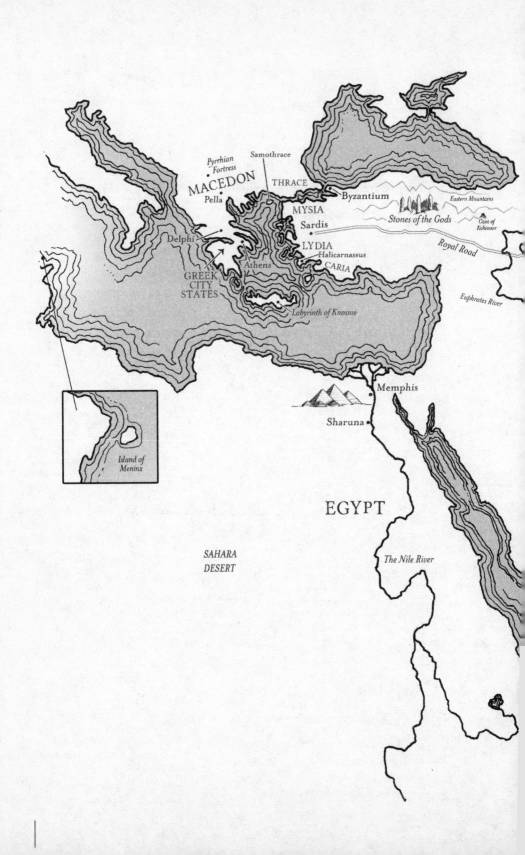

Pyrrhian
Fortress

Samothrace

MACEDON

THRACE

Pella

Byzantium

MYSIA

Eastern Mountains

Sardis

Stones of the Gods

Cave of
Kohinoor

Delphi

LYDIA
Halicarnassus

Royal Road

GREEK
CITY
STATES

Athens

CARIA

Labyrinth of Knossos

Euphrates River

Island of
Meninx

Memphis

Sharuna

EGYPT

SAHARA
DESERT

The Nile River

Tigris River

EMPIRE OF
PERSIA

Susa

*Palace of
the Great King*

Persopolis

ARABIA

ILLYRIA

DARDANIA

ERISSA

MACEDON

PELLA

MIEZA
(Temple of Nymphs)

EPIRUS

ORACLE OF
DODONA

THESSALY

AMBRACIA

GREEK
CITY STATES

Kat's Journey

DELPHI

ATHENS

CORINTH

OLYMPIA

SPARTA

CRETE

THRACE

BYZANTIUM •

TROY •

MYSIA

EMPIRE of
PERSIA

LYDIA

ROYAL ROAD

SARDIS

PERSEPOLIS →

APASA

SAMOS •

MILETUS •

CARIA

HALICARNASSUS •

EGYPT

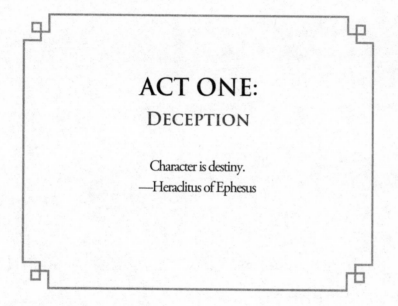

ACT ONE:
DECEPTION

Character is destiny.
—Heraclitus of Ephesus

CHAPTER ONE:
ZOFIA

ZOFIA, PRINCESS OF SARDIS, LEANS FORWARD and digs her heels into the beast's sides. Vata strains, shaking her mane, each beat of her powerful wings launching them higher into the sky. Zo doesn't need to look back to feel the dark energy of the thing—the horrifying, shadowy form hurtling toward her, gaining on her.

A roar splits the morning air.

Vata lets out a terrible whinny and banks hard to the left. Zo's heart plunges into her stomach as she begins to slip, frantically grasping tufts of cottony mane with both hands to steady herself. Far below her, the dry crumpled hills stretch to the horizon.

The Pegasus veers again, her mane whipping Zo's face as the wind stings her eyes and her vision blurs. A shadow falls on her and Vata. Something rakes her back. Sudden warmth floods through her tunic: blood.

She has only a second to register what has happened before white pain explodes across her body. In her agony, she is only vaguely aware that she has stopped holding on to Vata and that she's slipping, falling...

She slams into something brutally hard.

The pain goes numb.

Blackness drowns her.

Zo wakes in a sweat, flinging her arms and crying out in panic until she realizes that she is inside, lying on a little bed of straw and blankets. Panting heavily, she slowly understands that the flight and the chase were just a nightmare.

The Pegasus is not real—*was* never real.

Zo calms her breathing, taking in the moss-covered walls, daylight streaming in lazy diagonal shafts through the triangular cave openings. And for the third time that week, Zo forces herself to steady her heartbeat after the dream of flying and of falling.

Both the pain and the dreams are, Zo was told, the result of an avalanche that nearly killed her. Since then, she has lost her sense of what happened. Of what was real. She has images of a destroyed village, full of ash and ravaged bones and bright blood.

Red on Zo's hands, smeared on her thighs.

She tenses on her straw pallet, closing her eyes. No, those memories do not belong together. The blood was not the villagers' blood. It was *hers*. Her unborn child's. A moan falls from Zo's lips.

"My child?" Cool fingers suddenly trace her cheek, and Zo grabs the wrinkled hand. Blinking, she stares into the cloudy, violet eyes of her savior: Kohinoor the soothsayer.

Gradually, Zo's pulse slows, and her grief subsides. Being around Kohinoor eases her because each time she catches a glimpse of the old woman, she's reminded of miracles.

For it had to have been fate that threw the two of them together, first as captive slaves, then again, when the nearly sightless soothsayer had found Zo, battered and swollen, beneath the stones of the avalanche. Kohinoor had brought her to her home in the Eastern Mountains, allowing her to rest and recover from her wounds. She was there in the night when Zo screamed as her bruised body healed. She was by her side when Zo stood again, taking painful practice steps. And she was there to hold her when Zo had asked the terrible question. Kohinoor was the one who'd gently informed Zo that her unborn baby was no more.

Now Zo leans into the old woman for comfort. The knowledge that she has lost her child still catches her off guard, making her feel as though a giant fist has knocked the wind out of her. The agonizing loss is like another avalanche of rocks crushing her chest, making it nearly impossible to breathe or to think. Her sweet child would never see the world, never inhale fresh air or feel Zo's warm, loving arms. Long ago, in the slave cage, Kohinoor predicted that if Zo ever saw Cosmas again, she would cause his death. And now their child—her permanent link to him—is gone. So much is gone.

Kohinoor helps Zo sit up and hands her a warm mug of tea. Slowly, Zo sips the brew, which tastes like earth and roots and smells like fall leaves. Warmth curls inside her, soothing her and calming her heart.

"Better?" Kohinoor asks.

Zo nods but can't speak. An overwhelming weariness is settling upon her. For even when she sleeps, she does not rest. She battles the dark shadow of despair that threatens to engulf her when she thinks too much about all she has lost on this endless journey: her life as princess of Sardis; her five-year-old sister, Roxana, killed by the slave traders; Cosmas, the man she loves; and their baby. It is too much.

Before she can finish her tea, she lets sleep take her.

When Zo wakes, Kohinoor is gone. She's not sure how much time has passed, but from the absence of sunlight through the cave's roof, she guesses it is dusk. A tendril of fear rises within her—she hasn't woken up alone before. Kohinoor has always been here. She tells the fear to go away, that Kohinoor will be back soon, either from the fields where she picks herbs or the stream where she traps fish.

From somewhere far away, Zo thinks she hears a drumlike

pounding. Sitting up, she frowns, wondering what it is and why she's never heard it before. Though steady, the sound is muted, like the world's heart beating in the center of the earth. Curious, she stands and is grateful that her legs can again bear her weight after a month of healing and training. They no longer ache with movement. In fact, she feels strong. Much stronger than she has been in weeks.

She pours herself some water and drinks as the beat continues. What *is* it? Could it be the answer she seeks—the truth behind the dreams of flying beasts and monsters? Heart pounding with dread and hope, she feels around on the large table for the fire starter kit as if she were as blind as Kohinoor herself. She strikes iron on flint and soon holds a blazing torch that illuminates the cave. Her pallet rests on one side, Kohinoor's on the other. In between are tables with crockery, jugs, and mortars. Baskets of many different shapes line one wall.

She follows the sound to the back of the cave—nothing there. But through the solid wall of stone, she can still hear the rhythm. Turning her head, Zo presses her ear to the wall, and that's when she sees it. A small, dark opening in the shadowy corner, invisible unless you are looking for it.

"Kohinoor?" Zo calls. "Are you there?"

No response, but the beating is crisper now, louder, a drumbeat calling her to action. Curious, she ducks her head and steps through the opening into the passage. It is so narrow she has to angle her shoulders to get through, and even then she brushes against rock. She follows the passage for several minutes, the torch's light illuminating only a few feet in front of her at a time. Part of her says to go back to the cave, to lie down again before she exhausts herself. But a bigger part tells her to keep going. For the first time since waking in Kohinoor's cave she feels...alive. More awake. More herself. She's tired of days spent sleeping or pacing around the cave and is eager to see something new. To maybe, even, learn more about the Eastern Mountains and their dark secrets.

At last, the passage opens into another cavern, dark except

for the torch she holds, and there, in the center, sits Kohinoor. She hunches over a wooden plank, hammering a peg into one end. Relief sighs through Zo, followed quickly by another emotion: disappointment. There are no answers here, no clues to ancient mysteries. Just an old woman building something.

The hammering suddenly stops.

"You're here," Kohinoor says. It isn't a question.

"I am," Zo says. She hesitates before drawing closer, feeling as though she's stumbled upon something private. The old woman has already done so much for her. She doesn't want to be more of a burden.

"I woke and you weren't there," Zo rushes to explain. "And then I heard the hammering and followed it. I'm sorry to disturb your work."

"No harm. Shall we return? I will make you more tea."

"That's all right," Zo said. "Finish what you're doing. What are you making?"

"A table." Kohinoor suddenly slams her hammer into the peg again, and Zo starts as the sound rings around the cave. She is constantly astonished at the soothsayer's ability to see without eyes, and at the strength that allows such a seemingly frail old woman to lift heavy pails of water or this weighty mallet. As the woman returns to her work, Zo raises her torch and sees paintings brushed onto the rough walls.

"What are these?" she mutters to herself, walking over to hold the light closer.

"Paintings from the Hunor," Kohinoor says without turning her head from her woodwork. How can the old woman know what the paintings are without seeing them? Zo shivers.

The Hunor, Zo knows, are an ancient tribe here, in the Eastern Mountains. With her fingertips, she traces a green snake curling around a lotus flower. A few paces away, she sees men with horns dancing around a blazing pyre. Serpents in tall waves racing toward a city of temples and palaces. Three old women weaving on a giant loom atop a hill.

Their colors faded, these images are clearly things of the

ancient past, but for some unknown reason, they make Zo's heart pound. It's as though time has instilled a sense of weight to them, a thick patina of importance. Of truth.

The paintings curve around the entire length of the cave wall, and she follows them, her heart hammering in her chest. And then—

Zo gasps. There on the wall, flickering in her torchlight, is a Pegasus, white wings outspread, climbing into the sky. A girl with long dark hair, arms flailing in panic, has just fallen off its back and plummets to the earth. Falling. Falling.

Just like in her dream.

Next to the image of the Pegasus stands a walled city, Persepolis from the looks of it. There, by the gate, is King Artaxerxes's famous Tower of the Sun and Moon, with its great horned battlements, cracked in two, soldiers tumbling out as flames explode in all directions.

Zo can feel her pulse in her throat now. These paintings are ancient, centuries old at least.

But she knows that the tower was constructed within the past couple of years. Are these paintings some sort of prophecy...or warning?

She stares at the flaming tower in Persia's capital. The destruction. The ruin. The tiny figures of people, fleeing. As if in a trance, she reaches the last image and holds the torch close. A winged child, its arms encircling a wax tablet, rises from the earth as darkness descends from above.

She doesn't understand what that last symbol represents, but she senses that it's important—that it shows the culmination of this...this prophecy. Of the fall of Persepolis.

"Kohinoor," she breathes. "What *is* this?"

The hammering stops. "As I said, pictures from the Hunor."

"Yes, but what do they mean?"

"You know what they mean, child." Kohinoor's voice is but a rasp. "Danger breeds in the heart of Persia."

Zo's blood turns to ice as she remembers the rumors she and Ochus heard at taverns along the Royal Road. Entire villages reduced to ashes. Missing couriers. Empty farmhouses. Vanished horses and oxen. And the village she herself had wandered into the day of her injuries. Doors yanked off hinges. Bloody streaks on the ground. And below a shifting cloud of flies, a heap of bones—human and animal—gouged with deep teeth marks. She had thought, during these weeks of healing, that perhaps that memory, like the Pegasus, had been a dream. A fantasy born of rocks hitting her head.

But if these paintings are true, if they are prophecy…could it be that there was no avalanche? That Kohinoor had found her, unconscious and bloody among rocks, and had assumed she had been caught in a surging tide of stones? That Zo's dream of flying and falling was no dream at all, but a memory? That the Pegasus was real? And the creature that had raked her back with sharp talons… Was it a Spirit Eater?

"But who…what is doing this?" she asks.

The old woman turns sightless eyes to Zo and croons eerily, as if singing a lullaby to a baby, "Spirit Eaters are doing this, girl. The Spirit Eaters' hunger is sharp."

Spirit Eaters. Months ago, on the slave cart, Kohinoor had told Zo it was fated for her blood to mix with that of Prince Alexander of Macedon. *The only way to undo the threads of fate that have been woven for you is to find the Spirit Eaters who can negotiate with those goddesses who spin out, weave, and cut the threads of our fate,* she had said.

Where do I find these Spirit Eaters? Zo asked.

If they still exist, you will find them in the Eastern Mountains. That is where the Spirit Eaters sprang up from a fissure in the rocks, and there they still live. That is where you must go.

Zo had thought of these magical beings as gods, not monsters, and ridden east with Ochus to find them. Thinking once more of the pile of bones in the abandoned village, she realizes she almost did find them. Or they almost found her.

Mouth dry, Zo licks her lips. "Then we must go and tell the king. We must tell him what is to come before there is more death and loss."

The old woman sets down her hammer and looks up, her smile revealing a few brown teeth.

"Must we? All right, child, let us return to our living quarters to discuss it."

Her calm response unnerves Zo. It's as though she thinks Zo is addled, that she doesn't believe her...and maybe she is right. Maybe there was no Pegasus, no falling from the sky. Zo does remember something about an avalanche, doesn't she? What happened the day Kohinoor found her?

She shakes her head in frustration. There's so much in her mind, and though her thoughts feel sharper than they have in many days, they are still somewhat blunt at the edges, like a dull sword. It's as though she's been living life at the edge of sleep, as though she were downing a sleeping potion instead of water or...instead of tea.

A terrible thought crosses Zo's mind, and once she thinks it, it cannot be unthought.

"Come," the old woman urges. "The passage is over here." Her dry gnarled hand grabs Zo's wrist. The skin is leathery, like that of a crocodile. It's all Zo can do not to pull away in disgust. But Kohinoor rescued her, nursed her back to health. In all likelihood, Zo would have died without her.

So she allows the soothsayer to guide her to the opening in the wall. Just before she ducks into it, Zo notices something glinting in her torchlight: a large cage.

"What's this for?" she asks.

Kohinoor blinks. "I see that soon a dog will come here looking for food, and I will make him my companion. That is where I will keep him until he learns that this is his home."

But the cage is taller than Zo. A dog wouldn't need a cage that high.

"Did you make this yourself?" Zo asks.

The soothsayer laughs, not answering her, and starts down the narrow winding tunnel. As soon as they emerge in the cave below, Kohinoor sets about boiling water in her pot, throwing in leaves and powders, preparing the strengthening tea she has been giving Zo every day to ease her pains. But now the earthy scent makes her stomach roll.

When Kohinoor hands her the clay mug, Zo waves it away. "I...don't want any today."

Kohinoor pushes matted hair out of her face, and her bleary lavender eyes seem to stare at Zo beneath a furrowed brow. "You must drink. For your health." Her rasping voice suddenly seems as strong and deep as a man's.

Zo's discomfort grows. "Very well," she says, then pretends to sip. After a time, the old woman goes back to the jugs on the table, opening them, sniffing the contents, and exploring the inside with her bony fingers.

"You walked very far today, Princess. Are you not tired?" the old woman croaks.

Zo stares into her mug. "Yes," she whispers. She rearranges the straw on her pallet as if to sleep and silently tips the mug into it. A moment later, Kohinoor's clawed hand is there, ready to take the empty vessel from her.

"You rest," Kohinoor says. "I will go and gather more rosemary."

Obediently, Zo lies down and closes her eyes. She can feel the old woman staring at her a long moment, and then she hears her slip out of the cave.

This is the first afternoon Zo hasn't had any tea, and her blood hums with energy. Her thoughts are clear. All sense of lethargy and disorientation is gone. So. Her terrible suspicion is correct; Kohinoor has been drugging her...but for what purpose?

Zo sits up quickly. She doesn't know how much time she has before Kohinoor will be back.

Grabbing the torch, Zo again goes to the back of the cave, into the narrow passage, and back to the painted cavern. She first takes a closer look at the table Kohinoor was making. With her free hand, Zo pulls the wooden planks up, and feels her heart tumble into her stomach.

It's not a table—it's a cradle.

And at the moment, she feels a flutter in her womb. A tiny tremble.

Zo's hand flies to her belly. Her baby... Cosmas's baby.

She's still alive.

Zo almost sways with relief, happiness, and...horror. Not only has Kohinoor been drugging her—which Zo might have dismissed as a well-meaning attempt to prevent her from overexerting herself—but Kohinoor has been *lying* to her.

A cradle and a cage. One for the infant and one, Zo realizes with rapidly increasing horror, for her. The cage is for Zo.

She lurches back, and as she does, the torch sweeps an orange swath of light across the wall. The paintings are illuminated, and the winged child stands out in sharp relief. In the flickering light, the wings look as if they are beating the air. And as Zo stares at the prophecy, she feels her child kick.

Her heart now a hammer against her chest, her eyes flick to the image beside it: the girl, falling from the Pegasus—*her*. Her empire's capital burning. And a child, destined to save it from flames.

Her child.

She needs to get out of here, away from destroyed villages and soothsayers, away from iron cages and drugged tea. She must get to Persepolis, to tell the Great King about the missing villages and the warning on the wall.

To find answers.

To save her child.

CHAPTER TWO:
OLYMPIAS

THE MERCHANT SNAPS A BOLT OF GOSSAMER material into the air, and the fabric floats a moment, an unspooling iridescence of green and gold threads, something both beautiful and frail.

"I'll take it," Queen Olympias of Macedon says before the cloth falls to the ground. She sweeps her bangled hand to the merchant's wares, which overwhelm the royal chambers. Cloth of shimmering Tyrian purple, studded with tiny flashing amethysts. Kermes red, the color crushed from a rare pregnant beetle. A yellow as soft and creamy as new butter. A blue the color of lapis lazuli, threaded with silver. "In fact, I'll take it all."

The merchant gives a delighted gasp, and Timandra, the mistress of the queen's maids, sweeps forward to settle accounts, but not before giving Olympias a questioning glance. Timandra knows that King Philip has demanded a limit on extravagance as he prepares for war with the Persians. Enjoying this small stab of revenge on Philip, Olympias scowls at the handmaiden, who drops her gaze and prepares to buy all the fabric.

And why shouldn't Olympias buy it all? She has had to wait too long, for far too little.

Restless, Olympias rises from her gilded chair, wanders to her window, and looks out over the garden below. She watches the water of the Poseidon Fountain trickle down from the blue-bearded god's trident into the marble basin. She breathes in, trying to calm herself as the delicate scent of late roses wafts around her. The fragrance reminds her of another fall day, an eternity ago.

Over there, on that bench, was the place where her labor pains first struck her. Later that night, the then-new queen of Macedon gave birth not just to the son and heir so desperately desired, but to a girl, as well—a girl whose umbilical cord was wrapped so tightly around the son's leg that the doctors wondered if they should amputate his limb.

That was bad omen enough, but then she remembered the prophecy the royal librarian, Leonidas, had shared with her shortly before the birth. Stored for centuries in the royal archives, it was part of the Cassandra scrolls, prophecies supposedly uttered by the doomed oracle of Troy.

In the womb of the night
Twin stars struggle to shine their light.
The moon with great joy will blot out the sun
When the girl kills the boy and the world comes undone.

What does it mean? she had asked.

Leonidas's dark eyes had stared hard at the floor, then lifted to meet hers. *I believe it means you will give birth to twins,* he had said. *The daughter will be destined to kill her twin brother, unleashing tumultuous change into the world.*

The queen could not afford to lose a son, and she didn't need a daughter.

So Olympias held out the newborn girl and commanded her handmaiden, Helen, to kill her then and there. Helen asked to do it away from the palace, lest the killing of a newborn draw evil spirits. She promised to return with the bones as proof of the deed and galloped off with the baby... but never returned.

Olympias sought solace in her lover, a powerful demigod named Riel, who often took the form of a snake to hide in the palace, returning to a man's form only at night when the king was gone. But that night, when she pulled the large green snake to her, rubbing her hands across his cool, diamond-shaped gold patterns, he did not transform.

Instead of resuming the form of the tall, golden-haired god she loved, Riel remained a snake, his lidless eyes staring at her in desperation. His disguise had become his prison, and Olympias's heart shattered. Only a shard of her heart still beat, and it beat for her infant son: Alexander, her heir and her hope.

The boy who, soothsayers vowed, would achieve everlasting fame. He never fussed or cried, just observed the world with strange, curious eyes: one sky blue and the other dark brown. Olympias could stare at him for hours, twist her fingers around his pale curls, massage the scar winding around his leg like a snake. And yet, she could not fully indulge herself in motherhood—not when Riel remained in serpent form.

Olympias set to work studying King Philip's secret archive of witchcraft and sorcery to find a way to reverse Riel's curse. She was forced to wait sixteen years, until the Age of Gods ended, to perform a ritual involving Alexander's blood and her missing daughter's bone. And so, after many long days and inconsolable nights, she broke the enchantment, and Riel— the last of the gods—returned to human form.

But not as she expected.

Olympias can hardly stand to be near Riel. She can't look too long at his face, even though she still craves him, still wants that thing she felt sixteen years ago: that sense of invincibility, of possibility, of true power. Of—dare she say it?—real love.

As if the circumstances of his transformation weren't bad enough, Riel has been distant over the past month, refusing to speak of the future and slipping out of the palace on long, secret trips. But he is a fool to think she does not know where he travels. Olympias may be a mortal, but she is still a queen. Her guards have told her that all his journeys end in the same destination: the Temple of Apollo in Delphi. It isn't a huge surprise. The snake god has always had a fascination with oracles, whose words are delivered straight from the lips of the vanished gods, his brethren. And since Riel's return, his obsession with rejoining the gods has only increased.

"Thank you, Your Majesty."

Startled from her thoughts, Olympias turns her head from the window.

"Do let me know when you wish for more," the merchant continues. "We will soon receive a shipment of the finest Egyptian linen in every color of the rainbow, embroidered with filaments of Ethiopian gold. The most stunning cloth ever, truly fit for a queen!"

"I shall," she says curtly. After all, she needs new clothes. Ever since that Aesarian Lord Bastian poisoned her, her body has become skeletal. No longer can she wear her favorite one-shouldered sheaths, molded to her form and tightly belted. She will have these new fabrics made into fuller gowns with long sleeves and high necks, a symbol of mourning for her former self. A wave of loss moves through her, sickens her. She was stunning once—had been confident of it, full of the strength that comes with knowing one's own beauty.

"Send word when your shipment comes in," Olympias adds, "and I shall take all of it, too."

The man's eyes widen slightly, barely containing his greed as he bows. "Certainly, Your Highness."

As the merchant and his assistants stoop to roll up the cloth, the door flies open and there standing before her is Alexander, her son—and yet not her son. His eyes are like two emeralds, a stranger's eyes, and yet not a stranger. The change has not gone unnoticed. The priests postulated that the transformation of his eyes—from one blue and one brown to the bright emerald green—was an omen sent from the gods. But an omen of what, they could not say.

"Mother," he says, nodding his head in greeting. Olympias's stomach lurches. She feels sick, but she manages to compose herself. She claps her hands, and the merchants and all her ladies exit immediately.

"I bring good news," he says. Her son's smile never used to have any malice in it, no layers of deception and superiority and double meaning like it does now.

"It's about time," she replies, barely containing her frustration.

He puts his hands firmly on her shoulders. "Myrtale, listen."

Her heart skips a beat. It's her old name, her soul name, the one she used before Philip renamed her in honor of his chariot winning the Olympics—renamed her as if she had been his hunting dog.

She pushes her son's hands off her shoulders and starts pacing. "It's hard to listen when my imagination has so much time to run wild. You're never here. After all those years of waiting—as soon as you return you leave me at every opportunity!"

"What are you implying?"

"I know where you've been," she says, rounding on him. "I know you've been to Delphi, multiple times over—"

"Myrtale—"

"And yet," she continues over him, "you say nothing of it to me!" Her voice breaks, and she flushes with humiliation. But one last question—one last weakness—slips from her before she can stop herself. "What are you hiding from me?"

"Oh, Myrtale, really," he says, turning from her to pour himself some wine. "I have said nothing only because I didn't want to give you false hope. You yourself know that prophecies are never clear to mortals until after the events they predict have occurred. And you know that many of the oracles themselves are false—simply peasants who wish for honor and respect. I have spent *centuries* searching for an oracle, only to be cut off shortly after I found the perfect one."

Olympias's blood freezes at his words. The *perfect* one.

A memory of her former handmaiden's beauty flashes into her mind. Thick, golden-brown hair. Large blue eyes fringed by black lashes. A tall, lithe body and liquid grace of movement. Once, she and Helen were innocent and best friends. Then Olympias married King Philip of Macedon and everything changed. Their friendship transformed into mistrust, jealousy, and revenge.

"And is this new oracle also *perfect*?" she demands, hating the sharp, possessive notes in her voice.

He sets the cup back down on the olivewood table next to the window and turns toward her. Reaching out, he gently strokes her cheek. Those deep green eyes seem to burn from within her son's features. She wonders if this will drive her mad.

"Don't worry," he says. "I have a plan. A plan for *us*."

She doesn't like how close he has come to her in the full afternoon light. He must see how thick her makeup is to hide the ravages of the poison, how her skin—even her lips—are snow white beneath the paints, how much of her silver-blond hair is false, pinned on among her own scant tresses.

She pushes him away and retreats to a dimmer corner of the room. "I thought we already knew the plan," she says. "Remove Philip. It's simple enough. Doesn't require countless private prophecies from a beautiful young oracle..."

He sighs. "I've told you before, we must do it exactly as—"

"—exactly as the gods ordain it," she finishes, barely able to hide her fury. She draws herself up to her full height. "Well, what have they ordained? Or do you need to return to Delphi again to hear more?"

He shakes his head as he strides toward her, his muddy riding boots leaving marks on the priceless material still strewn about the floor. "This time the oracle has stated that Philip will die at the wedding of Cleopatra."

Olympias sucks in a breath. Philip sent word recently that he would take another wife in a few weeks, a young Macedonian noblewoman named Cleopatra Eurydice Attalida, Cleo for short. The wedding would be held in Byzantium, which his army just captured, as a celebration of the victory, he wrote. But it is more likely that Philip wants to marry the girl far away from Olympias, knowing she might throw a scene. She can picture the wedding guests eating, drinking, dancing, feuding, puking—civilians and soldiers alike. Utter chaos and confusion. No one guarding the king.

"Moreover, the oracle stated Philip will die by the hand of a lover," he continues.

Olympias scoffs. "There is not enough papyrus in the palace to write down all the names of Philip's lovers, male and female."

"I am sure you'll figure something out." He holds her gaze. "And when the king is dead, the new king, being so young, will rule jointly with his mother, of course."

Olympias feels warmth flooding her chest.

You follow power and I follow you, Riel had once said to her, so many years ago.

But uncertainty gnaws at her gut like the deadly growth the palace doctors found when her chief cook finally died last year. Black and slimy, it had coiled itself tightly around every organ like a deadly vine. Like a strangling snake...

She straightens her backbone. "Philip will not wed for six or seven weeks yet," she says, making an effort to sound persuasive, calm. "For now, you will stay here and pretend to run the government. The people are murmuring you no longer care about Macedon. They grow nervous that a woman alone is giving the orders. And next time you visit the oracle, I will go with you."

He smiles, leans in, his lips—the lips of her own son—dangerously close to hers. She gasps and there's a knock at the door just as she pulls away.

Timandra stands regally in her robes and veils the color of pearlescent mist. "My lady, my lord," she says, sweeping her gray gaze critically over the piles of fabric on the floor. "Dinner is served."

"Excellent. I'm starved." He turns toward the door, and Olympias watches the form of her son, the young and handsome prince, walk ahead of her—his broad shoulders, his confident gait. She notices Timandra staring at Alexander, too, but if the woman suspects something is amiss, she doesn't say.

And no one *can* know.

For the man who just left Olympias's room is not her son at all. He is not Alexander of Macedon. He is the god Riel, transformed and in possession of her son's body—*their* son's body. He is doomed to live as someone else, to inhabit the form of a Snake Blood descendant for the rest of his life. His old form—the form she loved and caressed, that drove her mad with desire—is gone forever.

This was the cruel discovery Olympias made when she performed the ritual to free him from his curse.

Now, as he leaves her room, the hope in her is wormed through with doubts. The words spoken by the Aesarian Lord Bastian just before he attempted to kill her with poisoned wine ring in her ears, an echoing warning: *It's ruinous for a mortal to trust a god.*

CHAPTER THREE: CYNANE

IN THE DAYS SINCE PRINCESS CYNANE ARRIVED on the shores of Illyria, fear has become as much a part of her as her own heartbeat, relentlessly thudding through her veins.

A royal picnic would seem to be a serene occasion—just one of many leisure activities with which the nobles fill their days—but Cyn can barely bring herself to swallow the thick, oversweet fig she has just bitten into. The back of her neck is beaded with sweat and her stomach feels like a horse has kicked it. Yet still she smiles and nods at the courtiers sitting beside her. The worst thing she could do is show fear.

Cyn always wanted to visit Dardania, one of the Illyrian kingdoms in the westernmost part of Greece and her mother's home. Audata used to sit on Cyn's bed and tell her about the sky like a powder blue vault, about the sparkling sapphire sea, and the charm of inland mountain villages. That is where Cyn is now, in a verdant field with a red-roofed village behind it and a sheer cliff in front. It's beautiful, perfect even, but as she watches a seagull dive over the side and wing its way toward the sea, all she can do is wish she could trade places with it.

"Princess!" comes the voice with its tone so sharp it could

scrape human skin off muscle. She straightens, inhales, then turns, flashing a brilliant smile.

"My love!" she calls, her disdain hidden—barely.

"How is our beautiful bride?" Amyntas replies.

Cyn hopes he doesn't see her flinch at the thought of to-night's wedding ceremony. Though he is not the repulsive troll she expected, any reminder of her wifely duties causes waves of nausea to grip her throat. Amyntas is her age, tall and handsome, with chestnut hair curling below his golden diadem, and alert blue-gray eyes. She could have been at-tracted to him, if he had been different.

She forces herself to stand from her cushion, delaying only a moment to smooth the royal skirts she's been forced to wear since her arrival, before striding over to him.

"I am well, Sire," she says. "This luncheon was another brilliant idea of yours. It is good to be away from the pal-ace and the trivialities of court." She studies his face for the slightest twitch of boredom, for the shifting of light in his eyes that signals danger.

"So glad you think so," he replies. "And the entertainment has not yet started!"

A shiver runs up Cyn's spine as he leans forward and waves his golden chalice. "I have a surprise for you," he says, smug satisfaction on every line of his tanned face.

"A surprise?" she says, careful to keep her smile in place even as her heart sinks. "How thoughtful of you."

She scans the surroundings with the eyes of a warrior, searching for the source of the assault. But other than some guards leading a crowd of brightly clad villagers, she sees nothing unusual.

At first, she thought that her weeklong journey to Dardania from Crete, chained to a wall in the ship's cabin by Queen Olympias's orders, would be the worst part of her marriage ordeal. The queen, unfortunately, was not a fool and knew of Cyn's warrior skills, made even more formidable because soldiers always underestimated a girl. Once, on that hot, interminable journey, when the black-bearded guard Herod came to bring her food, Cyn wrapped her chains around his neck and would have strangled him if Priam and young Jamesh hadn't heard the commotion and pulled him free.

Cyn's only consolation on the trip was that Priam was one of her guards. Tall, muscular, and devastatingly handsome, he had drawn her notice back in Pella. Every night on the journey, he volunteered to guard her in the cabin. It wasn't just his body that gave her pleasure. It was the feeling that, for once, she wasn't so completely alone. Wasn't the motherless girl people either ignored because she wasn't a boy, or made fun of because she wanted to be one. With Priam, she could just be herself. And talk to him about life. And hope. And hate. Priam actually listened to her, and told her similar things about himself. When Jamesh came to take his place each morning, Cyn felt lonelier—and hungrier—than ever before. And the days seemed far darker than the nights had ever been.

As the ship heaved into sight of Dardania, Olympias's women servants washed her and combed her long black hair with scented oils. Then they pulled out of a trunk the gown Olympias had sent for Cyn to wear when she first met Amyntas, royal blue with gold borders. "Kill me if you wish," Cyn had told them in a voice as steady and cold as stone, "but don't dishonor me." When she insisted on putting back on her filthy breastplate, leather skirt, and black boots, they were forced to call in the three guards, who pinioned her as the women dressed her in the gown and even pinned a wreath of roses to her head.

Numb with humiliation, Cynane allowed Priam to usher her onto the deck. The sun on her face felt like a caress, and the fresh breeze snapping the Macedonian flags on the mast reminded her of hope. Even the sharp clear cries of wheeling gulls overhead sounded like music after the oppressive atmosphere of the cabin.

Her ship entered a rectangular harbor where merchant and fishing vessels bobbed at wooden piers. Lining the harbor were white limestone houses packed closely together like teeth, their orange tiled roofs bright in the sun. White towers and walls snaked around the harbor and up onto the green hills behind the city. The water was the bluest Cyn had ever seen, and absolutely crystalline, reflecting her ship's double in its smooth undulations. Cyn, too, felt like a mirror image of herself: sharp and clear and disturbingly vacant.

The ship weighed anchor next to a long pier. As the sailors threw down ropes and set down the gangplank, Cyn looked at the crowded square. Hundreds of people cheered loudly for their new queen. Many were richly, though oddly, dressed, in ugly striped robes and lopsided caps. One of them would be her husband. She shaded her eyes and squinted, but they were too far away for her to see.

A delegation of old men with long beards walked down the pier, carrying ivory staffs of office. Priam helped her down the gangplank, one arm around her back, his other hand warm on her arm, and she momentarily imagined herself a mere puppet—a soulless wooden thing whose spirit was contained only in the hands of the man that made her move.

Halfway down the pier she spotted him, the only one wearing a crown. A large brown horse with a white blaze stood beside him. The king was tall, taller even than Cynane, she was delighted to see. And good-looking, though his eyes were, she noticed as she approached him, a bit too close together and too high up in his head for classic beauty. She also decided that under his billowing purple robes, he was thin, not the burly, muscled type she preferred.

She bowed before him, and he lifted her up with both

hands. A warm smile lit his face, making it luminous and beautiful. His teeth were white and strong. His pale eyes— which had a strange light in them—sparkled.

"Princess Cynane of Macedon, we are delighted to welcome you to the land of your mother," King Amyntas said in an accent that made him sound as if he were choking on fine pebbles. "You are just as beautiful as Queen Olympias told us."

"And you, Your Highness, are…" Cynane began. She was a warrior, with no talent for small talk with strangers. "You are very tall," she said.

He cocked his head, his bright eyes suddenly reminding her of the bay itself: limpid and blank, though at the time, this didn't send a blare of warning through her as it should have.

"We would like to introduce you to the chief minister of Dardania," the king said, "the only subject who we are sure would never plot any treachery against us. It was he who advised us to accept you in marriage."

Politely, Cyn looked at the richly dressed men standing around the king. None came forward. The king made a clicking noise in his throat and the brown horse shuffled ahead, wearing a purple saddlecloth, scarlet feathers on its head, and gold ornaments on its bridle.

"This is Aireon," Amyntas said, kissing the horse full on the lips, "who advises me wisely in all things."

Cyn heard Priam's sharp intake of breath at her side.

"What?" she asked as uncomfortable laughter bubbled up her throat. She clenched it down and swallowed, catching Priam's eye in her peripheral vision. He wasn't smiling, and the sudden realization that this wasn't a joke seized her chest.

The smile drained from the king's narrow face. "Do you not admire our Aireon, Princess?" he asked, a menacing edge to his voice.

Cyn had never heard so loud a silence. No one spoke. No one moved. There was no sound at all except for the boats bumping and jostling against the piers. Suddenly she understood: this man was not right. His mind was gone, deranged, mad. And dangerous.

Slowly and determinedly, Cyn calmed her breathing and placed both hands over her heart.

"I should have known this magnificent, loyal creature was your chief minister. How foolish of me."

The tension in his face relaxed. "Most women are foolish. We hear it is meant to be part of their charm." Aireon nibbled the back of the king's neck, and Amyntas's eyes rolled up slightly, as though he enjoyed the sensation.

"He wants to know if you will amuse us," the king said, turning around to rub the horse's nose. Those strange pale eyes fixed on her like the cold pointed ends of daggers. "Will you?"

Uncertain, she forced a smile. "I will do my best to amuse you, lord, until death parts us."

"Good," he said. "You will have your first opportunity immediately."

The crowd parted as they walked into the round stone tower on the harbor and through wide marble corridors lined with brightly painted life-sized statues of the gods—Apollo with his lyre, Zeus with his thunderbolt, Athena with her bow and arrow. Each one of them had had its head removed—Cyn could see the thin line around each neck—and Amyntas's head glued on, his mouth open in a ridiculous grin.

She and Priam exchanged alarmed glances as they followed the king and emerged into a small amphitheater crowded with spectators.

Cyn assumed the king had arranged a show for her, perhaps Illyrian dancers or a gladiatorial combat. She thought he would escort her to the royal podium halfway up the tiers of seats, but instead he guided her to a gilded chair on the sand, set among other chairs against the curved wall directly below him. Amyntas climbed up to his box while her Macedonian guards—Priam, Jamesh, and Herod—were led to seats on the other side of the arena.

The chair's metal rondels, hot from the afternoon's sun, burned through her thin gown. Something was off, *wrong*. Shifting, Cyn looked around. It took her a moment to realize what had unnerved her: the crowd was silent.

No careless chatter bounced between the spectators. No laughter. No applause.

Something tightened in Cyn. Her heart sped up, and her muscles contracted. This crackling anticipation of horror reminded her of waiting for the torture sessions, when she was held captive in the Aesarian Lords' camp. There had been the same tense silence right before the boots slapped on curling tower steps as they came to take her to be beaten, burned, drowned, making her almost mad with pain as they tried to determine why she would not die.

No matter how many times the Lords had cut her, her wounds had healed quickly, leaving unblemished skin ready to be sliced open again. At first, she'd thought it was because she'd at last attained her mother's legacy, a form of magic called Smoke Blood. But in her pain-filled days, a delusion had come to her, a being of smoke that had told her she was not Smoke Blood, not yet.

Casting her gaze around the amphitheater, she asked herself if she would she heal quickly now if Amyntas was planning to kill her. Her senses alive with the raw danger pulsating in the air, she could not answer. She did not know. She wished for the certainty of Smoke Blood.

"Welcome, Princess Cynane, our soon-to-be queen!" Amyntas announced. He had raised his arms as if to quiet the crowd, but there was no need. "Today we honor you with a queen's due."

He clapped his hands and called down to her, "Behold, my dear, your Queen's Guard!"

A dozen Illyrian men—old, toothless, lame, and half-blind—staggered into the arena under the weight of their shields and swords.

"These valiant soldiers will protect you from all danger," the king crowed from his nest-like seat above her, far from the arena. "From the raging battlefields…to this very moment."

Cyn suddenly made a frightening observation: *no horse*.

Whatever was going to happen, Amyntas didn't want his beloved chief minister anywhere near.

"And now," Amyntas continued, "my fool, Papari, will perform for us."

Papari? As in *testicles*? A slender, short man dressed in buffoon's garb cartwheeled onto the sandy arena. Strips of different-colored cloth sewn all over his tunic made him look like a wild chicken. He tumbled and leaped, doing backflips and somersaults, as the king and spectators clapped and laughed.

Amyntas clapped his hands again. Papari froze in the middle of the arena, miming absolute panic—large mouth open, watery blue eyes bulging almost out of their sockets, hands on his cheeks. Cyn clutched the edge of her seat, feeling the metal ornaments cut into her palms but not caring. Across the arena, the doors opened. She squinted in the bright sunlight, her eyes pinned to the darkness of the tunnel. For a long moment, nothing happened.

Then the blackness shifted, like shadow on shadow. Suddenly a bellow of rage echoed from the opening. A second later, a wild bull galloped into the ring.

Taller than Priam and five times as wide, the beast looked like a small mountain. Muscle and sinew rippled as it stamped and snorted. She could see its matted black hair clumping around the wounds that zigzagged across its back. The cuts had not been made to tame the beast, but to enrage it. As the bull shook its barrel-sized head, she realized with horror that its horns had been sharpened to cruel points.

Papari cartwheeled to the nearest marble wall and scrambled over several rows of spectators until he sat quivering in mock fear on a fat woman's lap, his head buried in her neck as she tried to push him off. Only one spectator laughed, and the sound of King Amyntas's mirth was like a whip to the bull's back. It roared in rage as wild bloodshot eyes locked on Cyn.

The bull pawed the ground as its red-brown eyes rolled. Then it charged.

Training took over. Cyn grabbed the sword and shield from the old man trembling beside her. He and the rest of her Queen's Guard fled toward the nearest door, as did the spectators in the bottom rows.

Finding her center, she braced herself as the bull bore down on her. The heft of the wooden shield and the sword's solid hilt gave her strength. It felt so right to have weapons in her hands again. She felt the blood pumping through her limbs, her heart racing in anticipation. The irony was that the king was doing this to harm her, but she had never felt so alive.

She counted the bull's stride as it thundered toward her. Five strides until it reached her. Three…

There was a movement in the corner of her eye, and Priam leaped in front of her. His sudden appearance startled the bull, and it swerved, breaking its pace. Cyn gnashed her teeth. What was he *doing*? She had the situation under control!

The two other Macedonian guards appeared behind the creature just as a kick connected with Priam's chest. An inhuman groan escaped Priam's lungs as he was tossed back, all the way to the wall, where he slid to the ground in a quivering slump.

Cyn froze, torn between running to him and defending herself. Herod and Jamesh stabbed the creature's back, but they'd misjudged the bull's agility. It swung its head and impaled Herod, horns piercing through leather breastplate, muscles, and bones as if they were butter. The tips of the bull's horns were visible through Herod's back as Jamesh, horrified, stumbled backward and vomited. As the beast shook his head, the dead man's arms and legs jerked hideously, like ribbons on an obscene hat.

Cyn stumbled back, bile rising in her throat.

Now. Now was the time to attack the beast, encumbered with the weight of the soldier.

"Over here!" she cried, banging her sword on the shield.

The bull, half-blinded by the body and half by rage, bellowed. It galloped in the direction of Cyn's voice. She wasn't sure if the spectators were still silent or not. If the audience had escaped or not. If Priam was dead or not.

Her entire world was hooves, horns, and fury.

Wait, she told herself, even when every particle of her being screamed at her to move. *Not yet…not yet… NOW!*

She dropped to her knees as the bull lunged.

With all her strength—with all her anger at Olympias, all her disgust at Amyntas's mad games, and all her bitterness of being nothing more than just a *girl*—Cyn drove her sword upward, into the bull's belly.

The force of the impaled creature wrenched the hilt out of her hands. She had only a breath to roll to the side as the beast tumbled, the weight of Herod's body, still attached to the horns, pulling it forward. The animal landed on its face with a sickening crunch, followed by a snap that turned Cyn's insides to liquid.

The bull gasped once, then was still.

Panting heavily, Cyn lurched to her feet. The remaining spectators sat frozen, eyes wide and mouths agape. But the king slouched on his throne, sipping his wine and frowning.

"You've ruined the game," he drawled, his voice carrying in the abandoned arena.

Without responding, Cyn walked to the bull, put one daintily sandaled foot on its stomach, flexed her muscles, and, with all the strength she had left, pulled the sword from the beast's thick, bleeding body.

The remains of Herod the guard had been thrown free as the bull fell, and she carefully stepped over him to begin hacking at the bull's neck—she had never seen such neck muscles, thick as sailor's rope. For a long, humiliating moment, her ears ringing so hotly she couldn't feel herself think, she feared she would not be able to separate the head, but at last, she managed to sever it from the body. It dropped to the sand, creating a dusty cloud. She picked up the head and held it aloft, her muscles straining with the effort.

"My lord king," Cyn said, her voice surprisingly clear to her own ears, "a mere bull is not worthy entertainment for majesty such as yours. A king of Illyria deserves nothing less than a Minotaur."

The king leaned forward, transfixed.

"Come with me," she muttered to Jamesh, and the dazed guard stumbled forward with her. Gritting her teeth, she walked toward the royal box. The still-warm blood dripped down her arms and splattered her new gown.

"Dance with it, if you want to live," she whispered to the guard, handing him the head. He cast her a questioning glance, then obediently took the head and held it in front of his own. He imitated a bull by pawing at the ground with his feet, then danced in weaving circles. Amyntas seemed fascinated, eyes fixed on the sight, mouth parted.

In slow, dignified strides, she climbed several steps toward the king's royal box and looked in his eyes. Now she knew what the light in them was: madness.

"Have I amused you, Sire?" Cyn asked, gesturing behind her to Jamesh, who danced and swayed, sprays of blood still spurting from the severed neck. "What other bride could offer you a Minotaur?" She faced her betrothed defiantly, chin raised. Watching. Waiting.

Amyntas mumbled something that Cyn couldn't hear. Then he wrenched his gaze away from the Minotaur and studied her as if he were seeing her for the first time. Every moment seemed like an eternity as her heart thudded heavily in her chest.

"Wonderful!" Amyntas finally said, clapping. "Yes, Princess, you are amusing indeed." He tilted his head and looked down at her with intense concentration. "And we have a feeling," he said in a low voice, as if to himself, "you will prove more amusing yet."

That was three weeks ago. Since then, Cyn's life has been a continual struggle to entertain the king.

One night, she marched into the banquet hall as Hecate, goddess of necromancy, in the goddess's traditional black robes, leading a great black dog with three heads—Cerberus, guardian of the Underworld—although two of the heads were fakes strapped on. Amyntas banged his goblet on the table and laughed madly. She held many animated conversations with the horse, Aireon, who always stood next the king at table, eating the finest oats on a golden plate. Day in and day out, she pushed herself to amuse the king, and all the while, she studied the kingdom.

She watched. She learned. She planned. For this was going to be her kingdom very, very soon.

A plan had come to Cyn: she would kill her cousin-husband and become the ruling queen. The murder would not just ensure her rightful place as ruler of her native country; it would also, she hoped, gain her the Blood of True Betrayal. Because a bride killing her husband on their wedding night is an abhorrent treachery. And with the Blood of True Betrayal, she would finally achieve her life's ambition: Smoke Blood, the

Blood Magic no one had heard of except Audata, Cyn's late
mother. With Smoke Blood and the king dead, she would control the government and become a ruling queen, commanding armies, as she'd always wanted—a queen with invincible
powers, one far greater than Olympias; greater than her mother
had been, too.

She would have liked to kill Amyntas immediately after the
bull attack, but something told her to reconnoiter the situation
first. The people, though afraid of their unpredictable mon-
arch, honored him as king, scion of a long line of Dardanian
royalty, and thought that his insanity came from being touched
by the gods.

Besides, before she killed him, Cyn would have to marry
the fool to achieve rank and respect as queen consort. Then
she would work to forge alliances with his advisers, the important families, and, above all, the military.

But now, watching the peasants—there must be a hundred of them, men, women, and children—take their places
around the king's luncheon tent, she must concentrate on
surviving another day.

Rising from his throne in long, gem-studded robes, Amyntas gestures to the villagers. "Today, my dear," he says, smiling
broadly, "we have an amusement for *you*. Today our people
are going to fly for you."

The villagers look around at each other in surprise and
alarm, as a spike of dread wedges between Cyn's ribs.

The king lunges forward and grabs the arms of a boy of
about thirteen. "Come, young man," Amyntas says. "Haven't
you ever wanted to fly like a bird?"

He pulls the boy forward, across the field to the edge of
the cliff, as Cyn and the others follow, the guards pushing
the villagers with their spears. Every muscle in Cyn's body
screams with the desire to wrangle the boy free of the king's
grip, but she knows that she cannot.

It's even windier at the edge of the cliff. Cyn's gauzy dress whips around as if invisible hands tug at it. She knows what the insane king is going to do. Everyone knows. A shrill cry of protest slices the air until a hand is clapped over it. The child's mother.

Amyntas has his arm around the boy's thin shoulders. The little peasant is all freckles, gangly limbs, and knobby knees. He looks up into the king's eyes, then down at the hundred-foot drop onto boulders. "Now, boy, let's see you…fly!"

He pushes the child hard, and the boy lets out a startled, terrified scream, clutching back at the king as if to grab onto his robes.

But it's too late.

Arms spread wide, the boy seems to hover in the air a moment, as if he really were flying, then Cyn's heart seizes in her chest as she watches his silent fall. His body strikes a jutting rock on the way down, then hits the ground with grotesquely splayed limbs and is still.

Cyn feels the heat of her fear and anger turn to something ice-cold and very strong, like iron in snow. She has killed men in battle, in a fair and honorable fight where she and her opponents tested their strength and skill. But *this*…

"You are disappointed, Princess," Amyntas says, "that that one didn't fly. We can see it in your face."

Cyn feels a hundred needlelike prickles in her armpits. Her face, yes. For a moment, she forgot to keep her face calm and smiling.

"We are disappointed, too," he adds, sighing.

Amyntas walks toward the trembling peasants, anger in his strange eyes. "If one of you actually does fly, we will be satisfied, and the rest may go home. But we want to see *someone* fly today. We are the king. We command it."

Cyn hears sobs coming from somewhere in the crowd.

"Who is that crying?" Amyntas asks irritably. "Bring her forward."

The crowd parts as two guards push a woman—no, a girl, really, no more than seventeen—holding a newborn baby in her arms.

"Can *you* fly?" Amyntas asks. The girl's dark eyes grow wide with terror. "Can you?" the king persists. The girl doesn't answer. Fear has rendered her mute.

Her pulse pounding in her temples, Cyn knows she must stop this. Dying for peasants wasn't in her plans for the day, but she can't stand idly by and watch all these people pushed to their deaths. Yet how can she divert the mad king's attention? It will have to be amusing. It will have to be...

Amyntas pulls the baby from the struggling girl's arms and says, "Well, if you are too mulish to answer, let's see if your child can fly."

It will have to be now.

"Let me be next, my lord," Cyn says, trying to suppress a shudder as she puts her hand on his shoulder. He looks at her in surprise. "I want to fly," she says, gently taking the baby from him and returning it to its sobbing mother. "Why should mere peasants have the fun of flying when their queen desires the honor?"

A slow smile spreads across Amyntas's narrow face.

"Yes," he says, a bit wary. "Yes, you are right. If you wish to fly, do it, by all means."

Cyn nudges the girl to return to the crowd and begins to strip, removing her gilded belt and sandals, letting them drop to the ground.

With downcast eyes and a shy smile, she takes the pins out of her long black hair, and it waves around her in the breeze. Conscious of the murmuring that spreads through the crowd, she pushes the shoulder straps off and pulls out her tanned, muscular arms. Then she lowers the garment, one inch at a time, below her breasts. Her waist. Her hips. Her knees.

The crowd of peasants has gone completely silent. Still holding the dress, she moves to the very edge of the cliff. Her entire body tingles with the sensation of complete freedom. She looks down at the long drop, at the boy's broken body splayed on the rocks. Ever since she arrived here, she has imagined herself dancing on the edge of a razor. Now she really is.

She turns back, facing the crowd of spectators. Their eyes are huge, their mouths open. Amyntas gazes on her with rapt fascination.

"Now, my king," she says, smiling, "watch me fly!"

Graceful as a dancer, she brings her arms above her head and flings her gauzy white gown into the air. The wind catches it and sweeps it up, billowing like a bird spreading magnificent wings, then bats it around as the dress floats over the plain below.

"Princess Cynane of Macedon has flown," she proclaims, arms raised above her head in exultation, "and in her place stands Cynane of Dardania, soon to be queen of the courageous Amyntas, best-loved of all the gods!"

For a moment, the king doesn't say anything, and Cyn wonders if he will throw her over the side to see her really fly. But then the tension of his face relaxes, and his usually cold eyes glow in delight.

"The queen has flown!" he announces, emitting a tiny squeal of a laugh. "Everyone must bow down before our flying queen!"

Peasants, courtiers, and guards alike kneel clumsily en masse.

"My lord," she says quickly, not knowing how long this will provide amusement, "as queen, I demand that the rest of these villagers take the path down the cliffs and find my old self that has flown away, capture her, and bury her with all the due formalities deserving of a deceased princess of Macedon."

"You are right," he says, snapping his fingers. "Do as she commands."

Eagerly, the villagers disperse toward the path.

Amyntas rubs his temples. "We are tired now. We must rest and prepare for tonight's wedding festivities."

Her mouth still pushed into a smile, Cyn stares at this murderous monster who will be her husband.

"Yes, my lord," she says, her disgust rounded to a purr. "It will be an eventful night."

In her breezy room overlooking the beach, Cyn soaks in a tub of warm water, unable to relax her tense shoulders, even when her Dardanian handmaidens rub her dry and massage floral-scented oil onto her skin. Then they drape her in her yellow wedding dress and clasp golden necklaces and bracelets on her.

A petite hazel-eyed girl, Rachel, combs her hair.

"We admire you, my lady," she says, tugging gently at a snarl with small, deft fingers.

"Whatever for?" Cyn asks, turning to study the girl.

"The king has had many mistresses here in the palace," she says, setting down the ivory comb and picking up a hair ribbon. "But none lasts more than a night. Some are never seen again. People say…" Rachel threads the ribbon through Cyn's thick locks as she whispers, "They say he kills them in a rage for boring him. Everyone thought you would meet with an accident or disappear long before now. But your cleverness has kept you alive."

But Cynane knows it is far more than cleverness that keeps her alive.

It is the will to strike. And to kill.

"My lady," Rachel says, knotting the ribbon at the nape of her neck, "do you need anything…arranged for tonight?"

Cyn stares at her blankly.

"Regarding the sheets?" the handmaiden presses.

Cyn smiles. Rachel suspects she isn't a virgin and is offering to help cover for her. Perhaps Priam's visits to her in the dark have not gone unnoticed.

For now, she shakes her head. "Thank you for your discretion, Rachel. However, I can assure you there *will* be blood on the sheets."

It just won't be Cyn's.

As soon as the girl has gone, Cyn uses a pointed fire poker to pry up the loose tile near the window and removes the bag of knives and vials of poison Priam has smuggled her over the past weeks. She must prepare for tonight…

Suddenly she feels that someone is watching her.

She turns around…but sees no one.

Shrugging off the sensation, Cyn straps the leather knife holders tightly to her thighs and slips the knives into their sheaths. Carefully, she selects a particularly deadly blade from the heap, admiring how the bars of sunshine floating in through the slatted shutters glint off its polished iron.

The hunting dagger's hilt is wood from a tree struck by lightning, imbued with the divine power of Zeus, Lord of the Gods, and overlaid with the winged lion of Dardania carved in ivory. Her mother brought this precious family heirloom with her to Macedon as a bride and gave it to Cynane shortly before her death. Olympias had callously distributed it, along with Cyn's other weapons, to her guards on the ship. *She'll never need weapons again*, the queen had said, laughing.

Well, Olympias was wrong about that, as she was about many things. As Cyn bends to slip the knife beneath her pillow, she hears someone clearing his throat. Someone *right behind her.*

Someone who can't possibly be there, because no one has entered the room.

Now every hair on her entire body is standing up, and she feels as if someone is nicking her spine with a dagger, one vertebra at a time. She feels a chill deeper than any she has ever felt, except the time she found her mother's snow-white body in the bathtub of blood, and the coldness that spread through her body like ice froze the tears that should have come.

She straightens and thrusts her shoulders back. She cannot panic. She is Princess Cynane of the royal houses of Macedon and Dardania. A warrior, trained in the arts of archery, riding, and swordsmanship. What harm can truly come to her, if she is ready for it?

Holding her knife, she swings around.

No one is there.

There is nothing but wisps of smoke.

And then, her stomach turns on itself, and fear blossoms through her chest, into her heart. Because before her eyes, the smoke shifts…and takes the shape of a man.

CHAPTER FOUR:
JACOB

JACOB IS LATE. *AGAIN.*

Quietly, he opens the door, hoping to slip into the Aesarian Elder Council without fanfare. He lost track of time as he studied High Lord Gideon's scrolls about Blood Magic. *Lost track* isn't quite the right way to describe it, though. It's more like time's jaws yawned open and swallowed him. More and more lately, he finds himself falling down a dark tunnel of anxiety and need.

Jacob needs answers. He needs to understand. More important, he needs to *suppress*—to keep the dangerous thing bubbling inside him hidden. If he can learn enough about Earth Blood Magic, then perhaps he can learn how to kill it.

Back in the Pellan palace, an infected wound on his arm healed itself as though of its own accord. On the battlefield, he seemed to heal a dying Katerina when he kissed her. Last month, after Princess Cynane attacked him, in his anger he somehow melted her chains, allowing her to escape. And when Timaeus was repairing the Hemlock Torch, the Aesarians' chief tool in detecting magic, Jacob held it, and it glowed red. Because of him.

But the more he chases answers, the more his duties lapse. It's a vicious cycle, and the awareness of it gnaws at his gut.

He clenches and unclenches his fingers as he moves toward the vacant seat.

"—evidence of a protective spell over the princess," Gideon is saying in his deep voice. He turns and adds, one black eyebrow cocked high, "Lord Jacob, you have decided to grace us with your presence, after all."

Jacob could swear he hears someone snicker and feels his cheeks turn beet red. "A thousand pardons, High Lord," he says, pulling out the empty chair. The legs scrape against the mosaic floor like a shrieking bird.

Gideon's dark face tenses with disapproval. "We were discussing Lord Timaeus. He writes that he has had the opportunity to talk to many—courtiers and servants alike—about Dardanian sorcery. He has discovered much that could explain why Princess Cynane healed from our torture so quickly. Timaeus is doing very well." *In contrast to you,* Gideon seems to be saying.

Jacob tries hard not to show his frustration in his face as heat races to his ears. Timaeus—his best friend ever since the two fought in the Blood Tournament in Pella earlier in the summer—is always joking, or uttering curses so foul they could strip the flesh right off your bones. But Jacob doesn't trust him anymore, not since Tim learned his deepest, darkest secret. A secret so dangerous that Jacob had been forced to find a reason to send him far away.

"I am pleased that *my* suggestion for Lord Timaeus's mission is going well," Jacob replies, faking a crooked smile.

"Indeed," Gideon says, frowning slightly before returning to the conversation at hand.

A warm breeze from the Corinthian Bay tumbles in through the open window of the little parlor the Lords use as a council chamber in this luxurious villa, home of a retired Aesarian Lord. The silver-green leaves of olive trees whisper and dance above the voices of men; it is the beginning of the olive harvest. And on the road below, Jacob hears wheels creaking and people singing—pilgrims, no doubt, winding their way to the sacred city of Delphi just a few miles west of here.

"And now let us hear about progress with the Hemlock Torch," Gideon says.

Instantly, Jacob's brief reprieve of calm collapses, and his pulse races.

Lord Ambiorix leans forward, his ice-blue eyes gleaming with excitement. "We are experimenting with making the torch more sensitive than ever before," he says in his guttural Gallic accent. "Instead of glowing red when magic abounds, we seek to make it specify the kind of magic around it. Violet flames for Snake Blood, green for Earth Blood, and red for other types of magic, soothsayers, and such."

Jacob's heart skips a beat. The dusty scrolls he has been studying posed no threat, but this torch is like a spear pointed at his heart if it can really reveal those who possess Blood Magic: Snake Blood, magic of the mind, whose wielders can mingle with the thoughts of another person or an animal, and sometimes even take over the physical form entirely. And Earth Blood, magic of the body. Those who have it can melt metal, cause earthquakes, and heal even fatal wounds.

The others around the table nod thoughtfully, and he hurries to do the same. Everyone knows that the Aesarian Lords, the most powerful fighting force in the world, are sworn to eradicate magic. But what most don't know—what, in fact, only the men around this table know—is that, for centuries, the Lords have been seeking magic wielders and taking them east to the Spirit Eaters, who devour them alive.

A single Snake Blood, a centaur or Pegasus, can keep the monsters satiated for years. But if the Spirit Eaters don't have magical victims, they will devour every human in the known world. The Aesarian Lords' goal is nothing less than saving the human race.

Sometimes the irony of Jacob's life overwhelms him. He entered the Blood Tournament, won it, and joined the Aesarian Lords to impress Katerina, to offer her something better than life on the farm so that she would marry him. Now here he is, with greater position and wealth than he could ever have dreamed. But Macedon is no longer an ally but an enemy, and Kat is forever lost to him. And the one thing he has sworn to destroy is within himself, in his own blood. According to the oath he swore, Lord Jacob of Erissa, the youngest member ever of the Aesarian Elder Council, should turn himself in as meat to satiate the hunger of the Spirit Eaters.

A strident knock on the door interrupts Ambiorix's discourse on modifications to the torch. "Enter," he says, his long blond braids trailing over his shoulder as he turns. "I asked Lord Turshu to demonstrate his progress."

Jacob goes from hot to frozen, like a rabbit cornered by a dozen foxes. He must get out. But how? His gaze rests on the painted wall across from him, where a life-sized image of Achilles drives a chariot around the walled city of Troy, dragging Hector's body behind him in a cloud of dust. Jacob sees his own face on the stiff, bruised corpse being dragged east.

Lord Turshu, the short, tattooed Scythian, enters, holding the Hemlock Torch. It's the length of a tall man's arm, its iron spikes thrusting out jaggedly like cruel thorns. In the center is a basket of what looks like wicked, twisted nails. On its long base are Aesarian symbols: a lightning bolt, a group of five flames, and a crescent moon. "My lords," he says, bowing to his colleagues. "We are still testing our work, but we shall show what we have accomplished so far."

Behind him, Lord Eumolpus enters holding a lit oil lamp, and Lord Gaius follows carrying a stone vial.

"In this vial," Turshu continues, taking it from Gaius and pulling out the stopper, "we have blood from the royal family of Caria, that nest of Snake Bloods." He pours a few drops onto the table. "Eumolpus, please light the torch."

Jacob's heart pounds in his chest. Drops of sweat slide down his armpits.

The torch flame bursts up, glistening white as snow under moonlight. Silvery smoke rises from it. "As you can see, it always starts off white," Turshu says.

Jacob exhales. *White. Stay white.*

Turshu brings it closer to the small puddle of blood on the table. It spits and sputters and...turns violet. The men around the table murmur and elbow one another. "The violet flame means Snake magic is nearby," Turshu says, evidently quite pleased. "So, we can see our new design is working."

"My lords, it is now green," Gideon says, pointing. "I just saw it turn green for a moment!"

Jacob's heart nearly stops. He, too, saw the curling ends of the violet flames turn green.

Turshu's face twists in a grimace. "As I said," he replies, disappointment in his voice, "we are not yet finished—"

Jacob pushes his chair back so suddenly it falls to the floor with a crash. "Forgive me," he says to the room full of staring eyes. "I—I don't feel well..."

He lurches out of the room, staggers halfway down the hall, and leans against the wall. Close. That was so close. Does anyone suspect he caused the flame to burn green? Or do they all think the torch still isn't functioning properly?

He becomes aware of a presence beside him and turns to see the hulking horned figure of High Lord Gideon, his powerful arms crossed over his chest.

"You have not been yourself lately, Lord Jacob," Gideon says. "The others say you've been quiet. Lost in thought."

Jacob straightens and bows to the Aesarian leader. "They are right," he says. It is time to tell the High Lord the truth.

Or, at least, part of the truth. "My lord, if I may speak with you? In private?"

Gideon stares at him, then nods. "Come, then," he says, clapping Jacob on the back. "Let us walk."

Gideon leads him down a wide staircase and across a fragrant garden filled with painted statues so lifelike Jacob thought they were people when he first saw them. Gideon unbolts a door in the wall, and Jacob finds himself in the downward sloping olive grove. Large nets encircle the bases of the trees for fallen fruit, and men in loincloths stand on ladders, baskets on each hip, plucking the olives and dropping them into the baskets in swift, graceful motions.

Gideon stops, closes his eyes, and lifts his chin, like a magnificent animal relishing the feel of the sun and wind. "Tell me," he says, "what troubles you."

Jacob almost laughs at the question—if Gideon only knew!—but something bars the sound from coming out. His throat tightens as he glances sideways at the High Lord, whom he has come to look up to over the past months. This man who wants to cultivate a greatness in Jacob—a greatness that he, too, longs for. This man who has entrusted him with the knowledge of the world's gravest danger, who has believed in him and trained him and even now wants to help.

This man who truly has no awareness of the dark seed of *wrongness* unfurling inside Jacob, despite everything.

Jacob swallows hard. "I have spent a great deal of time reading about magic," he begins tentatively.

Gideon nods. "I have seen you with the scrolls. It is the right of every member of the Elder Council to read them."

"High Lord," Jacob says, but he struggles for words. Perhaps it is best to be direct. "I believe that the Last God, Riel, lives in the Pellan palace, kept there by the witch-queen, Olympias."

Gideon's dark eyes narrow and he begins to walk once

more. "I have heard this suspicion before from someone who proved himself to be a traitor and a liar."

"Lord Bastian, yes," Jacob says hastily. "I admit, I heard him speak of it."

What Jacob doesn't say is that he was spying on Bastian when he first got the idea of finding the Last God. But that was before Jacob accused Bastian of sleeping with the queen. Before Bastian challenged Jacob to a Gods' Duel and ended up killing himself by mistake.

Arrogant, swaggering Bastian *was* a liar, a traitor, but Jacob believes that there is some truth to his story, and Princess Cynane confirmed it.

"After the Gods' Duel," Gideon says, "I assumed Bastian's stories of Riel at the palace were falsehoods created to obscure his affair with the queen."

"I believe it might be just the opposite, High Lord," Jacob counters. He passes a net covered with fallen olives the color of bruises: yellow-green and purple-black and dark red. "I think *because* of his love affair with Olympias, he might have known a great deal indeed. Riel, often called the Snake, according to the scrolls, is the originator of Snake Blood. The queen keeps a secret altar of snakes beneath her bedroom in the palace."

Gideon pauses, and Jacob stops, turning to face him. The lord's dark face hovers beneath the branches rich with purple olives. "Snakes are holy spirits," he says quietly, plucking an olive off a low-hanging branch and rolling it between his thumb and forefinger. "Even in Delphi the priestesses keep snakes in underground altars. Many temples and palaces do."

"No, there's more than that," Jacob insists. "In those scrolls, I learned that great Snake Bloods possess the power of transformation. They can put themselves completely into the body of an animal—a human, too, if they are a direct descendant."

His heart beats rapidly at Gideon's quizzical expression, but still he continues. "I believe that Riel has been living in Pella for many years as a snake. I believe it was *his* magic that caused the Hemlock Torch to explode during my initiation ceremony."

To their left, two men remove their hip baskets and dump their plucked olives into a large burlap sack. Gideon's eyes slide from the harvesters back to Jacob. "It was very powerful magic indeed that destroyed the torch, killed Lord Acamas, and brought the storm of crows. What makes you think it was Riel?"

"That last night, right before Princess Cynane melted her chains and escaped," Jacob replies, hoping Gideon doesn't hear the lie in his voice about Cynane's escape, "she told me something. She said that when she was a little girl, she found the queen in her secret chamber below. A snake was entwined around her body, and she moaned the god's name."

Gideon stops in his tracks and slowly turns the full weight of his gaze on Jacob. "And why did you never tell me this before?"

Jacob squints at the hundreds of olives trees on the slopes below. Somewhere, men begin to sing a harvest song.

"Because I wanted more proof of Riel's existence in Pella before I told you." He throws up his hands in a gesture of futility. "You are right that, so far, this is only a story told by a proven liar. Before I wasted your time, I wanted to find out if it is true and, if so, decide how to capture him. If we can deliver him to the Spirit Eaters, we will save the world from their hunger for centuries."

The High Lord studies him, and Jacob feels that Gideon knows he isn't telling him the whole truth, that he is holding back something important. So Jacob adds, "If I am right, I will win for myself the highest honor among the Lords."

The truth of that statement fuels him with confidence like new oil in a sputtering lamp. "I come from nothing, High Lord. I am a poor potter's son. Think what it would mean for me to have *my* name inscribed on the Wall of Honor in Nekrana."

It works. Gideon's face—all cheekbones and square jaw and tense brows—relaxes into a slow smile revealing blazing white teeth.

"Tell me how you plan to learn more," he says, flicking the olive into the grass.

"Prince Alexander has visited the new oracle in Delphi three times in the past month."

Jacob remembers Alexander's first visit, nearly a month ago. Guards on the walls surrounding the villa rang the alarm bell. Jacob grabbed his weapons and climbed to the battlements, where he saw the golden-haired prince on his magnificent black stallion galloping down the winding, hilly road with a dozen warriors, a cloud of dust trailing behind them. Borne on long poles by the flag bearers, the emblem of Macedon— a gold sixteen-pointed star on a blue background—glinted in the sun. Gideon, believing it was a ruse for an attack with a much larger force, made the men rig the estate with booby traps and stand guard all night with fire arrows—for an onslaught that never came.

Gideon had chosen Lord Imbrus's estate as the place to regroup after the Battle of the Pyrrhian Fortress because it was within the sacred precinct of Delphi—neutral territory. No one, soldier or civilian, can harm another person under penalty of death for breaking the peace of the god Apollo, who owns these hallowed lands. When Apollo slayed a giant serpent in Delphi, he even sent himself into exile and worked as a slave eight years as punishment for defiling the holy place. The High Lord assumed there would be no worries about Macedonian armies here, yet has been on constant alert for almost a month.

Gideon sighs. "We must remain vigilant, Lord Jacob. Perhaps Alexander hopes to lull us into a sense of false security and then attack us. He cannot allow our kidnapping of his sister to go unpunished."

"I do not think the prince is so irreligious, High Lord," Jacob responds. "Nor do I think he is so reckless as to call down upon himself the wrath of every Greek nation, for they would all wage war on Macedon if he spilled blood in Delphi."

Jacob passes a wiry gray-haired man tying up several bags brimming with olives. The old man smiles and nods at him.

"High Lord," he continues, "can you think of any other reason for the prince to make so many trips to Delphi?"

Gideon runs his thumb over the smooth ivory pommel of his sword hilt and says, "Alexander is a young man running a country by himself while his father is in Byzantium, planning to marry a girl who might bear a new son and heir. The prince is beset by enemies on all sides. He has had to replace his father's entire council for treachery, corruption, or ineptitude. It could be that the boy is frightened and wants advice from the gods."

Suddenly Jacob remembers his encounter with Alexander in the Battle of the Pyrrhian Fortress, the memory so vivid it seems more real than the olive trees and orchard workers. The prince steps out of the choking smoke in the courtyard, sword glinting, cool calculation in his mismatched eyes as spears and arrows hurtle past his head. His sword thrusts toward Jacob's neck, almost impaling it, but Jacob raises his shield just in time. Again and again their swords ring out as they circle and lunge, spin and jump. Even though Jacob is taller and broader, Alex possesses extraordinary grace and speed.

Instead of the olive workers' harvest song, Jacob hears the cries of attack and the screams of pain, the clang of iron on iron, the thump of swords against wooden shields. He feels again the sharp surprising pain of an arrow tearing straight through his left bicep. He feels the heavy shield drop from his grip and wet blood spray his arm. Expecting the death blow, he looks at Alexander, whose eyes meet his. The prince's eyes speak loudly of...compassion. Sorrow. Understanding.

Time stops. Noise drains away to silence. In slow motion, the prince lowers his sword. Then little Timaeus somersaults between them, grabs Alexander's weapon, and is gone. The prince looks in disbelief at his empty hand. The moment stretches out until one of his men hands him a sword. Time rushes back in a flood of smoke and noise, and in the melee, Jacob, his wound aching, flees from the bravest person he has ever seen.

"Alexander is not afraid," Jacob says firmly, shaking his head. "Concerned, perhaps. Unsure. But never afraid. There is some other reason for his trips to Delphi, I'm sure of it. With your permission, High Lord, I would like to ride to Delphi and continue my investigation. The oracle has met often with Prince Alexander. Perhaps I can persuade her to share with me her conversations with the prince."

"Oracles are all babbling madwomen," Gideon says, pulling off his horned helmet and rubbing his hand over his closely cropped hair. "I wonder if you could get her to say a word of sense. There's a reason the Delphic god is Apollo Loxias— Apollo the Ambiguous."

"But I can try, High Lord."

Gideon nods. "Go, then. It is a laudable effort, Jacob. Especially in light of the new reports."

Jacob frowns. "New reports?"

Gideon nods grimly. "Spirit Eaters have left their confines in the caves of the Eastern Mountains. Many villages have vanished, devoured almost whole, and entire fishing vessels have disappeared, though no storms were reported. If we can give those monsters the living body of a god, we will satiate them for years to come. But I warn you: if Riel is alive, he is very dangerous indeed. We don't want to lose you, brother."

Jacob feels a flash of terrible guilt. *Brother.* What would Lord Gideon think of him if he knew the truth?

He watches as Gideon puts his helmet back on, tightens the leather strap, and turns back to the villa. Over his shoulder the High Lord calls back, "Send a report soon."

★ ★ ★

In the quiet hour before dawn, Jacob's jaw is rigid with tension as he saddles a gray mare and makes his way slowly down the inky, winding road toward Delphi, the sacred city that Apollo made his home a thousand years ago. Many hundreds of years later, the wealthy ruler of Corinth erected the first treasury there, a miniature temple the size of a comfortable room, richly decorated with statues and filled with gold and silver. Other kingdoms soon followed suit, each one trying to outdo the others in ornate splendor, eventually making Delphi one of the richest, most glittering cities in the known world.

The air is chilly, echoing Jacob's mood. For in all that divine excess he must root out the whereabouts of the last living god. His own life—and possibly the safety of all mankind—rests on it. This used to be his favorite time of year, he dimly recalls, the early-autumn breeze whispering memories to him as though from a previous life: the golden days of his boyhood in Erissa, warm but not hot, the nights crisp and cool, excellent for sleeping. But winter will be here soon, he knows, with its cruel wind and smoky rooms.

He passes many inns along the road, dark and silent with sleep, and olive orchards shrouded in a pale fog. He hears animals *baah*ing up ahead and rides past large pens of goats, bred, most likely, for the sanctuary where pilgrims will buy them for an enormous price to sacrifice to Apollo in return for an oracular prophecy. Thunder growls down the steep granite mountain on his right, which seems to Jacob just then like a living, sentient thing, watching him closely and not altogether pleased. He halts his horse and stares up at craggy cliffs, fear spiking the back of his neck.

Lord Eumolpus told him that one hundred and fifty years ago, when the Persians sacked Greece and destroyed the Parthenon in Athens, they marched toward Delphi to steal all the gold. But the mountains shook in anger and bellowed their rage at the heathens' impiety. Rocks roared down the slopes, blocking the road. Terrified at the god's anger, the army turned tail and ran. Jacob listens for any sound of sliding rock. Nothing. He urges his horse forward.

He passes a perfectly round temple on his left, torches between its columns flickering in the lingering dark. Inside, women sing an ancient hymn, presumably begging the god of the sun to speed the dawn on its way. He knows that he, like them, should be praying for help. He should be thinking of the prince and plotting how he is going to extract confidential information from the oracle about the nature of Alexander's frequent visits. The prince's sudden interest in communing with the gods and the simultaneous rumor of an actual living god housed in the palace cannot be a coincidence.

But all that occupies Jacob's mind as he rides through the early morning—no longer black, but something between purple and silver—surrounded by the low throb of the priestesses' hymns, is a rough, scalding, complicated murmuring. It tells him he is as strong as rock, that his veins carry not blood but molten gold and iron. It whispers of whirlwinds and raging seas and toppling mountains. It is the Earth Blood that wants—he can feel it—to come out. To be unleashed.

He hears the spring before he sees it: the sounds of water slapping against itself and rushing over rocks. The Castalian Spring, he remembers: the spot where Apollo supposedly killed the giant serpent and washed off the blood. The holiest water on earth. Even his mother, a peasant woman who never left her tiny Macedonian village, knew of this spring. Sometimes she'd tease that all the Castalian waters wouldn't clean the dirt off Jacob's younger brother, Cal, when he'd come home from a day playing in muddy fields.

With sudden inspiration, Jacob halts his horse and ties her to a pine tree, then makes his way silently down a path toward the water. He will bathe in the spring. Maybe even drink from it. It's not that he really believes it will protect him... How could it, when the true danger is within him? But for reasons he can't quite justify to himself, he yearns for it. Yearns, perhaps, for the feeling of being pure again. Of being clean. Yearns for the days when life was uncomplicated and the possibility of love and happiness seemed just a breath away.

In the silver half-light stands a sheer rock face, scarred with countless cracks, a gush of water roaring from a cleft in the rock into a basin below. A little temple-like fountain encloses the cleft, with columns and a pediment, and steps leading down around the basin.

Something—no, someone—is moving in the pool below. White arms, long hair. A girl, no older than he is, splashes and mutters to herself in a language that sounds, to him, like nonsense. She turns toward him, and he ducks behind a bush, but she hasn't seen him. He, however, has seen that she is naked. And for a heart-stopping moment he thinks that she is Kat. That Kat has somehow left Pella and found her way here, to this spring, so that he could find her and they could be together again. He thinks of the pond in Erissa, where they kissed for the very first time. That was the night before they left for Pella and everything changed forever.

But as the air grows lighter with the pale gold of dawn, he realizes the girl is thinner than Kat, not as muscular. And her hair isn't a sandy brown, like Kat's, but a blend of blond and red.

The girl chants into the brightening air, begging Apollo to tell her true prophecies. Suddenly he knows who this is. The Pythia—a title for all of Delphi's prophetesses. The beautiful new oracle everyone is talking about. Previous Pythias were all over fifty—toothless old hags, from what Jacob heard. But this girl possesses such oracular powers that the Delphic authorities made an exception, permitting a mere teenager to hold the vaunted position.

She climbs out of the pool, dries herself with a length of linen, and puts on a white robe. Then she turns toward the city and slips into the shimmer of rising mist.

Jacob waits, stunned. So this is the girl he needs to win over to tell him about Prince Alexander's visits. How can he even talk to her when she reminds him so much of Kat?

Slowly he undresses and goes to the pool to slide into the icy water. She was here just moments ago, standing where he stands, this water touching her skin. He thinks of Kat's long hair, soft and wild as a breeze. Her skin, slick from moisture. Her hands, clutching his upper arms so that she could look him in the face. The way she challenged him, always—mentally and physically— and that sharp, determined blaze in her eyes, which could set a fire within him until he felt certain he would burn from the inside and die happy.

Even now, with these thoughts radiating through him, he can feel the waters of the spring trembling and bubbling, as though his desires have seeped from his skin and infected the spring, or caused the earth beneath it to react.

But that girl—that Pythia—was not Kat. And the fantasies, the memories—he knows those must die, or, at the very least, must be muffled into a small pile of smoking embers, never to be seen or lit again, like his own magic.

Like his true self.

He cups his hands under the torrent racing out of the rock and drinks the liquid that stings his throat and chills his mind with its immortal song of sky and mountain and earth.

Half an hour later, back on his mount and the dampness of the spring's waters nearly dry on his skin and clothes, Jacob watches the rising sun break through clouds and glint on something. Delphi. He has made it. The ferocious beauty of the city on the hill causes a terrible pain to slice through him and tears to sting his eyes.

Nothing has a right to be this beautiful.

Everything should be this beautiful.

He feels a sob rising in his chest, a reminder of pain and loss, of beauty and hope and fear, all balled up and begging to burst out. He puts his hands over his face. The pain slicing through him is so overwhelming, he wonders if this is a real city. Perhaps it is Mount Olympus, home of the gods, something that kills mere mortals to see. He looks again, unsure of what he has seen, needing to see it again, not caring if the sight destroys him.

Mist hovers at the city's base so that it seems to be floating on a cloud, incandescent and shimmering. On one side of the city, the long slopes of the Krissaean Plain, dedicated to Apollo and crammed with olive trees, roll down to the breathtaking turquoise of the Itean Bay. On the other side, two rugged crags of Mount Parnassus rise like the enormous gray shoulders of a giant, embracing the sacred city, protecting it, nestling it in powerful stone arms.

Rose-gold rays of the sun hit gilded rooftops, flash on golden statues and blaze on burnished bronze, painting the hundreds of white marble buildings orange-pink. Delphi is the most crowded place Jacob has ever seen, filled with temples, arches, colonnades, and massive public buildings. Here and there a slender, spear-shaped poplar tree adds a bit of dark green to the riot of shining color.

High up the hill sprawls the enormous Temple of Apollo, bigger than a palace. Jacob counts fifteen massive columns painted with blue and yellow lines. Behind them, bright paintings cover the enormous walls. To the side, a colossal statue of Apollo, almost as high as the temple, gestures to his sanctuary. And on the steep hill above the temple rise row upon row of marble seats in Delphi's famous theater.

Sucking in a deep breath, Jacob reminds himself that if he is successful in capturing Riel and delivering the god to the Aesarian Lords, maybe he won't have to hide his true self anymore. That one day he, too, could be like the grand statue before him: glorious. Powerful. Free.

He urges his horse forward.

CHAPTER FIVE:
ALEXANDER

CHURNING, SALTY WATER RISES AND FALLS, CAR-rying him with it. Rain pounds his head and lightning hits the water with a hiss, sending spray flying into the sky. As foamy breakers crash over him, Alexander treads water, reminding himself he's a strong warrior and good swimmer. But he can see no land in any direction...

Something wraps itself around his leg and pulls him down into the gray swirling depths. It's a serpent. No... Something enormous and ridged... a tentacle. It's squeezing his calf. He can't see much underwater, but he takes his knife from his belt and starts to saw away at it. Black blood swirls around him as an unearthly howl from below rips into his soul...

Prince Alexander sits up, yelling and spitting, slapping the sheets and...realizes it was a dream. Just a dream. That's all. Tonight he's had so many strange dreams, one sliding into the next.

His eyes adjust to his surroundings. He's in his room at the Pellan palace. Starlight floats through his louvered shutters and puddles on the marble floor. Alex feels as if someone has crammed raw cotton into his head. He feels groggy, slow, sick. He should call for Heph, who is always sleeping, sword at the ready, in his little bedroom off Alex's palatial one. As Alex slips unsteadily out of bed, he remembers. Heph is gone. To Egypt with Kat. And he hasn't come back.

But Kadmus... Yes, Kadmus is sleeping there now as the prince's bodyguard.

Clumsily—it feels as if his hands aren't quite following his commands—Alex throws open the door too hard and it hits the wall with a bang. Kadmus leaps out of bed in his sleeping tunic, sword in hand. Then he sees who it is and lowers the weapon. But his eyes, glinting ice gray in the darkness, remain suspicious, his posture defensive, muscles flexed.

"My lord," he says, a mistrustful edge to his voice. "Are you unwell?"

Alex shrugs and runs a hand through his sleep-tousled hair. "Sorry I startled you, Kadmus. Bad dreams tonight. Perhaps the oysters disagreed with me."

Kadmus stares at him a long moment, then goes about the little room lighting the lamps. Soon, a soft amber glow envelops them. "My lord, there were no oysters at dinner last night," he says quietly.

Alex presses his palms to his eyes and holds them there, finding brief clarity in the blackness. "No jokes, please. I really am feeling strange." When he removes his hands, he notices that Kadmus, too, looks unlike himself. Not ill, but strained. Alex tries to think of what might have upset his friend and can arrive at only one thing. Giving Kadmus a hard look, he asks, "Are you still upset that I appointed the Persian prisoner as an adviser to the council?"

Kadmus sinks onto his narrow bed and shakes his head. His face remains tense. "No, my lord. Cosmas is an asset, just as you predicted."

Confused, Alex frowns. "How can he be an asset when he hasn't been to a council meeting yet?" he asks.

Kadmus rubs his eyes and says in a tired voice, "He's been to several, my prince, meetings which you yourself chaired. Are you taunting me again?"

What by all the gods is wrong with Kadmus? Does he

have a fever? Are the dangers of his political intrigues affecting his mind?

"What do you mean by that?" Alex says sharply, crossing his arms.

The general composes himself and says, "My lord, you... have not been yourself lately."

"How so?" Alex snaps.

"You have rescinded many of your decisions, decisions which I had found to be good."

"Such as?"

Kadmus puffs his cheeks with air, obviously considering how to answer politely.

"Don't worry about offending me, my friend," Alex says. "Answer honestly. Brutally. Tell me the truth."

Truth—and trust—have come to define their relationship, even since Kadmus confessed to Alex on Samothrace that he was the spy on the council, working for the Persian Assassins' Guild, which had threatened to kill his family if he did not. Alex had stopped him from killing himself in shame, requiring only that Kadmus pledge loyalty to him—and to Macedon—and take on the perilous task of becoming a double agent. Kadmus looked into his eyes and agreed, coming close to confessing his love for the prince. Alexander trusts him completely; Kadmus wouldn't lie to him now.

Kadmus's eyes burn like snow thrown on flame. "Very well," he says. "You dismissed Sarina from the council three weeks ago, telling her she was the wayward spawn of a wayward race."

"Dismissed...Sarina?" Alex risked everything to make a former slave, a woman and an Egyptian, one of his council members. He doesn't remember sacking her. And why would he? He has come to rely on her shrewd wisdom. *Never* would he have insulted her.

"You have spent more time in Delphi than here at home," Kadmus continues, "despite your council advising against it."

"*Delphi?*" Alex practically yells. Panic mixes with anger, creating an infuriating brew pumping through every vein in his body. "But I haven't been to Delphi since Leonidas took me there four years ago."

"My lord," Kadmus says, his face flushing so deeply that Alex notices even in the pale, flickering lamplight. "You returned yesterday in high spirits."

Alex starts pacing. The room is far too small to pace effectively, but he needs to keep moving or his brain might explode right out of his pounding skull. Five steps one way, five steps the other. He rubs the back of his aching neck. What happened? He couldn't have been sick with the brain-fever, not if he has been riding to Delphi and chairing council meetings. There is some witchcraft afoot.

"What else have I done?" he asks, stopping in front of Kadmus. He's afraid to know, but he must know.

"When you've been in Pella," Kadmus says hesitantly, "you have spent a great deal of time with your mother, asking her advice on how to rule."

"My *mother?*" Alex knows Olympias has always wanted political power and has tried to coax it out of Philip for years, then tried to interfere with Alex's regency once Philip left to wage war on Byzantium. Now he has a suspicion, a horrible one. Has his mother—known the world over as a dangerous witch—given him something to drink to turn him into her puppet? Has she been ruling Macedon through a bewitched prince regent?

"The Aesarian Lords?" Alex snaps. "Have they returned to Macedon with reinforcements?"

"They are still outside Delphi," Kadmus replies in a reassuring tone. It seems he is beginning to understand Alex was sick in some way, under a spell, perhaps, but has found himself again. "I was wondering if you were meeting with them there."

Alex rubs his temples and says through gritted teeth, "I don't know. I can't remember." He sinks onto Kadmus's bed. "How long have I been like this? How much time have I lost?"

Kadmus suddenly looks much older than his twenty-five years, or perhaps it's the unflattering shadows of the oil lamps. "A month, my prince." And in his voice is all the weariness of the world.

A month. Alex throws open the louvered shutters and sticks his head out. It is the dark of the moon, but blazing stars cast the red tile roofs of Pella in a shimmering light. The air is pleasant, dry, without the heaviness of a hot summer night. Tomorrow will be warm, he knows, but tonight is cool with the promise of winter. It is the first month of harvest. Yesterday, it seems to him, was still summer. Yes, Kadmus is right. Alex has lost an entire month.

He turns back and says, "Heph and Kat?"

Kadmus rises from the bed and puts a hand on Alex's shoulder. "You received a message from them a couple of weeks ago and tossed it aside as if it were of no importance. I do not know what they wrote."

Alive, though. They were alive enough to send a message.

"My father's war in Byzantium?"

"He has conquered the city, my lord."

Alex sighs. Thank the gods. As much as he was dreading his father's return, perhaps it would be best now with Alex... bewitched. "And he'll be coming home soon?"

Kadmus opens his mouth and closes it again. Then he stares at the floor.

"Tell me, Kadmus."

"Your father will be staying in Byzantium to celebrate his marriage to Cleo Eurydice, niece of Attalus."

"*What?*" Alex demands, stunned, remembering the buxom, blue-eyed girl who flirted outrageously with him earlier in the summer. "I thought my fath—I thought King Philip hated Attalus."

"He does," Kadmus agrees. "Attalus is always plotting against him. But now he will no longer be Philip's enemy. Because if Cleo has a son..." He pauses, looks directly into Alex's eyes with a pained expression, and then looks down at the floor again. "He will be Macedonian on both sides. My lord, your mother came from Epirus. You are, therefore, only half-Macedonian. Attalus and his friends are calling you an unfit half-breed."

An unfit half-breed. Would Philip really push his warrior son aside as heir for a helpless newborn baby? Why would he unless... Unless he, too, has heard whispers that Alexander isn't really his son.

Alex remembers asking Aristotle on Samothrace, *Does my Snake Blood come from Philip or Olympias?*

Neither, the old man replied, and refused to say another word about it.

And if that's true, Alexander isn't even the rightful heir of Macedon. He pushes the thought away like a plate of maggot-ridden meat.

"What else, Kadmus?" he asks, rubbing his aching forehead. "What should I be asking?"

"Persia, my lord. The three brides the Great King Artaxerxes sent to replace the missing Princess Zofia of Sardis have died in a carriage accident, he writes. But my contacts tell me the Assassins have murdered them and will kill any other brides he sends. They want war with Macedon, not a marriage alliance."

Alex isn't surprised. Persia has been delaying the alliance for months. It's only a matter of time before their army launches an official attack and the two nations declare war.

"And Cynane?"

"You received word that she arrived safely in Dardania. Her nuptials are imminent."

Alex can't picture his independent-minded warrior sister obeying a husband and wonders how Olympias managed to convince her to agree while he and Kadmus were in Samothrace.

"Has Arridheus been found?"

Kadmus shakes his head. "There has been no trace of him since his abduction."

Alex sent his twelve-year-old half brother away in disguise—at Sarina's suggestion—to protect him from enemies who might wish to kidnap him from the palace. Slow, childish, simple Arri would never be able to rule on his own and would make the perfect puppet king controlled by Aesarians, Persians, or Athenians nervous of Macedon's growing power. But on his journey to safety, men with military skills captured him and killed all but one of his guards, which was what first led the prince to suspect there was a spy in Pella who had learned of his plans. Alex expected a ransom request or a coup attempt. What could it mean, after all these weeks, that there has been no word? Alex feels anger welling in his chest, anger at himself. If he can't even keep one boy safe, how can he protect all of Macedon?

"My lord," Kadmus says, reaching for an oil lamp. "May I look closely at your eyes?"

"My eyes?" Alex asks irritably. "Very well. But why?"

Kadmus holds the lamp up to Alex's left eye, and then his right. "Fascinating," he murmurs softly. "My prince, for the past month your eyes have both been emerald green. Now they are back to the way they used to be—one blue and one brown."

"Witchcraft," Alex says immediately. "It might have something to do with my mother, some spell she has put on me to gain power for herself. Or else... Kadmus, have you heard of Blood Magic?"

Kadmus nods slightly. "There are many myths—"

"No, not myths," Alex interrupts, but even as he tries

to find the words to speak—to explain—he feels something pushing them down. He feels the thing watching him from the corners of his mind shifting, growing impatient. Alex does not have much time, and there is so much to untangle.

Suddenly he feels that someone is watching him from the inside, that a raven sitting silently in the rafters of his mind has woken up from a little nap.

Kadmus pours a cup of wine from the *oenochoe* on the table and hands it to Alex. "You need a bit of strength, my lord."

Alex stares into the dark depths of the cup. "I am afraid, Kadmus, that I will go entirely mad."

"But you are back to yourself now!" Kadmus says. "The illness is over."

The wine in the cup starts to foam and swirl, and spill out over the top. Water pours in through the window as the room starts to spin.

"No, not over," Alex says, his lips feeling fat, his words slurred. He drops the cup. It breaks into several pieces, which are quickly swept away by the rising waters. A moment later, they swirl around his knees, sucking at his tunic, pulling him down. "Just a tem…porary break. Do you see the water?"

"My lord, there is no water!" Kadmus says, his voice rising with panic.

There is no time, but Alex must try to tell him. "Kadmus, you must make sure that when I am not myself, when my eyes are…green, I do nothing to harm Macedon," he yells over the roar of the water, hoping the general can understand him. "The army… The army must be prepared to defend us against an Aesarian or Persian invasion. Do whatever you must to prevent me from harming anyone. You…"

But the water is like ten thousand snakes, pulling him down into its boiling blackness. He looks up, and far above him, above the water, looms the alarmed face of General Kadmus. Then darkness obliterates him.

CHAPTER SIX:
HEPHAESTION

THE EARLY-MORNING SUN BEATS DOWN ON Hephaestion, already hot. Sweat drips into his eyes as he pumps his legs and arms. He can see nothing but the white glare of the beach ahead of him, hear nothing but the lashing ocean waves and the pounding of his own pulse. *Faster. Stronger. Better.*

Ever since he came here three weeks ago, he has pushed himself harder and harder, taking his body to the limits and then beyond. He has changed in that short time, he knows. His skin has become deeply tanned, and his arm muscles seem cut out of firm clay, taut and defined. Katerina has even teased him for the streaks of light in his dark hair, as if his unruly curls captured sunbeams and refused to let them go.

A cramp spikes his side, and he slows and bends, heaving, his legs throbbing. He has made it almost around the entire island this morning. His running isn't nearly as satisfying— mentally or physically—as wrestling with the prince, but those carefree days seem like another lifetime.

For five years, he and Alex spent every day together. Suddenly it's all gone. And rigorous training—honing his body into something faster, stronger, better—this is what keeps him focused, prevents him from sinking into the horrible realization that he has failed the prince. That he is stuck on the tiny island of Meninx in an endless purgatory, so close to the woman he has fallen in love with and yet unable to tell her, unable to touch her, unable to bring her home to Pella…and unable to leave without her.

He spies her up ahead, standing knee-deep in the water and gazing out to sea as gentle waves roll around her. Her tunic is dripping wet, molded to her legs and the curve of her hip. Though she no longer wears the garb of a princess, there is no doubt within him that no one, royal or peasant the world over, is as beautiful as she.

"Kat!" he cries, running toward her.

She turns and walks toward him, sloshing through the rippling wavelets. One glance from her green eyes sends raw intensity rushing through him. The sea breeze whips her wavy golden-brown hair all around her, wild and free. He wants nothing more than to run his fingers through it. To touch her smooth, sun-kissed skin. To take her in his arms.

But when he kissed her last month, she pulled away, became angry. He promised he'd never do it again. Still, he can't get the kiss out of his mind, how her body pressed against his, responding; how her arms tightened around his back and pulled him toward her before she pushed him away. Though he hated her when they first met—thought she was an ambitious peasant girl running after the prince—his feelings changed. Now, all day, all night, she's *almost* all he can think about.

And yet, he can't tell her. It would be unfair to burden her with his heart when she already carries such a heavy load. In only a few months, Kat has faced more loss than most people would experience in a lifetime. Queen Olympias murdered her foster family in Erissa, and her beloved friend Jacob became an Aesarian Lord, an enemy of Macedon. Kat also learned that Helen, the kind, loving woman who raised her, wasn't her mother, and that the horrible queen—who had been trying to kill her since infancy—was.

Friends, he tells himself. They are good friends, that's all.

He cries out as an unseen object stabs his bare foot. He stumbles, collapsing awkwardly on the sand. Wincing, he examines his heel. Drops of scarlet blood mix with sand as pain shoots up his leg.

"Are you all right?" Kat is next to him. "What happened?"

He gestures to a shard poking out from the sand. "I think I stepped on a shell," he says.

Kat reaches for it. "It's not a shell," she says quietly. "It's another piece of pottery."

She hands it to him, and he sees three red painted tentacles curling across a black glaze, one of them holding a struggling warrior.

The back of his neck goes freezing cold, as if a dead hand were caressing him, and he throws the shard back on the sand with a shiver. He and Kat have found many such pottery fragments about the island, along with toppled columns and broken walls, all of them elaborately painted with giant squids, serpents with human faces, and enormous waves towering above a walled city. Images of a civilization punished for its innovation, for its powerful magic.

Myths, gods, magic—Heph used to laugh at people who believed in them. But he has seen magic firsthand now, and something deep inside him has been altered forever. All myths have their roots in truth, he knows that now.

But each newfound image on this island—found among the trees, on the beach, rolling in with the tide—seems to pound Kat deeper into herself, bit by bit extinguishing her fire, grinding away at her courage and determination, the very things that make her Kat. Lately, he has been worried by her long silences, by the bruise-like shadows under her eyes, by her lack of appetite. Now she stares at the shard in the sand, her eyes dull, her lips slightly parted.

He shouldn't have brought her here…but taking her back to Pella would have meant the death of his best friend and prince. For before he and Kat left for Sharuna, that cursed city along the Nile, Heph discovered a prophecy that foretold Kat would kill her twin, Prince Alexander.

Heph knows she loves her brother deeply and sincerely, that she would never hurt him intentionally, but still… He also knows prophecies have an eerie way of coming true, despite logic and reason.

He knows he can't tell her, for as stubborn as she is, she would probably race back to Macedon just to prove the prophecy wrong. And more, even, than Alexander is at stake here. The last line of the prophecy pounds in his head: *When the girl kills the boy and the world comes undone.* What does an undone world look like? Is it the end of Macedon? Of all the kingdoms and empires in existence? The end of mankind?

Heph had been uncertain what to do, but then Alexander unintentionally helped him. The prince sent them on a mission: go to Egypt and bring back the powerful Princess Laila to be his bride and to strengthen his army with her soldiers. Heph was assigned as punishment for failing orders, while Kat was sent to keep her safe from Queen Olympias, who still sought to kill her.

Ultimately, their mission was unsuccessful. Princess Laila would not be Alex's bride. And so, as he and Kat traveled back north, up the magical, timeless Nile, he grabbed every opportunity he saw to slow them down. He needed time to think. Time to plan. And in Memphis, the Egyptian capital, near the Mediterranean coast, he found his distraction.

Kat and Heph came upon a Greek bard in a tavern there, and he sang the tale of Odysseus, blown off course by angry gods after sacking Troy.

Thence for nine days' space I was borne by direful winds over the teeming deep, the old man sang, strumming on a small harp. *But on the tenth we set foot on the land of the Lotus-eaters, who eat a flowery food.*

Kat gripped her silver lotus pendant so hard her knuckles turned white.

And the Lotus-eaters did not plan death for my comrades, the bard continued, *but gave them of the lotus to taste. And whosoever of them ate of the honey-sweet fruit of the lotus had no longer any wish to return, but were fain to abide among the Lotus-eaters, feeding on the lotus, and forgetful of their homeward way.*

Heph enjoyed the story, but Kat had seemed enraptured, and later that night, he discovered why.

"Who would create an entire civilization around eating lotus flowers?" Kat had puzzled throughout that sleepless night. "Ada told me the lotus has power to temper Snake Blood. And Princess Laila said it stimulates the powers of Earth Blood."

She had recently learned that she possesses Snake Blood—a notion that at first stunned and confused Heph but quickly became just one of the many factors in his fascination with her.

In the predawn darkness, she woke him. "I think I figured it out! That legend of the Lotus-eaters must have something to do with Blood Magic. Heph, what if the Lotus-eaters were a whole community of Earth Bloods, attempting to enhance their powers?"

It was then, as she questioned, that Heph began to see that Kat was not just curious but truly *tortured* with a burning need to better understand the history of this magic—the history of her own blood.

And he could empathize with that desire, that yearning to connect to where you came from—after all, Heph himself was estranged from his own family, and there wasn't a day that went by that he didn't question what would have happened if things had gone differently, what his life would have been like if he hadn't been forced to leave everything he knew behind. If the young prince hadn't discovered him, a ragged thief, in the Pellan marketplace, taken pity on him, befriended him, and given him a whole new life—and a whole new family.

When the sun rose, he sought out the bard and, with a few bits of silver, persuaded the man to tell Kat more of this land of the Lotus-eaters. After studying several maps, Kat got a possessed look in her eye, pointing out a dot on the map that, when looked at closely, seemed to have six points on it, almost like a star—or a lotus flower. This *is the island that holds the answers*, she claimed.

But the irony is that instead of finding answers here, Kat has begun to lose herself.

Kat retrieves the pottery shard and kneels next to him, rubbing her golden fingertip—the one Princess Laila magically gifted to her after Princess Cynane maimed Kat—over the faded paint. "In the water, just now," she says, "I entered the sea creatures again to learn more about the Lotus-eaters. But the images are still confused, passed down by so many generations. I saw towering waves as high as mountains again. I saw—"

The shrieks of seagulls interrupt her. Heph turns and squints up the beach at the bow-legged figure darting from the trees, a basket in one hand, the other flung over his head to protect it from attacking beaks—his old friend and mentor, Aristotle.

At first, Heph thought their journey to the land of the Lotus-eaters would be a short one—a simple delay while he figured out what to do with the doom-fated Kat. At least, that is what he wrote to Alexander in the message he sent from Memphis, along with the news of their failure to woo Laila and a request for his forgiveness.

But as soon as they splashed into the shallow waters surrounding the island and pulled their little sailboat onto the beach, their plan changed.

For, on this supposedly desolate island, they'd found Aristotle sitting on the beach, almost as if he were waiting for them. The old man had been just as surprised as the young adults, but he'd taken the turn of events in stride.

"There are no coincidences," he'd said. "Everything is as it was meant to be. Through observation we may understand the how and why."

And as student and teacher shared their stories, it became more and more clear that this was no coincidence. Aristotle was here because he'd received a message from Ada of Caria to meet her on the isle of the Lotus-eaters. While waiting for her, he conducted experiments on the natural world. But it was well past the time when she was supposed to meet him, and she had never shown up.

Kat had gone wide-eyed. "Her palace," she whispered. "When Heph and I went, it was woven shut by spiderwebs."

Aristotle, to his credit, remained calm, but Heph knew his teacher well and recognized the deep concern in his furrowed brow and the lines around his lips.

And so their journey to the island had taken on a new urgency.

Every day, Kat searches the skies with her thoughts and communes with birds, calls out to Ada with love and longing, but never has she received a reply. Sometimes, frustrated with the emptiness of the skies, Kat dips into the thriving world of the sea, joining with creatures to sense what happened to the tribe of Lotus-eaters that died out so many years ago. But that, too, has only frustrated her. He can see how she has folded into herself, how the fiery light has faded in her eyes, how she has made their tragedy her own. Sometimes he finds her sitting by the pools of lotus flowers that dot the island, staring at the waxy pink and white blossoms as if she is in a trance.

Aristotle, on the other hand, is thriving.

"Hello, my dears," the philosopher says mildly as he draws closer. Heph can see that gull eggs fill his basket. For the past few days, Aristotle has been gathering gull eggs and dissecting them in his makeshift workroom, examining the different stages of the embryos' development. The old teacher has made something of a life out of traveling from one island to another studying sea and plant life, measuring the myriad ways in which nature may help to better understand what it is to be human.

Now he looks at Katerina, and Heph recognizes a concern that is mirrored in his own. "Are you all right?"

"I'm fine," Katerina says, rising and brushing the sand off her knees. "I just need some time for myself...to clear the mind." She trudges across the beach, slips into the cool shadows of the trees, and disappears, taking the sweetness of her scent with her.

Heph wonders if he should go after her, help her in some way. But as he stands, Aristotle addresses him. "I need your help, young man."

"Yes?" He's still looking at the spot where Kat disappeared.

"I need you to find sea urchins for me."

This piques Heph's interest. Being marooned with Aristotle has stimulated the curious part of Heph that was so alive during his days with Alexander at the philosopher's school for noble boys in Mieza. "What for?"

"Most male sea urchins have five gonads underneath," Aristotle says solemnly. "Others only four. I want to see if it makes a difference in fertilization. So you must bring them to me live—females, and males with both four and five gonads."

Heph breaks into a grin. So today it's sea urchin gonads. He was used to the scientist's eccentricities at Mieza, of course: when he set up tall iron bars just outside the school hoping lightning would strike them, which it did. When he ate only unripe plums for a week, keeping careful notes of his digestive complaints. When he sent his students to raid the woods for spiderwebs and braided them into rope to test for strength.

"And there's one other reason I'm sending you into the sea," Aristotle adds.

"What's that?"

Aristotle smirks at him. "Because you stink."

Heph laughs, then stands. A swim, even one that is part work, is the right thing to distract him from Kat's melancholy mood, from the mystery of Ada, from mulling over how to redeem himself in Prince Alex's eyes. The only thing that gives him any comfort at all is the very coincidence that had so stunned him.

Finding Aristotle on this desolate island was enough to make him believe in something like fate, in the will of the gods, though the scholar has pointed out repeatedly that they were all drawn here for similar reasons, seeking answers from the mystic history of this place.

Leaving his tutor, Heph limps across the beach to a gathering of rocks where he strips off his tunic. He dives naked into the ocean, letting the cool water wash away the sweat along with his dark and puzzled thoughts. In the clear waters, he kicks out.

Seven sea urchins float in his bucket, their purple spikes waving slowly. As Heph dries off after his dive, he blinks at the sandy beach, sparkling with the silver-gold slivers of metal that he has noticed from time to time ever since he has been here. They are thin, shiny, and pliable like the mica Heph has seen in various rocky areas of Macedon, but there is something different about these flecks, most of them no bigger than a baby's pinky nail, glimmering in the sun. The shallow water, too, glints with scattered particles, which clump together and separate, dance and sway on the waves as if they have minds of their own. And yet...could they?

No. He has looked too long at these fragments of sun; he is too tired, has pushed his body too hard. Or has he?

His heartbeat ticks up a notch as vague wisps of an idea join and solidify in his mind. He scans the beach for a large shell. Finding one, he gathers up some of the glittering metal flakes before sprinting to Aristotle's makeshift workshop and busting through the door.

"Hephaestion!" his tutor calls out now, turning from his rough-plank table. "Do you have the sea urchins?"

"Yes," Heph says, putting the bucket on the table. "And this." He shoves the shell with several glinting metal flakes at him.

The man gives Heph a knowing glance. "What is that?" he asks, but Heph hears how his voice is abnormally light and airy.

"Something highly unusual," Heph responds. "Let me show you."

He searches the cluttered table among gull embryos pickled in jugs, giant balls of spiderweb, and an assortment of unusual rocks until he finds an empty bowl, which he fills with water. Then he takes all the precious metal he's been collecting and dumps it straight into the bowl of water. The metal flakes swirl randomly but then begin to drift to one side of the bowl.

"I got the idea by watching as the tide pushed them around," Heph explains. "Even when the waves pulled out to sea, they would shift together with no logical explanation for the phenomenon. It's almost as if they did it on purpose."

Heph hands Aristotle the bowl, and he moves it around, but the metal still sways to the same side, no matter how Aristotle holds the bowl.

"It seems like the water causes the metal to respond to some external force," Heph says. "It's as though the metal itself carries a directional knowledge."

For a moment, Aristotle's dark gray eyes take on an amused look, and he smiles broadly. "Well done, boy. And I used to think you were only good for wrestling and riding."

Heph ignores the jest at his expense; he's too excited by the discovery. "What do you think it is?"

Aristotle stares into the bowl, then he raises his eyes to meet Heph's. "I think I know what these shiny flakes might be, Hephaestion. I have seen them myself, experimented with them before you and Kat arrived."

He sets the bowl on the table and approaches the wide window overlooking the beach and the thundering breakers rolling in. "There is an old tale of something known as the Atlantean Mechanism," he says, "that was made of shiny bits of metal like this that they called *baruopa*, which meant something like 'glittering' in their language. It's said that the people of Atlantis built their *baruopa* mechanism shortly before their civilization was destroyed and sank into the sea along with it."

Heph is aware of the myths of Atlantis from his studies. He and Kat have talked about them over the last few weeks—the great vanished nation believed to have possessed extraordinary brilliance and unimaginable powers, especially when Kat began to suspect that the Lotus-eaters might have, in fact, been the survivors of the catastrophe that killed the Atlanteans. "But what did this *baruopa* mechanism do?" Heph asks, standing beside him.

Aristotle shrugs, turning. "Some say it could track the movement of the stars and planets. Others say it was the tides, and yet others the movement of armies. It is possible they could adapt it for a variety of purposes, tracking whatever they wished." Heph's heart pounds with excitement. He wants to ask a hundred questions but knows he must let his teacher tell the story at his own pace.

Aristotle watches a large gull dive into the froth and emerge with a glistening silver fish in its beak. He continues. "When

I was on Samothrace, Ada sent me word that she needed help in building a new Atlantean Mechanism to find something—or someone—to stop a great evil rising in the world. She bade me acquire the necessary materials and meet her here, on this island devoid of everything but myths of Atlantis and shiny golden flakes. And so I arrived with forges and molds, and drawings of the supposed Atlantean Mechanism that I copied from ancient archives in Egypt. But there are...difficulties."

"What difficulties?" Heph asks, unfazed. Difficulties exist only to be overcome.

Aristotle pushes out his lower lip and tugs on his graying beard. "First, Ada hasn't arrived, so I am not sure what it is that the mechanism is supposed to detect. Second, even if the flakes are *baruopa*, when heated, they melt down to almost nothing. We'd need ten thousand times more than your bowl of metal to forge a prototype mechanism to test it. That's years' worth of collecting them."

Heph's mind races ahead. Aristotle didn't say that it was *impossible*. He, Heph, could be part of one of the greatest discoveries since the fall of Atlantis.

"If we find enough *baruopa*," he says, "could we use the mechanism to find the missing Ada of Caria?"

Aristotle pauses, then a slow, sad smile stretches across his face. "You are worried about our Katerina, are you not?"

Heph nods. "If we could create such an instrument to find Ada, it would make Kat so happy," he says, as his mind races ahead. "And if we gave it to Alexander, he could track Persian armies and invading ships. He could discover the troop movements of all the regiments of the Aesarian Lords." *And he would finally forgive me*, he thinks.

Aristotle puts up a cautioning hand. "Others have tried, Hephaestion. I was not the first to copy the old drawings, nor, I think, the first to believe the shores of Meninx may be littered with *baruopa*. The third difficulty is that the instructions are incomplete, I think. There is some ingredient we need to add, but I have no idea what it is. I was hoping Ada, a Snake Blood, with her knowledge of ancient lore, would know. Without her, it's practically impossible."

Heph swats away Aristotle's warning as if it were an annoying mosquito. "We can keep experimenting, though. You have the diagrams and the equipment. And Kat is a Snake Blood, like Ada. She can help us." He needs to tell Kat about the mechanism. She has become that person now—the one he wants to run to with news, with discoveries, with secrets. And maybe it will cheer her up, distract her from her pain.

She's not in the palm hut they built when they first arrived, nor is she on the beach. He heads into the interior of the island, past the lotus ponds and the lean-to where Kat boils their laundry, past Aristotle's experimental vegetable patch. When he finally finds her, she is asleep amid the ruins of what he can only assume was once a temple. A cracked pediment lies behind her, painted in faded colors with people drowning in huge crashing waves. Her golden skin is sun-dappled, the swaying branches making shadows dance across her. Some patches of her skin have begun to redden and burn.

He stops, standing over her, staring at her softly breathing form. Carefully, he picks her up and carries her back to the palm hut. She murmurs something he can't quite make out as he lays her down on her blanket. He gently smooths her hair, but when she stirs, he pulls his hand away.

Though he wishes he could remain here in the cool shade with Kat, Heph knows that if he wants more peaceful moments like this in the future, he must leave. He must hunt for more of the mysterious metal and devise a plan for the mechanism. There's work to be done.

Chapter Seven: Rat

RAT PULLS THE BOW BACK AS FAR AS HE CAN, enjoying the feel of strength in his arm muscles. He was weak before. No one bothered to train him. He lets his arrow fly, and it sings through the golden air, straight and true, sinking deep into the painted target at the other end of the field, just a little off center. Rat cocks his head and studies it, his sadness lifting. It is so good, finally, to be like the others. To fit in somewhere.

Almost.

He goes to retrieve his arrows, but feels a heavy hand on his shoulder. Yuf glares at him, his bald head shining with sweat in this hot place with no clouds.

"No celebration until you have completed your mission," his teacher says. "Isn't that right, Rat?"

Rat nods, though somewhere in the back of his mind he remembers that he was once called something else. That his name wasn't always Rat...but what was it?

"And what have we done for you?" Yuf asks. His heavy kohl eyeliner is running in rivulets down his tanned cheeks.

"You have healed my mind and tongue," Rat says automatically. "You have made me strong."

Yuf nods. "And what will you do for us in return?"

An image floats in his memory of a golden-haired boy giving him honey cakes and playing games with him…but he can't grasp *who* it is. Someone close to him—someone who called him *Arridheus*. A friend, maybe. Or—

There's a crack in the air, and the tip of a whip lashes down on Rat's arm. He gasps in pain, but he does not cry. There are to be no tears in front of Yuf. The leather has only left a faint pink mark on his skin, but the small burst of pain has done its work. Rat remembers what he must do.

He draws back the arrow for a second time.

"Kill Prince Alexander of Macedon," he says, then lets the arrow fly.

It hits its mark.

CHAPTER EIGHT:
KATERINA

IT'S DARK, YET DAWN IS NOT FAR OFF, KATERINA senses. Only a sliver of moonlight slants in from their roof of palm fronds. Beside her, Heph sleeps, his strong chest rising and falling. He has always slept well on the island, unlike Kat. Sometimes there are a thousand chattering voices in her head at once, voices of birds, flies, fish, whispering to her of terrible things happening in Macedon. Terrible things that once happened to the inhabitants of this place, too. A whole civilization and their original homeland, drowned, washed away completely by the sea, save for the lucky few who made it to this remote sanctuary.

The Lotus-eaters. The survivors. The only ones who remembered the true glory that Atlantis once had been. Except now, they, too, are long gone.

Kat had at first been thrilled and inspired by the idea of coming here and exploring what she suspected had been the habitat of a tribe of talented Blood Magics. But by reading the paintings on the fallen temples and broken clay objects, and by listening to the worried, rambling, passed-down tales of the wildlife, she began to understand the true tragedy of the Lotus-eaters.

She had been right about who they were, but wrong about why they came. They didn't come to this island to reclaim their magical birthright, nor to rebuild the glory of Atlantis, nor to celebrate their legacy. It was quite the opposite: they came here *to forget*.

The Lotus-eaters couldn't bear the idea that their loved ones, everyone they knew, had sunk into the sea because of their powers. Kat didn't understand exactly what happened—birds and fish don't think in timelines with cause and effect—but they can feel, and sense the feelings of others, and pass these feelings on down the generations. In the luminescent blue vault of the sky, in the dark shifting waters of the sea, they felt the grief of the Lotus-eaters, the heavy guilt of surviving while all the others had slipped beneath the waves.

So the Lotus-eaters foreswore magic, becoming obsessed with eating the lotus flowers in order to suppress their powers. For they were all Snake Bloods, like her. All of them. Not Earth Bloods, who use the lotus to increase the power of their bodies, but Snake Bloods, who use it to decrease the intensity of their minds. They ended their days in an intoxicated haze, their magic flickering and dying within them.

And for some reason, this seems even sadder to Kat than the great tragedy of Atlantis. Because the Lotus-eaters chose to bring ruin upon themselves. They weren't punished by the gods as she had first thought—they punished themselves in a paroxysm of guilt and grief and loss. They hated their own magic for destroying their homeland, Atlantis, and almost everyone in it.

As for Kat's magic, she's not sure. It continues to throb and grow, unspooling within her, charging her with compulsions. She must listen to the voices around her, must send her mind away from herself…and yet she's terrified. What if mortals simply aren't meant to possess magic? What if, like the Lotus-eaters, she'll end up miserable and isolated, desperate to destroy the very gift, the very power, that makes her who she is?

She, too, aches from guilt and grief. Despite her magic, she could not protect the family that raised her, Jacob's family, from Olympias's murderous revenge. Nor could she save Ada of Caria—the woman who taught her everything she knows about magic in her mountain fortress near Halicarnassus—from whatever strange fate befell her when spiders wrapped her mountain fortress in giant webs. She calls to Ada day after day. *Where are you? Are you safe?* But never is there any response, never any sighting, not even a rumor of a rumor in the mind of a gull.

Now Heph has a plan to find Ada, a mechanism they will make if only they can find enough of the glinting flakes on the beach and some secret ingredient. Heph says the gold flakes are coming from somewhere; perhaps it is a mineral worn from rocks in the sea and they can find the source. Aristotle says it might be from a sea plant they could harvest.

She can't tell them that the plan seems hopeless, that they are helpless. Even if they find enough of the golden grains, what if it isn't *baruopa*? Ada is gone, and Kat feels sometimes that she is slowly joining her in oblivion.

On nights like this, when the voices and their overlapping stories of sadness and death overwhelm her, making sleep impossible, she yearns more than ever for Helen. To be held and comforted by the woman who will always be *mother* in Kat's heart. But it cannot be. Because Helen was murdered by the evil queen who turned out to be Katerina's real mother. Even putting the words *mother* and *Olympias* in the same thought makes her want to retch.

Since coming to Meninx, Kat has also pondered another relationship. Her father is not the wandering wool merchant Helen had told her about, the handsome young man who died of a fever shortly after Kat's birth. Her father is King Philip of Macedon. She's not sure how that makes her feel. She glimpsed the king before he left with his army to besiege Byzantium— he was a large, one-eyed man who drank heavily and loudly ordered everyone about. She wondered how he'd react to the news of a new daughter. Perhaps he would be glad, but more likely he would view her as just another trophy to be handed out to allies.

If Kat could slip away from this unending anguish into the sweet release of a pleasant stupor, would she? She's not sure, but the thought sends dread and heaviness through her veins. Sometimes, she thinks it *is* best, like the Lotus-eaters did, to forget.

It is hot in their small hut. Silently, Kat rolls off her sleeping mat and tiptoes outside, taking a deep breath. She lets the night breeze cool her off as she makes her way down the beach in the darkness lit by the glow of stars and a moon like a fingernail paring. The sea greets her as if it were an old friend. These past weeks, its rhythmic waves have calmed her frustration and panic until their lapping and crashing have come to seem like sounds she has known forever, even though she was raised on an inland farm and had never seen the ocean until a couple of months ago.

The crescent moon ripples silver-white across the blue-black water, and Kat wades out until the sand falls away beneath her feet. She treads water a moment, enjoying the feeling of utter weightlessness, then floats on her back, staring up at the million stars blazing like festival torches.

The whispering and weaving of myriad tiny voices, of shifting moods and feelings and urges, drifts up to her from the salty paradise below, vying for her mind's attention, crowding out her own worried thoughts. Small crabs scuttle sideways around rocks and shells, hoping to find a worm or dead fish. Sea urchins sigh with pleasure as water streams through their waving, needlelike spikes.

Turning over, she sees that a thousand small glowing orbs surround her, lighting the water. She stretches out her hand and, as if curious, they flutter around it so she can see her fingers clearly. The little glowing creatures pulsate quickly across her hands, feeling like tiny gentle kisses, except on her golden fingertip, which is numb, as always. She studies it now, in the luminescent water. While she is glad she no longer has an unsightly stump, she is constantly frustrated that the tip has no feeling.

A small turtle strokes its way toward the light. Effortlessly, she sinks into its thoughts. It loves fish and algae, and the feel of warm sunlight on its shell. It fears sharks, blood, and the screams that come thudding through the water when a creature is devoured alive.

She reaches to touch the turtle, to send it thoughts of comfort, but a coconut shell bobs in front of her. She picks it up just as a shaft of moonlight falls on it. For a moment, she is holding the head of Hagnon, Alexander's finance minister, crabs burrowing into empty eye sockets. She drops it with a scream and splashes away, but when she looks back she sees it is just a coconut shell, after all, rolling up and down on the tiny moonlit waves. She is imagining things, that's all, because she is worried about her brother.

Aristotle told her and Heph about Alex's visit to Samothrace, about his beheading of Hagnon, and how he almost executed counselors Gordias and Theopompus, as well. But Aristotle thought Alex returned to Macedon armed with wisdom, having learned an important lesson.

Kat hasn't told Aristotle or Heph about what the birds have whispered to her: that Alex isn't acting at all like himself; he has become impatient, cruel. That her twin is in trouble, that his eyes have changed color. She fears the worst: he is sick from not knowing how to control his powerful Snake Blood. And she's flooded with guilt. He needs her. She must go home.

The dry sand sticks to her wet feet as she quietly makes her way back toward the hut and its thick heat. Then a cry—or a caw—tears open the sky behind her. She turns to see a black form emerging from the darkness, as though a piece of the night has broken off from the rest. The shape grows larger, careens closer. A falcon. Furiously flapping its wings.

No, not flapping...faltering.

Falling.

It is not just any bird. Kat's golden fingertip tingles and throbs the closer the bird approaches. She throws her mind toward it, and her magic catches on a fizzing sense of someone else's magic.

Ada.

CHAPTER NINE: DARIUS

DARIUS REMOVES THE SMALL COPPER POT FROM the brazier and sets it on the marble table to cool. He is happiest working in his laboratory, part of his palatial suite of rooms in the Persepolis palace. Branches, seed pods, and blooms litter the tables and hang upside down from the rafters to dry. He spends his most meditative hours in here, mashing roots, brewing poisons, and crafting antidotes. Sometimes, he tries them out on the rats that scuttle in the twig cages next to the table. Now and then, he experiments with his concoctions on a convicted criminal.

As principal adviser to the Great King of Persia, affairs of state are never far from Darius's mind. Not just one set of affairs, but two—those of King Artaxerxes, and those of his own, very different goals.

For many years now, Darius has been chief of the Assassins' Guild, the real power in Persia. True, Artaxerxes has the title, the palaces, the armies, and the wealth. But the Assassins control politics in dark, secret ways, often working directly against the Great King. Those who interfere with their plans are either poisoned or—if a more dramatic statement is required—found with a bloody X slashed over their hearts.

He drops a grain of arsenic into the mixture and stirs until it has dissolved completely. Then he tips in a tiny vial of cobra, adder, and viper venoms, sprinkles in some wolfsbane, and adds a drop of hemlock and a pinch of dried jellyfish sting. Dollops of honey, myrrh, and cinnamon will hide the sting as death slides across the tongue and down the throat.

"Good morning."

Darius turns and smiles when he sees that one of his favorite members of the Assassins' Guild has entered his workshop.

"Good morning, Ochus," Darius says as he tips the mixture into a goblet of wine and stirs rapidly. "I see Rostam gave you my message." Tipping his head back, he drains the goblet and wipes droplets from his black beard.

"I don't know how you can do that," Ochus says, grimacing. "Poisoning yourself like that, daily."

"Life is full of venom," Darius says, setting the cup down with a hard clink. "Everything can be poisonous depending on the dose. Wine, certainly, water, even. Too much water will kill a man."

He briskly stacks his bowls and mortars in a washbasin. "Hate is poisonous in its very nature. But also...love. An excess of love can be deadly. We must inure ourselves to poison of all kinds, bit by bit, so that we get used to it. Otherwise, we are vulnerable."

Ochus shrugs. "I'm probably one of the least vulnerable people on earth."

Darius studies the young man stroking the gleaming tawny skin of the lion he killed in the western empire, the one that took the lives of two of his men and Princess Zofia. When Ochus returned to Persepolis, he waited eagerly for the courier to arrive from the tanner's out west where he had left it for curing. As soon as it arrived last week—complete with fangs, claws, and amber eyes to match Ochus's—the boy put it on, tying the front legs over his left shoulder, and hasn't been seen without it since. Now, studying Ochus, Darius realizes Ochus looks very much like the Greek demigod Heracles.

"Remember," Ochus says, smiling, "I dispatched this creature with my bare hands."

Darius nods approvingly. "Pity, though, you never found the princess's body."

He studies the Assassin for his reaction. Reports came to him from spies on the Royal Road that Ochus traveled east with a beautiful dark-haired girl he'd chained up, though the young man laughed off these stories. "I prefer my women to come to me willingly," he'd answered with a smirk.

Now Ochus continues to stroke the hide on his shoulders. "I can't imagine you summoned me here to discuss my attire."

Darius ignores the snide tone. "Come, walk with me."

He opens the doors into his Garden of Death, small and square, and surrounded by the rooms of his palace apartments. Life thrives here in the luxurious green of hardy plants, the rainbow colors of flowers, the cawing and flapping of his pet crows, and the buzzing of insects. But death lives here, too. All the plants are toxic: nightshade and hemlock, hellebore and henbane, digitalis and wolfsbane.

Darius folds his hands behind his back and walks toward the little fountain, water spewing from the gaping maws of underworld monsters.

"I met this morning with the Great King," the adviser says, picking off a brown hemlock leaf as he passes. "At eighty-five, His Highness is craftier than most men in their thirties. The man is not foolish. The murder of the three princesses does not seem to him like a coincidence, nor should it."

The Assassins, at Darius's own command, killed the three royal brides that were headed to Prince Alexander of Macedon, because Darius doesn't want an alliance. He wants one thing only, and he knows that there's nothing more dangerous to the empire than Artaxerxes's desire for peace with Macedon.

Ochus leans against the fountain, his eyes gleaming. "How many more dead princesses will it take to forge a path to war?"

Darius shrugs, glancing at the masterpiece of his garden, the rose he worked so hard to cultivate. Many would think it was white, but it is instead the palest pink, as if a single drop of scarlet blood fell into pure milk. Two red veins cross in its center, creating a vibrant, bloodred X. The Assassin's Bloom, he has named it. But autumn is coming, and the exquisite, fragrant roses will die soon. Just like the exquisite, fragrant brides.

Darius exhales slowly. "By now, most families realize it's not an honor for their daughter to be chosen so much as a death sentence. The Erez-razpas, the Mathra-vakas, and the Parash-turas—all the most noble families have told me their eligible daughters are sick with fever and cannot be seen."

Ochus laughs and runs a hand through his hair. "That seems understandable."

"It's only a matter of time now," Darius continues, ignoring him. "Spies tell me Macedon is growing restless. King Philip and Prince Alexander will become impatient with us soon enough, and the Great King will be forced to act. We need only one more bride, and this time I have a specific plan—"

The door to the laboratory flies open, cutting Darius off with a bang.

Rostam enters, wearing an expression of utter shock. Within three heartbeats, Darius has ticked off several possibilities. Artaxerxes has been assassinated. His sons have been assassinated. There is rebellion in the army. But on the fourth heartbeat he realizes that none of that could have happened without his extensive spy network catching wind of it first.

"Tell me," he commands.

"My lord," Rostam says, his voice shaking, "spotted over the city gates…a girl—riding a Pegasus!"

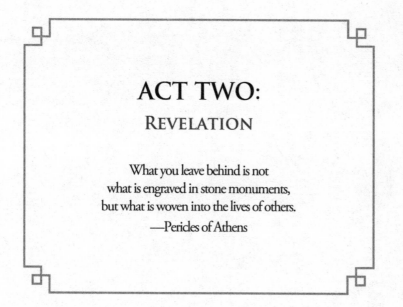

ACT TWO:

REVELATION

What you leave behind is not
what is engraved in stone monuments,
but what is woven into the lives of others.
—Pericles of Athens

CHAPTER TEN:
ALEXANDER

ALEXANDER FIGHTS AGAINST THE DARK WATERS
pushing him down, battling his way toward awakening.

You are strong, *comes the voice inside him.* But not strong enough.

Alex finds himself surrounded by explosions of light and song. A memory, powerful and ever-present, though not his own.

He must be trapped in another dream, one of the endless series of dreams and memories that wrap around him like tentacles and drag him down into a dark swirling abyss.

He catches only the briefest glimpses of faces, fragments of voices. Lightning strikes the parched earth and a pulsating silver spume flies heavenward. Waters rise, washing the world clean of men's evil. These are the dark waters, Alex realizes. The sense of drowning...

It is as though years, maybe centuries, pass within one moment, one memory.

Over time, the waters have receded into a clear blue pool.

The Fountain of Youth.

More time passes. People creep toward the pool and drink. A village rises beside it. The villagers grow tall, strong. But as the years multiply, those who drank of the waters turn dark themselves, grow wings, claws—become monstrous creatures, with a ravenous hunger.

Alex sees them roping a goddess, tearing into her glowing flesh with sharp teeth as her screams nearly shatter the sky, and then her light is gone. Other lights rise heavenward, away from the monsters, into a place of safety.

The gods.

They are fleeing.

He feels as though a light has been sucked out of him—he is emptied, and terrified.

He hears the shrieks of people being eaten alive.

We must destroy the fountain, *says a voice that he loves.*

The other gods have fled this realm, *he objects.* There is nothing to keep us here.

We cannot let the Spirit Eaters annihilate mankind. I will not leave this place until I destroy them.

And so, a war is waged.

And so, the last of the gods force the Spirit Eaters back.

Alex—though he is not Alex in these memories, this much he knows—lies on the ground, his entire body throbbing with pain, as if a giant has hurled him against a cliff face. His lungs are so tight he can hardly catch his breath.

Alex looks at his hands—which are not his hands but much larger—and feels them tingle and burn. But the rain stops hitting his face like needles. Storm clouds skitter away like women running with ragged, wet gray skirts, taking the rumbling thunder with them. Now Alex sees a sapphire-blue sky exactly the color of Brehan's eyes, and something twists painfully in his heart. Brehan. Brother. I have missed you.

Alex looks at his hands again, and blinks. They are his own hands. And they're sticky with something warm.

Blood.

He blinks, waking. The cracks in the muddy ground have become pink marble tiles with patches of early-dawn light filtering in through slatted shutters. He looks up. The blue sky over the fountain is now a coffered ceiling painted with the sixteen-pointed gold star of Macedon.

Strong hands grip his arms tightly behind his back. Alex struggles and twists. Standing behind him is Cosmas, his handsome face taut with determination. Mystified, Alex stops struggling and hears a loud groan. Kadmus leans against the far wall, his bloody hands gripping a dagger embedded in his side.

"Run, Kadmus!" Cosmas cries. "Leave the palace and don't come back!"

Panting with pain, Kadmus straightens. He pulls the dagger out of his side and lets it fall onto the floor with a clatter. Then he bunches his tunic into a ball and holds it tightly against the heavily bleeding gash.

He lifts gray, compassionate eyes to Alex. "It is not a mortal wound, my lord. Just a painful one. I've had worse." He forces an unconvincing grin. "Your eyes...they are back to normal. For now. Cosmas, let him go."

Reluctantly, Cosmas releases the tight grip on Alex's arms.

Alex takes a tentative step toward his wounded friend, his hand outstretched as a wary Cosmas shadows him. "Kadmus, did I...?"

"Not you, my lord. Never you," Kadmus replies, his voice thick with emotion. "I swear I will find a way to heal this sorcery which has taken you over."

He looks at Cosmas. "Keep this incident secret. If it gets out that the prince regent's mind is diseased, Macedon's enemies will pounce. Don't let him hurt anyone else."

Alex feels like he'll be sick. "Kadmus—" But when Kadmus shakes his head, Alex stops. His friend and guard bows once more, deeply, before he turns and limps from the room.

Panic ticks through the prince's veins.

How could this have happened? What sinister rage came over Alex when he was dreaming? How could he ever have tried to kill this man—his most trusted adviser, his friend? Why doesn't he remember anything? He pushes bloody hands into his hair and squeezes his skull as if he could force out the confusion and horror.

Think. He must quiet himself and think. He looks down at his tunic. Dark blue. That's not the one he was wearing the last time he woke up, when he asked Kadmus to keep him from doing harm. That night he was wearing a beige one. This is another day, then, perhaps weeks or even months later. More lost time. Alex's mind—that sharp, flexible instrument he has always prided himself on—has become his own worst enemy.

He suddenly remembers the thing, the being, living in the corners of his mind. It is still there, he knows, but resting, sleeping, like a bird whose head is firmly buried under its wings. He must hurry. There is very little time before it will awake to listen and watch once more.

"What happened, Cosmas?" he asks. "What did Kadmus say or do that angered me so much I stabbed him?"

The Persian studies Alex. "You don't remember anything, my lord?" he asks.

"No!" Alex wants to howl it, a loud wolflike wail, but he is prince regent. He must *control* himself.

"He gave you a message, my lord. Here." He picks up a small scroll off the floor and hands it to Alex. Written in what looks like blood is one line: *We will deliver war to Macedon's gate by the hand of her own prince regent.*

Alex shuts his eyes tightly and tries to think. Kadmus has been working as a double agent, claiming allegiance to the Assassins' Guild. Alex is aware that Persia seems ready for war, despite the actions of the Great King, who repeatedly promises him a bride to seal an alliance. But what could it mean that they intend to deliver war by the hands of the prince? He doesn't know.

"Did Kadmus say anything about it?" he asks. "What it meant?"

Cosmas shakes his head. "No, he asked me to join him here with you as he had something to share about Persia. He handed it to you. You read it and tossed it aside. And then you just stared at him for the longest time, a look that could melt iron. It happened so fast I couldn't stop you. You just stabbed him."

I didn't stab him, Alex thinks. *It wasn't me. But it was my... hand.* He looks at his hand, which is both narrower and longer than the hand in his dream. His head spins.

A familiar, sickening shadow spreads across his mind. It is back. Awake. He is no longer completely himself.

A voice pierces his whirlwind of thoughts. The voice is inside him, yet not him. One with him and yet separate.

True, you are not yourself, Alexander, the voice says, booming with power and yet utterly quiet. *Not anymore. Now you are...me.*

Alex feels as if this other being is choking out his thoughts, his very Alex-ness. He no longer has control over anything. What force has taken him over? Is it mania caused by uncontrolled Snake Blood? Or is this witchcraft?

No, not witchcraft. I am Riel, the voice states calmly. *I am a god. I am your father.*

Father, yes. Alex remembers something he learned recently. King Philip is not his father. A god is.

"But why," he begins, trying to tamp down the fear paralyzing his every muscle. Fear that this is real. Fear that it isn't, and he is going insane. The thumping of his heart reverberates through his head like a gong, drowning out logical thought. "Why are you...me?"

Alexander, the voice in his head says, clear and crisp against the rising roar. *Long ago a powerful oracle gave me prophecies direct from the gods in heaven.*

Alex sees in his mind's eye a girl with long black hair. She opens her mouth and the sound of her voice wraps around him, squeezing the breath out of him. *Beware Earth Blood! If you cannot find your way back to the gods in time, the blood of your brother's descendant will cause your death!*

How can I return to the gods in time? Alex-Riel asks, his voice tense with impatience.

The shrieking voice lashes him like a whip. *When the father begets himself, the father and son will be one. You may return to the godly realm when divine blood rules Macedon.*

Fighting hard, Alex pulls himself away from the voice, away from the water burbling at his knees. "But how," he says, "how did you get inside me?"

Olympias strokes his cool scales and says, *I just need a bone from my own offspring to give you a man's form again.*

"A man's...form," Alex repeats, his lips thick and tongue swollen. "My...form." Water rises fast and furious around him, buffeting him in strong currents, twisting like giant snakes all around his legs, his torso.

But before he sinks into the waters, there is something he needs to understand. "But how do you...how do you pretend to be me?" he wants to know. Does Riel recognize his counselors, his friends and servants? The layout of the palace?

He hears a ripple of laughter. *I can access the shadows of your memories, when I need to.*

This force within him, this god, has many secrets, Alex knows. As he feels the flame of his consciousness sputter, he resolves to keep some secrets himself. He will build a wall around himself, sealing inside it his knowledge that Cosmas knows and Kadmus lives. And if the enemy breaches that wall, he will dissolve all his *Alex-ness* into nothingness, taking this knowledge with him to protect his friends.

The black water submerges him, filling his eyes, his ears, his mouth. And then...there is *nothing*.

CHAPTER ELEVEN: ZOFIA

A EUNUCH ON EITHER SIDE OF HER, ZOFIA stands tall and straight as she waits for the imperial guards to open the bronze double doors to the Great King's throne room. Her heart thuds with anticipation, and a drop of sweat slides down the back of her neck. Her sheer green veils are no protection against the bright noonday sun.

Will the king send troops to rid the Eastern Mountains of the threat that lurks there? But that's thinking too far ahead of herself. Will he even believe her at all?

The day Zo learned of Kohinoor's drugged tea—the day she saw the cradle and the tall cage—she devised a plan. Clearly, she was unable to walk across the wilderness by herself again. She had barely survived the first time. She needed a horse, and she had a particular one in mind.

That night she slipped out of the cave, her footsteps muffled by the old woman's loud snores. But as she wandered the moonlit hills and gullies, she slowly began to despair. The Eastern Mountains were wide and wild. It seemed impossible to find the Pegasus in such desolation.

So she chose a direction, hoping it was west, and began to walk. Slowly, away from Kohinoor's mind-numbing teas, Zo remembered how she'd first met the flying mare. And how, when she'd first mounted Vata, the horse had flown around and around the mountain where her foal had died in an avalanche—the avalanche Zo had vaguely remembered and thought had injured *her*—as if unwilling to leave.

And she remembered, too, when the Great King visited Sardis two years ago, one of his war elephants had succumbed to illness. The other elephants linked trunks and swayed around it in a kind of mourning dance, bellowing peals of grief that echoed throughout the palace. Then they took their fodder in their trunks and sprinkled it over the body, as if burying him. When the elephant keeper tried to push them aside to remove the body, they almost killed him.

Animals mourn their dead, Zo knew. Especially their young. Vata was probably lingering near the mountain to be close to where her foal had died. And she couldn't be that far, Zo realized, for Kohinoor, half-blind and without benefit of a horse and cart, must have dragged or carried her back to the cave.

It took her time, but on the third night she found the location—the tumbled rocks, the dark open mouth of the cave against the cliffs glowing with moonlight. She sat next to the cairn of rocks that had trapped the foal. A few broken white feathers still poked out between them. She waited. And waited. The air was chilly. Autumn must be almost here.

Sitting still, she shivered, doubt casting frost on her heart. Perhaps it *had* all been a dream, a fantasy, and these feathers belonged to a bird caught in the landslide. She played the thought over in her mind, unsure what to believe, while above her, the dazzling stars circled slowly in the inky dome of the sky.

But then she saw it: a glimmer of motion in the corner of her eye. A falling star, perhaps, but those blazed across the sky quickly and disappeared. *This* was still there, moonlight streaming over muscled wings.

"Vata!" Relief and wonder vied for space in Zo's heart. Her throat grew tight with emotion as she waved her arms and let out a long, mournful whistle, the kind she'd heard ranchers use to call their horses. The Pegasus landed at a fast run, tucking in her enormous wings, her sweat-slick coat shining silver. She slowed to a halt several feet away from Zo and, glancing at the grave of her foal, whinnied and pawed the ground, sending pebbles flying.

"Good girl," Zo said, stretching out a hand for the horse to sniff. "You came. You're here." Vata raised her magnificent head and moved closer.

"I knew I would find you here," Zo said, and carefully stroked the cascade of wavy mane. "Will you help me?"

Vata stood still, then, slowly, majestically, the Pegasus kneeled.

The gesture overwhelmed Zo with its humility, and she felt tears trickle down her cheeks. Grabbing tufts of mane, she swung onto the broad back. Instantly, Vata took off at a gallop, gaining speed and spreading feathered wings. Then Zo's stomach lurched into her throat and an incredible sense of euphoria overcame her. They were airborne.

At first, waves of sickening dizziness assaulted Zo, but when she finally mustered the courage to open her eyes, she saw they were flying into the rose-gold embrace of the rising sun. Going east, toward Persepolis. *Pegasus is never lost. Pegasus knows the way.*

Below her, a river twisted through fields like a thin band of beaten silver. There was a savage beauty to the land, a wanton freedom of towering rock and slanting hills and the impossible shadow of a winged horse and rider sliding against rugged cliffs.

The wind streamed past her ears with the rushing sound of thousands of rippling feathers beating against the air. She felt the straining of mighty muscles beneath her. As she adjusted to the rolling movement of the powerful wings on either side of her, Zo felt she was no longer a skinny, exhausted runaway princess. She was a lilting, airborne song of joy—like Vata, Persian goddess of the wind.

They passed a cliff face, glowing red in the rising sun and carved with pediments and columns surrounding bronze doors that, if swung open, would do so in thin air. Tombs of ancient Hittite kings, Zo realized, their scaffolding removed to stymie grave robbers. She remembered learning about this vanished race from her tutor, who pointed out that civilizations are like individuals—they are born, grow great, grow old, and die.

Every few hours, Vata landed by a lake or stream to drink and eat grass while Zo filled her water skin and ate some smoked fish and dried figs she had brought from Kohinoor's. At night, Zo slept curled up against the warm body, shielded by protecting wings.

As they flew, a sense of urgency pounded through Zo that made her want a whirlwind at their back, pushing them forward faster. Even now the Spirit Eaters could be turning villagers into heaps of chewed bone. How long would it take for the Great King's armies to ride to the Eastern Mountains?

For two days they flew over deserts, then villages began to dot the brown banks of a river. Soon, Zo spotted a walled city and a great tower with horned battlements: the Tower of the Sun and Moon. Persepolis, the capital of the Persian empire and home of the Great King.

Vata had taken her where she knew Zo needed to be.

The winged horse circled the palace as people below cried out and pointed at them. Zo saw courtyards and gardens, a racetrack and theater, pillared porticoes and towers. Finally, Vata landed in the main courtyard of the palace. Guards stood with arrows nocked, but wonderment shone in their eyes.

And for a moment, travel-weary Zo saw herself as others must see her now: as a goddess.

Zo tries to remember that feeling of power now, moments before she will meet the Great King of Persia, Artaxerxes, the most powerful man in the world. On her left, Omid, a tall, gray-haired eunuch with heavy makeup on his lined face, plays with a tassel on his sleeve. On her right, plump little Zavan fans himself.

She feels stronger now, after a hot bath and hearty meal, after the harem handmaidens rubbed her with oils, combed the snarls from her hair, and dressed her in regal robes. She is a princess, she reminds herself. A princess.

A slight breeze whispers around the imperial courtyard with its stylized yellow lions stalking across glazed royal blue bricks. But even if the air were still, the emerald feathers trimming her robes would still tremble. She is afraid—and not just of meeting Artaxerxes.

What frightens her far more is the possibility that Ochus could be standing on the other side of that door. Ochus, who freed her from the slave traders only to handcuff her to himself when she claimed she knew where the last Pegasi soared. The whole time, she thought him a fool for believing her lies. Then, after several weeks of traveling east, he confessed that all along his mission had been to kill her.

He was a member of the Assassins' Guild, which disagreed with King Artaxerxes's plans to marry a Persian princess to Alexander of Macedon. He abandoned her in the middle of nowhere with no horse and very little food and water—all to save her life, he claimed. For his murderous brethren would track his horse, so he must lead them away from her.

There, in those agonizing hours of heat, hunger, and exhaustion, she'd come to the realization that maybe it wasn't hatred she felt for her captor. Maybe it was something quite different.

Or maybe it had just been the sun's merciless mocking as she stumbled over bone-dry fields.

But if Ochus is in the throne room…she's not sure what he would say. Which side he'd choose. Would he be the Ochus that electrified the air around her—who sometimes seemed to look at her as though she were the one pulsating with the violent power of the storm—or would he be the calculating killer who'd left her in the wastelands to "save" her from the Assassins?

Yet another problem she will have to deal with, and soon. For the palace of the king surely must be a haven for the Assassins. Though she knows they want to kill her, she also knows she must give the kingdom her warning.

Almost without realizing it, her hand drifts to her abdomen.

The bronze door opens. "Princess," a guard says. "He is ready for you."

Starting, Zo quickly drops her hand. She doesn't think that the guard noticed her stance, but she needs to be more careful. In the wild, she'd been allowed to be a protective mother-to-be, but here, she must be a virginal princess.

Zo lifts her chin. She has faced the mountains and the open sky. What is a king compared to the whole world? She enters.

It's cool and dark in the throne room, and it takes Zo's eyes a moment to adjust. As she makes her way between pillars ten times the height of a man, her gem-studded slippers tread on patches of light slanting in through the small, high windows. The Great King is ahead, sitting erect on his golden throne atop the high dais, purple robes billowing around him. Anyone in the world would recognize Artaxerxes the Great— even if they hadn't seen him before, as she has once. Tall and slender as a spear, with a long silver-white beard, and dark eyes hard as flints.

At the foot of the dais, she prostrates herself on the marble floor, the stone hard and cool beneath her cheek.

"Rise," the king orders, his voice sharp and commanding, "and tell us your tale."

Zo can hardly tell the Great King she ran away from home to avoid marrying Prince Alexander and to marry instead her lover, a common soldier. She has no choice but to lie... and lie she does.

She spins a web from fibers of both truth and deceit, of evil servants who sold her to slave traders, of soldiers who rescued her, and a lion who killed them, and finding, in the desolate mountains, one of the last of the flying horses.

As she tells her tale, the king's unblinking eyes fix on her, and she feels heat spreading through her chest and up her face. Can he tell she's lying? The only thing that gives her strength is the absence of Ochus. Perhaps he's not in Persepolis at all.

"A tale of marvels," the Great King says when she's finally finished her story. "I wouldn't believe a word of it if I hadn't seen the Pegasus with my own eyes."

"Indeed, highest of high," Zo agrees, her heart beating perilously fast, "it is marvelous, but there is also horror that I must now share with you, if you'll allow me to do so."

The king frowns, but nods.

"Danger breeds in the heart of the empire," Zo states, her voice strong. "In the Eastern Mountains, foul creatures from the Underworld called Spirit Eaters have destroyed entire villages, consuming everything alive."

The memory claws at her, chilling her blood, and the deep scars across her back prickle now. Though she hasn't seen a Spirit Eater, she has felt its devastation on her own skin and witnessed the utter, sickening destruction it can wreak. Still she keeps talking, informing the king of the prophetic paintings and their fiery warning for the end of his empire.

When she finally finishes, Artaxerxes stares into the dis-

tance and strokes a jeweled dagger on his belt. Has he listened
to a word she's said?

"If the Great King would give me troops," she continues,
desperate for him to pay attention, "I could lead an expedition back to the Eastern Mountains. They—"

Artaxerxes puts up a hand to stop her, and she notices that
his long nails have been filed to sharp points. She has never
seen anything like that before on a man.

"I believe that your heart is in the right place, daughter of
Persia, and I believe that you have undergone a terrible ordeal. What I am less certain of is the state of your mind after
such tragedies."

Frustration pulses in Zo's temples. "Surely," she says slowly,
fighting the rising urgency and anger in her voice, "the Great
King has heard of his couriers going missing. Of villages and
farms disappearing."

The king waves his hand as if swatting a fly, the gemstones in
his many rings glinting. "Yes, we are kept quite well-informed
of everything that happens in our empire. It is well-known
that some portions of the Eastern Mountains harbor murder-
ers, robbers, and brigands. This is nothing new."

"But, Great King," she protests, "no human could have—"

"If I may speak."

Zo turns slightly to see a spare man walking toward her
with the stealth of the pet panther her uncle kept in Sardis—
beauty, grace, and death fused together in liquid movement.
He is no taller than she is, but handsome—his features hawk-
like, a dark beard neatly trimmed, a smile white and gleaming.

He comes to a stop in front of her, just a bit too near for
protocol. "I am Darius, adviser to the Great King," he says.
Waves of ambergris and sandalwood float around her. After
all the months of smelling her own sweat, she should want
to dive into that scent, but instead she feels as if it might suffocate her. Her eyes fix on a rose pinned to his left shoul-

der, the only adornment on his rich black robe. It's a white rose—or almost white, it is hard to see in this room of shadows—with thin red veins crossing in the middle. Her heart skips a beat. The rose bears the Assassins' Mark, the bloody X of their victims.

She lifts her eyes to his and looks into black lightless tunnels leading down into nothingness, and fear strikes her heart. As if sensing it, he smiles more broadly, and she sees that his incisor teeth are longer than the others, like those of a dog. Could this be the leader of the Assassins' Guild, the one who sent his murderous minions to kill the princesses on their bridal journey to Macedon? An image rises before her of the three girls in the *harmanaxa* she found in the woods—their bodies bloated and green, deep slashes carved on the flesh of their chests. She hears the buzz of the flies. Smells the rancid-sweet scent of death and decay.

"Princess Zofia has a compassionate and womanly heart," Darius says, turning to the king. "It is my belief that she will make an excellent bride for Prince Alexander of Macedon. She was, after all, our first choice before she...went missing."

Zo's feels the blood drain from her face. Darius wants to send another bride to Macedon. To be murdered along the way, most likely.

"Yes," the Great King agrees. "That might work out nicely. We can pack up dowry goods rather quickly."

Zo can hardly believe her ears. She has just pointed out that the Spirit Eaters could spread like a putrid, festering wound, killing tens of thousands, and Artaxerxes has jumped to the topic of a *wedding*. After everything she's been through this summer, after everything she's learned, after all the danger and pain and exhaustion she survived—she is back to that first night she slipped out of the palace dressed as a boy, in search of Cosmas, nervous and excited about the adventure before her.

Everything is the same except for one, critical thing: now

she knows that she's with child. If the Assassins don't kill her, what will the royal house of Macedon do when they discover that she is not a virgin?

"But on second thought, I am not completely convinced," the Great King says slowly. He rises from the throne—and keeps rising, as Zo wonders how anyone so old could have a backbone as straight as a javelin. Fiery opals flash in his tall, conical gold crown. He steps down the dais and circles her slowly, his black eyes examining every bit of her as if she were one of his prize stallions. She half expects him to open her mouth and examine her teeth.

"She will be pretty enough once we fatten her up a bit, but she speaks a great deal for a woman, don't you think?" he asks, coming to stand in front of her. "Does King Shershah of Sardis permit his palace women to voice opinions to men?"

Darius, too, wheels around her, not coolly curious, like the king, but more like a wolf sizing up a lamb. He is so close his hot breath on the back of her neck penetrates her sheer veil and makes her hairs stand on end. She freezes, unable to inhale, until the breath moves away.

"True, Highness," he says, pivoting to a stop in front of her and folding hands into wide sleeves. "We could never marry her to a Persian—our men wouldn't stand for it. But the Macedonian barbarians like loudmouthed women."

"If we send her to Macedon, can you manage to keep this one safe?" Artaxerxes asks, sarcasm and accusation in his powerful voice.

"Indeed, Your Majesty," Darius says, inclining his head. "I will send my son as her personal escort."

Zo's breath catches as a figure detaches itself from behind a pillar and marches forward through the shadows. Before she can see his face, she recognizes his confident stride: *Ochus.*

Her heart skips, and it feels as if a bolt of lightning has dissolved into her blood. She's not sure if she wants to run away

or stay and fight with this odious man. Instead, she does neither. She looks at the ground, as if she were a silent, obedient
woman for once. But the fact is, she cannot look at him, for
if she does, she has no idea how she will react.

"Son," Darius says, clapping Ochus on the back. "Have
you heard the orders?"

"Yes, Father," Ochus replies as a hot pang of fear slices her
abdomen. Ochus is the son of the head Assassin who wants
nothing so much as to slice a bloody X deep into her chest.

Zo feels Ochus's amber eyes boring into her, but she refuses
to look up. The horrific knowledge that he is Darius's son
thuds through her head. Now she knows without a doubt that
Darius is head Assassin. The Great King Artaxerxes himself
clearly isn't aware the Assassins' Guild operates within the top
level of government. That the men responsible for the murder of the other three princesses stand before him. The irony
that he'd place her in *Ochus's* protection is almost laughable.

She is vaguely aware of a conversation about travel arrange-
ments, bridal chests of garments and jewels, and wedding gifts
to be hastily packed tonight. Her mind has gone numb. When
she is finally dismissed, she prostrates herself on the ground
once more, remaining just long enough not to appear rude
before she strides as fast as she can from the throne room.

Outside the doors, the two eunuchs fall into step with her
as she marches toward the only place Ochus cannot follow
her: the harem. Little Zavan almost runs to keep up with
lanky Omid's long strides.

"Oh, no, you don't."

A strong hand grabs her arm, and Ochus yanks her around.
But his grip falls a second later as Zo—with all her might and
frustration and fear—slaps him.

"Let go of me!" she yells loudly, shaking him off, not caring who sees or hears. The eunuchs, dark eyes wide in alarm,

thrust themselves in between Ochus and Zo, but Ochus, rubbing his jaw, just laughs.

"Give us a moment," he says, flashing a charming smile as he strokes the lion's hide on his shoulder. Omid and Zavan glance at him, at the skin of the fierce beast he killed with his own hands, and then at each other. They nod briskly.

Ochus stares at her, his eyes soft and searching. "Come," he says then, more gently. He nods his head toward a wide gate across the courtyard that leads into a garden.

"But we must see you at all times," Omid calls after them.

Ochus stops and calls back, "Please do! You might need to protect *me*." He casts that grin she has come to know so well, then turns, obviously assuming she's going to follow. And she does…but not for the reason he thinks she does.

He pushes through the gate and toward a large fountain where, she knows, it would be hard for anyone to hear their conversation over the splashing water.

Then he spins around to face her, but before he can open his mouth, Zo speaks first.

"How dare you," she seethes.

He looks at her, surprised. "How dare *I*? I told you to run! And now we're both in danger!"

Ochus is blaming *her*? Anger pumps through her with such force that for several heartbeats she can't even speak.

"I don't think," she begins, each word the stab of a tiny dagger, "that I can be in more danger *here* than I was alone in the wilderness with no food or water…*after you left me*."

"You know why I did!" He says it so loudly that Zo knows the fountain's trickle won't protect them for much longer. "What you don't know is that my father…" He glances around, then lowers his voice to the merest whisper. "My father is not just the king's adviser. He is the chief Assassin. It was he who sent the men to kill you before you reached Macedon as Alexander's bride. But then you ran away, and

his Assassins sent word to me to track you down. It was he
who sent the men to kill the three princesses we found in
the *harmanaxa*."

So. She was right.

"He heard reports of me with a chained girl traveling east
on the Royal Road," Ochus continues, "which I laughed off,
saying that the lion killed you, dragged away your corpse to
some unknown place. Now, with you here, he must be dou-
bly suspicious of me."

"I don't care what lies you told your father," Zo says, stepping an inch or two back, as though to protect herself, though
whether from his anger or the familiar smell of wood smoke
on his skin, she can't be sure.

"Why don't you understand? Why can't you listen to me?"
Zo is so furious she can't even bear to look at him and instead turns her focus onto the fountain's stream, slapping into
the basin. "This isn't about your safety or even mine—this is
about the safety of *Persia*."

She forces herself to lock eyes with him. "There is an ancient evil out there that will destroy us *all* if it isn't stopped."

Ochus sighs and shakes his head. "Of course, the Great King
and Father know of the danger in the mountains, but until it
comes to the steps of the palace, they won't care. Their attention is focused on winning kingdoms, extending the empire,
and you and I are just pawns in a complex game manipulated
by kings. We're not free to do as we want, Zofia. No one is."

"A fine speech," she says, chafing at his smug condescen-
sion. "I may not have a prince's education of politics, but I
do know that if you care about a place—or a person—you
do everything in your power to protect them. And nothing,
not dreams of destiny nor expanding borders—nor even the
Great King himself—gets in your way."

She turns from him, and unshed tears blur the palm trees
and ornamental bushes into splashes of green against glazed

blue walls. She feels his hand, warm and strong, on her shoulder, gently tugging her to face him. Blinking several times, she waits a moment before looking up at him. His eyes burn like firelight reflected in amber; his lips are slightly parted.

"You're right," Ochus whispers fiercely. "And I swear to you, that as long as I live I will never leave you alone again." His head tilts slightly. His jaw tenses. She can read the truth on his face…

She wants to believe that look—oh, how she wants to believe! And yet. This man held her captive. He left her to die, for all he knew.

Zo sways toward him, so close that her cheek grazes his and she can feel its light stubble against her skin. She's so close she can hear the pounding of his heart. She can feel his body tense beside hers.

Angling her head slightly, she murmurs into his ear, "I… don't…trust…you."

His head snaps back, and he steps away from her. She's left feeling cold.

"Then," he says, voice rough, "know that I will do everything in my power to win your trust." The surprise of his words fizzes and pops in Zo's mind like a too-strong drink, but before she can reply, the tromp of boots on gravel interrupts them.

"Commander Ochus. Princess," a black-bearded soldier greets them as he comes to a stop in front of them. Zo shuffles a few more steps away from Ochus. "Imperial Adviser Darius wishes to see you, sir."

"Right away," Ochus says. He turns to Zo. "Do you need to be escorted back to your rooms?"

Her mind wheeling from the sudden change of topic, Zo shakes her head. "No, I'd like to see Vata. Omid and Zavan are enough."

Nodding, Ochus swiftly bows to her and just as quickly

departs down the gravel pathway, leaving Zo and her swirling, tangled emotions behind.

As the eunuchs lead her across courtyards and gardens to the rear of the palace, Zo's mind races. Once she knows where the Pegasus is kept, she will find a way to escape the harem—she did it often enough in Sardis—and then free Vata, and together they will fly out of Persepolis…

But a heaviness thuds through her as she realizes she has no idea where she would go. Back to Cosmas's barracks outside Sardis, if he is even still stationed there? She feels a small flutter in her belly and puts her hands protectively over it. They could marry and raise their child. All she wanted, when she ran away from her uncle's palace, was a simple life with Cosmas. She has already paid such a great price for that life. She will never escape the sounds of her little sister's screams cutting through the night. Grief pulses through her. Roxana would have lived if Zo had never run away seeking to choose her own path. Does she want her sister's death to be in vain?

But how can she forget what she saw in the Eastern Mountains? The truth is, she *cannot*. She will not just let all those people perish, but to stop the Spirit Eaters, she needs an army—which she does not have. And there's another consideration: if she is fated, as Kohinoor predicted, to mingle her blood with Alexander's, should she continue to strain against her fate, or will she only invite more suffering, more pain and loss? The only problem is her pregnancy, now so far advanced she could never pretend the child was his. But fate, she has learned, plays unlikely tricks on humans, with random handouts of doom and salvation. Perhaps she should trust the fate that has brought her this far.

Or could she… She stops a moment, shocked at the thought. Omid and Zavan march on ahead of her, their pointed leather slippers crunching on the sandy dirt. Would Alexander of Macedon listen to her warning about evil in the east, an evil that could, once it has devoured Persia, easily move on to Macedon?

Perhaps the prince—an ambitious young warrior eager for glory, according to all reports—would be willing to launch an expedition. If her blood *is* fated to mix with his, as Kohinoor prophesied, perhaps it isn't in the form of a child they would create. Perhaps it is in battle fighting the Spirit Eaters *together*.

Prophecies are never clear, she knows. They often come true in ways no one could have guessed before the fact. Perhaps she has misinterpreted Kohinoor's augury from the start. For all she knows, her fate is to join Alexander so that together they can save the known world.

"Princess?" It is Omid, crunching back toward her. Zavan, still fanning himself, waits up ahead.

"Coming!" she says.

To Zo's surprise, the eunuchs lead her past the royal stables as Omid explains that the Pegasus isn't kept with the hundreds of other fine horses owned by the king because she couldn't fit in a normal stall. They cross a service courtyard to a former supply storehouse where, Omid says, Vata has been given the entire ground floor.

Two guards stand outside, blocking her path. From inside she hears angry whinnies and loud thumps.

"Stand aside," Zo says coolly. "I wish to see her."

The guards look at each other. "Too dangerous, Princess," says one. "She seriously injured three grooms and a guard this morning."

"What?" Zo asks, blinking.

"After you dismounted and went to the harem, they tried to lead her to the stables, but she resisted so fiercely they threw nets over her and hauled her there."

A stab of anger sears through Zo as another shriek of equine rage shatters the air. "I am the one who rode her here," she says through gritted teeth. "If anyone can calm her, I can."

The guards consider this. Finally, one of them says, "Very well, Princess. I will open the door just a handbreadth and you can slip in. Anytime we open it, she tries to bolt. We can't even get near her to tie her to a post inside."

Zo nods. The guard lifts the heavy cross-bolt on the door and opens it a sliver. Leaving her eunuchs behind, Zo slides into a shadowy room. Dust motes dance in shafts of light pouring in through high windows. A snort of warning comes from the other side of the room. Zo sees Vata glowing golden-pink, her moist dark eyes alight with fury. At her feet is a trough of oats she has kicked over.

"It's me, Vata," Zo says, tears stinging her eyes. *She* did this to the Pegasus. It's *her* fault she is here, imprisoned. The horse paws the ground angrily, her huge wings bristling.

"Hush, hush, my sweet girl," she says, stepping forward. The horse raises her head and bellows as she takes a step back. Zo realizes she must smell completely different from the sweaty girl on the journey. She has been bathed and per-fumed to meet the king, her hair combed with sandalwood.

Zo stands perfectly still for what seems like an eternity. Perhaps Vata recognizes something of Zo's scent, after all, because she takes a tentative step toward her, large round nostrils twitching.

"Yes, it's me," she whispers. "Don't be afraid."

The gigantic bulk edges closer as Zo raises her hand. Vata sniffs it, pulling her lips to reveal enormous teeth that could take off a hand in a single bite. The Pegasus whickers a kind of apol-ogy, an acknowledgment of recognition. Zo strokes her velvety muzzle and leans her head against the warm muscular neck.

"I'm so sorry," she says. She uses her fingers to comb out tangles in the long silvery mane as she says, "The Great King would treasure you as his most prized possession, that is true, but imprisonment would kill you. I brought you in here, my friend, and I will set you free."

Vata pricks her ears as she hears the nicker of a horse out-side. A man's low, modulated voice floats through the open window. It's a familiar voice—one she's heard recently. It puzzles her a moment, before it finally comes to her: Darius. Imperial Adviser. Ochus's father. Chief Assassin.

"...like to know what you were talking about," he says. "You think I don't know every move everyone makes in this palace? Within moments several reports came to me of you speaking to her in the garden."

"I need to get her to trust me," comes the calm response. *Ochus.* "She distrusted me enough to run off on the Royal Road when the lion attacked. I must win her trust if I am going to have the opportunity to do as you wish."

"And yet I sense reluctance on your part," comes the voice, smooth as silk.

"Unlike some Assassins, I don't enjoy killing the innocent, it is true," Ochus admits. "But I do it out of duty, out of ne-cessity. I have devoted my life to the Guild. Have I not given you sufficient proof? Do not doubt me now."

"But I do doubt you," Darius cuts in. "And this mission is crucial to our goals. If you succeed in making it look as if Alexander did it, the alliance between Macedon and Persia will be over before it begins. Tensions will flare into out-right war, and then we can vanquish the upstart Macedonians before they become a true threat. Artaxerxes's great age has made him weak. But we are not."

"Yes, Father, I understand."

"Understand what, Ochus?" Darius insists. "What must you do as soon as you arrive in Macedon—but no sooner?"

Ochus replies, his voice level, "Kill Princess Zofia."

CHAPTER TWELVE:
HEPHAESTION

FOR THREE NIGHTS AND THREE DAYS, HEPHAES-
tion has been forced to watch Katerina drain herself almost beyond recognition. As she sits on the floor of their hut, by the
lantern light, her face is lined with exhaustion as she strokes
the creature, murmuring words of comfort. She has not slept
and has taken only water and a few slices of coconut while she
strives to take care of some fool bird.

A kestrel, she said. *A royal princess—Ada of Caria.*

Heph had his doubts, of course, when Kat, in the dull silver light of dawn, came running into their hut wild-eyed and
babbling, holding a struggling falcon. He wrapped his arms
around her and ran to Aristotle's hut. The philosopher, caught
in the act of rolling up his sleeping mat, stared at her in alarm.

"It's Ada," Kat croaked, and Aristotle ran to one of his bags
and pulled out a vial of some sweet sedative. Though Heph
was thoroughly confused, he was able to help wrestle enough
of the liquid into the bird's beak. Moments later, it stopped
shrieking and finally fell into a deep sleep.

"What is happening?" he demanded as Aristotle wrapped
a blanket around Kat's shaking shoulders.

"It's Ada! I *know* it's Ada," she said. "I can sense her in the bird, but she's—she's lost in the creature's mind. And my fingertip! It has feeling…tingling… I think it recognizes Ada's magic."

Heph remembers how shocked he'd been at her words. How forlorn Aristotle had looked as Kat explained that she could sense Ada in the bird, but that Ada seemed to have lost all sense of herself. Aristotle shook his head, saying that he did not know much about the Blood Magics, but that Kat must try to call her back. If she didn't Ada would be lost and all her knowledge with her.

Thinking back on it now, Heph feels like swearing at his teacher. Aristotle should have known how Kat would take that. Should have known how much Kat would push herself to save her friend.

Heph's expression must show something stormy, for Kat looks away from the soft pile of blankets where the bird is nestled. "Can you go pick more lotus blossoms?" she asks. "We're nearly out."

They have been burning lotus blossoms—a suppressor of Snake Blood, Kat said—every hour, day and night, to try to loosen Ada from the kestrel. Heph doesn't want to leave Kat—she looks so tired—but he doesn't want to argue with her. Mutely, he nods and leaves.

Eyes adjusting to the dark, he picks his way down the path to one of the small ponds behind their huts and reaches across the starlit water to tear off lotus blossoms, wondering ruefully how he, once second-in-command to the Prince of Macedon and a menace on the battlefield, is now enjoying midnight flower picking. Though the sweet perfume of blossom mixed with the scent of the sea is delightful enough that anyone— soldier, Aesarian Lord, peasant girl—would enjoy it.

A bloodcurdling scream splits open the warm, dark night. Just like the scream he heard at the inn in Egypt when Cynane attacked Kat with a knife.

Before he can process what he's doing, Heph has dropped the lotus blossoms and sprints back to the hut, heart pounding, wondering if Olympias or Cynane has tracked them here. He curses himself for leaving his sword in his hut, but he will do everything in his power to protect Kat. Hurtling through the doorway, he stops short.

Kat kneels on the sandy floor before the sprawled body of a woman. The woman lies nude, tanned and lean; long black hair threaded with silver cascades over her like armor melting in a forge to be recast. Her eyes are closed, her breathing labored. Kat strokes her head, murmuring.

At first, Heph is far too stunned to move.

Kat was right, he thinks. Not that he doubted her—not really. It had just been too much to believe.

Now Kat looks up, as though sensing his presence, and her eyes catch his. They are full of weariness and fear.

"Heph," she whispers. "We must help her."

Without hesitation, Heph snaps into action, retrieving a cup of cool spring water, which Kat tips slowly into Ada's mouth. Soon, the lady blinks and whispers, "Katerina..." Then her eyes flutter again, and the woman drifts into sleep, the drug she drank as a kestrel still flowing through her veins.

Tears stream down Kat's cheeks, but Heph can't tell if they are tears of joy or exhaustion, and her entire body is shaking. Heph helps her cover the lady with a blanket.

She is beautiful, Heph sees, with high cheekbones and an aquiline nose, her skin smooth as a girl's except for a crease on either side of her mouth. He can't help but think she must be a goddess fallen from the skies. Beside him, he senses Kat slumping before he sees that she has practically fallen asleep sitting up.

"Come with me," he murmurs. But she's too tired to even nod, so carefully he picks her up and lays her beside Ada. He leaves the two women there and turns to go. He must tell Aristotle what has happened.

★ ★ ★

The sun has passed its zenith and started its westward descent when Kat and Ada finish their meal of bread, fish, and hot herb-infused wine. Both have come alive like wilting plants revived after a soaking rain.

"Ada," Kat says, pushing her plate away, "I was so worried when Heph and I went to your fortress. It was shrouded in spiderwebs and you had...vanished."

Ada's dark eyes take on a faraway look as she murmurs, "Yes. But before that, in the Alinda Fortress, birds came to me from the east, whispering of villages completely disappearing. Of loathsome, unspeakably evil creatures called Spirit Eaters or God Eaters, spreading from the Eastern Mountains to the shores of the sea."

Heph tenses, remembering where he saw those words before. In another time, another age—though it was only a few months ago—a boy much like him, but no longer him, had found an ancient map in a cave with Alexander. A map of the Eastern Mountains of Persia, where creatures named Spirit Eaters guarded the Fountain of Youth. Those long-ago boys had planned a great adventure to vanquish the Spirit Eaters and use the healing waters of the fountain to restore Alex's leg.

"I have heard of them before," Heph says. "What *are* Spirit Eaters exactly?"

Ada shakes her head. "I do not know. Helen—"

Heph sees Katerina flinch and grab her mother's silver lotus pendant, shining brightly against her tan skin. Ada must have noticed as well because she reaches out to touch Kat's arm before continuing. "Helen told me of visions she had about the world coming to a crossroads, ushering in a new age—either the Age of Monsters or the Age of Man. I think the rise of these monsters is a sign that the time has come."

Heph knows that whatever happened between Helen and Ada before Kat's birth cannot be easy for Kat to hear. But he cannot help her. He sits silently beside her on the hard-packed earth of the hut, his hands heavy and useless, and tries to focus on what Ada is telling them.

Ada sighs deeply. "I came up with a plan to meet Aristotle here. There is the slimmest of chances we could fight this great evil, but..."

"But?" Kat is gripping her hands together so tightly they've gone white. Heph wants to comfort her, to put his arm around her back, but his awkwardness—remembering how she cried when he kissed her in Ada's abandoned fortress—gives him more discomfort than if he had been wounded again in battle.

"Before I could depart, my brother interfered," Ada says softly. She swirls the herbs in the bottom of her cup and stares into them as if hoping to find answers.

"Madness runs in my family," she continues sadly. "Madness and foul incest. My brother, Pixodarus, has spent most of his days as a spider, rather than as a man. Given his increasing madness, the people wanted to make me queen, ruling jointly with him, steadying him. And so he possessed an army of spiders to wall me up in my home. I was able to escape in my kestrel form. I winged myself west, toward my meeting with Aristotle. My brother, I knew, would never follow me here. Like a spider, he sits in his web, watching and waiting, and doesn't stray far."

Aristotle, sitting cross-legged beside Ada, strokes his beard. "And yet I received your letter nearly two months ago. Why were you so delayed?"

Ada sets down her cup and shakes her head. "An enchantment I cast a long time ago suddenly...*broke*, I suppose is the best way to describe it. I was caught unprepared, flying over the sea when I felt the release of the spell I had cast so long ago. It took a physical toll on me, and I fell. Fell from the sky, faltered, unable to free myself from the bird's form. I was trapped that way for...I don't know how long. Longer than ever before. And I lost myself, my memories, my plans, my Ada-ness."

Her eyes take on a lost look, and in them Heph can see an endless horizon of bright blue skies and sapphire seas.

"Finally," she continues, "I became aware of someone calling me, softly, in the wind, in the sea below, in the chatter of other birds and the dreams of fish. I found myself drawn to it, not comprehending what it was—a call of love that drew me here. You, Kat."

Kat smiles at Ada, and leans her head on the woman's shoulder.

"But what sort of spell?" Aristotle asks. "It must have been very powerful for its echo to so disorient you."

"It was powerful," Ada agrees. "Seventeen years ago, Helen came to me asking for such an enchantment—one that would keep a Snake Blood in animal form. Though I admit, I didn't know much at the time."

Kat leans forward, her hair tumbling across her face.

"Over the years," Ada says, "I heard that Olympias was protecting a den of snakes. While many religious people keep a snake or two, there was something about the queen doing so that made me suspicious. My own Snake Blood family kept quite a few of them. So I researched old lore and discovered that all Snake Bloods—my own family included—are descended from a god: Riel the Snake. I began to wonder if Olympias had the Last God in serpent form beneath her bed. Or *in* her bed, as rumor suggests."

Heph slides his gaze from Kat's open face to Ada and says, "We learned of Riel from Princess Laila of Sharuna in Egypt."

"Yes." Kat nods. "Riel massacred Laila's people and put a terrible curse on her. He is the most evil man ever to walk the earth…" She trails off, her voice grown rough, and she doesn't have to say the rest for Heph to know what she must be thinking—what she's been troubling over ever since they left Sharuna: that she, also a Snake Blood, must be descended of Riel. Heph sees Kat collect herself. "You don't mean that your spell trapped *Riel*?"

"Yes—in his snake form," Ada says, beginning to sound stronger, the fierceness in her voice now matching that of her eyes. "From my studies, I believe that Riel, for some reason, was abandoned by the other gods to live in exile upon this mortal earth, his powers greatly diminished. And that ever since then, Riel has been trying to become a true god again."

"You said Helen's visions were terrible," Heph practically whispers. His throat has tightened so much that it's hard to speak. "What were they of?"

Ada fixes her eyes on him. They are black—not brown— with white rings around the irises. "She saw that Olympias's lover at that time, a Snake Blood man, would bring great evil into the world if not...contained."

Suddenly the truth of Kat's parentage is plain as day to Heph.

No, he prays silently. *No.* He hopes Kat won't see the horrible thing dangling right in front of her, invisible, yet threatening and real.

Ada stares at Heph thoughtfully, and now he feels as if something is gently poking and prodding his mind. Has she sensed his thoughts? If so, she gives no indication. Her strange eyes meet his once again, and there flashes between them an understanding.

He looks away. "Kat, I think Ada needs more spiced wine," he says, standing, and pulling her by the arm. "It's all gone."

But Kat is no fool. Staring hard at Ada, she shakes his grip loose and says boldly: "You're saying that Riel was Olympias's lover seventeen years ago." A quiet intensity buzzes in her voice.

Ada says nothing.

Kat continues relentlessly. "I've never heard that anyone

in the royal families of King Philip or Queen Olympias has possessed Snake Blood..."

"No," Aristotle says hoarsely. "They have not."

A sigh rattles through Kat's entire body. "Then that must mean..."

Heph stiffens, feeling the muscles in his arms grow hard, ready to defend Kat from the knowledge he knows that she must hear, but cannot bear to let her know.

"King Philip is not your father, Katerina," Ada says, glancing at Heph with something like warning.

Silence fills the hut like smoke, and it's all Heph can do not to cough. He blinks rapidly, trying to breathe in this new knowledge, and what it must mean for Kat. Sitting next to him, Aristotle sighs.

Ada's voice is quiet as she continues. "That is why both you and Alexander have such powerful Snake Blood, for your father...is Riel."

Kat crumples and puts her hands over her face. "So I'm to believe," she says, looking up, her voice breaking, "that I am the child of the most evil person—god—in the world?"

Ada leans forward, touching Kat's arm. "Katerina, listen to me carefully." Her words hum with urgency. "I come from the most despicable royal family ever—riddled with power lust, murder, and incest. But they are not *me*. I am myself, separate from them. You, too, are like that. Clean and brave and good, untouched by their evil."

Kat shudders and turns to Heph, her eyes brimming. "As upsetting as this is to me, what about Alexander? He isn't Philip's heir. How can we tell him such a thing?"

Heph marvels at Kat's thoughtfulness at such a time, even as a spike of panic shoots through him. He can't lie to Alex, can't withhold information this important even if he knows it will devastate his friend. He can't disobey, disappoint... Not again.

But Aristotle comes to his rescue. "I have reason to believe that Alexander suspects as much, based on a question he asked me in Samothrace. He is as quick as you, Katerina. He must have figured it out."

The new information weighs heavy on Heph, and if it's heavy for him, he can't imagine what it must feel like for Kat. But again she surprises him and shows her strength.

"So if you were the one who trapped Riel in snake form," Kat says to Ada, "and you say that your enchantment broke, Riel must now be free."

Fear prickles across Heph's back as Ada croaks, "Yes, the Last God is back."

Heph's mind whirls, clicking like the mechanism he and Aristotle talk about building. If what she says *is* true... "Ada," he says, "do you think this unleashing of the god Riel could be related to the great evil spreading throughout the world?"

Ada's strange eyes lock with his. Unblinking, they focus on him, prying into him, examining the most deeply hidden secrets of his heart. Heph feels exposed, vulnerable, and the spell only slightly lifts when she begins to speak. "Yes, I fear so. It can be no coincidence that the Last God is resurrected, and so are the God Eaters. I am afraid I have played a terrible role in ushering in the Age of Monsters."

There is a ringing silence as the four mortals take in what has happened...and what is to be.

"But you said there is the slimmest of chances we can prevent this evil," Kat says, determination flashing in her eyes.

"Yes," Ada says. "There is one drop of hope, one speck of light."

"Then tell us!" Aristotle says, practically shouting.

Heph's insides feel hollow. He knows that his teacher does not care for magic, instead preferring the power of man's imagination—he knows the situation must be grim indeed for his teacher to have such an outburst.

"There is a prophecy," Ada replies "A little-known group of predictions called the Cassandra Prophecies supposedly made by the great oracle, Cassandra of Troy."

Heph feels a shudder prick his spine. The prophecy he found in Leonidas's dead hand that indicated Kat would kill Alex had been identified as one of the Cassandra Prophecies. He has struggled to suppress the memory, has wanted nothing to do with it.

"Legend has it," Ada continues, "that Cassandra predicted Riel the Snake could only be killed by Earth Blood, by a descendant of his beloved brother, Brehan, the originator of the Earth Bloods."

"Why is this not more well-known?" Kat demands, pulling away from Heph. "Why has an Earth Blood not yet killed Riel?"

"There are not many Earth Bloods," Ada says. "I believe Riel has knowledge of this prophecy and has made sure that most Earth Bloods do not survive more than a few weeks past birth. But it may yet be possible to find one now."

Understanding glitters in Heph's mind as bold and bright as the metallic scales he has been collecting on the beach. "You want to create a copy of the Atlantean Mechanism with Aristotle to find an Earth Blood," he says. "An Earth Blood to kill Riel."

"Yes," she agrees. "It is our only hope. *If* the flakes that glitter on these shores are, indeed, *baruopa*, as some have surmised."

Aristotle clears his throat and says, "I think they come from unusual plants or rocks in the sea. Even so, they could be *baruopa*. Who knows what the Atlanteans used for their mechanisms?"

He glances at Heph and adds, "I have brought the diagrams, the forges and molds you requested. While waiting for you, we have been experimenting with the flakes. When we melt a bucketful, there is only the tiniest residue left, and that is too flexible for casting. To make even a small mechanism for testing, we would need a man's weight of the raw material and would have to add lead for strength. At the rate we're going, it would take years to obtain, I think. And all the flakes in the world won't help us if the substance isn't *baruopa*."

It is *baruopa*, Heph knows. If they could build the mechanism, they could find the Earth Blood, kill Riel, and save the world from his evil.

"By all means," Ada says, looking between the two of them, "let us help you collect this metal. The fate of the world may depend upon it."

The days bleed into one another on the island, fiery sunsets burning into simmering black nights full of stars that slowly melt into the cool light of dawn. Heph has scoured every beach on the island, looking for where the fiery flakes lie thicker on the sand. Some areas have more of them, some less, but there seem to be no signs pointing to a single source.

Mostly though, he kneels in the sand as he does now, shallow waves swirling around him. He taps the glinting grains from the strainer into a bucket. Over and over again. Morning into the heat of noon, and then all afternoon into dusk, until it becomes too dark to make out the flecks of shiny metal in the sand, until his eyes burn and his head aches and his muscles throb.

Back in Pella, he would have found the task mind-numbingly boring, but now he finds relief in doing something useful.

Especially because of what has happened to Kat.

Ever since Kat discovered who her father is, she has retreated to a place of sullen, wounded anger, and it's as though she has withdrawn into an actual cave—a place he cannot reach. He wants to comfort her. He wants to tell her his deepest secret, the one only Alex knows—that it's because of his own family he lost his home, his name, his position, and even his beloved sister. That nobody can pick who their relatives are or control how they behave. That the blood flowing through Kat's veins isn't Riel's. Isn't Olympias's. It's Kat's and hers alone.

But whatever he said would probably only upset her more. At least collecting the flakes has a purpose.

As the late-afternoon sun slips inexorably toward the horizon on one such day, he casts a look down the beach at Kat and Ada, who stand knee-deep in the surf as they attempt to call the metallic pieces to them with Snake Blood. The two of them have spent almost every waking moment together in long, private talks along the shore or walking among the old Lotus-eater ruins. Ada makes sure to keep Kat talking, keep her busy.

He's glad to give them time alone together, especially because it's so hard for him to be near Kat. To sleep in the same hut, listening to her steady breathing in the dark, is a kind of torture, when all he wants to do is touch her, kiss her, inhale the sweet scent of her. Even during the day, it's not much better. He finds he's jealous of the sea wind that whips through her unruly hair, the sun that warms her flesh, the rough-spun tunic allowed to touch her skin.

It's becoming harder and harder to stand next to the very person he wants so badly in every way but can never have. He's even thought about just leaving the island, going somewhere far away from disapproving princes and unattainable girls; after all, once before he left everything he knew and started a new life, and for years that worked out quite well. He could do it again.

But those dreams fade the moment he remembers that horrifying prophecy from the Cassandra scrolls about Katerina killing Alexander, and though it still seems unfathomable to him, he knows he must stay by her side to prevent it. He simply cannot abandon her and let those tragic words come true.

A shadow falls over him, and he twists around to find her staring down at him, her eyes lingering on the ropey muscles of his back. He quickly stands up. "Have you been successful?" he asks. "Were you and Ada able to call the flakes to you?"

Kat shakes her head. "It seems we can only call living things to us," she says, "and though the grains seem to have some memory of life, some inert intelligence, it isn't the kind of thing Snake Bloods can call." She's clearly upset at her failure. She looks as if she's almost about to cry.

"Don't worry," he says, his hand hovering over her shoulder. He pulls it back quickly. "We'll find a way to get enough of it for the mechanism."

"It's not that," she says angrily, staring at the hand hanging stiffly at his side. He looks at her in surprise. "Well," she says, "it is that, too. I can't seem to access my magic at all anymore, and how are we ever going to get all the grains that Aristotle says we need? It will take years, and we don't have that much time. But it's mostly..." She bites her lower lip, looks up at him with accusing eyes, and says, "You are being impossible!"

Heph runs a hand through his wind-tousled hair and asks, utterly mystified, "What do you mean? What have I done?"

"That's just it!" she says. "You haven't done *anything*. You ignore me. You walk away from me whenever you can, like today. You flinch every time you look at me, as if I'm so disgusting it hurts. Do you hate me that much?"

Heph feels his mouth drop open but just lets it hang there. When he kissed her back in Ada's fortress, she pushed him away and ran crying from the room. He had promised he would never kiss her again, and ever since then he has been pretending he just likes her as a friend. Somehow he has botched that, too, and hurt her feelings. Looking into her green eyes flashing with passion, seeing her beautiful mouth tremble, he wants nothing more than to take her in his arms and tell her why he's been avoiding her. But he can't. That would just upset her more.

"I… I'm sorry," he says, picking up the bucket and strainer. "I…didn't mean…" He turns awkwardly to go and feels a hard blow to his back that sends him tumbling facedown into the water.

"What was that for?" he splutters, grabbing the strainer before a small wave tugs it out to sea. He sits up, tiny waves rolling over his legs, and shoves wet hair out of his face. She just stares down at him. He starts to rise but grimaces and sits back down. "I think I've hurt my ankle," he says, extending a hand. "Help me up."

She scowls at him, then holds her hand out—and he pulls her into the sea next to him. She comes up coughing, one side of her hair dripping wet, and glares at him. But then she starts to laugh, and the sound is like music that makes the heart leap for joy. For a moment Heph is too stunned to move as she scrambles up and races away from him, deeper into the sea. Then he gives chase, careening through the foamy waves.

As he approaches her, she splashes him full in the face, and he splashes her back. He grabs her, planning to dunk her, but there's a look in her eyes that asks for something else. He bends toward her slowly, to give her time to back away if she wants. But she leans in and kisses him. Suddenly Heph is aware only of surf and wind and Kat. A large wave lifts them off their feet, and they float entwined in each other's arms, two sea creatures clinging to each other in the tide.

Heph feels the beating of her heart, the strength of her arms, the slender muscularity of her body. He kisses her face and it tastes like salt. He feels a tugging and lowering of the water as his feet find sand again. They break apart, grinning at each other, and Kat runs her golden fingertip over his chest. He grabs it and raises it to his lips.

"Can you feel that?" he asks, smiling.

"It can only feel magic," she says, grinning back. "So yes."
She giggles. "You have some *baruopa* on your mouth," she says.
Then she looks down and gasps. A jagged fear races through
Heph: Does she regret kissing him? Is she mad at him for
doing it after he promised not to?

"I know I promised..." he begins, the wind on his shoulders suddenly feeling cold.

"No," she says, looking in wonder at her golden fingertip,
shimmering now with the sparkling grains. "Look."

Against the gold of her finger, the grains look something
like scales on a golden-skinned creature.

"I think," she says quietly, examining the grains, "that I
understand what to do."

Chapter Thirteen: Jacob

As quiet as death, Jacob sneaks around the meandering tunnels under the Temple of Delphi. It's as if he's lost his way not just here, but in life. Everything he used to believe in—his love for Kat, his ambition to be become an important Aesarian Lord, even the person he always thought he was—has become twisted and confusing, just like these vapor-filled, undulating paths.

At the same time, he feels at home here, in the heart of the earth, surrounded by the crushing weight of rock. Something calls to him, something irresistibly desirable and yet dangerous, too, like the sirens who tempt sailors to their deaths on rocks. What is this tantalizing voice of the earth? How can he even answer it…and what will happen if he does?

He pushes the feelings back down into a tight, dark place, rolls a stone over them, and ignores them.

His torchlight slides over walls slick with moisture, and the greenish vapors rising from cracks in the wall almost make him gag, but he continues onward, trying to get to the underground pool where he agreed to meet Pythia tonight. If he can find out from her what Prince Alexander has been asking the oracle during his frequent visits, perhaps he can discover whether the

Last God, Riel, really is lurking in the Pellan palace. Then he can find a way to capture him and deliver him to the Lords, a silent apology for the strange magic that buzzes in his blood, the very thing that makes him their deadliest enemy.

Two weeks ago, when he first rode into the wondrous city of Delphi, he made straight for the Temple of Apollo, hoping for an audience with Pythia, the beautiful girl he had seen swimming before dawn in the Castalian Spring outside of town. But after waiting for hours in line with visitors from all over the known world—two kings, a queen, and three commanding generals, as well as farmers, milkmaids, and shop owners—the temple priests rejected him as soon as they saw his horned helmet, because they had something against Aesarian Lords. Jacob realized the only way he could see Pythia again was to wait at the spring the next dawn and hope she would come. He had wandered the city all day, dazzled by its richness, and taken a room at an inn so crowded he had to share a rather dirty bed with two other men.

Well before dawn he waited for her there, hiding his armor and helmet behind a bush. He saw movement first, a slice of white in the black air as the girl approached the edge of the spring. She removed her robe and slipped naked into the pond, where she bobbed and sang a hymn to Apollo asking him to give her true prophecies that day. After a time, still wearing his tunic, he slid silently into the sacred spring. She didn't hear him as he pushed out toward her, because she was splashing, kicking, totally submerging herself and coming up laughing and spluttering as if she were a small child. Then, when he was only an arm's length away, he whispered, "Don't be afraid! I mean you no harm. I need your help."

The girl turned, her pointed face frozen in fear. "Who are you? I will scream! I will call down Apollo's curses on you!"

"No, please! I just want to talk to you," he pleaded, hands outstretched in an imploring gesture.

She treaded water a long moment. "Do you know who I am?" she asked suspiciously.

"Based on the songs you sing, I imagine you are Pythia."

She stared, clearly deciding whether it was safe to respond. "That is what they call me," she finally acknowledged. "Who are you? Where are you from?"

"I'm Jacob, son of Cleon the potter from the village of Erissa in Macedon," he said, thinking perhaps he shouldn't mention the Aesarian Lords after the priests tossed him out of the temple. "Come to shore. I will hold up your robes and shut my eyes as you dress, I promise. I really need your help. Just listen to me, that's all I ask."

Moonlight rippled silver on the water around her. "If I do," she said, softer now, younger, "will you promise not to tell Apollo's priests I come here? I'm not supposed to leave the temple precincts at night, but it is so boring that sometimes I think I'll lose my mind if I don't get out. If they found out..." Her voice cracked.

"Of course I won't tell," he reassured her. "Even if you decide not to help me, I won't tell a soul." He swam in a wide circle around her—so as not frighten this delicate, fawn-like girl—and pulled himself up on shore, where he held up her robe and turned his head away. He'd been wrong to think she might be anything like Kat. She acted much younger, seemed more innocent, more nervous. He sensed an independent streak in her, but not with the same fire Kat has. He shook his head, willing away the thoughts of Katerina.

"All right," he said, "come out and I won't look until you tell me to."

He heard the water ripple, wet footsteps slapping on rock, and felt her tugging at the robe.

"Ready."

He opened his eyes and she was standing there, the setting

moon lighting her face. Pale skin. Large eyes. Were they green like Kat's? It was too dark to tell. Hazel, maybe.

"What do you want, then?" she asked, crossing her arms.

He considered a moment, running a hand through his wet hair. "First of all, please tell me how you left the temple without the priests knowing? Without the guards stopping you?" If Pythia could get *out* of the temple without notice, maybe Jacob could get *in*—and spy on Alexander the next time he came.

She twisted her mouth as if weighing how much to tell him. "There are many tunnels beneath the temple," she finally said. "One night, locked in there, I was so bored I grabbed a torch and started exploring. After a couple of weeks, I found a way that opened up outside the town walls. It's a bit of a walk, but I love coming here, breathing in clean, fresh air."

Jacob frowned. "Is there something wrong with the air in the temple?"

Pythia made a face. "It was built above two cracks in the earth that form a giant X. Vapors from Lord Apollo's breath rise up through those cracks, vapors that help me focus the voices that buzz in my head. Sometimes I just need to get away from them. I fear one day those fumes are going to drive me mad. Would you...?" She gestured to a towel draped on a nearby rock.

"I tried to see you today, but I couldn't," he said, handing her the soft length of fine-woven linen.

"Some people wait for weeks to see me," she said, using the towel to squeeze water from her hair. Clearly, she assumed he didn't get in because the line was too long.

"Can I ask you a question now?"

"For a prophecy, you mean?" she asked.

He nodded.

"No, not here," she said, wrapping the towel over her shoulders like a shawl. "I need Apollo's exhalations to hear the gods clearly. Even then, sometimes they echo so I can't understand them and the pilgrims go away confused."

"Was that what it was like with—" he hesitated, plucked a damp pebble from a crack in the rocks, and rubbed it nervously between his thumb and forefinger "—with Prince Alexander of Macedon?" he asked. "People say he's been here three times in the past month."

She nodded, eyes wide. "He's the worst one of all. The voices are so muddled when he's there, as if a hundred people are yelling different things. But there's one thing I can make out. Over and over again some of the voices say, *The father is the son and the son is the father.*"

Utterly mystified, Jacob dropped the stone into the pool of water. The tiny plunk seemed to echo in his silence. Finally, he asked, "What do you think that means?"

"I don't know. And the strangest thing was *he* didn't even ask what it meant. Just moved on to his other questions." She fumbled her damp feet into a pair of sandals strewn on the ground nearby.

"What other questions?"

She shook her head as she adjusted the strap on one foot. "Something about getting back to some place or other. Regaining his old powers again. And killing a king. The voices said he needs one of the king's lovers to do the deed."

Jacob frowned. What king would Alexander want to kill? Artaxerxes of Persia, perhaps?

"I can't really remember clearly," she added, rising. "The vapors...they make me dizzy. Everything is full of smoke and chatter and flashing lights. And when my head clears, it's as if the voices were a dream—not even my dream but someone else's."

She turned to walk back toward the center of town. "Don't follow me," she said over her shoulder, her voice a mix of warning and pleading.

"But wait," he called out. "That's...that's it? That's all you can tell me?"

She turned and cocked her head. "I don't know what you

want," she replied. The sun was starting to melt the darkness of the sky, rising behind her and setting her face in shadow.

"What *do* you know?" Jacob asked, frustration—no, desperation, hot and urgent—beginning to pound through his veins. He felt close to something, but he didn't know what.

She squared her thin shoulders. "I know that Alexander of Macedon must never come to the throne."

Jacob's mouth fell open, but he closed it quickly. "Why not?"

She shifted her weight, and he had the sense that at any moment she might flee—or turn into mist in the light of dawn. Finally, she said, "Horrible things will happen." He saw then that she was trembling. "I saw an unbearable darkness. So much blood. Images of giant snakes squeezing the life out of cities, nations, empires…"

Jacob thought of the Alexander he'd briefly met—thought of the moment they faced each other in the Pyrrhian Fortress. His overwhelming impression had been that the prince was brave, intelligent, and just. Why would horrible things happen in the world if this peerless prince came to the throne? It didn't make any sense, and something about her words— something more than the gruesome images they contained— set off an alarm ringing through him.

Pythia was staring at him, wrapping a wet lock of long hair around her finger. "If you really want a prophecy," she said, her voice uncertain, "there is a way."

"What way?" he said so fast and loud he could have bitten his tongue. The last thing he wanted to do was frighten her.

She bit her lower lip and looked at the ground. "You may trail me back toward town, but at a safe distance, in case someone sees us. Then watch how I enter the tunnel in the hill. Two weeks from now, three hours past sunset, when all the lamps are out, take that passage and always keep to the left if you have a choice of tunnels. You will end up in a rock chamber with a warm thermal pool. I will be waiting for you there."

Two weeks? He needed this information urgently. "Why not tonight?" he asked.

She made a face. "For a fortnight starting tonight I have to sleep in a special chamber with visiting priestesses and conduct certain rituals. But I will meet you as soon as they are gone and give you your prophecy then."

She turned to go, then faced him again, pulling her robe more closely about her. "But don't be angry with me if the prophecy I give doesn't make sense to you. They seldom do."

That was two weeks ago. Now, as Jacob pads silently through the tunnels, he goes over and over again everything he ever heard or read about Riel. What Lord Bastian said when Jacob was eavesdropping. What High Lord Gideon explained in Jacob's initiation ceremony into the Elder Council. What he himself has read in the ancient scrolls.

His mind keeps pondering one thing that doesn't make sense: the message his spy in the Pellan palace delivered ten days ago. Why would Queen Olympias throw temper tantrums about her son's visits to the oracle? Was the witch-queen afraid Alexander would receive some unflattering information about her? But no—the spy had said she was *jealous* of the younger woman, as if Pythia was a rival in love. Sometimes Olympias yelled at Alexander so loudly about the lovely young oracle that all the servants in her palace wing could hear every word she said, and they were all talking about it.

The tunnel widens, yawning into a small cavern where torches burn brightly. Before him, sulfurous vapors rise like ghostly fingers from a pool of yellow-green water. Others writhe out of cracks in the wall. Pythia, garbed in a loose, white wool robe, sits on a tall bronze stool, the *holmos*, the bowl-shaped seat of oracles, and before her white smoke rises from a tripod.

"Ah, there you are," she says in a sleepy voice. She smiles at him, but her eyes are fixed and glazed. The vapors, he realizes, must already be affecting her. Above her, he notices an ornate bronze grille, through which the vapors rise to a chamber above—perhaps the oracular chamber where she normally gives her predictions.

She throws something into the tripod, and soon aromatic smoke mixes with the sulfurous fumes—the exhilarating notes of oleander leaves and the heavy spice of myrrh and frankincense. She leans forward, her tumble of long strawberry-blond hair closing around her face like a bolt of gleaming cloth. When she sits back up, her wreath of bright green laurel tilts to the left.

"Know, Pilgrim," Pythia begins in a deep voice, her eyes cloudy, unfocused, "that the god who speaks neither reveals the truth nor conceals it, but only gives signs."

"I...uh...know," Jacob replies, unsure of the ritual response.

"What is your question, Pilgrim?"

Jacob looks around nervously. "I thought you would bring a sheep or goat to sacrifice," he says, setting his torch in a sconce. "Isn't that what all temples require?"

"The gods have had plenty of meat already today," she says drowsily, her eyes half-shut. "What is your question?"

"All right," he says, squaring his shoulders. "My question is this: Where is Riel?"

Immediately, Pythia's eyes roll back in her head so Jacob can see only the whites. Shaking as violently as if she had the falling sickness, she says, in a deep voice like that of a man, *"The last of us the last of us the last of us."*

Jacob is torn between feelings of relief—and terror.

She jerks, puppetlike, and says, *"The father is the son and the son is the father the father is the son and the son is the father."*

A shiver runs up Jacob's spine. Why is she saying the same thing to him as she did to Alexander?

Pythia convulses so violently that the tripod falls over, spilling a cascade of burning coals onto the stone floor. One of them rolls into the green pool with a hiss and burst of smoke. Now she teeters to the side on her high *holmos*, and Jacob grabs her as the stool slams onto stone with a crash. Her eyes are open, vacant, her lips moving as she mutters things he cannot understand. And she's thrashing so forcefully that he can barely hold her.

"Pythia, it's all right," he says. "Come back now. It's over." But she doesn't.

He looks at the wraithlike vapors rising all around them. She needs fresh air. He needs to get her out of here, away from these powerful fumes that seem to alter her state of mind. But the entrance out of the tunnels is too far.

In the corner, he sees a little staircase winding to the chamber above. Into the temple. He is forbidden there, but he must go, must rescue her. She shakes in his arms as he lifts her, and a string of drool slides from her mouth. Jacob's pulse races. What has he done? He folds her over his back and grabs a torch, then mounts the stairs, hoping no one is in the oracular room.

It is vacant, thankfully, a small chamber of white marble, bereft of furniture, with a set of double doors in the opposite wall. He sets his torch in a sconce and lays her gently down on the polished floor. But the air in this windowless room is no better than the vaporous cave below; as he suspected, fumes float straight up from the cave through the bronze grate of curling acanthus leaves. He takes off his cloak and throws it over the grate.

Then he opens the double doors a sliver and peeks into the main sanctuary of the temple. That, too, is devoid of human life; there is only the resounding but soft murmur of the last few crickets of summer. At one end, lit by torches, sits an enormous statue of Apollo strumming a lyre. His skin is a warm, glowing ivory; his hair shines with the luster of pure hammered gold; his lapis lazuli eyes blaze in the dancing, fiery light. A purple tunic of the finest Milesian wool has been draped on the statue's body, clasped with shield-sized brooches of amethyst and gold. At his feet are bowls of meat, bread, and wine left out for the god to nourish himself with their spiritual essence.

Jacob opens the doors wide, feeling a cool evening breeze clear the vapors from the oracular chamber, and carries Pythia to the threshold. As soon as the fresh air hits her, she mumbles something and opens her eyes. "Breathe in," he says, stroking her cheek.

She inhales deeply, closing her eyes, and smiles.

"You are kind," she says after a time, struggling to sit up. "Many respect and fear me. Others try to control me. Everyone wants something from me. Very few are...kind." She rubs her temples.

"Are you not happy here?" he asks softly. She reminds him of Kat again—but only when she first came to live with his family after her mother's mysterious murder—fragile, vulnerable, yet brave.

Pythia sighs. "It could be worse," she says, adjusting her laurel wreath. "I was born a slave." She pauses. "After years of earning a fortune through my predictions, a few months ago my master sold me here when the old Pythia died. But I am still a slave, I think, for I have less freedom now than ever before."

She gazes out into the sanctuary and says, "They even took away my name. Every Delphic oracle must be called Pythia after the first priestess a thousand years ago. I dress and act as Pythia is supposed to. I wear her clothes and answer to her name, but I am no more Pythia than that statue is truly Apollo. I am myself, pretending to be someone else."

With a sharp intake of breath, Jacob suddenly understands

what the gods meant when she said, *The father is the son is the father is the son.*

The certainty of it floods through him with thundering clarity. Just as this girl is acting as if she were Pythia, the ancient priestess, Riel is acting as if he were Alexander, who is his son, not King Philip's. He has somehow incapacitated the prince, hidden him asleep somewhere, and taken on his form. Or he has killed him and taken over his body. Alexander and Riel are one. The same. The father *is* the son. And the son *is* the father.

That also explains why Alexander—who attacked the Aesarian Lords twice and won—rides blithely past them on his way to Delphi without even glancing at them. Riel doesn't care about the Lords or their insults to Macedon. He cares about only one thing: regaining his divine powers and returning to the gods.

But how can Jacob capture Riel now, when he is, in the eyes of the world, the prince regent of Macedon? He can't just march into the Pellan palace, stride past the royal bodyguards, and drag the prince out of the city. He racks his brain for an idea, a disguise, a… Then he almost laughs at his foolishness. Why should Jacob seek out Riel in Pella when the Last God will surely return to Delphi soon for more prophecies?

"What is it, Jacob?" Pythia asks, worry creasing her soft face. "Did my prophecy disturb you? I hardly remember what I said, there were so many ringing voices…"

He looks down at her, torchlight making her hair flame a shining red-gold. "It took me a while to understand," he says gently, "but it makes perfect sense. Listen, Pythia, can I trust you?"

She laughs a little, wrapping her arms around her thin frame. "I've trusted you with my secrets," she says. "It's only fair you can trust me with yours."

Jacob smiles, the plan formulating in his mind. If he can't catch a god, maybe he can at least trick one.

CHAPTER FOURTEEN: KATERINA

SITTING AGAINST A PALM TREE, KAT WATCHES Aristotle and Heph drag the nets in from the stormy sea and squat down, inspecting them for the metallic grains. Just looking at the nets makes Kat feel trapped. Sharp skeins bite into her flesh, becoming tighter and tighter the more she flails and twists. Hers is a net she can never escape because it is made of her own flesh and blood, created by the coupling of two of the most evil people who ever walked the earth.

Her father isn't a wool merchant, or even a great king. He is a god. The Last God. A being of fathomless selfishness and cruelty. Worse, even, than this knowledge is the tickling, creeping question that comes unbidden: Would he love her? Be proud of her? What would it be like to have a relationship with her real father?

And the idea terrifies her. She berates herself for letting it rise to the level of conscious thought. Because if any of his innate malice slides hot and liquid through her veins, he would be the one to bring it out, to make it bloom and thrive, to turn her into something like himself.

The warm sun can't melt the block of icy fear in her heart. The brisk ocean breeze can't whisk away her aching despair.

Not all the waves in the sea can pound away the filth inside her, the filth that is her.

Ever since she learned who her father is, she has been unable to tap into her magic. What had become second nature to her—the exhilarating union with birds and fish, insects and animals, this ability that made life ring with universal song—is gone. Dark. Dried up. A dull, throbbing numbness is all that's left in the spot that used to contain the fizz and fire of her magic. Perhaps she has become like the Lotus-eaters without taking their drug.

Heph looks at Kat and grins broadly. Something lifts within her. A hope. A warmth. A gladness.

She smiles at him, a genuine one. No, she's not totally numb. There's Heph. The only times she has felt truly alive, truly herself, is when she is around him. Because Heph is happier than she has ever seen him, and she's humbled by his joy of knowing that she cares for him.

Over the past several days, Kat has found some relief from her nagging sadness by telling him stories of her childhood: how she liked to hide behind Helen's loom, playing with the dangling loom weights. How she could always seem to talk to goats and donkeys and was surprised to learn that no one else could. How she loved to fish and hunt and race the gazelles.

But she never mentions Jacob. When Heph asked about him once, she said that that story was a rolled-up scroll she would not reopen.

Mostly, though, the four of them have been studying the diagrams Aristotle copied in Egypt supposedly of the original Atlantean device. They examined the molds he had cast of tiny gears with a hundred teeth each, pin-and-slot mechanisms, dials, cranks, and levers to make a small test version, one that could fit in the palm of his hand. They practiced with the portable forge and bellows. They decided where they would get enough of the lead necessary to give strength to the soft, pliable flakes: Heph's sword.

Ada, who had spent many hours holding the flakes, her eyes closed, said, "Though the *baruopa* isn't a living thing exactly, it has just enough consciousness for a Snake Blood to access. I believe that if a wielder of Blood Magic adds into the mixture the thing that the mechanism should detect, the *baruopa* will seek out more. I think that is the missing ingredient."

And so they would add rock dust for Earth Blood, as well as snakeskin and feathers for Snake Blood. They are ready to go. Except they don't have nearly enough *baruopa*. They can go no further until they have at least the weight of a warrior in grains for enough molten metal to pour into the molds. So far, they have a few nearly weightless handfuls.

But Kat and Ada have a plan. When she showed Ada the strange paintings on the ruined temples around the island of tentacles wrapped around people, Ada speculated as to what sort of creature those tentacles could belong to. And whether the glinting pieces they have been collecting on the beach are actually remnants of crushed *scales*. That perhaps the Atlanteans bred a creature from which they harvested this magical substance. Aristotle—who studied living creatures all over the known world—is intrigued by this idea. But there's only one way to be sure: Kat or Ada must enter the mind of a sea creature, dive beneath the waves, and look around.

Beyond the breakers, a gray-brown ball bobs on choppy waves. At first, Kat thinks it's a coconut, but then the ball disappears and a gleaming tail slices up through the water. A seal. She should try again. She should calm her breathing and picture herself as the seal, reveling in the feel of the water buoying her up, the warmth of the sun on her head, the joy of fresh fish in her stomach. But she can't even try.

She groans aloud in frustration.

"Still can't?" Ada asks. She sits beside Kat, folding her long legs gracefully beneath her.

"No." The thudding of the waves is like the thudding of Kat's heart, heavy and repetitive. "My magic has left me!"

Ada looks out at the sea, avoiding Kat's eyes. "I think," she says cautiously, "that you know that is not the case. Your magic has not left you...you have left it."

Kat frowns. "Please stop talking in riddles, Ada. What do you mean?"

"I think that you are scared to wield your abilities now that you know from where they came. I suspect you believe that if you accept your magic, you are accepting the evil dangers of your father."

Kat flinches. "That's a bit dramatic. The truth is I'm just tired from the heat and sun."

"You are not," Ada says gently. "But when you stop denying yourself, we'll be able to locate the source of the *baruopa*. Everything depends on getting enough."

Anger floods Kat, bright and hot. Why does she have to do it? Hasn't she been through enough?

"You do it," she flares. "Go into a seal or fish and look around down there to see if we are right."

But Ada shakes her head. "I will not be doing any Snake magic for a while. I am still not recovered from my ordeal. Besides," she says, tilting her head and staring at Kat, "something tells me this is your journey."

Her journey? She's had her fill of this journey. For weeks now she's been asking herself what purpose magic even has other than evil and danger. Yes, she used it to help Alex in the Battle of Pellan Fields, but she couldn't save her foster family, and she couldn't stop Jacob from slipping away from her into the fold of the enemy. What use is any of it? It's all too much.

Kat puts her head in her hands. She wishes with all her heart that Helen was here now, to comfort and love her—to affirm that she was whom Helen knew her to be: Kat, a gentle, loving daughter. She longs to be a child again, an infant, wrapped safely in her true mother's arms.

A sharp memory suddenly cuts through Kat's ocean of sorrow. The memory of Helen's turquoise chest…with the bones of an infant inside.

"Ada," she asks quietly, "where did Helen find the bones of a baby to prove my death to Olympias?"

"It was her own daughter, I think," Ada says sadly. She resettles herself, brushing sand off her legs. "I think she took you to Erissa hoping to raise the two of you together," she says. "But her child was either born dead or died soon after birth. Helen must have put the bones of her own baby in that box just in case the queen ever found her. She would have hoped that Olympias would believe those bones were yours, Kat, so you would be safe."

"Poor Helen," Kat says quietly, sadness sweeping over her. "I would have loved to have had a sister."

The women look out at the sea together, a comfortable silence sitting between them. Slowly, the wind picks up, whipping Kat's hair. She reties the leather thong around her ponytail and says, "Lately, I wonder if I even want my magic anymore. Knowing the evil my father… No, I'll never call him that, just like I'll never call Olympias mother."

She lets her hair fall to her shoulders and sighs. "Knowing the evil Riel did with his magic. Seeing you trapped in the hawk's form. Knowing that the entire civilization of Atlantis was destroyed for using such powerful magic…"

"I think," Ada says slowly, "that Atlantis didn't sink beneath the waves because of its magic. I think it is possible they hid themselves there from some great evil, perhaps the very one that now rises in the Eastern Mountains."

She stares at the sea as if hoping to get a glimpse of painted marble columns just beneath the lilting white caps. "Maybe they are still there, waiting for something." She turns to Kat and says, "Go for a swim."

Kat looks at the water, a roiling sapphire blue glistening with streaks of silver, capped by foamy breakers. "I'm too tired right now," she says. "Maybe tomorrow."

"Katerina," Ada says, and her voice is low and deadly serious, "we both know you must do it, not just for the sake of the mechanism, but for yourself, as well. You can't let your magic wither inside you. You can't let yourself fear the very thing that makes you *you*."

Yes, she's right, Kat knows. But still, there's something important that she needs to understand. "Ada, tell me, how can the same force that makes me who I am make that horrible monster Riel who he is?"

Ada pushes a stray black tendril behind her ear. "How can fire be such a boon to humankind—providing heat and light and cooking food—and yet destroy entire cities, fields, and forests? Because fire is neutral, Katerina. It is a thing. Magic, too, is a neutral thing. It can be used for good or evil, for selfish or unselfish purposes. You have magic. That is a fact. A neutral one. The key question is how you will use it. For the good of humanity? Or to enrich and empower yourself? There is a third choice: you can ignore and deny it instead of using it to help others, which is an evil in itself."

Kat hangs her head. Ada is right. Knowing who her father is means she just has more to prove when it comes to wielding her powers for good. She must try harder. Risk more. And yet...

"Ada, what if I..." Kat feels her face crumple and sees Ada's look of concern as she utters the most frightening thought of her life. "What if I become like him?" she asks, her voice a cracked whisper in the wind.

Ada, her eyes gleaming with compassion, strokes Kat's hair. "You are not like him," she says. "You will never be like him, because you are you. You have already proven your courage and goodness. But you cannot stop, Katerina. You must continue. And right now, you must swim and seek answers."

Thunder rumbles on the horizon. Kat looks at the storm clouds rolling in, charcoal and pewter striated with gold from the late-afternoon sun. "All right," she agrees. "But it's going to rain."

"Good," Ada says. "You can concentrate on the rain hitting your face and the rolling of the waves. Don't try consciously to use your magic. Just relax and slide into the rhythm of the sea and the creatures in it."

"All right," Kat says again. She stands and walks into the sea in just her light tunic. It's unusually rough; the waves pummel her with froth and foam as she pushes past them. Beyond the thundering breakers, smaller waves slap her face like angry hands. She floats, weightless, feeling the shift and pull of the water, losing herself in its rhythmic power. Feeling the first fat drops of rain hitting her face.

The familiar warmth of oneness is so indescribably sweet it hurts. Her veins are on fire, her flesh tingles. This is unity with all living things. This is...this is Riel's power. Now terror flows through her. And disgust. And anger. And fear of what she might become. But no, this is *her* power. Hers. Katerina of Erissa, princess of Macedon. Sister of Alexander. This is hers—no one else's—and it feels so very good. A surge of magic rolls through her. She has missed this. She is this.

Suddenly she is a thousand creatures at once: fish, crabs, clams, seaweed, and tiny pulsating beings too small to see. She feels what they feel: hunger, the contentedness of drifting in the womb of the ocean, fear of the coming storm. All sea life tumbles through her consciousness like the tides: *We are here. We are here. We are one.*

She darts farther out to sea, away from the dangers of pounding waves, to hide in calmer, deeper waters between rocks. She moves past dozens of barnacled amphorae rolling in slow motion back and forth on the sandy bottom. She finds the safety of a shipwreck, the rotting planks of its curved hull like the moldering rib cage of a human giant.

But something deeper calls to her, a low moan, a buried meaning. The sea has a secret, pulsing and dark and very, very powerful. An ancient song echoes through the murky depths, calling, calling.

And then: sliding smoothly toward her is an enormous gray-black creature with a square head—a whale. The sound is coming from its body, a sort of watery lullaby that reverberates through Kat as if it were her own. She slips into the song, becomes one with it. She is the whale, and the song of the whale, and the echo of the song.

She is large and ancient, gliding through inky blackness splashed with shifting shadows and occasional beams of light. The song continues to pulse through her lungs—it's a melody she knows without knowing how. It is the oldest song of the earth, the song before men were created, before the gods, even. A song to love, depths and depths away. The song has no words yet throbs with meaning. *Home. Welcome home. You are home. We are one.*

She drifts, her mind and body one with the whale, learning to see without seeing. Learning to sense—moss-covered rocks and water currents, small nervous fish, and mollusks creeping over sand on one slimy foot. She must remember she is Kat. She must remember her purpose here: find the creature with the glittering scales, if it exists at all.

She glides farther out to sea, deeper into cold darkness.

Long hours go by and she feels the pull of the ocean's rhythms, luring her away from shore, away from certainty, away from even the memory of herself.

And then the shadow comes, a transformation of the darkness into shape.

Suddenly it is as though a sun—not the sun in the sky, but a strange subaqueous source of light—has broken through the blackness. The water churns with flashing scales and snapping serpents' jaws. It is no sun, but a marvelously reflective array of shimmering surfaces, of *skin and scales.*

The sea beast.

There are several of them, five, six, seven heads with fiery eyes and cruel teeth. Claws shred her slick whale skin and she roars in pain. No, there is only one of them, one body. With seven heads on long twisting necks like tentacles.

And it is attacking her. Killing her.

Its thick muscular tail wraps around her, squeezing, dragging her lower, away from the sun and air that even a whale needs. Terror and awe mingle as she begins to suffocate, but the beauty of the scales—those dazzling, precious scales—captivates her. She and Ada were right. The metal was no metal at all, but something natural, once living. Something magical. A thrill of excitement rolls through her.

Now she is the monster, feeling its need for flesh and rich blubber. She has a fleeting vision, a memory, perhaps, of a city on the bottom of the sea, with many-columned temples and palaces, markets and roads, and people gliding forward, their long hair and full robes trailing behind them in the sea currents. But then the memory is gone, replaced by ravenous hunger.

Jaws close on the whale's back, and pain reverberates through her. She is dragged down, down. For a moment, Kat panics. If the whale dies, will she die with it? She twists—she is one enormous, powerful muscle—and bites off one of the vicious, fanged heads bobbing in front of her. Six other heads howl in pain. Together, entwined like lovers, Kat and the monster hurtle down into the black depths.

And then there is a startling, blinding zag of light. Lightning. The storm.

She feels a sudden surge of strength, and...

★ ★ ★

"Kat!"

It's Heph. She wants to open her eyes, to say something. But she can't. She hears wind and thunder, a crash of lightning. She feels wet sand beneath her and little waves rolling over her legs. Rain stings her face.

"Is she breathing?" Ada, her voice a stab of panic in the darkness.

"Kat! Please! Wake up!" Heph.

"Get her into the hut, out of the rain." Aristotle.

Someone—Heph—picks her up and carries her awhile, then gently lays her down on something soft. The strong smell of lotus blossom under her nose clears her head, as it always does when she gets lost in Snake magic. She opens her eyes and sees Ada's worried face hovering above her, holding up a bright pink flower.

"Kat," Ada says softly, "are you all right?"

"The whale..." she croaks.

Ada turns to the men. "Leave us alone, please. I think this is a matter for Snake Bloods." Heph doesn't budge, just strokes Kat's head. She smiles at him weakly and nods, and then he goes.

Ada slowly rouses Kat with sips of watered wine and more lotus scent. Finally, Kat is able to tell her what happened.

"We were right," she says, her voice ragged. "Those metallic pieces are crushed scales from a sea creature, just as you thought. Four long legs with webbed feet and claws, a serpent's tail, and seven long serpent heads."

"A hydra," Ada gasps. "In the age before Troy fell, Heracles killed one of them. And before that, the Atlanteans must have raised them, bred them for their scales."

A burst of wind throws open the shutters as nearly horizontal rain pounds into the hut. Ada rises and closes the shutters, bolting them securely.

Kat rubs her throbbing temples. "For a few moments," she says, "I was the hydra, hungry, frenzied to kill and eat. And I had a memory of Atlantis, of a city beneath the sea with people living there. But that vision came and went so quickly I'm not even sure what I saw."

Ada stands motionless by the window, staring at Kat. Outside, thunder rumbles loudly and waves angrily pound the beach.

"This time, my experience was different," Kat continues. "I've often felt like I shared minds with animals, but this time I felt like I was sharing the soul of the whale. I wonder if it died, if the hydra killed it down there. And if so, how was I able to extricate myself?"

Seating herself on the floor, Ada looks at her in evident surprise. "Well," she says, affecting a light tone, "under the circumstances, I think your abilities may astonish us all."

The next morning, Kat wakes early. For some reason, she feels the sea beckoning her. Quietly, she slips out of the hut and makes her way in dawn's darkness. When she arrives at the surf's edge, she walks in, allowing the waves to run over her skin and toss sand onto her feet. And in the darkness she waits, not certain of what.

Slowly, pink tinges the sky, becoming fiercer as the sun begins to rise. And as the first rays hit the beach, Kat sees a glimmer. And then another…and another.

She gasps. For in the light of a new day, the entire beach shimmers a silvery gold. No—the beach *is* silvery gold. It's covered with scales. Kat shrieks with joy, running her hands through the scales as if they were gold coins washed up from the deep.

"What is this?" she hears someone gasp. Whirling around, she sees that Aristotle, Ada, and Heph have joined her. Heph picks up a bit of gleaming gold and tries to bend it.

"*Baruopa*," he says, examining one in his palm, "but these grains are much bigger than the ones we've been collecting."

"Not grains, Heph," Kat says. *"Scales."* She picks one up and bends it. "These are bigger because they are fresh. They haven't been crushed by waves pounding them against sand and rocks."

Aristotle raises a bushy eyebrow. "What did you do, Katerina, when you were down there?"

"I think," she says, "I killed a hydra."

Heph grabs her and pulls her close to him, burying his face in her neck. Over his shoulder, she gazes at the sea, calmer now, a shining lapis blue dotted with small whitecaps. And there, in the distance, she sees a whale's spout.

CHAPTER FIFTEEN:
CYNANE

CYNANE LUNGES TOWARD THE GUARD'S LEFT; then, as he raises his shield to deflect her blow, she jabs him hard in his right shoulder. The guard curses and spits a wad of saliva onto the sand of the practice arena.

Another guard, Perdix, laughs. "Karpos, the men will love it when I tell them you got beat up by a girl," he says, leaning on his shield.

Cyn kicks a hard blow to Perdix's wrist. He cries out in pain as his sword flies out of his hand. Then she drops her practice sword, snatches up his shield, and, armed with two shields now, pummels him backward until he falls on the ground with his arms crossed over his face.

"Not a girl, whelp of Cerberus," she barks. "Your queen. And better trained as a warrior than you."

Karpos bursts out laughing, a long, screeching rasp like a handsaw scraping through wood. "Who's the girl now, Perdix?" he asks.

Cyn stands back, panting, as Perdix pushes himself up, grunting and cursing. The leather lining of her helmet is slick with sweat, her hair is stringy with it. Her tanned skin gleams. Life pumps through her muscles, throbs in her veins. This is ecstasy.

"Now get up and fight me like a man," she growls. "From what I've seen so far, *you're* the girl."

The wooden swords thwack and thump against each other and the cowhide shields. For Cynane, the training is a dance to the pulsating rhythm of her heart. She spins and leaps, agile and lithe, while the two burly guards are no match for her speed.

Her morning training sessions are the only time she can raise herself out of the pit of misery that her life has become. Here, now, she can release some part of her pent-up anger, frustration, and fear. Each day, Amyntas becomes more and more threatening, and Cyn feels as if she has never left the cliff precipice where she stripped and allowed her clothes to dance on the wind. She is still there, perilously close to the edge, waiting for Amyntas to push her off. And it's all *his* fault. Taulus.

She knows now that's what—that's *who*—appeared in the bedroom as she was slipping the dagger beneath her pillow. The figure made entirely of smoke.

Though at first she'd been terrified, sickened even, by his presence, she had quickly calmed down and recognized him. It was Taulus who had put the protective spell on Cynane; after the most horrible torture sessions at the hands of the Aesarian Lords, Cyn's shattered bones and torn flesh would heal within moments. He first appeared to her in her cell after one such session, and then again when she was wounded in the Labyrinth of Knossos. She always wondered if he was a hallucination born of pain and desperation. But now she knows the truth. He is real. And she will never die of a wound as long as he lives.

The shadowy ghost of a man is, in fact, Cyn's great-great-grandfather, Taulus, a legendary figure Dardanians whisper about in awestruck wonder. Cynane's mother, Audata, used to tell her bedtime stories about the man who turned into a phantom, who melted silver with his breath and could slip through walls and reappear hundreds of miles away in an instant. It was Taulus who steered his grandson, Bardylis, from the life of a lowly coal miner to becoming king of Dardania, building it into the most powerful of the Illyrian kingdoms. Taulus is the only person on earth with Smoke Blood.

And he has forbidden Cyn to attain it.

It was Taulus who convinced her not to kill Amyntas on their wedding night as she had planned. She first had to build up alliances, he said, make influential friends, persuade the Dardanian power structure that she would advance their interests more than the mad Amyntas ever could.

Cyn's anger builds to a crescendo as she jabs Karpos hard in the gut—he drops his weapons and keels over—and hits Perdix at the base of the throat. He just stands there with something like a death rattle gurgling out of his slack mouth. Really, if this is all Amyntas's army has to offer, it's a miracle another kingdom hasn't invaded and taken over.

"Pathetic," she says, throwing her weapons on the ground. "Tell your commander tomorrow I want to fight men, not kittens."

Perdix, still coughing hard, pulls up his colleague. They bow clumsily and stagger off. Cyn hears one of them mumble something about "a cheating bitch" and is about to call them back and make them pay for the insult, when the air in front of her shimmers.

Even in the broad, hot daylight, her skin prickles with chills. The air is suddenly thick with mist. He appears to her frequently like this, and she wonders if he is always watching, even when she can't see him.

The two guards have left the arena, but Cyn glances around to make sure there are no other prying eyes as the mist thickens into smoke, which slowly begins to take shape, like she knew it would, finally coalescing into a tall, well-built man in a full robe with long, wide sleeves. Though it is hard to see his face in daylight, she has seen it fairly clearly in twilight. Silver hair frames a wide, proud visage with dark, hooded eyes and an aquiline nose. He pulls out of his robe a sword of sparkling crystalline mist that turns into something like glass as it cuts through the air.

"Fight me, my child," he says in a voice of cinders and ashes. "What I just saw here was no training at all. You will lose your form practicing with such men as these."

Cyn cannot disagree—or resist. She picks up her weapons and rounds on him. Taulus is the most challenging opponent she has ever had, and his weapon is not nearly as insubstantial as it looks. He surges toward her in a swirl of vaporous robes so fast she can barely afford to blink. She raises her sword to hit his, but she slices only air as his sword appears in his other hand and hammers down on her bronze helmet. Her skull rings out like a bell. Even her teeth are ringing.

Furious now, she spins, eyes on the glimmering air that is Taulus standing behind the raised sword. A mouth opens in the smoke, and she hears low gravelly laughter. Then the smoke shifts into the form of a little girl with long braids and a sweet face. "Don't hurt me," the child says in a soft imploring voice, her plump fingers curled around the crystal sword.

Cyn hesitates only a second—she has seen Taulus's shapeshifting tricks before—and in one swift movement she engages his sword, pushes it away from her, and thrusts her shield into the smoke girl. But she just parts the smoke, which sweeps around her and reforms into Taulus behind her. The heart. She needs to hit him in the heart, the only part of him with any substance left. She sizes up the undefined shape, picks her mark, and lunges, hitting something solid, something almost flesh.

Taulus grunts in pain. The wisps that make up his form dissolve, and his sword disappears. Cyn curses as she twists right and left, looking for the coming assault. He has hidden his sword in his robes again, making it, too, vanish, until he is ready to use it.

"This is cheating!" she says, raising her weapons. "Show yourself!"

A hard blow to her back knocks the breath out of her. She stumbles forward and drops to her knees. Taulus stands before her, the smoke of his face curling into a wide grin.

"You must always protect your back, Cynane," he purrs.

Grunting, Cyn stands and dusts off her leather skirt. "I would, if I could become invisible on the battlefield like you," she says. "Why won't you let me attain Smoke Blood when you use it yourself all the time?"

The figure swirls around like fog disbursed by wind, and she raises her shield just in time to feel a hard whack on its cowhide surface. "Warriors do not give sharp swords to toddlers," the voice teases. "You are not ready."

Cyn has had enough. Enough play. Enough mystery. She throws down her sword and shield. "I am more ready than you could ever imagine," she says, her teeth grinding together. "I cannot continue to live like this, Taulus. Every moment of every day—and let us not forget the nights when that cackling fool touches me—is more painful than an eternity in the deepest pits of Hades."

She steps toward the two eyes glinting behind a sparkling white veil of smoke. "If you do not let me have Smoke Blood, I swear to you I will kill Amyntas myself tonight. And if that doesn't work, I will kill myself. Do you understand me?" She is so close now his smoke swirls around her, causing goose bumps to rise on her arms and the back of her neck.

Taulus steps back and shimmers over to a bale of hay where he settles himself.

"Very well," he says, all levity drained from him. "Though I will not give you Smoke Blood, I can at least tell you why."

Cyn approaches him warily. Now they are getting somewhere. "Why?" she asks, her voice as flat and hard as an anvil.

Taulus sighs, and the smoke of his face flows outward before withdrawing back into itself. "Because the desire for Smoke Blood is what killed your mother."

The training pit fades from Cyn's view, replaced by a ghastly white face under red water, long black tendrils floating around it like the tentacles of an octopus. Dark eyes wide open in horror. A ragged wound like a gaping mouth in her chest. Audata was murdered in her bath when Cyn was only eight years old.

Against her will, Cyn walks to Taulus, her chest tight with foreboding.

"But," she says, hating the little crack in her voice, "she was betrayed by the royal court... Or was it the Lords?"

Cyn has always suspected Olympias as the most likely culprit behind her mother's murder. Olympias's jealousy of Audata had been widely known, even though she was a lesser wife of Philip, and not the queen. But recently, Cyn has begun to wonder whether the Aesarian Lords knew of Audata's knowledge of ancient magic lore. Perhaps they had something to do with her death.

His face is a mist, too hard to read, but his words are clear and sharp. "No," Taulus says. "Neither Olympias nor the Aesarian Lords killed Audata." As he inhales, it's as though he's breathing in his own image, making himself disappear, and then reappear on the exhale.

"Who did, then?" Cyn shivers. It hasn't occurred to her before that Taulus might know more about her mother's death than she does, and now it's as though he's baiting her to ask.

There is a pause, the smoke over the bale of hay wavering until she's sure he has gone for good. But then his voice penetrates the air and his answer leaves her shaking.

"*I* did."

Shock numbs her for a moment, then gives way to confusion, and then a rage like she has never known before. It pounds through her, making it hard to think.

"Why?" she chokes out, taking a step backward.

His smoke eyes are dark, shadowed. "To save you."

"Me?"

"Your mother felt threatened by Olympias, abandoned by Philip, and targeted by the Aesarian Lords. She desperately wanted Smoke Blood to protect herself."

Cyn shakes her head. She *knows* all this. Why is he telling her this? The daggers of memory are dragging through her, merciless. Her mother's blood. *Don't look. Don't look.*

"Think, Cynane. She needed the blood of betrayal in order to gain that power."

Cynane is physically shaking—as though beaten by an opponent twice her size and speed, even though she is standing perfectly still.

"But whom could she kill to get it?" Taulus continues mercilessly. "What murder would be loathsome enough to be the Blood of True Betrayal?"

Cyn feels faint. The training pit spins wildly around her. Buffeted by waves of nauseating dizziness, she clings to one thought like a blood-slick sword in battle: *it can't be true.* The awful, terrible thought that he has raised within her is a lie.

"Say it, Cynane," he barks. "Don't be weak."

"A mother's murder of...her child," Cynane croaks out. Her stomach heaves, and she puts her hands on her knees, bowing her head to steady herself.

But her mother *was* love—was the only light in a world of darkness and deceit. Cyn has never truly believed in the gods. She has never believed in anything except that her mother was good. That her mother was *hers*, was everything. It was always the two of them against Olympias, against Philip, against the entire world. Audata would *never...*

Cyn falls to her knees. Anger rushes out of her like wine from a staved-in barrel. She is suddenly not a warrior of nineteen but a child, lost and afraid. Love vanishes. Strength disappears. Because everything Cyn ever believed about her mother—the bond they shared, the love, the loyalty—was a lie.

"I am sorry, child," Taulus says. "I did not want to tell you this, not ever. But you see how the temptation of Smoke Blood can drive people to unthinkable ends. Let this be a lesson to you."

Cyn can't reply. She isn't even sure if she can breathe.

Smoke engulfs her in a calming embrace. "Come," he whispers. "Walk with me."

Numbly she follows him, aware she is following a ghost, an invisible figment who holds so much sway over her. They move past the barracks and enter the walled sculpture garden, where the statues of all the gods—even Aphrodite bathing naked—have had their heads replaced with a grinning head of Amyntas.

They walk past withered flowers and around the tiny temple her husband has built to celebrate his own divinity. Usually she avoids this place, but now she feels as if she is seeing all this through someone else's eyes and none of it matters.

Somehow she finds herself walking up a tightly spiraling staircase and emerging onto the top of the palace's highest tower, overlooking the town and the sea. Amyntas often eats dinner up here under a canopy with a few friends, watching the sunset over the Adriatic. Red wine stains from last night's repast blotch the floor like blood.

Cyn won't look down. She takes off her sweaty helmet, closes her eyes, and inhales, the fresh sea air filling her lungs with something akin to life. Cleansing tendrils of wind run though her hair and cool the back of her neck.

She will survive this.

"Yes, you will," Taulus says, turning from his place against the battlement. "And all of this will be yours." He gestures sweepingly to sea and harbor, to palace and town, to rugged gray mountains rising behind them. "*If* you remain focused on our plan. *If* you remember this throne is not about a battle, but about patience."

Cyn walks to the battlements and sags against them. Below her, a fishing boat tacks against the wind out of the harbor, right and left, right and left, two fishermen struggling to maneuver the square sail. Sometimes there is no straight path to where you want to go.

She turns to him and says, "I am better at battles than patience. Battles are quick. Fun. Over. This..." She gestures to the sprawling palace complex behind them. "Every day here is an agony for me. And the nights..." She shudders.

A dark eye glints with sympathy in the writhing smoke. "Have you found a suitable candidate from among the leading families that you can make your king consort?" he asks. "One you can control?"

Cyn sniffs. "Dardanian men are weak."

"So much the better," he replies, nodding so quickly his head disburses before reforming. "Only after you have secured this alliance can you kill Amyntas. If you act too quickly, the people will see you as a newcomer, an invader, and worst of all as a woman, unworthy to rule on your own. As Amyntas is without an heir, one of the leading families will take the throne and either kill you or marry you off."

Which would put her right back where she is now.

A small figure emerges from the half-open door to the staircase. It's Aesop, a ten-year-old servant boy, carrying a sloshing bucket and scrub brush. He bows his head and sets his bucket down in the corner, where he proceeds to scrub last night's wine stains.

Cyn hesitates, wondering if she should leave. But Aesop is mute. Amyntas had his tongue torn out for some reason or other. She decides to ignore him and turns back to Taulus. Something has been niggling at her mind. For the first time, she's driven not by the desire for Smoke Blood but the desire to *understand* it. As though perhaps if she does, she will be able to understand—and forgive—her mother.

"Everyone says Earth and Snake Blood came from the last two gods," she says. "If that is true, where did Smoke Blood come from?"

"What no one remembers anymore is that there were three last gods," Taulus answers. "Una, the sister, was the progenitor of Smoke Blood. She killed herself when they were abandoned by the rest of the gods—but though she wasn't fully divine, she wasn't fully human, either. She didn't die, only dissolved into smoke. In this way, she lived on, helping her mortal descendants as her divine family never helped her. She taught a nearly vanquished tribe in these lands how to heal and how to change their physical forms or disappear when danger came their way. For centuries, Smoke Blood could be earned only through deeds of bravery and self-sacrifice."

Cyn frowns. "What happened? Why did it change?"

"The same reason everything changes," Taulus says smoothly. "Somebody's ambition."

He gazes at her, his expression shifting. "One of Una's descendants wanted Una's power, even though she was long gone, a victim of the battles of gods and monsters. He devised a spell called the Blood of True Betrayal and killed all his clansmen to draw their combined powers into himself. It worked."

For a moment, Taulus pauses, gazing out over the water. Cyn shifts uncomfortably, and finally he begins to speak again. "This man became the most powerful Smoke Blood in the world—the only Smoke Blood, in fact.

"He could change his physical shape to look like anyone, male or female, young or old. He was so potent his body could no longer contain his soul, which started to leak out of it like smoke."

Cyn's breath catches. "You," she says accusingly. "It was you."

The smoke form shifts away from her as if in shame.

"Yes," he whispers. "That was how I helped my grandson rise from coal miner to a powerful king of Illyria. Yet each year I became more and more insubstantial, until I became as you see me now, a thing of smoke and mist. I am but a phantom. Mine is a cursed life—*a life not worth living.*" His last words spool around her face, coating her with horror and sadness.

"But…for many years, you *had* flesh and blood," Cyn persists, trying to shake off the curse of his melancholy. "And your incredible powers."

He nods. "Until one day I looked in the mirror and could see the morning light slanting through my flesh. The only part that is left of my soul now—and even that is fading—is my heart. I will eventually be disembodied consciousness buffeted about by the wind, hither and yon, forever." He turns to her, his swirling face inexpressibly sad.

"And you, as my flesh and blood, would suffer the same fate, I think."

"I'm willing to risk it—" Cyn begins, but Taulus disappears like steamy breath on a winter's day.

The door slams open, and Amyntas bursts onto the tower, followed by the two guards she recently vanquished in the training pit. On their heels is Papari, wearing grapes in his stringy brown hair, his nose reddened with cinnabar, and a leaky wineskin in one hand, obviously costumed as the god Bacchus.

"Ah, wife, there you are," Amyntas says, eyes darting around the tower. "Papari told us he had seen you come up here." That comes as no surprise. The fool always seems to be everywhere underfoot. The king raises a long, manicured finger to his lips and swivels around in obvious perplexity. "To whom were you speaking just now?"

"This slave boy of yours," she says, gesturing to Aesop, who stops scrubbing as his wide brown eyes open in fear. "I said I was willing to risk losing my royal dignity and beat him if he didn't do a better job scrubbing the floor." She turns to the child and commands, "Get hot water this time, Aesop. That water is barely lukewarm." Nodding, the little boy grabs his bucket and runs off.

Amyntas, with the sixth sense of the hopelessly deranged, still suspects something. Sunlight glistens off his bejeweled robes as he walks to the edge of the tower and looks down. Then he turns around, sweeps his gaze over the entire expanse of the tower, and even puts his hand over his eyes and looks up. Finally satisfied there is no one else there, he shrugs.

"Well, we have an amusing assignment for you," he says with a cold smile.

Cyn feels a flutter of fear in her chest. "Yes, Sire?"

"You must visit a brothel."

"Of course," she says, forcing a smile even as she wonders if he will make her prostitute herself. "Which one?"

Amyntas tilts his head to one side. "We would, of course, only send our wife to the best brothel in town: Aphrodite's Grotto, run by the most talented whore of our grandfather's time, Madam Locusta. Our guards will take you there."

Cyn stares at the leering guards. Surely Amyntas doesn't want her to—

The king cackles again. "We're not interested in sharing you, dear wife. We simply want you to kill one of the girls there to make an example of her to the others."

"An example of what, my husband?" Cyn asks, voice stiff.

"Those whores have been saying terrible things about us. They claim we're not touched by the gods—just simply mad.

Can you imagine? Naturally, we can't have all the women executed, or hundreds of Dardanian men will be pounding on
the palace doors complaining. One executed whore should
do," he says. "For now."

The two guards grin at her. Perdix is missing most of his
teeth. Karpos has all his, but they are stained with wine and
riddled with brown holes. Now she understands the purpose
of this task. The guards complained to Amyntas that since
Cyn fights like a man, perhaps she should kill like one. This
is punishment for her besting them with weapons. Well, the
joke is on them. They don't know that she has killed before,
or how easy it was. How enjoyable. She drops a mocking
curtsy in the king's direction and heads to the stables, her
unwelcome companions at her heels.

When Cyn announces to the brothel guards that she has
come in the king's name, they step aside. She, Perdix, and
Karpos march through an atrium richly painted with naked
gods and goddesses and into a surprisingly large, sunny courtyard surrounding a long pool. A fountain stands in the center
of the pool, where three life-sized statues of mermaids spray
water from their breasts and hold a scallop shell on which sits
an inebriated, burly man wearing the blue wig and beard of
Poseidon, waving a sharp iron trident.

Two girls, wearing the sparkling blue tails of mermaids and
nothing else, swim around the fountain splashing and giggling. Standing on enormous sculpted scallop shells in the pool
are more naked girls in wigs so long the hair reaches their
knees. Ah, yes. The myth of Aphrodite's birth: she sprang
fully formed as an adult from the sea on a scallop shell.

But the frolicking stops as soon as they see the queen and
the king's guards.

Cyn surveys the courtyard for potential danger. Colored
drapes hide what she supposes are tiny bedrooms on all sides.

"Everyone out!" she cries in her most commanding voice. "In the king's name!" No one moves. "Now! Or I will arrest all of you!"

Curtains peel back slowly, revealing people covering themselves with sheets and hastily throwing on tunics.

"Out where I can see you!" she orders. "No weapons!" Men and women reluctantly shuffle toward her. Girls climb off scallop shells. Mermaids hoist themselves dripping out of the pool.

"All the girls, gather around me!" she barks. Looking at the women, her heart sinks. These are no worthy opponents in battle. No brutal soldiers. Like her, they are trapped by their gender, unable to survive unless they please powerful men. It's not right to storm in here and kill one only because someone here has said the truth: Amyntas is mad.

But Cyn, too, needs to survive. Best to do this unpalatable job quickly and get it over with. Her gaze falls on a girl of perhaps fifteen clutching a sheet to her body, her face still round and full like that of a child, her brown eyes huge with terror. No, not that one. Too young.

Beside the girl is a lithe young woman with the burnished bronze skin of a North African, her eyes wide and dark, her painted lips like luscious fruit. Not that one, either. Too beautiful.

Cyn turns in a slow circle, hand on her sword hilt, rejecting this girl and that, as the people instinctively withdraw slowly to the edges of the courtyard like water receding after a flood. To her surprise, one girl remains rooted to her clamshell in the pool. She's about eighteen, tall and shapely, with a long red wig. Her stormy dark eyes meet Cyn's with defiance. Not her. Too brave.

In contrast, on the pillar above the girl, the drunkard playing Poseidon trembles so hard his trident shakes.

A dignified woman—Locusta, Cyn assumes—sweeps in

wearing a long-sleeved crimson robe, her silver hair twisted into an ornate coiffeur under a gleaming diadem. Her face is deeply lined and heavily made up, though Cyn can tell by the magnificent structure of the bones that she must have once been devastatingly beautiful. Cyn judges her to be about sixty, though the wide blue eyes that size her up seem to be more like a thousand years old. This woman has seen everything... and probably has done everything, as well. She will do.

"What is this?" the woman asks, narrowing her eyes at Cyn and the guards. "Why have you forced your way into my establishment?"

"I am Queen Cynane," she begins, "and I am on my husband's business."

"I know who you are," Locusta says. "But you are more puppet than queen, jumping as high as the mad king wants whenever he snaps his fingers."

Cyn clenches her jaw, not at the insult, but at the truth of it.

"I am the queen," she says, standing to her full height. "And you are...um, were...a whore. Used by men for their foul needs."

Locusta's slash of a red mouth opens in laughter, revealing a full set of yellow teeth. "You have it backward, my lady. *We* use men. We take their wealth, their hearts, and even ruin their marriages and families, if we wish. With our riches, we have true freedom to go wherever we want, do whatever we want, buy whatever we want."

Cyn feels a pang of envy as she unsheathes her sword with a scraping ring. "Be that as it may," she says, "King Amyntas Cleitus has commanded me to execute one of you as punishment for spreading the wicked slander that he is mad." She looks straight into the madam's eyes.

A cold understanding passes between them.

Sighing slightly, as if a client has run off without paying, the madam straightens and says, "Let it be me. I have lived my life." She turns to a black-haired woman in her thirties and says, "Xanthe, my will is in the Temple of Hera. You are my heir and will inherit this establishment."

Xanthe covers her mouth with her hands and moans.

As Cyn raises her sword, she's aware of movement in the corner of her eye. The redheaded girl on the scallop shell has grabbed the iron trident from the openmouthed Poseidon behind her and hurls it in Cyn's direction. Cyn ducks. The girl's throw is forceful and true. It hits Karpos in the shoulder, sticking deep in his flesh and knocking him over. He howls and curses, thrashing on the ground. Perdix moves toward the girl, who's still standing motionless on her scallop shell, but Cyn grabs him by the arm and wrenches him back.

"Leave her!" Cyn bellows. "Or I will tell the king his guards are too useless to stand up to a naked whore on a scallop shell. That ought to *amuse* him."

Quickly. She needs to do this quickly and painlessly and have it over with. The more time she gives the madam and her girls, the greater the horror. She marches back to Locusta and in one clean blow slices off her head.

It flies to the fountain and bobs in the water, the blue eyes open in surprise, the silver diadem still in place, gleaming in the sun. The water around the head turns rapidly red. Like Audata's bathtub. Cyn rubs her eyes.

"We are done here," she commands, and strides out of Aphrodite's Grotto, feeling sick, her head echoing with screams—she knows not whose.

Cyn tosses and turns in her bed. The nights are cooler now with the anticipation of winter, which should help her sleep. But the image of Locusta's head bobbing in the fountain torments her. And what she said about Cyn being a puppet was right. Cyn needs to kill Amyntas before he kills her. She can't wait any longer. And to rule Dardania—to make the people fear and respect her—she needs the powers of Smoke Blood.

Her conversation with Taulus goes around and around in her head, the things he told her tangling together until she's dizzy, seething in anger, confusion, loss, and something else, too...the suspicion that she's missing something. She plays over his words once again. How he tried to warn her that Smoke Blood is a curse. That being a Smoke Blood *was not a life worth living.*

The old man was rarely so direct. He usually spoke in riddles, baiting Cyn, goading her. Had he been, in fact, warning her, like she had at first assumed? Or did he have another purpose?

Not a life worth living.

He'd been speaking of his own mistakes, his *own life*: a miserable half life, caught between human and spirit.

What else had he said when they were sparring? That the only human part left of him was his heart, and once that had dissolved, he would never be able to die. It was almost a coded invitation. A request, made indirectly.

Cynane sits bolt upright, the strange thought that's been budding beneath the surface breaking through at last, seizing her with conviction. Taulus told her not to wish for Smoke Blood anymore...but what if he didn't mean it? What if he was baiting her again?

It suddenly makes so much sense... Why else would he have told her what he did to Audata, if not to enrage Cyn, to make her hate him?

And what greater betrayal is there than to turn on the man who is not only her forebear, but her protector and trainer? A betrayal that great would be certain to bring her Smoke Blood of immense power, even if she did lose his protective spell.

With a cold confidence, Cyn realizes what she must do.

She must kill Taulus.

CHAPTER SIXTEEN: PAPARI

PAPARI MAKES YET ANOTHER LOOP THROUGH Queen Cynane's wing of the Dardanian palace, skipping and singing to himself. The palace is just waking; wafting over from the kitchens is the comforting smell of wood smoke and a whiff of fresh bread that makes his mouth water. Outside in the harbor, fishing vessels head into the brightening day; above the sighs of the waves he hears the snap of sails and the voices of men.

He plays with the words in his head, making a few substitutions, and tries it out again.

> "Liars, cheaters, traitors all
> Whom can a smart king trust?
> Useless people, large and small
> Like weapons full of rust.
> There's only one to trust, of course
> He's not a man; he is a horse!"

He will sing it for the king at dinner, and Amyntas will bang his goblet and clap his hands and whinny with laughter as that strange light comes into his eyes. Oddly, the courtiers call Papari "the fool." Well, people have always underestimated him because of his size. He's used to it, and sometimes it is a great advantage. Little do they know he could cartwheel around the banquet hall skewering them all with their own dinner knives before they even knew what was happening.

"What are you doing here?" asks a deep voice.

Startled, Papari turns to find the queen's Macedonian guard, Priam, blocking his path. Papari does a backflip and rolls into a handstand, waggling his feet in the air. Upside down, he says, "Please don't beat me, majesty. I am just practicing songs! I am quite creative at dawn, you know."

Priam does not seem amused by the formal address…and why should he be? Regal and handsome as he is, in station, he's barely above a slave—like Papari.

"Stand up straight so I can look you in the eye," Priam growls.

Papari flicks upright, opening his large watery blue eyes as wide as he can, putting both hands on his cheeks as if in fear, and sings.

"He's so tall, that handsome Priam,
I'm so small, I'd like to be him."

Priam's lips twitch. "Enough nonsense. You have come back to this hallway several times now. Are you looking for someone?"

Papari looks around as if he has no idea where he is. "I am a fool, great king, not a mapmaker. Where am I, then? Isn't this the latrine?"

Priam rolls his eyes, sighs, and says, "Never mind. Be off with you."

"May the gods bless you, my queen!" Papari says, kneeling

before Priam and kissing his hands fervently. Priam pushes him away.

"Stop that!"

"If you say so, great Zeus!" he says, cartwheeling down the hall as Priam shakes his head and rounds the corner. Papari laughs out loud. Who was the fool now? He is expert at talking in circles—just as he is at talking to the air, as he has seen Queen Cynane do on several occasions when she didn't know he was watching her.

Many people talk to themselves, he knows, but few wait for answers, leaning forward, listening, considering, seeming to hear what no one else can hear.

Oh, but she is interesting, interesting, interesting...

Footsteps clatter up the stairs, sending him ducking behind a statue, another advantage to being so small. Finally, his effort is rewarded. It's her.

Queen Cynane, looking tired and drawn, walks down the hall and *into* her chambers—not out. *Where has she been?* Hovering over a bonfire, from the smell of her, and the smears of smoke and ashes on her face.

No ordinary bonfire, though. For her hands and tunic are covered in the thick sticky red of blood.

Long after the bedroom door closes, he sits motionless in a little ball behind the statue, thinking. *It is time,* he decides. He will send the message to High Lord Gideon today.

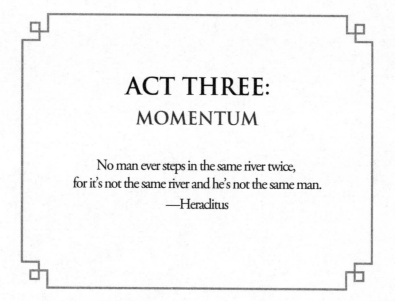

ACT THREE:
MOMENTUM

No man ever steps in the same river twice,
for it's not the same river and he's not the same man.
—Heraclitus

CHAPTER SEVENTEEN:
ZOFIA

THE TORCHES OF APASA DIMINISH UNTIL THEY are tiny orange pinpoints in the silver-blue dusk. Zofia walks to the other side of the ship as sailors crawl along creaking ropes like spiders moving deftly across a web, securing the snapping sails for the night. She stares at the utter blackness of the horizon where Macedon waits. Two days from now—if the weather holds—she will arrive there, ready to face whatever that means for her.

Right now, she won't think about it. She savors the fresh salt air, the freedom to move about the ship. Thirty-three days she was trapped in that box of a *harmanaxa*, jolting and dipping over ruts and potholes, listening to the twittering mindless gossip of handmaidens and eunuchs. The interminable journey took her over blinding desert and stinking swamps, across rich fields as men harvested cotton and rye, and through forests so thick it was dark even at midday. Her muscles quickly became cramped and sore, but she did have plenty of time to think. To plan.

She daydreamed of meeting Prince Alexander of Macedon, of convincing him he would win worldwide renown by vanquishing the Spirit Eaters. She saw them scouring maps by lamplight, tracing a route along the Euxine Sea to avoid Artaxerxes's armies. She fantasized about herself, courageous and determined, sun glinting off her silver breastplate as she pointed toward the cave where the creatures lurked.

If she were a hero who helped save the known world from destruction, no one would care whom she married or what she did. What would her life look like if she could go anywhere? Do anything? Though a better question is: *Who* would she want to be? Perhaps it was the cold breath of Death at the hands of Assassins on the back of her neck, but on that endless rattling journey she realized she had wasted her time on earth, focused on frivolous trivialities. She had had the finest tutors in the world and barely paid them any attention. There is so much she would like to learn, to do. If, against all odds, she survives long enough to raise her child, she wants to be a better mother than her mother was to her. She wants to teach her child the value of wisdom, of courage, of true knowledge.

That is, if Ochus doesn't obey his father's commands and kill her.

Even if he does, at least Zo could die happy in the knowledge of what she did for Vata. The last night in Persepolis, she asked the harem doctor for a large flask of poppy juice to help her sleep on the journey west. Then she poured it into a pitcher of fine wine and gave it to the men who guarded Vata's stable—a thank-you, she said, for looking after the Pegasus once she was gone. Within half an hour, all three of them were flat on their backs outside the door, snoring loudly.

Zo held the lantern high as she slipped inside. Vata whickered loudly, a groan of both protest and recognition. Zo saw hoofmarks in a wide circle around the central post. Vata stared at her with hurt eyes. Her wings sagged, tufts of ungroomed feathers poking out. Then she started pacing, around and around the post. The trough of oats still lay on its side, the food untouched. She would die in here, Zo knew. A wild creature meant to fly could not be tamed.

"My love," Zo said quietly as she approached the creature. Vata stopped and hung her head low. "You have saved me. And now I am going to save you. To get you out of here."

"Are you now?" A voice emerged from the shadows.

Zo whipped around. Ochus. She would know that voice anywhere—it could cut iron or melt butter, depending on his mood.

As he stepped into the glow of lantern light, she whipped her small knife out of her belt. Vata whinnied, stamped her hooves, and flapped her wings. Ochus didn't blink. His eyes moved from Zo to the Pegasus. "Beautiful," he said, extending his hand, palm up. Zo expected Vata to shy away or bite his hand off entirely. Instead, she stepped forward and sniffed it, black nostrils quivering, and grunted in satisfaction before taking a step back.

Zo grabbed her knife more tightly. "Ochus, I know what you are." Her jaw was set so hard it hurt.

"A fool for not telling them to put you back in chains?" he asked, crossing his arms over his chest. He glanced down at her knife, then turned his eyes up as though amused.

No—*she* was the fool. For having ever thought she loved this man who had treated her so badly, had held her captive and dragged her across the country in chains. It sickened her, the idea that she could have let her heart seize and sting, had allowed herself to cling to the idea that maybe he'd held her against his will. That maybe, *maybe*, there had been something else between them, something *real*. In the warmth of his rare smile. In the intensity of his gaze. In the way his arms held her when they shared a horse. In his halting confession that he'd delayed because he could not bear to kill her.

And yet he had abandoned her, left her to die. And now, he planned to finish the job.

She stepped closer to him. "I heard you," she seethed.

"What?"

"I. Heard. You." She let each word stand on its own, have its own weight. "What your father commanded—"

In one swift movement, Ochus clapped his hand over her mouth and knocked her knife to the ground. She struggled, but his muscular arms held her so tightly she couldn't budge. She felt hot breath behind her ear as he said, his words a low hum against her skin, "Promise me you won't scream, won't make any noise at all, and I will tell you what you do not know."

There was something in his voice—not anger, as she'd expected, but a rough sort of emotion she might have mistaken for tenderness, had she still been a fool.

She was not a fool anymore.

But she was curious.

She nodded, and he released her, taking the warmth with him.

He looked toward the door and pulled her by the elbow to the back of the room, behind Vata. "I *wanted* you to overhear that conversation, Zofia," he whispered.

She stared at him, though it was too dark now to read his expression.

"I was the one who suggested to my father that we go for a ride. Then I spoke to him about our plans as we passed, hoping you would listen, that you would learn of the danger you are in. You had to know—it would be safer that way."

"Why?" she asked, trembling, though from fear or anger she couldn't tell.

"It's...complicated," he said, low.

This maddened her even more. The man was so full of riddles and excuses. He was a killer. She was a prisoner. "There's nothing complicated about you being a murderer," she nearly spat at him. "Though you can't kill me here, now, can you? Artaxerxes would know you and your father were behind it all if he lost yet another princess on Persian soil. You have to wait until we reach Macedon. Make it look like Prince Alexander did it."

Ochus nodded. "True," he said quietly. "What are you going to do?"

"If I scream, guards will come running and arrest you. I imagine your father can save you from hanging, but you will never be allowed to escort me to Macedon. I am the one with power now. Not you."

His eyes gleamed golden in the dancing lantern light. "There is no need to scream. And what power you have will not keep you alive once you arrive in Macedon, as you said, especially if I am not beside you. Frankly, I think my father is suspicious of me as far as you are concerned. I wouldn't be surprised if he has others in your entourage who will kill you if I don't. But I have a plan that will keep you safe."

"You have a...*plan*?"

He put his hands, warm and strong, on her shoulders. "I will never harm you, Zofia of Sardis," he whispered, his voice thick. "I vowed never to leave you again as long as I live, and I will keep that vow. You must trust me."

She scoffed and turned away. Heat flooded her face as she tried to sort out what to say. There was something about him that made her want to believe his words, but a greater part of her knew that was a deadly trap.

Ochus dropped his hands, moved around the horse's bulk, and picked up something glinting in the straw. Her knife. "Here," he said, handing it to her. "I doubt this could peel an apple. Perhaps I should get you a bigger one." He almost smiled.

She yanked the weapon out of his hand and thrust it into her belt. "Prove to me I can trust you."

He cocked his head. "How?"

She looked at Vata, who stared right back, snapping her tail. Ochus could help her do what she came here for. The Pegasus should be wild and free, a spirit of air and rain, of wind and sun and moon, of sweet grass and cold streams.

Zo cleared her throat. "I don't want her to be the petted toy of a debauched king. It would kill her to stay here." As she spoke, Zo knew she was also talking about herself, and her heart was breaking with the pain of it.

Ochus sighed. "Artaxerxes will be furious." He paused, then sighed again and gave a quick, curt nod.

They opened the warehouse doors and stepped into a dark service courtyard, the windows around it dark and empty like the eyes of skulls. Zo had many things she wanted to whisper to Vata before she flew away: that she deserved freedom. That Zo would always love her. But there would be no time for that. The Pegasus roared out of her stable with the force of a white-hot bolt of lightning and raced around the courtyard, kicking up the dirt in joy. Then, spreading her enormous wings, she soared.

The last sight Zo had of her was of a silver streak flying toward the moon.

The Great King was furious, of course, when he discovered what she had done. Ochus told her he would have punished her severely if he hadn't had his heart set on an alliance with Macedon. As it was, he refused to honor Zo by personally bidding her farewell the next morning. Without the Great King's blessing, she was escorted to the caravan that would take her as far west as the shores of Lydia. There she would board a ship to Pella and, perhaps, dock in the black arms of Death.

Now Zo draws her cloak more tightly about her, feeling the dip and roll of the ship. As she strolls between coils of rope and barrels, a barefoot sailor with a long, matted beard and filthy bandanna lands in front of her from the rigging above, giving her a start.

"Did I frighten you, Princess?" he asks, his smile revealing rotten teeth. The whiff of sweat and rancid fish nearly makes her retch. A man like this has no business talking with her. If her eunuchs were here instead of sleeping off their wine in the little cabin, they would beat him black and blue. She casts him a disdainful look and moves forward.

He blocks her and she nearly slams into him. "My name is Zubin," he says. "What's yours?"

"I am Princess Zofia of Sardis." She snorts. "Now stand aside."

"That's not very friendly, now, is it?" he asks, his smile fading into something hard and cruel. "I hear you're a bride, going to marry a prince. Royal brides are supposed to be virgins, aren't they? Are you?"

Her fingers itch to slap him for his impertinence, but she is aware of his strength. He isn't tall or broad, but the taut wiry sinews of his bare arms look like braided rope. Then the fire of her anger chills to panic. Why is he talking about virginity? Has he noticed the gentle swelling of her abdomen? She is four months pregnant now and hides it under loose robes. If he has noticed it...perhaps others have, too.

The door of her cabin is thrown open. She turns to see one of her eunuchs, Chosroes, stagger out, throw himself against the rail, and heave his dinner into the sea. When she turns back, Zubin is gone, an undulation in the ropes far above.

Pulling her veil closer, she walks to the other side of the ship and leans on the rail. She smells his aroma first: musk and wood smoke and something sweet all his own. Then she feels the heat of him. She has not seen him, not heard him, even, but every part of her being knows he is there. He, too, leans against the rail, looking into the endless blackness of the night sea.

After a time, she asks quietly, "What awaits me there?"

Ochus shakes his head. "I can't tell you my plan yet. Trust me."

She is silent. He knows her answer to that. She can't, she won't, she doesn't.

After a moment, he gives her the wry grin that both excites her and makes her want to slap him at the same time.

"What?" she asks shortly.

"I have obviously failed in my attempts to show you that you *can*. Trust me, that is."

"Indeed, you have failed. I will not soon forget the shackles you bound to my wrists day and night on the Royal Road." Her throat closes up at the memory of it—the humiliation, the fear, the physical exhaustion of being dragged about like a possession to be sold or gotten rid of. The added insult of how he teased her, how he seemed to look at her and through her and *know* her.

The fact that he knew, the whole time, that she'd been lying about the cliffs and the herd of flying horses, but played along, anyway.

His smile has vanished, and he looks so intense she is once again afraid—not of what he might do to her but what he might *not* do.

The boat dips into a sudden trough that makes her stumble against him. "But I can think of one thing that might make us even," she whispers.

Moments later, they are standing inside the low, dark storage deck, and he is holding a length of chain, and a lock, in his outstretched hands.

"What explanation will you give for doing this to me?" Ochus asks as she wraps the chain around his wrists and secures it around a beam.

"The truth," she replies, snapping the lock shut with a satisfying little click. "Your impudence."

There's that grin again. He nods. Then he slides to the ground and crosses his legs.

She briefly wonders why he's allowing her to do this. Is he tricking her into trusting him? Or is it his way of sincerely proving he will do anything to win her trust?

Lantern in hand, Zo makes her way back to her cabin on the prow, but stops with her hand on the latch of the door. She turns and sees moonlight streaming silver through clouds and shining in bright patches on a black sea.

Entering her cabin, Zo steps over her sleeping attendants on the floor, climbs into bed, and listens to the slap of water against wood, wondering. Eventually, the sea rocks her to sleep.

The following morning, as Ochus dips his bread in the bowl of stew, his manacles clank loudly, just as Zo's did at all those posting station taverns. It gives her a surge of gratification every time they clatter and chink. Their eyes meet, and he gives her a knowing look.

"Fair is fair," he says, and takes another bite of bread.

And yet…for all the joy of revenge, part of her feels sorry for him. He must truly want to win her trust to let her chain him up like an animal in this stuffy dark hold smelling of old wine and littered with rat droppings. But, of course, it could all be just another trick.

"Thank you, Princess," he says, offering her the bowl. She bends to take it and hesitates, staring at his lips. Strong, yet soft. She remembers their only kiss that last day in the wilderness, how desire almost consumed her when he wrapped her tightly in his strong arms, when she felt his broad chest against hers, when he arched her backward and her lips parted and…

And he rode off on the horse and left her.

She grabs the bowl and climbs the ladder back up to the deck.

For the rest of the afternoon, Zo's attendants gossip behind their hands about Ochus, chained up in the hold. She can hear bits of their chatter, carried on the brisk tangy wind that sweeps across the deck.

"What he did was truly impudent. He pinched her rear

end," Chosroes says confidently, clearly unaware that Zo is standing on the other side of the mast. "I saw it myself last night on the deck."

"You mean between bouts of vomiting?" Parmina, Zo's fierce little handmaiden, asks. "I heard it was because he said she was getting fat."

Zo flinches. People *are* beginning to notice her swelling belly. But no one has the right to ask her why she chained up Ochus. Or the nerve. She is grateful when evening falls and a man high up in the ropes cries, "Macedon!"

Looking off the side, Zo spies a few twinkling lights on shore. Tomorrow morning they will enter the estuary of the Axios River and sail up to Lakeport, and from there ride to the capital.

Thinking of all that could await her there, it is impossible to fall asleep. Sometime around midnight, she gives up. Throwing on a cloak, she slips onto deck. The lights of Macedon have been doused for the night. She can make out only a darker line against the darkness of the horizon.

"You're out late, Princess," says a voice like the scrape of iron on stone.

A foul miasma engulfs her as she turns. Zubin. The sailor with the long, matted beard, the one who yesterday swung down in front of her from the ropes as if to scare her, is standing far too close to her for protocol. And unless the ship was sinking, he really shouldn't even address a royal personage of Zo's status at all.

"Do you need an escort to your bed?" he asks.

"Thank you, but I know my way," she says frostily, moving around him.

"Well, that's a rude reply to a kind and generous offer." Suddenly he grabs her and pushes her against the rail. "I've never kissed a princess before. Give me a little kiss."

She feels her face twist into a mask of disgust. "Get...off...

me," she croaks, pushing him away. How does he think he can get away with this? That she won't run screaming for help the moment he releases her? That the captain won't hang him from the mast? Maybe he doesn't. Maybe he plans to violate her and throw her overboard into the cold, black water. People will think she fell. Or jumped.

His filthy hands rip the neckline of her robe and as she opens her mouth to scream he uses that same hand to clamp down on her throat. She can't reach her knife! She can't knee him, either—he's too close, against her, all over her. His reeking mouth presses on hers, the hand around her throat only letting up just enough for her to choke down a tiny breath. He doesn't want her to die—at least not yet, she realizes. He just wants his way with her. And then…

Bitter bile rises in her throat. She twists her face away and tries to scream again, but it's more like an animal's whimper. He is pushing her down, too… The two of them sink against the wooden deck.

"Hold still," Zubin hisses.

No. This isn't happening. *No.* She lets out a strangled cry, as loud as she possibly can, using all her strength to wrestle away. But still he holds her down, clambers on top of her, heavy for his size, and she feels as if a wall has fallen on her, a wall of hair and muscle and stench and filth. She is choking. She sees stars explode and—

A thick chain dangles in front of Zubin's face and tightens against his neck. And then suddenly, the weight of him vanishes.

She looks up and sees him floating above her, eyes wide open in surprise. She scrambles away, into a pile of coiled rope, as Ochus stands behind the sailor and yanks a chain tightly against his neck. Zubin's eyes and tongue bulge out; his fingers pluck uselessly at his neck. "You'll swim to Macedon if you know what's good for you," Ochus growls, "because if you try to come back on this ship I swear I will gut you and feed your intestines to the fish."

And with that threat, Ochus swings the sailor overboard as easily as if he were a doll. Cowering against the rope, Zo hears a scream and then a splash.

She can hardly catch her breath, and her mind reels. That couldn't have happened. It almost did. She is sick with the idea of it, her body on fire with the pain of it. *Her child!* Her hands rush to her abdomen.

Ochus kneels beside her as she clutches her ripped robe over herself. "Zo! Are you all right? Did he—?"

"I'm fine," she says shakily. "You were in time."

The realization of what could have happened breaks over her, and she begins to shiver uncontrollably.

Ochus's warm hands move to her face, his fingers tracing her neck, where she is sure bruises must be forming. Gently, he lifts her to her feet, and she lets him.

"Let me take you to your cabin," he says, his strong hands gripping her elbows. "You're in shock."

As she clutches her torn robe together, her mind begins to clear. "I… I thought you were chained." Her teeth chatter.

He shrugs, a bit sheepish. "I had an extra key to those chains. But they did come in handy, now, didn't they?"

She knew it. Even his grand gesture of letting her chain him up was fake. A lie. All he does is lie.

"Please don't be angry," he says, correctly reading her expression. "I saw how that sailor watched you the moment we boarded, and I know how you like to wander at night, freeing Pegasi." He gives her a small smile. "I thought I had better be on deck…just in case."

And Zo—exhausted, tired, sad—finally believes him. At least for this night. And she is grateful. Truly, deeply grateful.

Zubin's reek lingers in her hair, on her skin. She can't go

back into that stuffy cabin. She wants to stay out here so the brisk night air can wash it off.

"Sit with me out here awhile?" she says, hesitant.

He leads her to a wooden chest, where she sits heavily, then settles himself beside her.

Tears suddenly slip down Zo's cheeks. She's unprepared for them, didn't know they were coming. Tears of relief and confusion...and sadness, too. For everything she has lost. Tears of horror at what almost just happened. Tears of fear for her future, her baby's future. And beneath all that, the agonizing knowledge, like a dark water, that has nagged at her mind for weeks now: there is an evil destroying entire villages in the Eastern Mountains...and Zo hasn't been able to do a thing to help. And if Prince Alexander doesn't listen...

It's so much to bear all at once. She's been trying so hard to be strong, but maybe she just can't do it anymore. She rubs her eyes with the heels of her hands and swallows the rising ache in her throat. If she lets Ochus see a moment's weakness, he will never let her forget it. He will always remind her of it in his mocking way. He will—

He pulls her close to him so that her head rests on his shoulder. "Cry," he whispers into her hair. "If you can't be strong anymore, lean on me. I have enough strength for both of us."

Feeling warm and safe in his arms, she cries long and hard until there are no more tears. Then they sit together in a tight embrace, looking up at the stars wheeling slowly around the black vault of the night.

CHAPTER EIGHTEEN: HEPHAESTION

HEPHAESTION'S HEART HAMMERS IN HIS CHEST as he stares down at the mechanism—small enough to fit in an outstretched hand—that Aristotle has set on the sandy ground. The four of them—Heph, Kat, Ada, and the old philosopher—sit cross-legged around it. Shafts of light pierce the trees like glowing spears in this still, silent place at the center of the island. Here, unlike closer to shore, there is no breath of wind, nothing that could move the mechanism's needle other than proof that it works.

It *must* work. For more than two weeks they have spent almost every waking moment laboring on it. The entire time, the urgent need to finish it raced through Heph's veins like fear before a battle, causing him to work harder, rise earlier, and continue laboring by torchlight long after the sun set. They boiled cauldrons full of scales to a fine reduction and scraped away the sticky, malleable residue. In the forge, they mixed in a bit of Heph's melted lead sword for strength, and Ada added rock dust for Earth Blood and pulverized feathers and snakeskin for Snake Blood. Then they poured the bubbling metallic mixture into molds of gears and levers and wheels, let them cool, and assembled them according to Aristotle's drawings.

It was sweaty, smoky, backbreaking work, and Heph has grown both thinner and stronger for it. Though he has no Blood Magic, he has had the uncanny feeling that the wind and the surf, the birds and the trees, whisper to him night and day. *Time is running out. Time is running out. It's almost too late.*

They must use the mechanism to find an Earth Blood to fulfill the prophecy of killing the Last God, Riel, and preventing a new age, the Age of Monsters, from destroying the earth. The stakes for everyone in the known world are so high they simply can't fail. And then there's his personal need for the mechanism to work. Heph failed Alexander in the Battle of Pellan Fields and in his mission to Sharuna. He quakes at the thought of returning to Macedon empty-handed. But if he could bring the mechanism to Alex, surely the prince would forgive him.

"Well," Aristotle says, his deep voice cracking the stillness as he tugs nervously at his beard. "Let's give it a try, shall we?"

No one speaks.

The metallic sheen of the mechanism seems to wink at Heph, glittering like nothing he has ever seen. It is more radiant than gold, yet darker, something more like new bronze, warmed by an inner fire.

"Ready," Kat says, her expression serious.

Aristotle winds the crank on the side of the mechanism, which gives tension and energy to the gears inside that move the needle mounted on a dial on the face. Then he slides the lever above the dial until it clicks in a groove labeled with the drawing of a snake, and places the mechanism back on the ground.

Nothing happens, not the slightest tremble. Heph tells the needle, *Move. Move.* But it is as still as a block of stone. He groans loudly. All that work, for nothing. The sweat, the heat, the sore muscles lifting all those… The needle quivers a bit. No. Perhaps there is a breath of wind here, after all. Or the needle reverberates with his pounding frustration.

"Look!" Kat says quietly. "It's moving."

Jerkily, almost unwillingly, the needle lurches to the right, back to the left, then right again. Now it swings wildly around the whole face of the dial, like a top a child has set spinning. Heph feels his heart beating in his throat now. *It works.* Or does it? Why doesn't it stop?

Ada sighs. "Perhaps you wound it too tightly," she says. "It doesn't seem to…"

The needle stops suddenly, pointing directly at her and Kat. Snake Bloods, both. Heph takes a deep breath, the first, it seems, in many minutes.

"It works," Kat says in wonder, tapping it with her golden fingertip. Then she breaks into a wide smile. "It works!" she says more loudly.

"Yes," Aristotle says, mopping his brow. "At least it works for Snake Blood. But we really need it to work for Earth Blood." He moves the lever above the dial to the groove engraved with a diamond that represents Earth Blood, sets the mechanism back down, and waits.

For a long time, nothing happens. Then the needle shudders, as if it were cold. Now it is spinning wildly around and around the dial so fast Heph can see only a gleaming blur of motion. Finally, it stops, quivers, and settles, pointing directly away from Kat and Ada.

"Northeast," Heph says excitedly. "Our Earth Blood is northeast of here. Though it doesn't tell us how far. He could be standing just behind that tree, or thousands of miles away."

He picks up the mechanism and stands, brushing the dirt from his tunic. "Come. Let us try it at different places on the island to see if we get the same result."

No matter where they go—to the large toppled temple on

the other side of the island, to Aristotle's experimental vegetable patch in the clearing, or any of the beaches—they get
the same result. The mechanism works.

The light Egyptian wine fizzing down his throat mirrors
the bubbling sense of victory Heph has enjoyed all day. A
quarter-moon glistens on the ocean, and a fresh breeze in-
vigorates him. With a crash and a shower of ashes, a log rolls
into the pit as Aristotle and Heph clean up from their last
meal on the island—local fish, its skin blackened, meat flaky
and oozing with rich juices.

Kat has already returned to their hut and lies sleeping on
her mat when he enters a little while later. Moonlight floods
in from their open window, making her face glow. Her hair
sweeps over her pillow in waves, her lips are slightly parted;
her eyelashes are thick and dark against her cheeks.

He knows he should sleep, too. At dawn, they will be leaving for Carthage to seek a ship to Athens. Once there, Aristotle will disembark. He has already told them that this is
not his battle to wage—he is too old, and must focus his tal-
ents where they may be of most use. He has already aided too
much in a war of gods and monsters, a war of magic. *After all,*
he explained, with that cryptic lilt Heph has come to love in
his old tutor, *in the end, man's fate doesn't have to do with magic
at all. The highest training of the mind is to see fate's strings.* Heph
didn't know exactly what it meant, only that he might not
see the old man again for a long time, and that the prospect
of what came next, without Aristotle, both thrilled and terrified him.

As for Ada, she will find a vessel bound for Caria. Birds
have told her that chaos has descended on her land under the
rule of her mad brother, that Spirit Eaters are advancing on
civilization from the Eastern Mountains, and Persian princesses are dead or have disappeared.

Once in Athens, Heph and Kat will be on their own.

And Heph has a feeling this journey will be their most dangerous yet. If what they fear is true, if the Spirit Eaters really are on the move, they may not survive this one. But they have to try. They must find the Earth Blood, confront Riel, and do everything in their power to destroy the god whose rule would usher in a time of monsters, an era of bloodshed, and possibly the end of man.

But there's something else Heph must do, too. Something small and private and of no consequence to the fate of the world but of desperate consequence to him: he must tell Kat. Tell her everything...even though the thought of doing so roils his guts and turns his legs to jelly. The nagging claws of fear—that she'll reject him, that she'll be horrified by his true nature—have been holding him back. Funny, he thinks, that he is less afraid going into battle—where he could easily lose an arm, a leg, his life. But the desperate truth is that he can have no life, anyway, without her in it.

He turns away from her and listens to the sound of the waves, the heartbeat of the sea.

When he wakes, morning has yet to break. Gulls cry out on the horizon, and the night sky is just beginning to blush in the east. Kat is gone, her sleeping mat rolled up and tied to one of her neatly stacked bags. Aristotle and Ada must still be sleeping.

He finds Kat just where he thought he would—sitting on a dusty fallen column, staring at the cracked and faded paintings of the Atlanteans, barely visible in the waning darkness. Though she wears a torn, dirt-splayed tunic, she is majestic, her long bronzed legs powerful-looking, like a wild animal's, her face cut into an expression that's profound, serious, distant. She is a royal princess—no, more than that, a god's daughter—capable of inconceivable feats of magic and courage, and yet she also is of the earth, tangible, invigorating like a cold mountain spring to thirst. There is only one girl like this in the entire world. There is only Katerina.

Her eyes dart up to meet his, and she doesn't have to explain. He knows she is making her silent goodbye to the Lotus-eaters. "Are they ready to leave?" she whispers.

He shakes his head and sits down beside her.

Kat looks around at the trees bending over the ruins, an expression of weariness—or protection—in the arc of their thin trunks. "I will miss this place," she says, echoing his thoughts. "It was a kind of bubble, wasn't it? A time outside of time."

"Yes." He could lose himself in her green eyes, crisscrossed with shadows. He wrenches his gaze away. "Before we head into the unknown, I must...tell you something. About myself." He pauses. "Over the past few weeks, you have told me so much about your past, and I have told you almost nothing about mine."

"Heph, you don't have to—" She puts her hand on his cheek.

"No," he says quickly. "I do."

She traces his jaw, but he gently takes her hand and holds it in his. And as he stares at her, searching for the right words, he realizes he has forced the memories down into a dungeon and barred the door for so long he's not sure how to let them out now.

The silence is thick between them.

"I was eleven," he begins shakily. His tongue feels swollen. Sweat beads on his forehead and prickles his underarms. He thinks of home, the only home he ever really had, a large villa in the hills outside of Pella. Suddenly he is back. He hears the wind whispering through the elegant rooms, the slap of his father's sandals on the marble floor, the musical notes of his mother's laughter. The chatter of his older sister, Polyneices, as she flirted with her betrothed, Lykos.

And then slowly, haltingly, he tells Kat his truth.

How when his parents died, their boorish cousin Myron and his brothers came to live with them at their estate.

How Myron watched his sister with predatory eyes, until one day, Heph, still a child, heard a heart-chilling scream.

How Heph rushed into the room to see Myron on top of her, kneeing her legs apart...and how Heph grabbed a pair of gilded embroidery scissors from the table, a delicate-looking thing made in the form of two facing herons, their long thin legs forming the blades, and plunged them into Myron's neck. How they escaped the wrath of Myron's brothers, but Heph had to disappear completely. Because he is a murderer. A killer of his own kin.

He feels a warm arm around his shoulders. Heph looks up, almost surprised to see it is Kat's.

"Heph," she whispers, "you're shaking."

He tries to still the tremor in his body, taking a slow deep breath. But exhaustion hits him like a dark wave. His past—the gruesomeness of it...a child murderer—has taken up so much room inside him that he now feels a great emptiness where it used to be. He feels dizzy from the release, washed out, but not deliciously free so much as panic-stricken at the enormity of the aching void inside him.

"What happened after you left Poly?" Kat asks quietly.

He calms his breathing, runs a hand through his hair. "I sent word to Lykos to come and get my sister," he says quietly. "But I made my way to Pella where I survived—barely—by running errands, begging, and stealing. Until that day when I stole Alexander's money pouch in the marketplace and he caught me."

Kat raises her eyebrows in surprise, and her lips curl into a half-smile. "That's how you met?"

Heph nods, warmth flooding him along with the memory. "King Philip was going to have me hanged on the spot, but the prince told him he had dropped his purse and I was returning it. Alex invited me to the palace for a meal—it must have been clear I was starving—and I never left."

Kat nods. Early dawn light has begun to trickle through the foliage overhead, streaking her face and limbs in silver. "That's what he did with me, too. Took me in and never doubted me. Even when he should have."

Ah, Heph thinks. *But he* has *doubted me.*

The thought pains him, and yet it spurs him on, makes him want Kat even more. She is so different from the prince in so many ways, and yet she is his twin, shares some part of his soul, and Heph can feel that, can feel how it connects all three of them. He cannot bear not to be loved by them both.

And he cannot bear the thought that one could be responsible for the other's death, as prophecy has suggested. But he pushes that fear back into the shadows.

Kat's hand entwines with his in a fierce grip. "You and I both have a murder in our childhood that changed everything," she says.

"Yes," Heph agrees. "But you didn't commit the murder that changed your life. When I killed Myron, that was the first time I…completely lost control. Each time it happens, it ends badly."

He cuts off, remembering how he slayed High Lord Mordecai in battle instead of taking him prisoner. How he'd disobeyed orders and broken trust with the prince, all because, in that split second, the only thing he knew was rage, and rightness. It *had* been right, in the moment, to kill Mordecai, a mortal enemy to the throne, just as it had been right—he'd felt it deep in his bones—to kill Myron. But everything afterward told him that these things had been wrong. He couldn't trust *himself* when passion went to his head. How could he expect Alexander to?

And how can he expect Kat to, either?

"I know what it means to have regrets, Heph," she says now, quietly. "I have many."

Guilt clogs his throat. He knows she must be thinking not of him but of Jacob.

"Do you…" His voice is so low he isn't sure if he's even speaking at all. "Do you regret—" he gestures between the two of them *"—this?"*

Her hands find their way to his shoulders. "Heph."

"Because," he bursts out, unwilling to hear her response, unready to, unless it is the response he wants, the response he needs, "I want you. I need you. I—I love you, Kat."

She sucks in a breath but doesn't move away. She has one hand running through his hair now. There are tears in her eyes. "Always," he plunges on, the words nearly uncontrollable now. "I can't imagine what it would be like to live without you. If we survive our next journey, I want you to marry me, Kat. I—"

"Shh," she says, her hands finding their way back to his face. She is kneeling on the column now, inches away. And then she is kissing him, and he can feel her body moving against his, and he swears he can feel the truth of it—that she loves him, too, that she understands. The whole flood of his confession turns from language into liquid feeling, and he is kissing her back, hungrily, as they sink from the column into the sand and grass.

The morning sun sends a wild scattering of bright light all around them, and he feels as though they are inside a many-faceted crystal. There is light everywhere, all is rightness, all is touch, all is Kat.

CHAPTER NINETEEN: JACOB

THE HEAT OF THE SMALL CAVERN SEEMS TO match the intensity leaping inside him. Jacob wipes sweat off his brow, then takes another log from the pile and tosses it onto the fire beneath a large cauldron of bubbling water. He throws in another handful of bright yellow sulfur crystals, and nearly retches at the smell. Golden steam carries the foul sulfuric odor up through the grate in the ceiling—just as he had planned.

The Temple of Apollo is set atop a source of natural gases said to emit the very breath of the god through vents in the floor—it is these vapors that aid in the mysterious work of the oracles. However, today, Pythia will not be performing her normal prophecies. Today she will be working with Jacob, faking the voice of one god in order to fool another, who still walks among them.

That is, if Jacob's plan works. But it all depends on keeping the real fumes suppressed. He has laid long wooden covers across the vaporous pool and hung wet blankets over all the fissures in the walls. There shouldn't be a single thread of the stuff wafting up through the bronze grate into Pythia's oracular chamber and sending her into a trance.

It feels good to work in the hot, tiny cavern belowground. He has been waiting—a skill Jacob has perfected. There's been nothing in his life that he hasn't had to wait patiently for, carefully laying the groundwork, setting the trap, then hiding out and watching, watching. Three years ago, after losing their fall harvest to drought, Jacob's family faced starvation in an unusually harsh winter. For two days, Jacob and Kat tracked an enormous ten-pointed buck into the snowy woods, suffering cold and hunger, wondering if they would even make it home or die out there from exposure. Finally, with persistence and patience, they wore the buck down, found him, and brought back enough meat for the family to feast.

Every day for the past three weeks, High Lord Gideon has kept a round-the-clock watch on the villa's towers for the Macedonian retinue thundering past, but it wasn't until late yesterday afternoon when Jacob was on watch that the prince rode by on his huge black horse, sunshine glinting off his golden armor, his guards carrying the sky blue flag with the sixteen-pointed gold star. Beside him cantered Queen Olympias, her fur-lined purple cape flying out behind her. They would appear at the temple at dawn, Jacob knew, and he would be ready.

"Jacob!" a voice whispers. Pythia is hurrying down the narrow winding stairway into the cavern, wrapped in her white robe. Her whole body trembles, her long hair cascading around her shoulders. "He's here, with Queen Olympias." Tension chokes her voice. "They just slaughtered the goat in the courtyard. He's—he's coming."

He strides over and puts his hands on her shoulders—so narrow, so delicate—and sees a flush rise in her pale cheeks. "You'll be fine," he says quietly. "We've practiced. Just adjust the prophecy a bit based on his question."

She nods and breathes slowly, then coughs from the strength

of the fumes. She waves a hand in front of her face, her eyes watering. "Yes. Yes, it will work. We've practiced." Scared as she is, Jacob knows she's doing this for him. Courage, he realizes, is a far greater virtue than fearlessness. Courage is doing what you need to do despite absolute terror. Courage is putting one foot in front of the other as you push yourself forward, deeper into your worst nightmare, knowing truth lies on the other side.

"Will you be all right down here?"

He smiles. "Of course."

She nods again. "Then I'd better get back up there." She turns. Her sandals click against the stone stairs and she begins to climb.

"Pythia, wait."

She turns back, hovering near the top step, her pointed face questioning.

"Thank you," he says.

She nods for the third time, and then disappears. The door to the chamber above snaps shut.

Jacob climbs the ladder next to the fire pit and peers up through the grate, hot yellow steam coating his face and rapidly cooling. He can't see Pythia. She must be sitting in her *holmos* behind the brazier burning aromatic herbs. That smoke, too, should mask what is really going on down here.

Jacob waits.

And waits.

He begins to feel faint from the power of the sulfuric gas, the smoke clouding his vision. He begins to feel like he is no longer himself at all but a spirit, disembodied, made of steam and heat and tension.

His hands, slippery, grip the ladder, but he feels unsteady.

He reaches out to touch the stone wall. Almost without realizing it, some part of him slips inside the rock *itself*, feeling its strength as his strength. He pulls his hand back as quickly as if he touched molten metal.

He should fight against this. This is *wrong*. This is the very evil he has sworn his life to eradicating. He is a warrior, strong and disciplined. He must...

His hand, unbidden, strokes the stone again, as if it were a lover. He places the flat of his palm on the rock, and leans his forehead against it, succumbing with a shudder. The Aesarian Lords are not here. Here there is no reason to resist the power of the earth calling to the core of his very soul. He extends beyond himself, into the rock, dark, silent, and brooding. He is as ancient as time itself, and more majestic than any king. He is the earth, rocks and soil, mountains and islands. He is the encircling sea, angry and turbulent. He is the wind tearing through forests, chiseling stone with his sighs, somersaulting across endless fields. He is lightning, cast from the mighty hand of Zeus like javelins, splintering trees.

The earth, he realizes, is not a lifeless mound of dirt and water, but tingles with energy. With power. He shudders at the realization... Or was it the earth around him trembling? Steaming water squeezes out from beneath the wooden covers he has put on the pool. He isn't sure what is happening but...

Above him a door opens and footsteps clatter, bringing him back to himself. Jacob looks up and sees small feet and a long purple skirt pass overhead. The queen. Then the black shape of a boot sole rests squarely on the grate. If the prince looked straight down, surely he would see Jacob peering up. He pulls his head back so quickly he nearly falls off the ladder.

"Pythia, Voice of Apollo," Prince Alexander greets her.

"Know, Pilgrim," Pythia replies, her voice deep and controlled, "that the god who speaks neither reveals the truth nor conceals it, but only gives signs. What is your question, Pilgrim?"

The feet pace restlessly, back and forth, back and forth over the grate. "You foretold that a…great calamity would befall a great and noble ruler on the day of his wedding."

Jacob wonders if he is talking about the marriage of King Philip to Cleopatra.

Pythia murmurs something unintelligible.

"That it would occur," Alexander goes on, his voice dropping low and rough, quiet, "by the hand of the king's lover. Will that lover be his wife?"

Now Jacob understands what Pythia told him that morning by the spring: that only a lover could kill the king that Alexander wanted dead. He had thought the king might be Artaxerxes. But now it's as clear as day that Alexander-Riel wants Philip dead so he can take power. And he wants Olympias to do the job.

Jacobs hears Pythia mumble, almost unintelligibly, "Wives are lovers are wives."

Alexander grunts in satisfaction and continues. "But the gods did not specify in what *manner* and by what means. I know how prophecy works, Pythia. I know that the gods often trade in truths only to lure men into their fates. But I am no ordinary man."

Pythia murmurs again, beginning to chant. "No, no, you are not like other men." She sighs and groans, going through the motions of a trance. Jacob can picture her, eyes closed, body swaying.

Now she mutters in a deep voice, *"The last of us the last of us the last of us. The son is the father is the son."*

"Yes," the prince breathes, in a voice unlike his own. It is so quiet Jacob is unsure whether he really heard it.

Silence hangs heavily in the oracular chamber.

Then Pythia begins to chant again, this time more clearly.

"I, Apollo, speak through my daughter
You must take of the deadly water
There at the base of the eastern mountain
From what's left of the cursed fountain
Slip it in King Philip's wine
And he will die before his time."

More silence. Lingering, heavy. Jacob finds he is holding his breath. If their ruse works, the prince will take this information to heart, and will pursue the Fountain of Youth for a poison fit for killing a king. There, Jacob and the Aesarian Lords will be waiting to ensnare and destroy him forever. Food for the Spirit Eaters. Enough magic to keep the evil at bay for centuries to come.

But he must believe that the gods have willed it so.

The quiet is so stifling, the smoke so thick, Jacob almost doesn't hear what follows...the slick of metal against leather, the distinct sound of a dagger sliding from its sheath.

No.

There is a gasp, and a loud crash, and before Pythia can even utter a scream, Jacob has leaped off the ladder.

There's a hissing sound as burning coals skitter across the grate and hot ashes rain down on him. Brushing them out of his hair, he bolts up the staircase.

He pushes the door open and sees many things at once: the brazier knocked to the floor, the purple back of a silver-haired queen, and Alexander's hands around Pythia's neck. "Who made you do this?" His demand is rumbling and quiet as distant thunder; his arms flex, ready to kill.

Jacob feels blood pounding through him in a mighty torrent as he stands in the doorway. The prince looks directly at him, and his eyes are not those of a man but of a god, blazing and powerful, in a face shining so white it hurts Jacob's eyes to gaze upon it.

Something cracks inside Jacob, a release of rage, and the ground shifts. He starts to fall backward, down the steps, but grabs the door handle to steady himself, and pulls it tightly shut against him. A groan issues from the earth, like the death rattle of a huge beast. In the chamber beyond, something crashes. The queen's scream slices the electric air.

Jacob tries to open the door, but the ground heaves again, as if vomiting. Jacob flies backward, hits the curving wall, and slams onto the stairs. Rocks crash to the ground in the chamber below him. He fights his way back toward Pythia, who is crying now. Alexander—Riel—must have released her.

"Leave her!" Olympias shrieks from somewhere amid the chaos.

Another crash. Dust and smoke everywhere.

And then, there is a brief window of eerie silence.

Flinging the door open, Jacob sees Pythia on the floor, her eyes closed, a wooden roof beam crushing her chest.

He races to her just as the floor behind him caves in, the marble tiles cascading into the abyss along with Pythia's bronze *holmos*. Vapor—real vapor, this time—rises like curling yellow fingers around him. Screams echo from the sanctuary as something heavy thuds to the ground.

He bends over the girl. His heart hammers. He tries to lift the beam, but it's too heavy. A huge zigzag crack appears in the wall behind her. Blocks topple onto the floor as Jacob throws his body over the young oracle, shielding her as stone pummels him relentlessly.

He searches himself—and the raging earth below him— for answers.

He has done this.

He has unleashed this power like a mighty catapult stone he cannot bring back. He squats low, channeling the power of the earth, the roar of the waves, and the ferocity of the whirlwind into his back, his arms, his legs, feeling the energy spark and stream within him. Groaning, he slowly raises the fallen pillar, his teeth grinding, sweat dripping off his brow, and sets it down behind her with a thud.

Blood seeps from Pythia's chest, staining her white robes. Her ribs must be crushed—she appears to be breathing, but faintly. Jacob hears a threatening rumble in the earth, echoed by moaning walls inside the sanctuary. There is no time. He picks her up as gently as possible and carries her out of the oracular chamber.

In the sanctuary beyond, part of the far wall has toppled to the ground, and several of the life-sized statues of gods lie shattered on the floor. Riel and the queen are nowhere in sight.

The ground shifts, and Jacob struggles to keep his balance as the floor tiles in front of him burst and buckle, rising up like giant writhing snakes. To his right, a stone Aphrodite wobbles on her platform and plunges to the ground. Her head rolls off and comes to a stop near his feet, her wide, painted blue eyes looking up at him imploringly. In front of the colossal statue of Apollo at the far end, pitchers of fine olive oil, offerings to the god, skitter and fall, cracking open. Flames from the lit silver lamps at the statue's feet lick across the floor. And the colossal statue of Apollo strumming his lyre leans forward as if to inspect the racing fire, and starts his own slow dive.

Still carrying Pythia, Jacob runs over buckled tiles and fragments of statue to the wide doorway just as, behind him, Apollo hits the floor in an explosion of stone and ivory. On the temple porch, Jacob gapes as the buildings around him jitter and jump. People race through the streets, hands on their heads, screaming. Flocks of birds swoop through the city as riderless horses stampede past, neighing in panic.

This can't be real. He is trapped in a nightmare.

The ground below him rises, nearly causing him to fall sideways, and he sees the columns in front of him pitch to the right. He races down steps that jump up and down under his feet like a galloping horse and leaps into the street, turning back to look. *Know Thyself*, commands the inscription on the wobbling pediment, and Jacob feels hysterical laughter rising in his throat. He knows himself all right. *This* is him. The real Jacob, unleashed.

All six columns fall, slowly, with a kind of grace, as Jacob runs farther into the square of the agora directly in front of the temple. The pediment of painted statues crashes to the ground, spewing a hailstorm of white dust and tiny stone shards, some of which stick in the backs of his arms and legs like knives. The fluted column sections careen around him like loose carriage wheels; one smashes into a souvenir shop, sending statuettes of Apollo flying in all directions. Another strikes an old man standing in front of a shop, knocking him to the heaving earth, and keeps bounding forward as he lies still.

Jacob makes his way down the hill, avoiding the collapse and ruin. From this vantage, he can see most of the city, where some of the treasuries have fallen, revealing golden statues and silver platters. In the nearest treasury, three men frantically raid the loot, scrambling over heaps of coins and jewels and gleaming armor, stuffing their pockets full, even as the one remaining wall wobbles...

"No!" Jacob calls out, a warning too late.

The wall collapses on the looters: punishment, no doubt, for robbing the gods.

Jacob passes a white-robed priest, kneeling and praying out loud, flinging dirt on his head and beating his breast. He flies past the still-standing bronze statue of the Three Fates—laughing toothless crones working the woolen threads of human lives—and sees a red-faced toddler crying just as the stone wall next to her begins to shift, bulging outward. Settling Pythia over his left shoulder, he swoops low and picks up the child with his right arm just as the wall tumbles into the street where she stood.

"Apella!" cries a woman with a ripped robe and blood on her outstretched arms. Jacob deftly hands her the screaming girl without stopping. He passes a collapsed house where men and women pick up stones, calling in desperation to those trapped beneath. Jacob wishes he could stay in the city to help them all, with his strength, with his healing powers, but Pythia lies white and still on his shoulder, bleeding. Pythia, who risked everything for him.

Up ahead he sees the gate, still standing, though the rear wall of its gabled tower has fallen, exposing a staircase that dangles in midair. Beside it, a horse rears and screams, its traces caught in fallen rocks. Jacob unsheathes his sword and cuts the traces. The horse bolts out the open gate, and Jacob follows. Cradling Pythia as gently as he can, he runs away from the crashes and screams and smoke. He hears more panicked hooves and veers out of the way just in time to avoid a man driving a horse cart filled with wailing children and large silver vases.

After a time, Jacob pauses to catch his breath. The violent upheavals have stopped, and now the earth is merely trembling, like the heaving of an ox that has run too far and fast. He looks around. People stand in front of houses and taverns along the Delphi road in the early-morning light, staring slack-jawed, pointing in disbelief.

Jacob can barely bring himself to look back, and when he does, a fresh wave of horror rolls through him. On his left, the sea boils with anger, foamy breakers crashing on the little beach below. On the long sloping hill, Apollo's ancient olive trees have been uprooted and snapped in two, lying like dead and dismembered warriors. And the city… Jacob's heart nearly breaks. Delphi no longer stands like a glorious poem between the sparkling azure sea and the protective embrace of the mountain. Smoke rises from shattered buildings. Flames leap from wooden beams. The colossal statues have all toppled. Walls have collapsed. Countless people must be dead and injured.

He did this.

He hears a loud whinny and turns again to see the horse he saved at the city gate shifting its weight as if unsure where to go. He walks up to it, clucking reassurance, and pats the horse's bristly muzzle. Speaking words of encouragement, he lays Pythia on its back and climbs up behind her.

Minutes later, Jacob dismounts next to the sacred Castalian Spring, which is…empty. Water trickles out of a new-formed cleft in the bottom of the rocky pool. He pulls Pythia off the horse, concerned about her breathing, which sounds as if water is bubbling inside her chest. He lays her beneath a tamarind tree and unties her bloodstained white robe to examine her. There is so much clotted blood it is hard to see her injuries.

He jumps into the rocky pool and scoops water from a puddle with the leather cup hanging from his belt. Then he tears off part of her ruined robe with his dagger and gently washes her wounds. He was right; her ribs are crushed, broken, jagged edges poking through shredded skin and probably into her lungs, as well.

His stomach turns but he wills himself to remain calm, to keep the magic urges in control.

He holds his hands just over the wounds, channeling the healing energy of the earth—its warmth and fire and creative forces—through them and into her. His blood sings ancient songs of stone and storm. His hands grow warm. Hot. He feels love pulse through his veins, joy dance inside him. He opens his eyes and sees a golden light radiating from his hands and sinking into her torn, bruised flesh. His head spins with the pleasure of the life-giving, healing force moving through him. But he is tired now. So tired.

The warmth drains from him and he feels suddenly cold and alone, as if someone has pulled off his fur cloak and he stands naked in a blizzard. He shivers, lost in the freezing emptiness, but a groan pulls him back to the present. Pythia is coming to, her breathing calm and deep. He explores the pale flesh below her breasts with his fingertips. There are still smears of blood, but the wounds are closed, the ribs knitted firmly together.

Pythia pushes up on her elbows, staring at him groggily, then down at her exposed chest. Eyes wide in horror, she clasps her arms around her breasts.

"You were injured," he says, pulling back awkwardly.

Pythia runs one hand over the bloodstained skin. "Were?" she asks in confusion.

"A scratch only," he says, "but the gods must have healed you." He takes off his cloak and drapes it over her. "Wear this for now."

"What happened to Prince Alexander...?" she asks.

Is the Last God lying crushed under a wall? Can a god die so easily? Jacob sincerely hopes not. His future—and the future of mankind—depend on it. He starts to say he doesn't know, but something shifts inside him, and he feels hooves pounding earth and wind tangling hair. Riel and Olympias made it out of the city unharmed.

"I have the feeling they are alive," he says. "But the temple, your temple, Pythia, is destroyed."

She seems startled for a moment. Then she says, "Good."

He is so surprised by her response that for a moment he can say nothing.

She shakes her head as if to clear it, then stares at him with intense moss-colored eyes. "Everyone will think I died in there. Alexander won't come looking for me and neither will the city priests. I don't want to go back, Jacob. Take me away from here."

"All right," he agrees, though he has no idea where to go.

A smile lights Pythia's sweet face, and Jacob is overwhelmed by her faith in him. She trusts him. With a sharp pang in his heart, he's reminded of... No, he won't think about that.

"Where will we go?" she whispers.

He stares at her, thinking. He can hardly bring a woman to the Aesarian camp. And does he even want to go back there with the knowledge of his catastrophic failure? With the earth bubbling in his blood, sinister and wild and beyond his control—a manifestation of everything the Aesarian Lords stand against?

No. Jacob can no longer deny who and what he is.

And accepting that, he must also accept that he will never be free—will always be hunted by the Lords if, or *when*, they find out—unless he can offer up a god to stave off the Spirit Eaters and their hunger for magic blood.

There is no looking back.

He *must* ensnare Riel, by whatever means necessary.

And he knows exactly where Riel is headed next: the wedding of King Philip and Cleopatra in the north...

He touches Pythia's face, knowing his caress is cursed; his touch is both powerful and devastating. That it can give life and take it away.

"We will go to Byzantium," he says.

CHAPTER TWENTY: RIEL

FEAR POUNDS THROUGH RIEL AS HE GALLOPS away from Delphi—it's a feeling so ancient and so deep he hardly recognizes it. It's been a very long time indeed since Riel has felt afraid. Though his powers are greatly diminished from what they were, still they are far greater than any mortal's.

But now... Now he has reason to fear. The man he saw just for an instant in the doorway of the oracular chamber, though mortal, was built like Heracles himself, his dark eyes glowing with volcanic fire. Riel felt the man's raging Earth Blood power and sensed it was almost as great as that of his brother, Brehan, who also caused the earth to shake when angry.

This is a power, perhaps, to rival Riel's own diminished abilities. Enough to fulfill the Cassandra prophecy he has feared for nine hundred years. Despite Riel's systematic culling of Brehan's descendants, one Earth Blood still lives. One who could be Riel's killer.

The rhythmic sound of Bucephalus's hooves hitting the road seems to say, *Your death is near. Your death is near. Your death is near.*

"Slow down!" Olympias calls to him shrilly. Reluctantly,

he pulls on the reins, slowing the stallion to a walk. The horse tosses his head and grumbles loudly. He is a sensitive creature, the first to realize Alexander is not Alexander. It has taken all Riel's concentrated power to force Bucephalus to carry him.

"What happened back there?" she asks, gasping for breath as she comes up beside him. He eyes her critically. Sweat runs down her cheeks, making bone-white streaks where it has taken her makeup with it. She looks gaunt, haggard. Gone is the luscious, passionate beauty he loved, replaced by this woman who has become a symbol of all his past failures instead of his future hopes. Still, she is a valuable tool.

"What did you do?" she demands.

"I did nothing," he says, furrowing his brow. "It was not me."

"What do you mean?" Olympias says, her face wrinkling in alarm. "Are you telling me that this was someone else's doing?"

He needs to think. How can he do that with this woman always skewering him with questions? Seething in frustration, he turns. "You didn't see him? He was standing in the small doorway of the oracular chamber."

She looks at him blankly.

"I've been compromised," he murmurs. "Someone knows—knows that Prince Alexander is not who he appears to be."

Pythia betrayed him, that was certain. Her prophecies were true, up until today. Then she tried to play him for a fool. But who was the man in the doorway? How could he have figured out Riel's true identity? True, General Kadmus suspected him, staring at him with those ice-chip-gray eyes, silently prowling about his room under the guise of protecting him. Then, one day when Kadmus showed him some message about Persians, Riel's eyes locked with his and he knew that Kadmus knew the truth about him and slaughtered him on the spot. He would have killed the Persian adviser, too, Cosmas, if he had seen the same knowledge in his eyes.

Mortal enemies are laughably easy to subdue. Only the Earth Blood is dangerous. Riel must get as far away from here as possible, make sure Olympias takes care of business in Byzantium as the oracle prophesied, and return to Macedon as the new king. Then he can rid himself of her and devote himself to regaining his divinity…before the Earth Blood finds him again. But the appearance of the Earth Blood is not the only recent cleft in the fabric of mankind's destiny.

He looks back at the ruined city in the distance, at smoke rising from toppled temples. Many there spoke of troubles in the east, of entire villages devoured. Sailors reported black winged creatures swimming beside fishing vessels, climbing the sides to grab a crewman and dive back into the deep. Riel knows what those creatures are.

Much is changing in the world. He can feel the shift. But the rise of the Spirit Eaters does not concern him. Because of them, he lost his divinity and became trapped here with lesser powers. He will not try to stop them again. Let them devour the entire world. Let them slake their hunger with the whining Olympias, if they can stomach her. It matters not to him. He will be with the gods soon.

Riel looks at the queen, and sees that her face is taut; hurt is etched into her every line. Smiling a sweet smile, he beckons her.

"Come, my love," he says cheerfully. "It is too dangerous to stay here." He kicks Bucephalus, who launches forward like a loosed arrow.

CHAPTER TWENTY-ONE: CYNANE

RIPPLING LAUGHTER FLOATS ABOVE THE RHYTH-mic tap of drums and the shrill of pipes in the palace court-yard. Fires burn high in numerous iron cressets, providing not only plentiful light but also keeping the worst chill out of the autumn air. Cynane, arms crossed over her black robe, watches her guests—powerful ministers and noblemen—and the girls she has hired to entertain them, prostitutes from the brothel whose madam Amyntas forced her to kill. This is not a party so much as a tactical move on a battlefield.

Taulus was right. She will need these men on her side be-fore she goes through with her plan. It is one thing to kill a mad king, and quite another to inherit the throne from him. She must first earn trust from those in power, must prove she is the superior choice.

She has been in Dardania two months now and has worked hard to win the most influential to her side. She has given dowries to daughters, jewelry to wives, and has persuaded Amyntas that his horse wanted him to bestow honors and ti-tles on the men and their sons. Now it is time to go further. These men, too, she knows, are just as terrified of their mad king as she is. She must use that fear to her advantage.

If Taulus could be here tonight, would he be pleased with her strategy? She'll never know.

Taulus is dead—by her hand.

She killed him in this very courtyard after she arranged to meet him here shortly before dawn three weeks ago. She had asked to hold his crystal sword, then lunged with it, piercing his heart, the only part of him still made of human flesh. Hot blood burst all over her—so much blood for a man composed mainly of vapor.

Then the smoke of his leaky soul curled around her rapidly like a whirlwind, spinning faster and faster, tightening in an agonizing embrace, choking the breath out of her, coating her with cinders and ashes that made her cough and retch. Smoke poured down her throat like acidic wine, charring her lungs and burning through her veins until she was certain she was going to die.

Slowly, the pain lessened. The smoke winding around her lifted and dispersed, rising skyward as the flame of Taulus's spirit was extinguished. The flinty eyes were the last thing to disappear, surprising her with their expression of deep satisfaction.

She had been right. He had wanted her to kill him. He had warned her of all the dangers of Smoke Blood, yet hoped she would kill him, anyway, freeing him from his eternal suffering.

Still, the memory of it, the guilt, washes over her with the repetitive, pounding insistence of angry waves. Taulus saved her life so many times. His wise advice guided her. The regret tastes bitter in her mouth, like ashes. But it *should* taste bitter—after all, that is the taste of True Betrayal.

Since that awful, unforgettable deed, Cyn has felt different at times, experienced a dark bubbling in her blood, felt soot coating her insides. But then it's gone, like smoke blown away. She has developed no powers that she's aware of yet... She certainly cannot vanish and reappear like Taulus, or change her shape, or cast the powerful protective spell he had put on her, but he himself told her his abilities increased with time. And she's been experimenting. Pain, she's found, focuses the magic, causes it to spark and throb and grow stronger.

"Wine, Your Highness?" Alecta, the girl who threw the trident at Cynane that awful day in the brothel, now stands before her holding up an *oenochoe*. She, like all the other girls, is dressed as a bacchante, a sacred worshipper of the wine god, Bacchus, her loose, wild red hair crowned with a laurel wreath. She wears a white wool robe and a leopard skin thrown over her left shoulder. Cyn is amazed once again by her fierce beauty.

"Highness, where is your cup?" Is it Cyn's imagination, or is Alecta smirking at her?

Cyn waves her hand. "I need a clear head tonight." She sighs. "Come to think of it, I need a clear head every night."

Alecta raises her eyebrows. "Even though our lord king hasn't graced your first party as queen consort with his majestic presence? Surely you can relax a little."

Cyn stares at her, suddenly on guard. It is not the woman's place to speak so openly to a queen.

She is surprised to see Alecta crack a grin. "What important business keeps our lord king away?"

She is mocking her. Cyn doesn't know whether to slap her or to laugh.

"He has gone to the cliffs to debate with the stars," she answers, because it is the truth. "Last week he ordered them to shine more brightly, but it seems they have stubbornly refused." She is playing a dangerous game, Cyn knows, by admitting to the king's madness before a mere servant, a prostitute at that. But she finds there is something intriguing and bold about Alecta. Something she likes. "He has threatened to launch catapults against the stars if they don't comply, which should provide a show if we can catch it. He aims to douse their light."

Alecta's laugh is low and sultry. "As long as he doesn't douse *your* light, my lady."

Cyn feels a shiver. She doesn't like that Alecta has surprised her yet again. That her quick wit has caught Cyn so off guard.

"That's enough," she says, waving her off. She's not going to thank the girl for her compliment. She knows too well that flattery and familiarity are both simple strategies to disarm someone, and she will not be so easily distracted.

Cyn wanders through the crowded courtyard until she comes upon three men chatting among themselves—each of them nearly as influential as Leonidas was back in Pella. Trusted counselors, to whom the others listen. Cyn needs to win all of them to her side.

She bumps in between the elbows of the first two. "I thank you for coming, gentlemen," she says, inclining her head. "As you know, I would like a much *closer* relationship with all of you."

General Georgios, commander of the army, looks over his shoulder and says in a low voice, "We know, my queen." He's a lean, bearded man in his forties, missing most of his left ear and two of his right fingers.

"But there's nothing we can do," whispers Kyros, minister of the treasury. Cyn is astonished by bags under his eyes so puffy a small fish could live in each one with room to turn around.

"Nothing at all, unfortunately," says Simon, minister of religion. He snaps his fingers and the mute slave boy, Aesop, comes forward with a tray of lamb-stuffed olives. He is chained at the wrist to his slave master, a burly man with eyes that float in two different directions, who offers slices of goat cheese. Simon helps himself generously to both. It takes a great deal of food to keep oneself shaped like a wine barrel.

"Who among us is next to suffer and die at his whim?" Cyn asks. "You, Georgios? Simon? Kyros?"

Kyros flinches and nods. "True. But there is no male relative to replace him."

"What about a strong female relative?" she counters.

"Real Dardanian men would never allow themselves to be led by a woman," Georgios scoffs. "It would be humiliating. I know what you want, my queen, and it is not possible—nor *natural*."

Cyn's entire body shakes with anger at how easily he dismisses her claims, like flicking a speck of dust off his coat, but she says nothing.

"It's a pity about Pyrolithos," Simon says, licking his fingers.

"Who is that?" Cyn asks. The name is only vaguely familiar.

"Who *was* that," Simon replies, picking a quail wing off a passing tray. In one swift move, he sucks off the meat and flings the bone over his fat shoulder. "Amyntas's first cousin. He disappeared a decade ago when he was only a boy. The family had just returned from a pilgrimage to Delphi, and he joined some men on a boar hunt. Pyro disappeared. They searched the woods for days and found no trace of him. Either a beast devoured him or he died of starvation."

Cyn has heard this story before. Shortly before her death, her mother told her about a young nephew who'd disappeared. Smart, funny, dark-haired and dark-eyed, he had been the delight of the Dardanian court.

Kyros lifts his painted *rhyton*, formed in the shape of a horse's head, and drinks deeply, smacking his lips. "I think the loss of him killed his parents. He was a strong, likable child, unlike Amyntas. He would be the heir now, had he lived."

An idea—vague and shifting—forms in Cyn's mind. She rejects it. Outlandish. Farfetched. And yet...

"How tragic," she murmurs.

General Georgios, tapping his foot impatiently, says, "Getting back to your plot, my queen—for we all know that is what it is—there *is* a way for you to rid yourself of that maniac."

"What?" she asks, something like hope rising in her chest, but immediately, distrust chases it away. Nothing, she knows, comes easily in this world.

The man looks around suspiciously, and though no one is standing nearby, he whispers in her ear, "Arrange to marry one of us. That man will kill Amyntas, claim you as his bride, and rule through your blood-right. The others will follow him. It's the perfect solution."

Cyn stares at the unpalatable trio, doing her best to mask her disgust. The man's suggestion is degrading on many counts. That she should stoop from marrying a king by right to marrying a mere counselor. That she should stoop to marrying any man as detestable and deformed as these three. That she would not be ruling queen but merely queen consort— which she already is. That she has so vastly failed to be understood. That men have, for uncountable centuries, failed so deeply to understand all women.

"Of course, I will be delighted to consider that option," she says, nearly choking on her own spit.

Simon chimes in. "It would be a great advantage over where you are now."

Cyn feels frustration boiling inside her, feels the same ancient howl of unfairness, of something she can't change no matter how hard she tries.

"And in the meantime," she says, voice diamond-hard and diamond-clear, "you are willing to put up with a mad king who makes you worry that every day might be your last?"

"A mad king is not ideal," Georgios says, dark eyes narrowing, "but a female ruler is just as bad, if not worse. Women are unfit to rule."

In one swift move, Cyn unsheathes her dagger and sticks the point directly under his bearded chin.

"Call me unfit to rule again," she snarls, no longer able to keep in her rage. Like a wild beast, it must be allowed out.

A murmuring crowd quickly gathers around them.

"Sheathe your tiny claw, kitten," Georgios says, disdainfully pushing the dagger away.

Suddenly Cyn feels a firm hand on her waist and turns to see Alecta, smiling broadly, a smile that doesn't reach her eyes.

Alecta, too, holds a dagger, and she slowly spins Cyn around in a kind of dance. The musicians are behind her, also dressed as bacchantes—Thalia playing a flute, Halie shaking a sistrum, Kyra tapping a drum.

Cyn, aware that all eyes are on her, realizes Alecta is trying to save her, turn her embarrassing threat into a dance. She follows Alecta's slow graceful moves, longing to engage in *real* combat, but surprised, once again, by Alecta's almost mesmerizing effect on her. The girl's expressive dance reminds Cyn of a song played in motion, a song of love and hate, fear and sorrow, pride and sacrifice—everything it takes to be human. She feels awkward in comparison, a reed flute offering a few notes compared to her partner's full-throated concert of many instruments, but does her best to keep up. Finally, Alecta bows, as does Cyn a beat later, to uproarious applause.

"Come," Alecta says, grabbing Cyn hard by the wrist. She pulls her across the courtyard and into the shadows of the peristyle.

"You have a strange way of making allies," she says, her smile gone.

Cyn tries to close her gaping mouth. Alecta is onto her, watching her.

"Women," the girl reminds her, "have *other* means of persuasion, if you know what I'm after. Means that men simply do not have. The question is, how can you persuade them to get what you want?"

Cyn scoffs. "I know how to persuade a gentleman in the manner of which you speak," she says, eyeing Alecta, the way she moves with confidence in her body, as though every gesture were a preamble to something sexual. There's power in it, and hunger, too. But these things are nothing new to Cyn.

Alecta stares at Cyn, undaunted by her, arms crossed over her chest. "Well, your tactics so far haven't accomplished much. I only meant to help."

She walks—swaying her hips in a most enticing way, Cyn notices—back toward the crowd, but Cyn calls out, "Wait!" and she stops.

Alecta turns. "Yes?"

"Why?"

The girl approaches again, slowly. "Why what?"

"Why are you interested in helping me?"

Alecta's eyes lock onto hers, and Cyn feels a kind of undoing, as though her heart has gone to smoke, guttering in the wind. "Why wouldn't I?" the girl whispers.

And then, with only a few easy strides into the moving throngs, she is gone.

Cyn remains in the shadows, unsettled, pacing the perimeter of the party. Alecta is right about one thing: her tactics *haven't* worked, and her patience is thinner than ever; in fact, it hardly resembles patience at all, more like a wound rubbed raw.

As she passes a banquet table of dishes mostly scraped clean, a silver tray winks at her in the torchlight. She picks it up and stares at her reflection. Her face is strong for a woman's, her forehead broad, her nose long and straight, her cheekbones high. But her pink lips are soft, her lashes long and thick, her jaw delicate.

It is, undeniably, the face of a woman. A woman who is

not allowed to rule, even though she is now the only one in all the world with Smoke Blood.

Once again, she reaches down inside herself and taps into the swirling darkness in her heart that appeared the moment Taulus stopped breathing. In her mind's eye, it's like ink added to water, sin added to the soul, and from here she can feel the Smoke Blood's power, shifting and floating away, just beyond her grasp of control.

Cyn sets down the tray, takes her dagger, and pricks her finger. The pain nudges the smoke in her soul to billow forth in swirling gusts. As her cut skin tingles, she picks up the tray and studies herself, trying to shift her features. A stronger jaw. A thinner, more determined mouth.

The braying of laughter strikes dread in her heart as the crowd parts and applauds.

"Where is our queen?" asks that high-pitched voice she despises. Amyntas has returned—early. Her breath catches— what will he do when he realizes she threw a party without him?

Pushing her face into a smile, she sets down the tray and strides through the crowd. "Aha!" her husband shouts, leading Aireon into the courtyard, followed by Priam—who gives Cyn an alarmed look—and the ever-present Papari, dressed tonight as the messenger god Hermes in a winged helmet and winged boots.

Frowning, the king looks around and asks, "What is this?"

Bowing low before him, Cyn rises and says, with a sweeping gesture, "This is a surprise celebration for you, my lord, to celebrate your victory over the stars of heaven. For I knew you would vanquish them."

"A surprise party for us!" he cries. He tilts his head back and looks down at her with his strange pale eyes. She waits, her heart palpitating. "What a completely wonderful night!" he says. "You are right, wife. The stars have hidden their faces for shame at our eloquence during our debate. And you have planned a party for us!"

Cyn looks up. Clouds cover the night sky. She lets out a breath.

"Now that the king is here," she calls, clapping her hands, "the play may begin!"

She leads Amyntas to the front row of seats at one end of the courtyard. Within moments, he is mesmerized by the scenes unfolding among the bright torches and drinks heavily from a goblet Alecta refills many times. The play is *Medea*, the story of a powerful witch-queen who murdered her husband's young betrothed with a poisoned gown and then killed her own sons. The girls from the brothel all wear masks, playing both the female and male parts—breathtakingly scandalous, as usually male actors play both parts. Women aren't supposed to be on the stage, but Cynane knew such a shocking reversal of roles would titillate her audience of jaded middle-aged nobles. The chorus bewailing the tragedy is especially powerful. For the tiniest sliver of a moment, Cyn almost loses herself in the fiction.

At some point, Alecta sidles up to Cyn with a goblet of wine and whispers, "A good choice of play, my queen." Then she is gone, her delicate lavender scent sweetening the air.

Cyn wonders if perhaps Medea was also Smoke Blood—if that's why she killed her children, just as Cyn's own mother planned to kill her. But obtaining Smoke Blood isn't the only reason women betray and plot and kill. Cyn looks at the prostitutes before her, playing men so believably. They are strong, smart, willing to do whatever it takes to survive.

She twists her head around to look at the men in the audience. Most of them are old. Drunk. Useless. Suddenly she realizes she's been going about it all wrong—she doesn't need the noblemen's permission to be queen. All she needs is her own group of loyal supporters who are willing to defend themselves. Her warriors could be female, couldn't they?

Her heart beats faster when she realizes the added advantage of women fighters: the advantage of stealth. No one would suspect danger coming from a band of women. They could be spies, assassins, swinging swords out from under their robes and striking before Cyn's enemies had any idea what was happening. Men seem to think that Penthesilea, queen of the Amazons, who died by Achilles's spear at Troy—was myth only, an erotic tale for those who liked their women athletic.

Loud wails interrupt her racing thoughts. On the stage in front of her, King Jason has found the bloody bodies of his two young sons. Medea, laughing uncontrollably, flies upward on a barely visible rope and disappears into the trapdoor over the stage. The actresses take their bows to tremendous applause.

Waving a cup, Amyntas stands—none too steadily—and says to Cyn, "We're soooo booooored." Spittle flies out of his mouth and hits Cyn on the cheek. "Lesss usss depart... Tonight, I will schleep...in your chamber."

Cyn recoils. The thought of even sleeping in the same bed with him makes her skin crawl. But she nods, and when he stumbles, she catches him.

As they cross the courtyard, he leans against her heavily, then suddenly she doesn't feel his weight at all. She turns and finds her husband sprawled out facedown on the paving stones.

Papari is there in an instant, as always, hands on his cheeks in his habitual comic gesture of surprise. "His Highness has seen fit to leave the realm of Bacchus and enter the realm of Morpheus," he says solemnly, looking down at the slovenly, unconscious figure. "Praise be to all the gods."

"Take him to his chamber," she commands sharply. Though he's as small as a girl, Papari has the strength of a large warrior, she knows, combined with an acrobatic skill she has never before seen. She has often wondered where he came from—his accent seems Macedonian—but the one time she asked him, he merely said, "The moon," bent over backward, raised his tunic, and exposed his bare rear end. She never asked him again.

Now Papari stares at her with his huge, watery blue eyes. "What is it?" she asks impatiently.

"It's just that I never noticed before how square your jaw is, Majesty," he says, and for once he speaks like a normal person instead of a fool. He tilts his head and adds, "I saw King Philip once, and for the first time I can see your resemblance to him."

Then Papari, who can never be serious for more than two sentences, starts batting his eyes at her and giggling. "But I imagine being married to Amyntas would make a man out of any woman if she's going to survive!" he crows, hoisting the king over his shoulder and staggering off.

A burst of excitement shoots through Cyn like a meteor blazing and crackling across the night sky. She grabs a torch off a column wall and hurries through the dark corridors and curling staircases to her room. She sets the torch in a wall sconce, then picks up her silver hand mirror from the cosmetics table and stands next to the brightly flickering light. It's hard to be exactly sure in the changing shadows—she'll wait impatiently for daylight to make certain—but her jaw, once round and soft, now seems squared and sharp.

She runs a finger across her chin, and smiles.

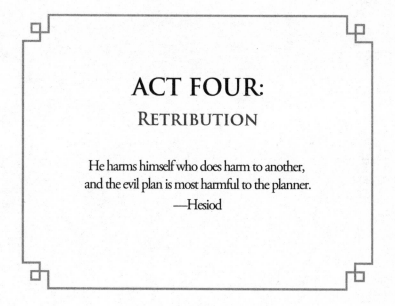

ACT FOUR:

RETRIBUTION

He harms himself who does harm to another,
and the evil plan is most harmful to the planner.
—Hesiod

CHAPTER TWENTY-TWO: RAT

RAT HONES HIS DAGGER ON THE WHETSTONE the way Yuf showed him, angling the blade slightly so that it winks in the sun, and dragging it slowly across, then turning it around to do the other side. It makes a horrible shriek that hurts Rat's ears, but if he complains Yuf might strike him again.

Now the large man strides across the courtyard toward him, his bald head glistening in the heat, and Rat feels a little spike of fear. What has he done wrong now?

"She's here," Yuf says gruffly. "The priestess is here. Come with me."

The priestess.

For weeks now, Yuf has talked about the priestess, their leader, the wisewoman who arranged for Rat to come here, for both his training and his healing. Rat must show her his gratitude, Yuf said, show her his absolute obedience. For if it wasn't for the priestess, Rat would still live in the cold gray north, his tongue thick and unwilling, his mind slow, his body weak.

Rat slips the dagger into his belt and runs beside Yuf out of the courtyard, down the dusty street lined with small shops and houses, and outside the town gate. The Nile waters are receding now, revealing a new layer of thick black earth in which the farmers will plant grain. In the summer, the river rose all the way to the village itself, lapping against this outer wall.

Yuf and Rat walk on the raised walkway down to the river landing, over black mud and sloshing, ankle-deep water. At the landing, stepping off a brightly painted barge, is a heavily veiled woman, petite and slender, holding a lidded basket in the crook of her elbow. There's something about the graceful way she moves that reminds Rat of a girl in that other life…

Yuf bows to her and cuffs Rat, who hastily follows suit.

"Priestess," Yuf says, "all is as you directed. I think you will be pleased."

The woman pulls aside her veil and smiles at Rat, and he feels his mouth drop open.

For standing in front of him is someone he knows he knows. Someone from his other life. Someone who'd been kind to him, played with him, comforted him when he was scared.

And slowly, the name comes to him, bright and shining.

"Sarina!" he gasps.

Her eyes are large and black, fringed by thick lashes, and they smile at him. "I am so very glad to see you again, Rat," she says. "That is your new name, I hear. A new name for a new boy."

"Yes," he says, barely able to contain his joy.

"I have a present for you." She opens her basket and takes out a long brown rat, shiny black eyes blinking in the bright sun, pink nose twitching.

"Heracles!" Rat cries, gathering his pet into his arms. "I thought I would never see him again." He puts the rodent on his shoulder, near his neck, where he always liked to be, and Heracles settles there just as if they had never been separated.

"He wandered around your old room in the palace looking for you," Sarina says. "I fed him cheese, and when I left I took him with me. Come, Rat. I need to show you something impor-tant so that you will understand why I have brought you here."

She offers him her hand. He looks at Yuf to see if it is all right, but Yuf just says, "Do whatever the priestess tells you," and marches back to town.

Hand in hand, Sarina and Rat walk toward the Temple of Sobek, its golden limestone walls rising square and solid out of the still-receding water. In the winter, the non-flood, it is on the banks of the Nile, and pilgrims from the village walk up a long staircase. In the summer, it is an island, reached only by the floating bridges they walk on now.

At the entrance Sarina drops a coin into the basket of the temple guard, who smiles, revealing brown stumpy teeth. They cross the courtyard and enter the sanctuary with its enormous, brightly painted statue of the crocodile-headed god standing solemnly at the far end, torchlight flickering off his gilded snout and pleated white kilt.

"You have been here before, I think?" she asks.

"Yes, the priests have given me medicine," he replies. But the best medicine of all is having Heracles back. It feels so good to have him perched on his shoulder again, to feel his whiskers tickling his neck.

She nods. "Do you know how old this temple is?"

He shakes his head. He was never very good at understanding time, and the priests haven't been able to fix that. In that other life, people were mad at him when he missed meals or sat hungry at an empty table two hours early. "Older than me?" he guesses.

She flashes him a brilliant smile. "It is much older than twelve years," she agrees. "It is more than two thousand years old, in fact." She pauses, evidently to let that sink in.

He can't quite wrap his mind around such an age, but he says, because it seems like the expected thing to say, "That is very old indeed."

"Look at this," she says, sweeping over to a wall covered with the funny picture writing the Egyptians use. Birds, hands, feet, snakes... They must be fun to draw, more fun than the Greek letters his tutor tried to get him to learn in that other place before giving up in frustration. "This is a prophecy, my friend. A story about something that will come true."

Rat stares at the picture writing. Heracles, too, arches forward, wringing his paws. "What does it say?"

Sarina gestures to the symbols, her golden bangles clinking on her slender brown wrist. "It says here that a golden-haired prince of the north, a young man with one blue eye and one brown eye, will conquer Egypt. If we don't stop it first." She turns to Rat. "Have you any idea who this prophecy could be talking about?"

Rat sees him so clearly in his mind's eye. The hair shining like the sun, one eye dark as Nile mud, the other as blue as the midday Egyptian sky. He remembers his kindness, his patience, his laughter, when everyone else was mad at him.

"Yes," he says sadly. "My bro—" No, not his brother. He isn't allowed to say that anymore. Not even to think it, or Yuf will beat him. "The prince of Macedon," he says, squaring his shoulders.

"Correct," she says, tilting her head to study him. "Three years ago, Rat, the Persians conquered us and killed or sold into slavery my entire family, including myself. I will not let it happen again. Not to Egypt, and not to me. Before I left Macedon, the prince showed me his darker side—cruel, selfish, arrogant—which just proved to me I was right in bringing you here."

Rat stares at his dusty toes poking out of well-worn sandals. He doesn't understand. What she is saying can't be true.

"We are not ready to deal with him yet," she says, tilting his head up with one cool finger under his chin, "but soon. Very soon. Do you understand?"

Rat feels that his head is impaled on her finger, but the rest of him slumps. He wants to argue with her, to tell her that the prince would never hurt anyone like that, that the prince is good.

But it is easier to say, "Yes."

CHAPTER TWENTY-THREE: ZOFIA

"PRINCE ALEXANDER IS GONE, PRINCESS."

Gone? Zofia blinks in confusion. Is it possible she has misunderstood him? The accent of Radamanthos, Macedonian royal chief of protocol, is strange, much harsher than the soft, gentle tones of the Greek speakers of Sardis who have been living there so long their cadences sound almost like Persian.

Radamanthos bows, the top of his silver hair gleaming with oil. "Gone," he repeats, spreading his hands. The royal counselors waiting with him at the dock in Lakeport seem as embarrassed as he is. They shift their weight, playing nervously with their gold chains of office and adjusting the folds of their bright red cloaks that flap in the brisk autumn wind.

Zo is speechless. Her only hope to slay the Spirit Eaters has gone. All the fine speeches she memorized, all the daring plans… They were for nothing. Her nervousness at meeting her betrothed ebbs away, along with her final chance of salvation.

He is gone. The words rattle around in her head like the last autumn leaves scuttling in little circles in a courtyard before the gardener sweeps them up.

"Where did Prince Alexander go?" she asks, her voice a flimsy, brittle thing.

"To Byzantium, Princess, for his father's wedding," Rada-manthos replies in his rich ringing voice.

"When will he be back?" she asks. *Soon.* He must come back very soon.

Radamanthos shrugs, his arms outstretched in the ancient gesture of not-knowing. "We have no idea," he says. "He may come back immediately after the wedding, or perhaps he will stay awhile and visit with his father, the king. I am so sorry for the inconvenience. We expected you earlier in the summer and only just received word a week ago that you would arrive, possibly on this very ship."

Ochus steps forward, and the Macedonians eye his lion skin with admiration. "We understand," he says, so agreeably that he's almost unrecognizable to Zo. "This is no one's fault. But now the princess needs to bathe, eat, and rest."

"Of course!" Radamanthos says. "Please, Princess, let me escort you to the carriage we have brought for you and your servants."

Staring out her window as the coach rattles along, Zo sees a prosperous land of fields and orchards. The walled city of Pella isn't so different from Sardis, well-dressed people bus-tling about busy streets filled with shops and taverns. It is only when she passes the tall gates of the Pellan palace that she can tell at a glance she isn't in Persia anymore. Here the architec-ture is lighter, more open. There is a lilting delicacy, from the tapered columns to the ethereal wall paintings, while every-thing in Persian palaces—the heavy square turrets, the frescoes of enormous lions and monsters—speaks of a warrior's mind.

She studies the Persian soldiers riding smartly alongside her, the handmaidens and eunuchs in her carriage, and wonders which one is an Assassin, sent to kill her if Ochus doesn't. As she settles into her luxurious rooms, Zo stifles the urge to look under the bed and behind the tapestries. She reminds herself that with Alexander gone, she is safe for a time. For a very little time.

On Zo's first night in Macedon, Timandra, mistress of the queen's maids, sees to her bath, a meal, and rest—the traditional offerings of hospitality the world over. A tall woman of about sixty, iron-haired and straight-backed, Timandra issues orders like a general. Zo's Persian attendants, aided by new Greek ones, unpack her trousseau, marveling over her spangled robes and thick gold jewelry. Iris, a plump, motherly handmaiden, bustles about Zo's room lighting the lamps.

During the long days of waiting that follow, in the prince's sustained absence, Zo wallows indulgently in the freedom of being alone and unwatched. Her attendants are in the room next door, instructed not to disturb her each night until morning. Here there is no one to herd women into confined spaces like farmers do chickens. For the first time ever, she can roam a palace by herself instead of being constantly accompanied by eunuchs. When she walks down the palace's long, unfamiliar corridors every morning, the servants replacing the wall torches don't even glance at her. It is as if she has the magic power of invisibility, and the heady liberty that comes with it.

Perhaps, she begins to think, she may have time to figure out how to escape this noose growing tighter and tighter around her neck the more her belly expands. Her thoughts roam constantly to the freedom of escape. She could throw a servant's cloak over her head, put a basket over her arm, and just saunter out of the palace gates, into a new life for herself and her child without the threat of Assassins or an outraged Macedonian royal family.

Whenever she mentions escaping to Ochus, he assures her

that he has a plan. One he can't tell her about, but she needs to be patient. To wait.

What is his plan? How will he keep her safe? Zo wants to believe him. And, true to his word, he never seems far away. At night, when she lies sleepless in her four-poster bed, watching white smoke rise from her brazier and reach like long curling arms to the freedom of the window, she hears his footfall outside her door. Confident, steady, yet quiet, too, like the steps of a watchful lion. Sometimes his footsteps are like a lullaby, lulling her anxiety until she finally tips over into sleep.

Twice, she watched him in martial contests held between Macedonian and Persian soldiers in the odeon, a small theater-in-the-round in the palace compound. Whether it was wrestling, archery, or swordplay, Ochus always ended up the winner with his lithe grace, quick reflexes, and keen eye.

To celebrate, he obtained fine Persian wine for her, calling the Macedonian vintages as sour as vinegar mixed with sheep's piss, and instructed the palace cooks to make Persian delicacies for her table. Yet when he shares a meal with her and her attendants, he never looks at her or speaks a word. Just sits there, staring into his stew as if all the wisdom of the world lived among its lentils.

He cares for her—except when he doesn't. She wants to kiss him, wants to feel his arms around her. Yearns to feel safe again, the way he made her feel that last night on the ship. But she doesn't know how to make that happen and wonders if she will have the time to go mad, or if Prince Alexander will return first. If only Ochus could seem interested in her long enough, she would unburden herself of the enormous weight of her secret. Each evening, she tries to tell him but fails, the words withering on her tongue, the truth rattling her bones, making her cold even beneath her thick woolen bedcovers at night. And this particular night, she can't sleep at all. The child within her is turning, pulsing, keeping her awake with its own heartbeat, its will to live, to be known.

No one here knows, though her handmaidens have hinted that they have all gained a bit of weight on the long trip west, shut in the *harmanaxa* all day with baskets of food and nothing to do but eat. She is lucky that Persian robes are fuller, looser, than Greek ones. But someone soon, perhaps Timandra or Iris, will ask her when she expects to bleed so the cloths will be ready. And what will she do then?

She gets out of bed and dresses in her robes by the tiny flicker of an oil lamp, which she uses to light a torch. Another walk in the moonlit gardens might calm her nerves and still the churning within her womb. She sweeps down a wide marble staircase, torchlight playing against the walls and railings, and onto a colonnade surrounding the largest palace garden, the Poseidon Garden. It's not yet very late—many nobles are still awake and socializing, passing her tipsily with hardly a glance. Servants throw wood from wheelbarrows into cressets along the paths, creating a fiery orange glow in the courtyard. Standing with her hand on a cool white marble column, she hears men's voices coming down the path and the crunch of boots on gravel.

"…that Klaccus asked her eunuch to drop his pants for two gold staters and he did," says a Macedonian native in his harsh language. "I've never seen such a horrifying thing in my life. It pains me even to think about it."

Zo winces. Her tutors had always said barbarians would never understand eunuchs. How homeless boys who would otherwise starve to death or live in grinding poverty are given education, employment, even power. She truly loved some of the eunuchs at the Sardisian palace, their kindness, their humor and loyalty…

The other man chuckles, a low, warm rumble that reminds her of something sweet and safe. "I knew of one palace eunuch in Sardis who actually carried his amputated balls around with him in a tin," he says, his Macedonian softened by a Persian accent. The sound of the man's voice sends Zo back in time, back home to Sardis. She hovers nearby, hoping to catch and savor more of his accented lilt—even if his jokes are bawdy and ill-fitting the ears of a princess.

"I hope they don't bring the foul custom here," says the Macedonian, stopping in front of a cresset to warm his hands. From where she's standing she can see the backs of the two men, their chains of office glinting gold around the back of their red capes, the uniforms of royal counselors. "And I hope they send back to Persia the ones that arrived with the princess. It makes me nervous just looking at these half-men."

"You will never understand our culture, any of you."

"Quite a culture you have there, cutting off people's balls."

In response, the Persian laughs loudly, a rolling, delightful sound.

Suddenly Zo is paralyzed. The laugh...it has unlocked something inside her. It is rich, heavy, warm. It is...*familiar*.

"I wish I could have been here to welcome the Persian entourage at Lakeport," the Persian says. "The entire time I was in Athens arguing about trade with wily old men, I worried about leaving Prince Alexander's side, but he hasn't been here, anyway. Now I can relax and enjoy myself with my fellow Persians, speaking a cultivated language instead of your barbarous tongue. Have you heard what part of the empire the princess is from?"

Zo *knows* that voice. She ventures a few steps from the colonnade just as the Persian turns a bit from the cresset, warming his hands. The dancing firelight hits his face and she sees him: Cosmas.

Her first and only lover, and the father of her unborn child.

Zo's blood turns to ice. She is stiff, freezing, unable to move. She can only stand there helplessly gaping, taking him in, still unable to fully believe that her mind hasn't played some horrible trick on her. His face seems leaner, more severe. Why is he dressed in a white Greek tunic, and in the red cloak and gold chain of office of a royal counselor?

"Persepolis, I think," says the other man, oblivious to her presence. "The caravan came here on some kind of forced march."

The two men stride forward, only a few paces from her now. Zo's heart thumps so loudly she is surprised they can't hear it. Cosmas seems commanding, more confident than the shy soldier she fell in love with. His face looks both strange to her and yet so familiar. It's a face she never thought she'd see again...*couldn't* see again.

With horror, she remembers Kohinoor's prediction. *You will see the child's father again, but only once before his death. You will be the cause of his death.* A sickening lump of terror turns in the pit of her stomach, and she thinks she will vomit.

Before either of the men can spot her, she turns and runs back toward the stairs, knocking into a gentleman's elbow along the way. Her heart practically beats a hole through her chest. When she reaches her room, she grabs a nearby washbasin and retches over it. Has she condemned the father of her unborn child to death?

She straightens and stumbles to pour herself some wine to wash the acid taste from her mouth. Her fingers tremble as she pours, but she only splashes a little. Taking a sip, she tries to sort out what she knows.

Cosmas—*her* Cosmas—is in the employ of the Macedonian royal family.

And Kohinoor is both a soothsayer and a known liar. She lied to Zo about the loss of her child, but she also knew of her baby's existence before Zo was aware of it herself.

She moves to the window and gazes out on the garden through which Cosmas just walked. He is so close. Perhaps even now he stands over there where lamplight seeps out of closed shutters, or maybe he's gone into that ground floor room at the end, where men sing and slam mugs on tables. If she asks around, she can probably find him again within minutes.

He doesn't know of his child. The thought thunders through her, leaving her stomach turning again. *A man should know his child. A child deserves a father.*

But she can't risk it, can't risk testing the veracity of Kohinoor's prediction. Besides, something else is holding her back, too. This dull, leaden feeling in her chest, heavy and sad. It's Cosmas himself, she realizes. How he has changed.

No. How *she* has changed.

She leans on the windowsill, taking in the night breeze. She used to feel waves of tingly heat rise from her belly, flood her chest, and burn her cheeks when she saw Cosmas. She used to feel a rush of pleasure just saying his name, over and over again, to herself. Her heart leaped with excitement when she wrote his name and hers on a wax tablet, then used the warmth of her fingers to push the letters together.

Zo first saw him as she stood behind the lattice in the women's viewing room overlooking the male banqueters in her uncle's palace. King Shershah was honoring several soldiers who had rushed into a flaming apartment building and rescued the inhabitants. Cosmas was a head taller than the others, and darkly, devastatingly handsome. Tucking food into his pockets, he left the feast early. Zo found him in the courtyard, feeding stray kittens. And so, their romance had begun. Stolen moments, secret meeting places, ciphered notes, all aided and abetted by Zo's toothless old nurse, Mandana. Until that last night in the cellar storage room, where she insisted they consummate their love. And he complied.

Just now, looking at him in the cresset's glow, he seemed

almost a stranger. An extremely handsome, confident stranger, but a stranger nonetheless. Her heart has moved on.

Zo's breath catches in her throat as Ochus enters without asking. He closes the door behind him and walks into her room holding an oil lamp.

"How did you enjoy tonight's fig cakes?"

She turns to him. "What?"

He has done this every night since their arrival, coming by to ask about some dish or other. She suspects he does it so that it is both common sight and common knowledge to see the Persian princess confer with her head guard. So that if, should the time ever come, he must relay a message at a strange time of night, no one would consider it out of the ordinary. But tonight, as Zo contemplates life and death, the scorching flames of love and its cold ashes, it seems particularly ridiculous. If they are not going to have a sensible conversation, they shouldn't be having one at all.

"You are visiting me to ask about fig cakes," she continues coldly. "Last night it was the lemon yogurt. And the night before that the cheese-stuffed olives."

Ochus stiffens and sets down the oil lamp on a table. "I need to make sure you are pleased with Persian specialties amid all the barbarian cuisine," he says. "You are far away from culture here."

Zo shrugs. "It seems I am doomed to live among barbarians the rest of my life. For however short a time that is."

In two strides, he is in front of her, too close for courtesy, yet not nearly close enough for satisfaction. She wants to sway into his scent, the warmth she can feel emanating from his skin.

"If you could live anywhere in the world, Princess," he says, his voice rich and thick as dark honey, "where would it be?"

To her horror, she realizes her head has nodded toward him. She pulls back awkwardly and paces slowly around an

ivory-inlaid table, trailing her finger over its smooth polished surface.

"I have heard much about Babylon," she says, wondering
if he will laugh at her. "Of hanging gardens and ancient zig-
gurats that reach up to the sky. For three thousand years, as
empires rise and fall, Babylon has remained a center of learning, of mathematics, astronomy, medicine, engineering, art,
philosophy. There is a great library…" She trails off, embarrassed, and stops in her tracks.

He swings in front of her and tilts his head to one side,
his eyes shining. "I never knew you were interested in those
things."

Her eyes shift to avoid his face. "I…wasn't," she admits.
"Until recently, I thought all my tutors' lessons were a waste
of time and barely paid attention. All I wanted to do was gossip." She turns and starts walking the other way around the
table. "But on the interminable journey here, I had plenty of
time to think. I asked myself, if I survive the dangers here, if
the world survives the Spirit Eaters, and if a jinn comes out of
a lamp and tells me he will send me wherever I want, a free
woman, where would I go? And I decided, Babylon. I want
to learn so many things."

She feels his strong hand on her shoulder and turns. "Do
you?" he asks quietly. "I would like to learn them, too. I have
spent too much time learning how to kill. And death is more
of a waste than gossip, I assure you."

Death, yes. The image of Cosmas's face flickering in the
light of the flames hovers before her. She will be the cause
of his death. Though the thought of Cosmas no longer sends
her heart aglow, he did at one time mean so much to her—
everything to her.

"I must leave here, tonight," she says, realizing as the words
burst from her mouth that it's true. She has perhaps delayed
too long already. Now urgency quickens her pulse. Kohi-

noor's words loop in her head. Her thoughts scatter—it's too strange to be coincidence. Why is Cosmas here? She must go. She must—

"Zo, I don't understand," Ochus says, and she can hear the frustration in his voice. "The prince will be away from Pella for at least another fortnight, according to council, quite possibly longer. Nothing can possibly happen to you until his return. You know that."

What she knows is that her dreams of defeating the Spirit Eaters with Alexander by her side were foolish, childish fancies.

"Tonight," she says, feeling as though her throat is going to close up. He needs to understand. She grabs his upper arms, trying to make him see.

"I've told you, Zo, I have a—"

"Plan, I know, but there's no time and you've told me *nothing.*"

Ochus looks at her, and emotions seem to war in his eyes. "I can't," he whispers. "You'd only try to stop me." He has told her this before. He has told her she must wait, must be patient. This same lines, over and over—and she can no longer tolerate it.

"It doesn't matter, anyway," she says, her voice thick with a confusing mix of panic and helplessness, as though the very threads of fate have twisted around her limbs and throat.

"Please, Zofia. Tell me what's made you so upset. If someone in the palace has harassed you, has threatened you or your safety, I'll—"

"No," she gasps out. It's time. She must tell him.

"No," she repeats again, shaking her head. "It wasn't anyone else's doing. Not exactly. This is all my own fault. I..." A tidal wave of regret rises in her chest, and she's going to drown in the truth of it. Because this *is* all her fault...or all her fate.

"Zo." Now his voice is soft, so soft. He touches her cheek.

"You know I will never let any harm come to you." His arm is trembling with the intensity of his promise, his muscles flexed, and she knows—knows in that moment that he means what he says, that he will kill anyone who might hurt her.

And that crushes her more than anything else. That he *can* be trusted; that *she* is the one who has lied.

"But what if you can't prevent it?" she asks; her lips hardly move, the words hardly have a sound to them all.

"I don't understand," he says. "There's nothing I can't prevent."

She shakes her head, working so hard to hold the tears down inside her now that she is physically shaking from the effort. She turns her face away. She can't tell him Kohinoor's prophecy about Cosmas. He wouldn't understand, wouldn't believe, or perhaps wouldn't care. But she can tell him about herself. He will recognize the danger to herself and her child if anyone here in the palace realizes her condition.

And, if she is right about the prophecies on the cave wall, somehow her unborn child may save the world from the Spirit Eaters. She must protect the child at all costs. For everyone.

"The greatest threat to myself…is myself," she says.

"What do you mean?" he asks, frowning in confusion. "Are you going to…hurt yourself?"

"You don't understand," Zo bursts out, her voice breaking completely now. Her entire body has become a leaf in a windstorm. The words will undo her.

He rubs his thumbs on her shoulders, his eyes searching her face. "No," he whispers. "I don't."

She pulls away from his grasp, moves to the bed, where shifting shadows on the sheets remind her of blackbirds stretching and folding their wings. Wildly, fleetingly, she thinks of her little sister, Roxana, who loved the blackbirds that would alight on the blue-tiled fountains in the Sardis harem gardens, preening and flapping and splashing.

Even thinking the name—*Roxana*—causes a stab of sweet painful memory to lance the very core of her heart. Such a beautiful child.

Say it. She must say it. *Child.*

"I am with child, Ochus." The words are out. She is shocked by their heaviness, and sways now with the worst of the weight having been removed. "I am four months gone," she pushes on, turning now to catch his expression in the dim light. "I will show very soon. Don't you see? The future queen of Macedon is carrying another man's bastard to the bridal altar."

She feels his silence, how hard and how cold it is.

"Your soldier?" he asks, his voice flat. "The one you ran off from the palace to meet?"

She nods, squeezing her eyes shut. "Cosmas, yes. We were together one time..." she whispers.

In the interminable pause that follows, she wonders if he will slap her, throw her to the ground, call her names, leave and never speak to her again. She wonders if she can bear it.

Then he says, very quietly, "One time is all it takes, I hear."

She opens her eyes and sees him regarding her with something she can't read. It's not anger. It's...tenderness.

The shock of it is like a bolt of lightning through the middle of her, shooting hope through her and making her knees wobbly with its force.

"I had no idea," he says, shaking his head. "And to think... Everything you've been through... Everything I—"

"That doesn't matter now," Zo says. "What matters is that Prince Alexander can't return and find me...like this. Even in his absence, others might discover it. I must... I *must* leave. Tonight."

He starts pacing, hand on his sword hilt. "We will get you out of here..." he says. His eyes take on a faraway look. Already he is scheming.

Warmth rolls through her, mixing with gratitude and joy. Almost without thinking, she throws her arms around him and then he is turning his face down toward hers, and she can feel the slight bristle on his chin as it brushes her cheek—the clench of his jaw softens and their lips meet.

She kisses him, her own mouth parting at his touch.

She feels him inhale, and after an instant of surprise, he is kissing her back. Heat rushes through her like an inferno, though she is not sure if it is her heat or his, or both.

Somehow they are on the bed, and he is so gentle with her she can hardly fathom that he is the same man who easily strangles another with his bare hands, who slays two foes in the blink of an eye without making a sound. An *Assassin*.

"I love you." The words slip out of her, as light as the wind, as though spoken by it and not her. "I think I always have."

He kisses her tears away. "Zo," he says, stroking her hair, "I can't. We can't. I—"

"Please," she whispers.

He moans softly against her, then kisses her again. And again. Then he pulls away, enough to say, his words a whisper across her skin, "And I love you."

Gray light filters in through the cracks in the shutters, and Zo feels the familiar hot slice of panic she always does on waking. Then she remembers she doesn't have to be afraid anymore. Ochus.

But the tangle of sheets beside her is empty. She rolls over onto his side, savoring the musky notes of his cologne on them, and realizes they aren't warm. He has been gone for some time. She sits up, looking around the room. His sword and helmet, his precious lion skin, everything is gone except his blue cloak draped over a chair.

Sudden shouts ring out from the garden.

A scream pierces the air.

Zo leaps out of bed and opens the shutters, her feet cold on the marble floor. There's a commotion outside as guards with spears and shields race through the garden paths. All around the garden, other people are throwing open their shutters, leaning out and squinting down at the uproar.

Zo throws on a robe and a cloak and slides into slippers. Her handmaidens Barsine and Parmina burst into the room in night robes.

"Princess! Is there a fire?" Barsine asks, her wide face white with fear.

"I don't smell smoke," Zo says, pushing her way between them and into the corridor.

"Princess!" Chosroes call after her. "You must stay…"

But Zo is out of earshot. She's flying down the staircase and into the chilly garden, following the Macedonian guards down the path, past the fountain of a blue-bearded god holding a pitchfork, and to a door at the far end.

A guard bars her way with his spear. "Go back to bed, Princess," he says. "This is official business."

"I am your future queen, you fool!" she says, pushing his spear out of the way. "I demand to see."

The guard hesitates, moves out of the way, and bows.

Zo steps inside but isn't sure at first what she sees in the dark room. The air smells stale, thick and coppery. One of her shoes sticks to something, the other slips. Blood. There's blood all over the floor.

A guard throws open the window shutters and she sees bodies sliced open, guts tumbling out, heads nearly hacked off. Blood-caked swords catch the light and gleam dully. Her heart pounds like a battle drum. Calm. Stay calm. A guard turns a body over. It's one of her Persian soldiers, but next to him is a corpse in a Greek helmet and breastplate.

One of the bodies lies facedown, wearing a scarlet cloak. Many men here have scarlet cloaks. It could be anyone.

But when the guard turns this body over, she gasps and covers her mouth with her hand.

You will see the child's father again…

…But only once before his death.

Cosmas.

His white tunic is ripped open, and a gold chain of office dangles over a bloody X carved in the man's chest. It's the Assassins' Mark.

Something deep inside Zo knows—just *knows*—that Ochus has gone from Pella. The heat of him has drained from her, leaving ice in her veins. She let slip Cosmas's name, didn't she? Did Ochus somehow learn he was here, in the palace, a royal counselor? But Cosmas is a common Persian name. And why would he kill him, anyway? After last night, when their bodies and souls mingled, transforming into one, Ochus must have known Cosmas posed no threat.

Staring at the still, white face of the father of her child, Zo doesn't know if Ochus did this, or why he has left.

She only knows this: she cannot stay here. To save her child and herself, she must run.

Chapter Twenty-Four: Olympias

AS OLYMPIAS MAKES HER WAY THROUGH THE marble corridors of the Byzantine palace, she fights to keep her head above the rising waves of hope, then dread, then despair—one barreling after the other. If she is successful—*if*—she and Riel will finally rule together.

The Delphic oracle said Philip would die at the wedding of Cleopatra, the foolish girl he's going to marry tomorrow, making her Philip's seventh wife. Pythia said, too, that a lover would kill him. Even though Philip has had more lovers, male and female, than anyone she knows, Riel expects her to take care of it. He doesn't trust anyone else.

Not that she blames him. She would hate to leave such an important task in the bumbling hands of another. And she *wants* to be the one to make Riel's greatest dream come true, to secure his eternal love and gratitude. Ever since he's come back, she feels that he has been slipping away, pretending to still love her.

Once they have rid themselves of Philip, surely Riel's next step will be to discover the magic to make her young and desirable again. After all, Riel is a god, and he will find a spell to liberate Alex's body from his grip and reclaim his old form, giving her back both their son and her lover. Then she and Riel will rule the world, just as they dreamed when she was an ambitious but emotionally scarred girl named Myrtale, who longed for more.

After days of bad weather, during which she despaired that they would miss the wedding, their ship entered the great harbor late yesterday afternoon. The sky behind the hills of the city was lit with the coming sunset, painting the countless towers and temples the color of ripe melons. It was only steps from the dock to the grand palace on the hill.

Philip was glad to see Alexander, who seemed uncharacteristically obedient, and less glad to see Olympias, whom he evidently feared was here to ruin his wedding. She knew she needed to provide a selfish reason for her arrival or Philip would remain deeply suspicious. If she didn't play her role just right, he might even confine her to her quarters.

After she sent Alexander to his rooms, she told Philip she had come for their son's sake. Though Alexander excelled in battle, he had made many mistakes in his statecraft. And the priests, alarmed that his eyes had suddenly changed to green, foretold that some great change was afoot. Philip should come home, she said, wringing her hands with the convincingly wretched concern of a fearful mother. He could bring an entire Byzantine harem of new young wives as far as she was concerned, but he should come home and help Alexander.

He finally grunted his assent. Now she has free run of the palace. And she intends to make very good use of it.

Olympias nods at the two Macedonian guards in front of the young bride's door—men she knows from Pella—who uncross their spears and step aside, murmuring greetings. Opening the door, Olympias looks inside. She vaguely remembers the girl they call Cleo, niece of Attalus, from her visits to Pella earlier in the summer. The girl stared so brazenly at Alexander it became the brief but all-consuming gossip of the court. And now here she is, marrying Alexander's father.

Cleo sits before her cosmetics table as her handmaiden removes a hot curling tong from the brazier and rolls a long lock of black hair in it. Cleo is plump, voluptuous, like a succulent plum ready to be plucked. No wonder Philip desires her.

The handmaiden—a dark-haired woman of about thirty—slides the tong out of her hair and lays it back down on the brazier as she tugs on the springy curl and then pins it into place.

"He said I could wear the family's lapis lazuli necklace," Cleo says excitedly. "And the Egyptian emerald set."

Over Olympias's dead body.

"Wear them with my blessings," Olympias says lightly, slipping into the room as the girl and her maid look up in surprise. "They are for the young and beautiful. When Philip gave them to me, I was about your age."

The bride's face sets into hard, sullen lines. "That must have been a long time ago."

Olympias feels a stab of rage in her chest but she covers it agilely, smiling with just a trace of wistful sadness. Looking at the girl, her blue eyes flashing both fear and challenge, her anger subsides. She would have said exactly the same thing. Come to think of it, she *did* say similar things to Philip's other wives, and worse, driving them away until she was the only one left.

"Longer than I will admit," Olympias agrees pleasantly. She walks to the window and looks through the carved and painted slats at the breathtaking view of the harbor below. She adjusts her purple, fur-lined cloak—the wind off the water is cold and whistles through this open palace of balconies, peristyles, and wide windows. It must be delightful in the sultry heat of summer; less so now.

Olympias turns around to face Cleo. "I wanted to speak

with you before the wedding to reassure you that I am not your enemy. I have been ill lately—perhaps you've heard—and am planning to retire from court. Soon I will return to Epirus, where I was born, and live with my brother there."

Cleo and the maid exchange glances but say nothing.

"I know I have the reputation of being a jealous queen," Olympias says, sighing, "and it was true when I was younger. But not anymore. In fact, I am glad Philip is marrying you. Perhaps you can persuade him to stay away from less worthy laps."

Cleo frowns. "What do you mean by that?"

Olympias *tsks*. "Oh, nothing. Forget I mentioned it."

Cleo stares at her through the mirror. "I don't like secrets being withheld from me."

Olympias sighs. "I *told* him it would be unseemly to have the wedding here in Byzantium rather than home but, of course, he no longer listens to me." She smiles gently at Cleo. "I'm sure *you* will hold sway over him, though, even if you must first suffer through this small embarrassment."

"Embarrassment? It is *your* embarrassment, I should think." Cleo snorts, tossing her head like an angry horse. "He told me he wanted to have the wedding far from Pella so you couldn't ruin it."

"Hmm, how amusing of him," Olympias says. "I suppose he didn't share his favorite tales of this city with you, then."

"Tales?"

"Of all the amazing things the women in Byzantium can do with their bodies—apparently he is quite addicted to the life he has created for himself here."

Two angry pink circles bloom on Cleo's cheeks. "Well," she says, opening a cedar wood *pyxis* to reveal a heap of shining jewelry, "he won't need them once he has a young wife."

Olympias nods, fingering the item hidden beneath her cloak. "I can only hope his attraction to your charms will be enough to bring him to his senses. He knows what a terrible liability so many mistresses can be. But, Cleopatra, perhaps you can convince him to return to Macedon."

Cleo stabs her fingers into the mound of jewelry and plucks up a huge golden earring in the shape of a warrior's shield.

"I doubt the king wants another wife nagging him about what to do," she says, threading the wire through her right ear. Just like every member of the Attalid clan, her tongue is sharper than her wits.

"Of course he doesn't," Olympias concurs. "What man does? The secret is to persuade him that your ideas are his ideas, and then applaud his infinite wisdom. That way you can get whatever you want from him, for yourself and for your *family*." The Attalids, known for their unquenchable thirst for wealth and power, have always reminded Olympias of a pack of rather stupid, very hungry wolves.

Cleo, holding the second earring, arches a black eyebrow with interest and turns to Olympias. "Why are you trying to help me?"

"You remind me of myself when I was young," the queen says. "And I've never had a daughter."

A lie, of course, but Cleo's eyes no longer seem as narrowed. Now to reel in the fish.

"I have a gift for you," Olympias continues. "Something I know he has always favored." She proffers an exquisite tiny painted clay jar in the shape of a hedgehog, its eyes polished green stones.

Cleo takes the jar and asks suspiciously, "What's in it?"

"A lip color," Olympias says. "Made with red dye from the pregnant kermes beetle and other unguents, an aphrodisiac worth its weight in gold. It always drove Philip wild with desire when I wore it."

Interested now, Cleo removes the stone stopper and sniffs. "Smells lovely," she murmurs, then looks up at Olympias, her eyes narrowing. "*You* put some on," she says, thrusting the jar toward her.

Suppressing a chuckle, Olympias dabs her finger in the red jellylike mixture and rubs it on her own lips. Then she takes the silver hand mirror from Cleo's cosmetics table and studies herself. "What I like about it is that kissing doesn't take away the color. It's a dye that stains your lips. You will wake up with some color still on them."

Cleo stares at her and says stubbornly, "You might have taken an antidote. Eumakia, you try some."

Reluctantly, the handmaiden dips her finger in and smears the salve on her lips with a shaky finger.

"It seems all right," she says, her voice tremulous.

"Lick it," Cleo insists.

The handmaiden's pink tongue darts out, slides over her lower lip, and retreats from view. They wait. Nothing happens.

"You are very smart to be careful," Olympias says approvingly. "Always have everything tested—even clothing—before you eat it or use it. Remember Princess Glauke."

Glauke was a young princess of Corinth whom the hero Jason planned to take as his second wife. But his first wife, Medea, was so angry she gave the girl a gorgeous gown lined with burning poison that consumed her flesh when she tried it on. She died in agony.

The similarity between the two situations should be alarmingly clear, but Cleo must be too stupid to understand. She is, after all, just an Attalid. And the silly girl returns to putting on her earring. A long, slow smile spreads across Olympias's face.

"Wear the lip color for the festivities tomorrow," she suggests. "He won't be able to resist you on the wedding night. And if that goes well, you'll have him in your power, I have no doubt. No doubt at all."

The big blue eyes stare boldly back at her. "What do you want in return?" Cleo demands.

No, this one isn't stupid exactly. She has the street smarts of a cunning olive merchant. Olympias wrinkles her face into what she hopes is an expression of worry.

"Just a bit of kindness toward my son," she says, "when I am gone, and you are the most powerful woman in the kingdom."

The girl shrugs. "We'll see."

We will indeed, Olympias thinks.

For mixed in with the kermes red, the honey and rosemary, the myrrh and lemon rind and rose oil, is a concentrate made from the fleshy purple pulp of rare Persian mulberries. Olympias still recalls years ago when she wore an oil with the berry's sweet essence—harmless to anyone else. But when Philip leaned in to kiss her neck, he began to choke just from the scent. His eyes watered and his face broke out in red blotches.

Palace physicians agreed the berries were a poison to him—and him alone. Some people have a strong reaction to certain foods or plants, they said, and she knew they were right. Shellfish gave Olympias's father itchy red welts. Her brother vomited when he ate pork. But Philip's extreme reaction to just a whiff of the berries in oil meant a single taste of it would be more deadly than arsenic, according to the doctors. She gave away the mulberry cream.

But she has not forgotten.

CHAPTER TWENTY-FIVE: JACOB

JACOB THROWS AN OLIVE PIT INTO THE FIRE AS cold fingers of wind curl the smoke around him. Drunken songs float in the chilly night air as a glow of torchlight slides across the blackness above the garden wall. The Byzantines are already celebrating tomorrow's royal wedding of their conqueror, King Philip of Macedon, to young Lady Cleo, niece of Attalus of the house of Attalid.

How quickly people change sides when it offers an advantage. Whose side is Jacob on? He thought he had devoted himself body and soul to the Aesarian Lords, but he didn't even send word to High Lord Gideon that he had survived the Delphi earthquake. He and Pythia walked the short distance to Kirra, the port nearest Delphi, boarded a ship for Athens, and there found another headed to Byzantium. The late-autumn storms were atrocious, waves beating them back toward Greece like giant gray fists, and there were times standing on deck that his impatience almost pounded right out of his head. They arrived only this morning, a mere day before the royal wedding.

So little time to carry out his plan to capture Riel.

The very name sends shivers down his spine. He will never

forget the evil power of the god posing as Alexander in the oracular chamber, the blazing green eyes staring directly at Jacob. He will never forget the pure loathing in them, and the horror that made his blood freeze in his veins.

A cold gust whips up the fire, causing the logs to burn more brightly. Pythia wraps her arms around herself. Jacob wishes once again that he'd been able to find them a room in this sprawling city. But when their ship docked in the magnificent harbor, they found Byzantium crammed with soldiers, diplomats, merchants, and country folk hoping to see a spectacle. All the inns were booked; he knocked on doors up and down several streets asking for a room in a private home, but they, too, were taken. Finally, a spice merchant, struck by Pythia's obvious exhaustion, agreed they could camp under the laundry lean-to behind his house for a steep price.

Pythia sets down her plate, her meal half-eaten, and stares at him. He feels her gaze first, a kind of heat on his face, then turns and sees her large eyes reflecting the fire's flicker.

"Well," she says in a soft voice, "we've made it. Have you decided on our plan?"

"Not *our* plan. *My* plan," Jacob corrects her. He takes a deep swig of wine, relishing the rich fragrant liquid slipping down his throat. "You can't get anywhere near Riel, even with your disguise. It's too dangerous."

Not just Riel, but any of the thousands of pilgrims who have sought a prophecy at Delphi might recognize the pale, slender girl with golden-red hair, so unusual in the southern Greek lands. Jacob kept Pythia veiled until they got to Athens, where he bought her a long black wig and makeup. With black brows, heavily lined eyes, and bright red lips, she looked nothing like the young, fragile oracle.

"Since a fake prophecy is out of the question this time, will you fight him?" Pythia persists. "You look stronger than him."

Jacob shakes his head. "He is a *god*," he says, setting the wineskin down in the dirt. "Even the strongest mortal can't overpower him single-handedly. But if I can't fool a god, or trap a god, maybe I can lure a god to me."

"Lure?"

"Growing up, I used to hunt to provide food for my family." He pauses a moment, remembering when life was simpler. Helping his father bake pots in the kiln. Milking the goats. Hauling water from the well. Back before he knew of kings and gods and oracles. Before he knew of evil, of loss, and of the strange magic humming in his blood. Back when he was naive enough to think he perfectly understood who he was in the world.

A log cracks and falls, creating a shower of blazing sparks that instantly cool to ash. He continues. "I would lure animals into traps with something they couldn't resist. So, I've been thinking. What could I get to lure Riel to me? And the answer is clear: the queen."

"The queen?" Pythia frowns. "Olympias?"

"Yes," Jacob replies, leaning closer to her, excitement pumping through his veins. "I will kidnap her tomorrow, and then ride for the Eastern Mountains and the Fountain of Youth. I'll inform Riel—Prince Alexander—that I have his 'mother' and will ransom her if he comes personally with the money. But when he arrives at the appointed place, he will find himself surrounded by the mightiest Aesarian regiments. Not even the Last God could fend off an army of such warriors."

He turns toward her. "It will save the world from Riel's evil, and the Lords will make me one of their most powerful leaders."

And forgive him for his Blood Magic.

But he can't say that. She doesn't know, nor does she know about sacrificing magic bearers to the Spirit Eaters. He has kept that Aesarian secret.

Pythia looks at him with sad eyes. "What if he doesn't love

the queen? Sometimes…you love someone who doesn't love you back. Or, at least, not enough."

Jacob considers the question. He has no idea of the relationship between Olympias and Riel. Still, as a soldier he understands tactics.

"It doesn't matter if he loves her or not," he says, "he still needs her. Riel believes only Olympias can kill Philip. He told you that much at Delphi. I just need to capture the queen before she kills the king."

She sighs. "Do you ever feel like the thing you want is just outside your grasp?"

The firelight flickers. "Sometimes…yes," he says, thinking of his goal of capturing Riel, but also of something else, something even deeper. He's thinking of Kat. What if he was having this conversation with her? He imagines her analyzing his plan in detail, pointing out its weaknesses, making suggestions, arguing with him, making him laugh. But Kat is far away from here, in Pella. Safe in the palace all these months.

Or perhaps she has returned to his family in Erissa—her family, too, ever since they took her in after her mother's mysterious murder. He imagines Kat baking bread with Sotiria, helping Cleon sweep out the kiln, making sure his little brothers have clean tunics and plenty to eat. How he misses the boys. At twelve, Phinias is gangly like a colt, all arms and legs, but a hard worker with a talent for pot making that Jacob never had. Linus, two years younger, can do any sum in his head, and already helps with tallying costs and income. At eight, Calas is interested in everything. Pot making. Farming. Hunting. A ball of tireless energy unperturbed by the bruises and cuts he wears like badges of honor from playing too hard.

Jacob sent them most of his bag of gold, the prize he won as victor of the Blood Tournament in the summer, with a note suggesting they buy more land and improve the farm. Ever since he became a member of the Elder Council, he has been meaning to send Cleon more money to build a second kiln and hire an assistant. He wants to give his mother a bright red gown and a pair of golden earrings, luxuries she always dreamed of. He wants to send his little brothers to a real school so they will know more about the world than Jacob did.

"Tell me," Pythia says, shifting his focus from the warm memories of home to the dark chill of the here and now. "Why am I still here? Why have you brought me all this way?" Her voice trembles. "You don't need me with you, and without Apollo's vapors, I never know when I will go into a trance and prophesy."

Jacob opens his mouth but nothing comes out. He couldn't just leave her alone, not after she risked her life for him. Not after he almost killed her by setting off the earthquake that toppled the roof beam that crushed her ribs.

She looks at him expectantly, hopefully... The black wig lies beside her on her sleeping mat; she has washed the makeup off her face, and without it she looks so soft and sweet. He wonders what it would be like to hold a girl like that in his arms, to stroke her long hair, gleaming with golden firelight. To maybe, even, kiss her.

The last time he kissed a girl was during the Battle of Pellan Fields, when Kat lay bleeding. He remembers thinking, *This is the last time I will ever kiss her*, and his lips touched hers...

Suddenly—he's not sure how—he and Pythia are kissing, gently, carefully. He pulls slowly away, wondering if this is really what she wants. A flush suffuses her pale cheeks, and her eyes shine with happiness.

He goes back for more, enjoying the warmth of her, the sweet fragrance. Feeling her in his arms, her heart beating against his, he realizes how wretchedly lonely he has been. Back in Erissa, he always had Kat, ever since he was seven years old. They ate together. Worked together. Laughed and played together. But after they came to Pella and he lost her to the prince, he has felt as if a piece of himself were missing.

He moves his hands inside Pythia's cloak, encircles her slender waist, and draws her closer to him. She gasps, kissing him back, pulling him even more closely toward her. Wind hurls itself beneath the little roof of the lean-to like a catapult stone, causing the fire to wave wild orange arms in all directions and smoke to wrap around them.

Immediately she stops and pushes him away, clutching her head. "The Voices," she whispers, coughing and shaking violently. "The lights... They... Oh."

She rocks from side to side, murmuring nonsense words, or perhaps she is speaking some ancient language known only to the gods. He waits, wondering if he should bring her back to herself or if he should sit quietly and listen; perhaps the gods have a message for him.

"Girl," she practically growls. "The gazelle girl."

Jacob's heart skips a beat.

"She is on the water," Pythia continues, rolling her head. "The gazelle girl is on the water, very close now."

"What gazelle girl?" he asks, though he already knows.

"Coming, coming. She's coming. For your heart," Pythia says, and suddenly she lets out a low moan, a sound of ache and fury. "No, wait, she *has* your heart! She always had it... she always *will* have it!" Pythia shakes as she screams.

Jacob grabs her by the shoulders and pulls her to her feet, away from the fire, and into the cold clear night air beyond the lean-to.

"Pythia!" he cries, shaking her. "Pythia! Come back!"

She thrashes from side to side, coughing. Then, suddenly, she is sapped of energy and goes as limp as a rag doll. He catches her as she slips to the ground, and slowly lowers her to a sitting position. "Pythia," he whispers in her ear. "Please."

Her eyelids flutter open. She stares at him as if she has never seen him before. "Why do you call me that?" she asks, her voice loud and raw.

"Are you all right?" he asks. "I think the smoke caused you to go into a trance."

"I know," she says, hanging her head. "I remember." She shakes her head, her eyes squeezed shut. "The Voices are never clear, but I understood enough...enough to know...that you love someone else."

He can't deny it.

He will always love Kat, even if he lives to be a hundred and never sees her again. His love for Kat is as much a part of him as the beating of his heart. It will never fade, never disappear, until death. And maybe not even then.

Pythia's eyes plead with him, but he can't lie to her. That would be even crueler than the truth.

That night, they sleep side by side, close to the fire. Pythia falls asleep immediately, or pretends to. Jacob lies awake, trying to think of ways to get into the palace tomorrow, but thudding in the background of his racing thoughts is Pythia's prophecy. *The gazelle girl. She's coming across the water...she's coming for your heart.*

He pulls his cloak more closely around him as the cold wind howls and checks to make sure Pythia is well covered. He's sad he's hurt the sweet, brave girl who risked her life for him, but the heart doesn't always choose whom to love. He knows that better than most, and as he drifts into sleep he wonders why the gods delight in tricks such as these.

Hours later, the ragged cries of roosters wake Jacob. He sits up to see a gray, chilly morning and a dead fire. Turning, he finds that Pythia is gone...as is her sleeping mat and water skin, though the black wig lies on the ground like a dead animal.

He jumps up, looking around the backyard of this town house. Chicken coop. Smokehouse. Latrine. No Pythia.

Stunned, he notices something at his feet, words etched

into the dirt with a stick. Words that cause his heart to fall into his stomach with sadness and self-reproach.

You never asked for my true name. I am Patra.

Jacob marches down the chilly marble corridors of the Byzantine palace, nodding to the guards he passes. He's grateful that the nosepiece and cheek flaps of his Macedonian helmet hide much of his face; one of these guards might recognize him as a former colleague who joined the Aesarian Lords, now Macedon's enemy. Still, his training as a Macedonian guard gives him the confidence to play one.

He started scouring the streets and taverns early, looking for an off-duty Macedonian soldier diving headlong into wedding celebrations. Pushing his way through the narrow, winding streets teeming with parades, dancers, musicians, religious processions, and hawkers of bread, wine, sausages, and head wreaths, he looked everywhere for a red cloak and a red horsehair crest on a bronze helmet. As the sun rose higher, Jacob began to despair of finding one. And his thoughts took a prohibited turn: Pythia's prophecy that the gazelle girl who had his heart was coming, coming here to Byzantium. The mere thought of Kat pulls something apart in him, like claws relentlessly picking at a fraying thread, and threatens to unravel him entirely. He must not think of Kat coming here, of seeing her, touching her, or he will go mad.

Then he saw him, a tall man, like himself, staggering away from a tavern. Jacob sprang into action, clapped the man on the back like an old friend, pulled him into an alley, gave him a quick punch that knocked him unconscious, and took his uniform.

Getting through the heavily guarded main palace gate was ridiculously easy. The crowds watching the jugglers and acrobats performing in front of the gates parted willingly for a Macedonian solider. He marched right up to one of the guards, saluted smartly, and said, "Erastus, sir, reporting for duty."

When the guard asked the password, Jacob, who knew

Philip used his mistresses' names, scratched his neck, made a face, and said, "Phoebe. Alcmene. Melia. I'm sorry, sir, but I can't keep up with them."

The guard had shaken his head and said, "There's a new one. Maia. An *acrobat*." He winked.

"If only he'd give us his leftovers," Jacob said, shaking his head. Laughing, the guard opened the gate and let him in. It had been as easy as that.

Inside, he stopped a guard to ask for the location of the queen's rooms. Now he rounds the corner and sees another guard standing in front of the double doors.

"I'm here to relieve you," Jacob says to the small, wiry man.

"Really?" the man asks, a hopeful expression on his narrow face. "So soon?"

"Orders," Jacobs says, nodding.

"Thanks be to all the gods. I've had to pee for over an hour." He starts to go, then turns back and asks, "The password?"

"Maia." The guard nods and leaves.

Jacob waits a long moment, then opens the door a crack and peers in. The queen sits in front of a little table by the window, studying herself in a silver hand mirror. The table is littered with bottles and makeup brushes. She takes a hairpin and pushes it into a mound of silver-blond curls, admiring the effect. Jacob feels Pythia's black wig, tucked under his tunic. Once he has knocked the queen unconscious, he will put the wig on her and pretend she's a drunken prostitute he has been ordered to remove from the palace grounds.

Silently, he enters and closes the door behind him. She must see him in the mirror because she asks, without turning around, "Well, what is it?"

He approaches her on silent feet.

"Are you mute?" she snarls. "It's not time yet. Or have you brought me a message?"

She slides gracefully around on her stool and looks at him questioningly. His heart skips a beat. It isn't the queen. Or is it? The person who stands in front of him looks like an older, somewhat skeletal sister.

"Queen Olympias?" he asks, unsure.

"Of course it is, you fool," she snarls. "What do you want?"

He hesitates. What happened to her? Just months ago, she was beautiful, voluptuous, desirable. "You've changed," he says in shock.

Her jaw tightens, and her green eyes rake over him in bright fury. "I know you," she says slowly. "You were the victor of the Blood Tournament, weren't you? You were the friend of that girl, Katerina."

"Y-yes," he says, unsure now.

A slow, unpleasant smile spreads across her face. "My condolences," she says with mock courtesy.

Condolences? Is she making fun of him for losing Kat?

He makes a dismissive gesture. "It doesn't matter," he snaps.

"What?" she asks archly, tilting her head. "The loss of your entire family doesn't matter?"

Loss of his family? Jacob's heart drops like a stone. He can't speak. Can't ask. Doesn't want to know but must know...

"They've changed, too," she says triumphantly, feeding off the shock and misery in his face. "Now they're burned bones. A far greater change than even I have experienced, wouldn't you say?"

He suddenly feels he is a mouse, batted back and forth between the paws of a sadistic cat. She is toying with him, torturing him, and enjoying every moment of it.

Is she telling the truth? Or is she punishing him for injuring her vanity? No, there's something about the look in her eye. This is real. His head starts to pound. Every part of his being shrieks a silent *No*.

"What..." he begins. "How..."

Olympias cocks her head, studying him. "Your family wouldn't tell me where Katerina was, so I had my soldiers kill them all. We burned the house to the ground."

His vision swims red and black. The room in front of him pulsates, in and out, along with the thudding of his heart. She's still talking, though Jacob can only make out some words in between the gong ringing in his head. "Blood... Screams... Flames."

Her eyes glisten with pleasure. That painted, scarlet red mouth pulls into a mocking sneer and keeps moving. She's clearly savoring the pain she is inflicting on him, each word like the blow of an iron-tipped whip.

"Quiet," he says, putting up his hands, then clapping them over his ears. "No more. *No more.*"

The raging anger inside him slips deep into the earth and rock beneath the palace, causing the hill to shudder. Through the open window, he sees the waves in the harbor jumping, roughly jostling the boats. Inside the whirling, ringing maelstrom of hatred and despair, he tells himself to control his powers. He doesn't want to hurt innocent people, as he did in Delphi. He wants to hurt only one person—the one sitting in front of him, laughing as she continues to describe his family's death agony.

But he needs to stop that mouth and the words that are knives, sharp and serrated against his chest. She must see the rage reflected in his eyes, because her face turns white as she says, "There is a guard just outside that door, you fool. If I scream, he will slice you in two."

Jacob shakes his head, feeling like the sacrificial bull stunned by the priest's hammer.

"I am the guard," he roars.

He lurches toward her, reaching for her throat. He will make her take back her words, take back what she has done.

But before his hand touches her flesh, she whips an ivory hairpin out of her coiffure and swings wildly at him. The double-points meet his outstretched arm and he recoils, but not before she has cut him—a twin set of long ragged marks running from his elbow to his wrist. Blood blooms from the wound, but Jacob feels nothing. He catches her slender wrist, crushing bone in his grasp, and she screams out in pain as she drops the hairpin.

He looks into Olympias's frightened eyes then, and the power of his fury moves through him as he slams her head hard against the table, shattering delicate glass bottles of scent and paint. She slumps to the floor, red and blue face paint smeared on her cheeks, shards of glass in her scalp. Blood flows from the wounds, turning her silver-blond hair bright red and pooling on the floor.

He breathes heavily and, slowly, kneels beside her. The queen's head, its bloody curls falling out of their pins, lies next to a mosaic of Medusa, her tendrils ending in snake heads, the sight of which turned men to stone. Jacob feels as heavy and numb as stone right now.

As he stares at her, a coldness sets into his bones. What has he done? No. *No.* All his plans…

Quickly, frantically, he leans down to feel her neck. He can't feel a pulse. Is she breathing? He can't tell. She looks so pale. Her glassy, open eyes. The torrent of blood. Silver hair saturated red. He feels faint. Realizes now that hers isn't the only blood dripping onto the floor. Her hairpin cut him deeply. He stares at his arm—blood oozing from the long scratches, puckering lines on either side of the wounds, bright pink against the pale skin.

He tries to stand but sways, dizzy. He has killed before, of course, but only in battle. Never like this. But she was cruel. Destroyed his whole family—his whole heart—his father and mother and brothers. He has lost everything.

And now, he has lost his means to capture Riel.

He stares at her unblinking eyes. There is no question in his mind now.

The queen is dead.

Jacob runs.

CHAPTER TWENTY-SIX:
HEPHAESTION

HEPH GRIPS KAT'S ARM AS THEY WEAVE THROUGH the riotous crowds celebrating in the streets of Byzantium. Every balcony is cram-packed with revelers. People even sit on the roofs, eating and drinking. This morning, their ship could hardly find a space to dock in the crowded harbor. And all the inns were full to bursting. When they asked what was going on, they learned that Philip of Macedon was marrying again. They finally found a tiny room in the attic of a private house for an exorbitant amount of money.

As they washed and unpacked, Heph worried about who else from Macedon might attend the royal wedding. Would Olympias be here, still seething with the desire to kill Kat? Would the prince? Even if they were here, there was very little chance he and Kat would run into them in such a crowded city. And yet, the shadow of the prophecy has lingered in the back of Heph's mind since he discovered Leonidas's remains after the palace fire in Macedon: the prophecy that indicated Kat would be the cause of Alexander's death. *In the womb of the night, twin stars struggle to shine their light...*

The moon would blot out the sun, the daughter would kill the son. It still seems, after all this time, unthinkable. But the memory won't go away, either. It's like an open cut, causing uncertainty to fester in his heart.

As Heph glances at the mechanism, making sure they are still following the arrow leading them to their Earth Blood, something nags at him—a tight lyre string plucked again and again in the back of his neck. Something is wrong, or about to be wrong.

The irony is, he had had no idea he would travel to Byzantium. But a few days ago, in Athens, the Atlantean Mechanism indicated their Earth Blood was still northeast.

"We could get a ship to Byzantium," Heph said, frowning at the needle, "and hope he or she isn't more northeast still—in the snow lands of the northern Scythians beyond the Euxine Sea."

Kat's jaw tightened, and her eyes narrowed, an expression that meant it would be pointless to argue with her. "Even if the Earth Blood is in the snow lands beyond the Euxine Sea, we must go there," she said.

A chilly wind hurls itself off the water and down the street, clearing for a moment the smell of fresh bread, spiced sausages, and urine. Heph pulls his cloak more tightly around him. Halfway to Athens they noticed the drop in temperature and sat shivering in their light summer cloaks. Meninx, just off the coast of North Africa, seemed to exist in an eternal summer. Heph had lost track of time but realized it must be almost winter. In Athens, they bought heavy clothing. They sorely needed new things, anyway, for while patched, stained tunics did not matter on an isolated island, their garb was no longer fit to be seen in public.

Now Kat, pushing through the crowds while sneaking glances at the mechanism, looks almost unrecognizable to Heph in a long, dark green robe and burgundy cloak, her hair in a neat bun. He will always think of her as the sea nymph of Meninx, her skin sun-kissed, her untamed hair whipped by the wind.

They turn a corner and see, atop the hill, the royal palace. Turrets, balconies, and columns, in green and pink and white marble, stand against silver-white clouds dappled like the scales of fish.

"The palace," Kat says in wonder, glancing down again at the mechanism in Heph's hands. The needle spins wildly, then stops, pointing directly at it, then spins and stops again. "The Earth Blood is in the palace. Look at what the needle is doing."

Heph's heart skips a beat. He cannot allow Kat into the palace until he finds out who else is in there. He tucks the mechanism into the pouch on his belt.

"A coin for a hungry man, my lord!" cries an old beggar, kneeling before Heph with uplifted hands. Heph reaches under his cloak for his money pouch and pulls out a bronze coin.

"Tell me about this royal wedding," he says, handing the coin over. "Are any of the king's relatives here from Macedon?"

The beggar rises stiffly, nodding. "His son, Prince Alexander, is here," he says. "Arrived yesterday."

Heph's heart sinks. He looks at Kat, who beams with excitement. What can he say to prevent her from marching right into the palace to find him? Between one prophecy, that an Earth Blood is required to kill Riel, and another saying Kat will be the cause of Alexander's death, Heph fears they are playing a dangerous game. He thinks of Aristotle's words. That magic has little to do with the fate of men. *The highest training of the mind is to see fate's strings.*

"He came with his mother," the beggar cackles, giving Heph a knowing look. "People have been saying the queen will try to ruin her husband's wedding to a girl less than half her age."

Kat's expression falls. Yes, this is exactly what Heph had been hoping to hear. An excellent excuse for keeping her away from the palace. Away from Alex.

He pulls her aside, under the canopy of a cheese shop. "You can't go to the palace with me," he says firmly.

"But—" she begins.

"No," he says, his fingers digging into her arm. "Last time the queen got a fingertip. This time it would be your head. I will find the Earth Blood and will let Alex know you're with me. You can't be anywhere near Olympias."

Or Alexander, the horrendous thought whispers.

The prophecy cannot be realized, not here, not ever. No matter how much he loves Kat, he must also protect Alex, his best friend.

Kat purses her lips in that stubborn way of hers, then, to his great surprise, instead of arguing with him, she nods and says, "You are right, Heph. You do it for both of us." She throws her arms around him and embraces him.

When he can finally pull himself away from the smell of her hair, he says, "Look, over here," and points to a large tavern on the corner. Despite the chilly weather, the out-side tables are filled with revelers drinking hot spiced wine. "There's an empty seat at that table. Take it, and I will meet you back here soon."

She turns sideways and slips between drunken people stag-gering out of the tavern singing, then takes the seat at the table, murmuring something to those already there. Relieved, Heph turns toward the palace and rejoins the river of human-ity flowing uphill.

He has to shove some people out of his way to reach the main palace gate, where King Philip has hired acrobats and jugglers to entertain the masses. The spectators enjoying the show don't move willingly. One man curses him. Another elbows him in the side.

Finally, near the front, he studies the guards standing stiffly, spears outstretched. The first two he doesn't recognize, but the third one, a bearlike older man with a weatherbeaten face, is Diodotus, their trainer and captain of the guards from the Pellan palace.

"Diodotus!" Heph says, striding around the jugglers and smiling broadly.

"You!" the guard says, lowering his spear and grinning. "Lord Hephaestion! It's good to see you. We heard you went on a mission for the prince some months ago. It will do Prince Alexander a world of good to see you again. He hasn't been himself since you left."

Heph blinks. Kat had warned him something might be wrong with Alex. "I can't wait to see him," he says.

"Well, sir, please, go right in. The servants will show you into the feasting hall."

Heph crosses the courtyard, climbs the marble steps, and enters the palace. There's no need to ask for directions: he hears the wedding celebration from the entrance. Following the sounds of music, laughing, and clapping, he goes down a long corridor and through the open double doors beyond. A large, two-story dining hall is hung with brightly colored bolts of material and a dozen Macedonian flags, blue and white with the gold sixteen-pointed star.

As Heph inserts himself into the room, he spies an enormous man with greasy bits of meat in his beard helping himself to the rich food heaped high on the buffet table. A young nobleman dips his cup into the *krater* of unmixed wine, throws back his head, and pours the dark liquid down his throat. In the center of the room, the fire pit, as wide as a man's height, burns brightly, smoke rising through the hole in the roof far above.

Heph feels a bead of perspiration slide down the back of his neck. It's hot in here, a soup of humanity slow-cooked by the fire and the crowd, and it smells of roasted meat, perfume, and sweat. The long garlands wrapped around the columns are already wilting; their green leaves drop to the floor below and are immediately crushed by heavy boots and soft doeskin dancing slippers.

Behind a troop of dancing girls in flimsy costumes, he catches a glimpse of King Philip—the only one wearing a black eyepatch and a crown—clapping a fat, dark-haired man on the back.

Alex—where is Alex? Heph's heart beats with anticipation at finding his old friend, at recounting his and Kat's extraordinary adventures in Egypt and on Meninx. But where in all this writhing mass of humanity is the prince? And which one of these people is the Earth Blood they've been seeking?

The mechanism can find both Snake Blood and Earth blood. He fumbles in the leather bag hanging from his belt... but the bag is empty.

For a moment Heph panics. He is a fool to have lost it! And then, in shock, he realizes the truth: Kat must have taken it from him when she embraced him. She tricked him!

His rising anger cools, chilling his blood. *Alex.* He can't let her get anywhere near Alex. He races down the marble steps into the courtyard, out the gate, and back through the steep, crowded streets toward the tavern.

But when he gets there, he finds that an old woman has taken her place at the table.

Kat is gone.

CHAPTER TWENTY-SEVEN: RIEL

"MORE WINE, FATHER?" RIEL ASKS, HOLDING the silver *oenochoe* over King Philip's gold horse-head *rhyton*.

Sitting on his throne, one meaty hand on his bride's knee, Philip grunts something Riel can't hear, but he pours the sparkling scarlet liquid, anyway. He has avoided drinking any of the wine himself, in case his mistress-mother has poisoned it. All the muscles in his body are tense, and he wonders now whether it was in fact wise to trust Olympias with this most precious of tasks. Maddeningly, she had refused to tell him her scheme, merely smiled and said it would be a surprise. But no—if there's one thing in this cursed world of which he can be certain, it is Olympias's devotion to him and him alone.

He remembers her when she was just Myrtale, a wild and abused girl-child of the Epirote king, how she came to him so effortlessly, and yet with such fierce passion in her veins, he sometimes wondered if she, too, wasn't part god. Over time, she became his greatest advocate. His most treasured pawn. Now, even gaunt and aged, she has her uses. She will not let him down. He has made certain, over the years, that all her happiness came from him and him alone. She will do her part.

But how? If not poisoned wine, he thought perhaps she had

tainted the king's ornate purple wedding tunic, but Philip shows no signs of itching or burning. Time is running out to kill the king at the wedding of Cleopatra, which is how the oracle said it must be done. Soon bride and groom will be bundled off to the nuptial chamber with rowdy songs and raucous jokes.

Where is she? He dislikes the idea that his entire future rests in the hands of a mortal. And a woman. His jaw aches with the tension of it. But soon, soon, he will be a full god again, and none of this will matter. Until then, he must only suffer a little longer.

Again, he scans the room for a petite woman with silver-blond hair. Lute girls play, bending their sinuous bodies like snakes. Dancers with bells on their ankles and wrists sway their hips and wave their arms to the beat of drums and flutes. Matrons with dark or gray hair eat and chat. But no Olympias.

Two men not much older than Alexander—members of the extended Attalid family—saunter slowly by, curl their lips in sneering smiles and mutter something about a "legitimate heir." Riel's hand squeezes the neck of the *oenochoe* so tightly it breaks, and the clay spout comes off in his hand. The Attalids have been mocking him—as the prince—ever since he arrived here yesterday morning, and Philip allows it. Riel has never put up with any insults before. He would have already killed all the Attalids if he weren't playing the part of Alexander, a mere mortal.

Nor is it just the Attalids' insults that have him tight as a bowstring. Far more dangerous to him than those pompous fools is the Earth Blood who toppled the city of Delphi with his rage. Riel can't afford to let his guard down for a moment.

"Well," one of the Attalids says, casting a gloating glance back at Riel, "at least the new heir won't be a cripple." Riel grits his teeth, imagining killing them with a thousand cuts.

"I'm sorry, nephew," Xander says, tight-lipped with anger.

Olympias's brother, the reigning king of Epirus, apparently feels the sting of the insults, too, against his family's house. His pale blue eyes glitter with anger. "But consider the audacious impracticality of the plan. Even if Philip and Cleo had a child in the next nine months—and assuming it was a son—they would have to wait at least another sixteen or seventeen years before he could lead an army and take the throne. Do they really think you would sit obediently on the sidelines all that time?"

Riel shakes his head. "Doubtful. The Attalids would probably try to assassinate me as soon as a son was born."

"We—your mother, your friends, and I—would take action before then," Xander promises grimly, running a hand through his white-blond hair. "And the full power of the Macedonian army would be behind us. They love you, Alexander, for your courage in the victories of the Pellan Fields and the Pyrrhian Fortress. One day you will learn that love inspires greater loyalty than fear."

Riel feels his face slide into an expression of horror at his uncle's stupidity before he can stop it. Then he forces a smile. "I'm sure you're right," he says, trying to calm the roiling anger in his gut with the knowledge that none of this will happen. There will be no need for troops to protect him from the Attalids. Before the day is out, Philip will be dead.

Olympias will kill him, fulfilling the oracle's prediction that he would die by the hand of a lover at the wedding of Cleopatra.

If she hasn't met with some accident.

If she hasn't lost her courage.

Anger—at Philip, at the Attalids, at the absent Olympias— throbs in his head, rings in his ears. That he, a god, should be reduced to this is beyond endurance. Now, watching Philip caress his curvaceous bride, he wants nothing more than to shatter the king's neck as he has just done to the wine pitcher—if only the prophecy would allow it.

"The wedding kiss! The wedding kiss!" cries the bride's ambitious uncle, Attalus, as he saunters up to the royal dais. He's a round man with a black beard and red face. Riel feels a twist of fury that Attalus wears a purple robe with wide borders of gold trim, as if he himself were a member of the royal family.

The musicians' last notes hang sourly in the air. The jugglers catch their balls and the dancers cease their twirling as the crowd surges forward.

"It is time for the wedding kiss!" Attalus repeats, grinning lasciviously and winking. The guests laugh and clap. Cleo—made up like a Corinthian temple whore, Riel notes—turns her artfully painted red lips to Philip, who bends down to kiss them.

"One moment! One moment!" Attalus cries, raising his chalice, his countless rings flashing on plump fingers. "I would like to propose a wedding toast! Here's to the future heir King Philip and Cleo will give us! A fully Macedonian legitimate heir with two good legs!"

Riel squeezes the broken neck of the *oenochoe* with such force it crumbles to dust. His other hand grips the bottom of the pitcher so hard that it bursts; red wine, black lees, and clay shards hit the marble floor. He can stand it no longer— the insults, the crudeness, the laughing faces, and constant frustration. For sixteen years, he was trapped in the body of a snake: speechless, limbless, forced to glide on his belly across the floor. Finally, in a spell that shattered his snake form, he found himself in possession of a human body. But he is almost as trapped as when his spirit was bound by a coil of green scales. He, Riel, made from starlight and cosmic storm, is now imprisoned in the flesh of a youth with a limp. A youth disrespected by these mortal oafs.

The boy is almost gone now, just a shadow in a room lit by a guttering lamp. Alexander has stopped resisting Riel's takeover, stopped pounding angrily against the locked door. Riel senses that he has sealed himself up, yielding to the annihilation that is soon to come. Riel is disappointed. Clearly this is a son not worthy of a god.

On the dais, Philip grins, placing an arm around Cleo's shoulders. "We're wasting no time in begetting a legitimate heir!" he says. "In fact, we've already started trying!"

Cleo's smile freezes and a beet-red blush rises from her neck to her cheeks, while many in the crowd roar with laughter. Some look quickly at the prince and away.

The remnants of Riel's magic course through his veins like smoldering embers of a once-great bonfire. He can stand it no longer. He feels Xander's restraining hand on his arm, pushes it off, and strides to the dais, carefully hiding the limp this imperfect body has.

Hand on his sword hilt, he bellows, "What am I, then, a bastard?"

The laughter stops. Silence hangs in the air like smothering smoke.

Philip turns his flushed face toward Riel, his one eye bloodshot and heavy-lidded. "You!" he cries, dropping his *rhyton*, which falls to the floor with a loud clatter. He grips his own sword hilt. "You *are* an ungrateful little bastard."

As he moves forward, he forgets there are two steps between the dais and the floor and falls forward heavily.

The crowd pulls back, gasping, as Philip lies stunned a moment, then pushes himself up on all fours and roars, reminding Riel of a wounded mountain bear. He strides over, and laughs loudly.

"This man wants to conquer Persia," Riel scoffs, "but he can't even conquer a step."

Xander throws back his head and guffaws, as do Alexander's friends and supporters. Other guests murmur in disapproval. Philip barks something incoherent, while Attalus and another man struggle to pull up the unwieldy king. The bride sobs, throws her yellow veil over her face, and races out of the servants' entrance behind the dais, trailed by twittering handmaidens. *Like all of Philip's queens*, Riel thinks, *running at the pivotal moment.* No one can be counted on. Prophecy be damned. Riel will kill Philip himself.

He starts to slide his sword out of its hilt but suddenly half a dozen Attalids surround the king. Riel pulls one by the back of his cloak, spins him around, and punches him, sending him into a table as guests scatter. The man's companion unsheathes a dagger from his belt and swings it at Riel, who knocks it out of his hand and kicks him hard in the gut. The man flies backward across the floor, slamming into two women, who fall over screaming.

Another Attalid barrels toward Riel, but Xander grabs his cloak as he passes and uses a wrestling move to push his feet out from under him, sending him hurtling into the fire pit. The Attalid screams and leaps out of it, but he is too late, his cloak on fire.

A young servant whips the tablecloth off a table—sending plates and cups flying—throws the burning man to the ground and smothers the flames with it.

Phrixos and Telekles, Alexander's good friends, are suddenly at Riel's side. That is, they had been Alex's good friends until the prince had started acting *erratically.* That was the word Riel read in their eyes. Along with *cruel* and *irrational*, though Riel, a god who'd walked this earth for more years than these buffoons could count, knew that what they misinterpreted for cruelty was merely leadership, and irrationality, power.

The warriors stand beside him, bristling for a fight. Phrixos says, "They're the bastards, my lord. Do we have your permission?"

Riel nods. Phrixos and Telekles, surprised, smile grimly before plunging into the group of Attalids. All Riel can see are swinging arms and, now and then, Telekles's long golden hair.

The entire great hall has erupted into a violent melee. Benches and pitchers fly through the air. A table hits the floor with a crash, and silver platters roll like wheels into the crowd. Riel sees a man helping what must be his elderly mother navigate a safe path out of the room.

A frightened girl pulls a young man toward the door, but he shakes her off, balls up his fists, and dives into the fight. A servant deftly picks up silver spoons and slips them into the large pockets of his apron.

Riel looks around for Philip. The king must die—tonight. But then he sees that Attalus and his relatives are pushing him out the servant's entrance. At the other end, Macedonian guards tromp in, shields up and swords extended.

Diodotus, their grizzled commander, appears at Riel's side. "We'll take care of the insulters for you, my liege." He offers a grim smile. "Now best get yourself to safety." Shouting orders, Diodotus flings himself into the brawl.

Rage pumping through him, Riel turns, pushes through the servant's entrance, and takes the curling stairs three at a time. Philip has slipped through his fingers. He will not die at the wedding of Cleopatra as the prophecy predicted. At least not this Philip, or not this Cleopatra. He wants to kick himself for not remembering how tricky prophecies can be, how unreliable it is to accept their most obvious interpretation.

Now the Earth Blood has all the time in the world to hunt Riel down and kill him.

He needs to find that untrustworthy bitch Olympias and demand answers. Is she cowering in her chambers? He will find out. Now.

Chapter Twenty-Eight:
Katerina

KAT KNEW SHE SHOULDN'T HAVE STOLEN THE mechanism from Heph, but the words *Find the Earth Blood* were pounding through her body with the rhythm of her heart.

For days she thought of nothing else. And Heph couldn't understand what this meant to her. She cares for Heph— maybe even loves him, or something as close to love as she can allow herself to feel. But even still, she fears he doesn't truly *know* her. Doesn't understand why this is the most important moment of her life so far.

On the island, Heph spoke of the pain of his past, sought her forgiveness. He wanted to open up, to share everything with her that could be shared. And she wanted that, too— wanted *him*. He had become so much more than the cocky best friend of the prince, the young man whose sarcasm and pride used to make her bristle with anger. She had begun to see his determination and brilliance, the incredible loyalty of his heart, the strength of his ambition. She knows that Jacob loved her once, too, but this love feels different. Heph's love is not steady and deep, like Jacob's. No. Heph's love is full of fire and anger and *need*.

And yet, neither of these men understand who Kat *really*

is—that she is not a girl in need of saving and protecting. That she can never be whole, can never love either of them back, until she confronts her true self, her true past, her true parents. She needs to prove that despite her father and her mother and all their evil, she is not them. She is selfless, strong, a warrior of light, a force for good. She will not wait meekly in the tavern while someone else courageously acts to save the world. She will do it herself, safety be damned.

And so, when Heph insisted she stay behind so that Olympias couldn't harm her, her choice was clear: she would lie to him. And she would find the Earth Blood herself.

After leaving the tavern, Kat squeezes toward the front of the crowd watching the performers at the main palace gate, and sees behind them the Macedonian guards standing at attention, holding long spears. How is she going to get past them? Then it occurs to her that perhaps she knows one of the guards from Pella. If one recognizes her as Prince Alexander's companion, surely he will let her in. But it is hard to see the guards' faces clearly; their helmets have long nosepieces and cheek plates, and acrobats tumble and leap in front of them.

A large bald man shoves her out of the way. "Make way! Make way!" he cries, as those he pushes grumble. Behind him are a dozen beautiful women with long flowing hair, heavily made-up faces, and revealing robes despite the cold.

Hetaerae. High-class prostitutes, known not only for their sexual services, but for their entertaining conversation and musical skills. An idea strikes Kat, and she curses herself for not wearing makeup.

Pulling the hairpins from her bun, she lets it fall in a wild golden-brown tumble over her shoulders and down her back. Then she removes her cloak and readjusts her robe, revealing her shoulders and much more cleavage…and takes her place at the end of the line.

The *hetaerae*, she notices, hold their heads high, staring around boldly with wide smiles, and swinging their hips as they walk. She tries to copy them as men whistle and make lewd comments while the women call them names.

The acrobats cartwheel out of the way, and the guards open the gate, eyeing each *hetaera* appraisingly as she slips through. Just as Kat is about to enter, a guard grabs her wrist and her heart sinks. He must know she doesn't belong.

"Meet me later," he says with a wink. "I'll make it worth your while."

Kat tilts her head back, looking at him through her lashes, and smiles, hoping he doesn't hear the pounding of her heart. "I'm sure you will," she says sweetly, and slides out of his grip and through the gate. It clangs shut behind her.

She is in.

The other women cross the courtyard, and she follows them up the entrance stairs and into the marble hall. The *hetaerae* turn right, heading in the direction of music and laughter. Skirting the little knots of people chatting in the hall, Kat pulls the mechanism out of her bag and examines it. The needle points straight ahead. But when she passes the stairs, it starts to spin wildly.

Upstairs, then. Her Earth Blood is upstairs.

"You missed it!" cries a bearded man with wine stains on his white tunic, stumbling into the entrance hall. Three men, who have been chatting in front of a statue, look up.

"What happened?" one asks.

"Attalus just insulted the prince regent!" the bearded man cries. "Said with this marriage to his daughter, King Philip can have a legitimate, fully Macedonian heir with two good legs!"

"He didn't!" says a tall, thin man in a red tunic. "How did the prince take it?"

"Not well, as you can imagine."

Poor Alexander. Kat knows how sensitive he is about his leg, believing it makes him less of a person, fearing it will make him less of a king. She aches to find him in the great hall, to comfort him, but Olympias must also be in there.

Suddenly Kat hears shouts, screams, and the sound of benches and tables hitting the ground and pottery crashing. The *hetaerae* who just disappeared around the corner race back out, holding their colorful skirts above their knees. Others follow—men, women, servants, wide-eyed and panicking—pushing their way out the front door and into the courtyard below.

In the confusion of wedding guests running and yelling, Kat runs up the wide staircase. At the top, she looks at the mechanism.

It seems the little machine is confused. At first, it points in the direction of a window. She looks through the slats and sees a large inner courtyard thronged with revelers. Some of them sit on the basin of a splashing fountain. A tall Macedonian guard pushes his way wildly through the crowd, probably on some important errand for the king. She loses sight of him, and the mechanism twitches to life again, this time pointing down the corridor.

As she passes brightly painted walls and marble statues, she realizes that her golden fingertip tingles, just as it did when she was in Ada's presence. There is Blood Magic, nearby, she knows it. The needle swings wildly when she passes the fifth door, then stops, pointing directly at it.

Kat stands before the door, breathing deeply, the mechanism like a tiny metal heart humming inside her palm, the arrow like a dagger pointing the way to her fate. The Earth Blood is behind that door. The person who can save the known world from the evil of Riel.

From the evil of her father.

Now that she is about to set Riel's death in motion, she hesitates. Sounds from the wedding chaos echo distantly from another wing of the palace, but the hall around her feels eerily still. She wonders where the Last God is, and whether he even knows that she exists. There are a thousand questions she might ask him, a thousand things she might say.

But he's evil, she knows, the most evil being on earth, or so the prophecies say. And she believes everything Ada told her—she trusts Ada more than anyone in the world. She remembers, too, what Princess Laila showed her in Egypt—the destruction of the entire city of Sharuna, thousands of innocent people murdered.

Kat raises her fist to knock on the ornately carved door painted with two facing griffins, wondering who she will find on the other side. But doubts prick her once again. Maybe she should have waited at the tavern for Heph. Maybe she shouldn't have taken matters—and the mechanism—into her own hands.

No—she's hesitated long enough. She casts one final glance at the mechanism and is startled to see it is pointing toward her. The Earth Blood is behind her, in the courtyard, it seems to say. Then it spins around again and points toward the door. Could there be two Earth Bloods in the palace?

Well, she will try this room first. Taking a deep breath, she raps on the door.

There is no sound from inside, no answering voice, no soft thud of footsteps. Kat knocks again, more loudly. Her heart ticks up a notch. Perhaps she should run downstairs and into the courtyard. But she must first make sure the Earth Blood isn't really in this room, asleep or passed out from too much wedding wine.

She opens the door slowly and goes inside, closing it behind her. "Hello?" she calls. "Is anyone…"

Shafts of gray afternoon light float in through the open slats of the shutters. Coals glow in the bronze brazier next to a bed with rich scarlet covers and tasseled pillows. But as Kat scans the room, she notices something wrong. The stool in front of the cosmetics table has been knocked over. Is the Earth Blood a woman, then? Little bottles on the table are shattered. Kat bends over and touches a strange wine-colored design on the floor, then draws back quickly. It's not a design.

It's blood, thick and sticky. There are several such puddles, some littered with glass. Signs of a struggle.

And blood smears across the floor, as if someone has dragged herself—or been dragged—to the small servants' door in the wall. Her chest feels tight. Something isn't right. Something has happened here. She can feel the room closing in on her, trying to swallow her like a dark throat.

Her hand grasps the door knob. She forces herself to open it. But all she sees in the passage beyond are drops of blood disappearing into darkness. If she had a lit lamp, she could follow the trail… But is the injured person the Earth Blood?

She checks the mechanism again and sees it is pointed at her, behind her. The Earth Blood is not the person who bled in the passage.

Reminding herself to breathe, to be calm, she follows the needle toward the cosmetics table, lifting her robe and stepping over the thick sticky messes on the floor. There, on a mosaic of Perseus fighting Medusa, is an ivory hairpin in the form of a snake with flashing emerald eyes. And its twin prongs are coated in what looks like blood. This is a room of blood.

A wave of nausea hits her.

She can't move, staring at the hairpin. Something about it is familiar.

Then the hairs on the back of Kat's neck rise as she realizes where she has seen this before. Back in the Pellan palace, she noticed that Queen Olympias had hairpins just like this. She glances around, beginning to panic. This must be Olympias's room. But what has happened here? Was the queen injured? Or did she beat a handmaiden in a fit of anger? What if the queen comes back? She must flee…

But the mechanism led her here. Why? Could it be broken, after all this? Should she run into the courtyard and see if it finds the Earth Blood there? She wants to weep with the uncertainty of it, with the terror that is pushing through her veins, making it hard to think.

She leans forward, trying to push herself back up to standing. There is blood on her hands. Blood from the floor. She gasps, trying to wipe her hands clean. She looks down at the hairpin, and then at the mechanism. No matter how she moves, the needle continues to point at it. *What happened here? Where is the queen?*

Kat picks up the curving ivory ornament and holds it up in a bar of light. The long prongs at the bottom are coated in blood.

The door is thrown wide open. Kat gasps, expecting Olympias to stride in. But her heart leaps with happiness when she realizes it's Alexander.

Kat runs up and throws her arms around him. "I'm so glad it's you," she says. He holds her a moment, stiffly, then slowly pushes her away to study her. Something is wrong. His eyes—they have changed color, just as she heard, but didn't want to believe. How is that even possible?

"Well," he says, looking her up and down, his eyes lingering on her mother's silver lotus pendant. "I know who *you* are."

Kat falters. It's such an odd thing to say. In fact, everything about Alex seems off. Instead of greeting her and overwhelming her with questions about where she's been and what she's been doing, he just stares at her with disdain etched on his proud face. On Meninx, the birds held stories in their minds, flashes and images of Alex behaving strangely, of being changed, and even *cruel*. She didn't know what to make of them. No, that's not true—she just didn't want to believe them. But now she sees that she must.

"Where is the queen?" Alex looks impatiently around the room.

"Are you all right?" she asks him. "I've heard you weren't... well. And I have been worried. I have wanted to see you for so long..."

Alex stares at her, a look that freezes her blood. He walks

to the vanity table, peers at the broken cosmetics jars, then squats down and looks at the pieces of glass in a puddle of blood on the floor. He stands abruptly.

"Where's the queen?" he demands again, more loudly.

"I don't know," Kat says. "I just got here and she was gone."

His glance fixes on the streaks of blood on the floor leading to the servant's door, and his eyes narrow. He turns to her, a question on his lips, but stares at the mechanism glinting gold in her left hand as the light strikes it.

"What is in your hand?" he asks.

"It's..." But she hesitates. For a brief moment, she doubts him. Almost immediately, she feels guilty. Of course she should tell him. He's still her brother and the prince regent. He needs to know what they have created.

"It's a copy of the Atlantean Mechanism," she says, holding it up. "A powerful tool to locate whatever you want."

Alex takes it, frowning. "Symbols," he says, turning it around slowly. "A diamond and a...a snake." He looks at her, tilting his head, then flips the switch to the snake. The dial points directly at him, then swivels to Kat, arcing back and forth as though it is tracing a crescent moon.

Understanding dawns upon his face. "This device can track the Blood Magics?"

She nods, uncertain of his new demeanor. When they have found the Earth Blood, they will go to Halicarnassus to seek out Ada together, and the queen will help Alex train in Snake Blood powers so that he will find his way back to his own mind again. She will help him. Heal him. But first things first.

"Yes," Kat says. "Because we need an Earth Blood to kill Riel—oh, but you don't know who he is, do you? There is so much to tell you!"

He face takes on an expression so delighted and so menacing at the same time that it sends a shiver up her spine. "It will find Earth Blood?" he asks, rubbing his thumb over the diamond etched on the surface of the mechanism. "Really?"

There is something about his gaze makes her shiver. This is not like Alex. Not at all.

He laughs. "No," he says. "I suppose I'm not like Alex, am I."

Kat frowns. It's as if he's read her thoughts. But Snake Bloods can't read each other's thoughts unless invited to. Which means... This person standing before her is no ordinary Snake Blood. He is not her brother.

"Correct. I am indeed no ordinary Snake Blood," Alexander whispers—again reading her thoughts. "I have greater powers than those. And you are also right about something else, dear Katerina."

Alexander lunges forward and grabs Kat by the arm. She cries out in pain as his fingernails dig into her skin.

"I am *not* your brother."

Kat's heart stops. Her entire world becomes the glowing green eyes of the man in front of her.

"Silly girl, I am your father," Alexander hisses, his voice wrapping around her, squeezing her with sinuous power. She stares at him, unable to process what he is saying.

"I am Riel," he says, leaning toward her. "I am the Last God."

Suddenly she thinks she understands, and for a moment she can't breathe. "You have made yourself look like Alex," she gasps out, "except for the eyes."

His fingers dig deeper into the flesh of her arm, bruising it, but she's stopped straining away. All she can do is stare in horrified fascination at the man who is, somehow, both brother and father.

"No," Riel says, the right side of his mouth twitching up into a twisted smile. "This is your brother's body. The only human body a Snake Blood can fully possess is one belonging to his or her own descendant."

"But where is Alex, then?" she asks, her voice rising in panic. "Is he still alive? Or have you killed him?"

He laughs. "Oh, he's alive. Barely. I have pushed him down into darkness. Soon he will not be there at all. With his body, flawed as it is, I will rule Macedon and conquer the world until it is time for me to return to the gods."

"Please," she begs, blinking the tears away, "don't hurt him. Leave his body; let him come back."

He casts her a grin of molten malice. "And where would I go?" he asks, the acidic venom of his voice curling around her.

"I, too, am your descendant. Use my body—I will let you have it."

"What use would I have with a girl's body?" he sneers. "A girl couldn't rule the world." Then his expression changes, as if something new has occurred to him.

He lets go of her arms and walks around her, his hand on his chin. "You are beautiful," he says appreciatively. "Strong. Intelligent. A fitting daughter for a god. Clearly, you have been poorly educated. Misinformed about the gods...about me, too, I see. I was going to kill you. But I could give you a chance. I could *teach* you how to wield your magic to help others."

Kat feels the room spin around her. He knows her weaknesses. He knows exactly what to say to persuade her. He knows *everything*.

Riel plants himself squarely in front of her. "I will keep this body, Alexander's body. Though it is flawed, it is at least male. But you and I can be allies. Join with me, flesh of my flesh, blood of my blood, and we will rid ourselves of Olympias. You will no longer live in fear of her. You will have your revenge."

Suddenly Kat isn't in this room anymore. She's back in the little cottage she lived in with Helen just outside Erissa. From her hiding place in the wool box, six-year-old Kat sees Olympias say, *Kill her*, and two guards run their swords through Helen, kneeling before the fire pit in their little cottage. Helen falls backward onto the packed earth floor.

Now Kat is in the field behind the Pellan palace just three months ago, and the terrifying image trapped in a gazelle's mind shows her a house in flames. Smoke. Murder. Screams. She sees bodies in the courtyard. Sotiria lying next to the well, her dark hair streaming into a widening puddle of blood. Cleon next to the gate, an ax head buried in his broad back. Jacob's younger brothers, broken and lifeless, lie in the dirt. A silhouette of white-gold stands against the burning red of flames. Olympias, smiling.

Anger wells up in her. Yes, she wants revenge on the queen. This man—this *god*—could get it for her. Her *father* would help her.

A look of victory crosses Riel's face. "Yes, daughter, she has harmed you greatly," he says, his voice warm and caring. "I will get you the revenge you seek. But ask yourself, what happens then?"

Kat, who has been imagining the queen's dead body, shifts her focus back to Riel.

"What do you mean, what happens then?" she asks.

"Do not underestimate yourself," he says, stroking her hair and smiling in a proud, fatherly way that suffuses her with un-expected joy. "You are not just any Snake Blood, Katerina." The way he says her name reminds her of a flute player, blow-ing four lilting notes from a reed pipe, notes that hypnotize a snake. She finds herself half closing her eyes, slowing her breathing, agreeing with every word he says.

"You do not have generations of weak mortals diluting your blood," he continues, and she nods, knowing he is right. "You are one-half divine. I sense that you have barely begun to develop your magic. I will show you how. You will have powers only gods ever had. And with Olympias dead, to-gether you and I can rule the world, Katerina."

His persuasive voice rises with excitement. "Picture it. A god. And his sister-daughter. I could teach you such things…" He takes her by the wrist and leads her to the window.

Throwing the shutters aside, he gestures to the city and harbor below. "We would rule this great city, and all the great cities and harbors, temples and fortresses on earth. And when I return to the gods in the divine realm, my daughter will remain here, empress of the world. You will ensure justice prevails. You will punish evil-doers. You will bring an age of righteousness and abundance to all the earth."

She sees herself atop a throne on a tall dais, dispensing justice. Punishing the evil. Rewarding the good. Building hospitals and orphanages. Feeding the hungry. If she were empress of the world, imbued with godly powers, she would...

Not be Katerina.

Not be herself.

For if she accepted her father's offer, she would be consigning her twin—her other self—to the unknown abyss, crushed and mindless inside Riel's consciousness. Riel would already have made her selfish and evil, like himself. She stares at him, at the face she so loved as Alexander's, and realizes the face has changed. It is stamped with selfishness and cruelty—he is using her love of justice, of kindness, to tempt her.

She thinks of what Aristotle told them. *The highest training of the mind is to see fate's strings.* Her fate is tugging at her now, but what is it saying? Where are its strings?

Then she remembers Ada's words to her on Meninx, when Kat first learned who her real father was. *I come from the most despicable royal family ever—riddled with power lust, murder, and incest. But they are not me. I am myself, separate from them. You, too, are like that. Clean and brave and good, untouched by their evil.*

Riel's eyes take on a wary look, and he tilts his head back, waiting for her reply.

She wants to tell him he has nothing to do with her other than one act of pleasure many years ago. That she is herself, very different from him. She is not evil or cruel or selfish. That she will not let him corrupt her. That she would die rather than let him keep Alex a prisoner inside of him. That she would never accept his offer.

But even as these thoughts race through her mind, she sees his jaw tighten and a vein pulsate in his temple.

Because he can read her mind. And he can snap her neck with one hand.

She cannot pretend she didn't have those thoughts. But she can add to them. Quickly she pictures herself, instead, reigning as empress of the world, dispensing justice, kindness, and mercy to all who deserve it. She forces herself to feel the joy of it sweeping through her. She sees Heph in a purple cape and dazzling crown sitting on a throne beside her, and revels in calling him her own.

The pictures, and feelings, and sounds and smells are so vivid, surely Riel, too, can see them. He does. He must. His face relaxes. He is waiting for her answer.

She shuts her eyes and shakes her head. "I want what you offer," she says, shakily, "but losing Alex would be so...difficult. I have mixed feelings about it all. I need time. To think."

Riel springs on her, grabbing her arms. Smiling, he shakes his head. "Daughter, there is no more time," he says. "Not for you, anyway. You think I don't know what you just tried to do with your thoughts? To cover the true ones with lies? You are not so adept in your Snake Blood training to hide them from me."

Her blood has turned to ice. Why did she think she could fool a god? "Yes, why did you?" he says. "*You*, my daughter, were a mistake. And, knowing what you now do, you must, of course, die."

She screams and cries for help, but he just laughs. "They won't hear you," he scoffs. "With all the fighting, the music, and drinking. No one will hear you scream, Katerina. No one will hear you die."

Wildly, she twists and turns. His hands encircling her wrists are like tight iron manacles. She tries to kick him in the shin, knee him in the groin, but despite her training with Ada and her brief experience on the battlefield, she is not a born fighter. Her blows are ridiculously weak and poorly aimed, which causes her to struggle harder, even as fear drives a spike through her.

"Let me go, Alexander," she manages to shout.

"Don't call me Alexander," he snarls, hurling her to the floor. Her head hits the mosaic tiles and lights explode in front of her eyes. He kneels beside her. "Call me Father and I may just let you live," he says almost lovingly.

He's toying with her. He won't let her live no matter what she says. She cannot fight him, but she *can* leave this life defying him. "I would rather die than acknowledge someone as cruel and evil as you as my father," she says and spits at him.

The wad of saliva slides down his cheek. His eyes narrow. "So be it."

He starts to squeeze her throat. Immediately she feels like she's going to throw up. She coughs, but the air is trapped in that viselike grip. She needs to do something—anything—to get those hands off her. As she tries to pull his fingers away, she realizes she's still holding the bloody hairpin in her right hand.

She raises it, but he's not looking at her hand. He's looking at her face, enjoying the pain and panic he sees there. With a clumsy, uncertain movement, she scratches his neck with the hairpin.

It's not enough, she knows. It won't slow him down one bit.

But then his hands release her throat and his eyes open wide in alarm. Blessed air fills her aching lungs as she coughs and gags, rolling out from under him.

Gulping air, she stares at him in surprise. How could the wound have had any effect on him at all? It's just two slender scratches on the left side of his neck, the kind any man might give himself with a straight razor as he shaves.

Now Alex grasps his neck and makes a choking sound, as if she had slit his throat wide open. He sits back on his feet, gurgling, sputtering. She scrambles away from him toward the door, wanting nothing more than to run away. To find Heph. To do *anything* but stay here with this monster who just tried to strangle her. But Alex is in there somewhere. She can't just leave.

She watches in horrified fascination as Riel gasps for air and shudders. His face contorts and he falls on his side, arms and legs thrashing. Suddenly he is still, and he looks at her with an expression of utter shock. The large pupils of his green eyes have turned to slits, like those of a snake.

Forcing herself to approach, she kneels beside him, her hands over her nose and mouth, unsure of what she has done, of what she should do.

"You," he gasps, choking. He grabs her hand so hard it hurts, but she doesn't care.

"Alex!" She is crying, her voice heavy with wet sobs. "Alex, if you can hear me, it's Kat! Come back to me, Alex. I love you! Fight your way back through the darkness and find me! Don't let him win!"

The hard grip releases.

The head falls back.

The snake eyes close.

A final, awful gurgle rattles out of the open mouth. He is white as snow and completely still. Kat waits, staring at him. Riel is gone, she knows. It is as if a great furnace has gone out. She can feel the sudden loss of heat and light. But surely Alex isn't gone, too. Surely Alex will come back.

But the chest no longer rises and falls.

No. No. No.

Alex is dead...and *she* killed him.

Boots pound on the floor in the corridor outside. She looks up in confusion as Heph bursts into the room.

"No," he cries, a long howl of pain. He kneels beside Alex, feels his throat for a pulse, then his wrist. He looks up at Kat, his dark eyes angry and accusing. "What have you done?"

CHAPTER TWENTY-NINE:
PAPARI

PAPARI HOLDS THE OIL LAMP ABOVE THE BED. The flame casts dancing golden shadows over Amyntas, who sleeps with his long arms and legs sprawled out and his mouth wide open.

Will tonight be the right time? He has been waiting to act until he is certain the king trusts him. Pure trust is necessary for pure betrayal; that much he has learned from spying on Queen Cynane. But with someone as unpredictable as Amyntas, it is almost impossible for Papari to tell.

The king has said the only person in the world he trusts is Aireon, his chief minister. A horse.

The king certainly doesn't trust his wife, Queen Cynane, or his advisers, generals, or subjects. Once, when Papari asked him how someone could win his trust, Amyntas thought about it and finally replied, "We will give our trust to whoever makes us the Man in the Moon. Because being on earth bores us so."

The king likes Papari, that much is clear, for keeping him constantly amused. Papari promised him the sweetest bed companion ever; that night the king dove into his sheets to find them smeared with honey and laughed for hours.

Another time, Papari redecorated the banquet hall by turning the furniture upside down. Courtiers were forced to sit on the underside of benches on the floor and eat from the underside of tables. No one complained; they knew that if they did, the king, sitting on his upside down throne and eyeing them critically, would execute them.

For the king, he knows, is not just fond of silly humor. He is a sadist, dark and blood-hungry and inhumanly cruel, in a way that only the truly mad—and truly powerful—can be.

And this man, this horror of a king, likes Papari.

Papari can't wait any longer, though. It must be tonight. He has received a message that everything is in motion. All is ready, even the moon.

"Sire!" he hisses, gently shaking the king. "Wake up!"

Amyntas murmurs something, then opens his pale eyes. In an instant, he is sitting bolt upright. "What is it?" he asks in alarm. "An invasion?"

"No, Sire," Papari replies matter-of-factly. "It's morning. Time to get up."

Amyntas looks around the room. "It's still dark. I can see moonlight in between the cracks of the shutters."

"It is merely a trick the gods are playing on you, Sire. They want to see if you are foolish enough to fall for it, sleeping forever, or if you will defy them, rise, and go about your business like a wise man."

"Ah," Amyntas says, his eyes taking on a crafty look. "In that case, we will most certainly defy them because we are very wise." He slides off the bed and Papari helps him slip on his fur-lined night robe.

"I have your warm shaving water over here, Sire," he says, pointing to the table by the window. "I think, despite the chill, we must open the shutters so I can shave you by the light of the moon, which is brighter tonight than any torch could be. Here, I will roll the brazier over by the window for a bit of warmth."

"Very well," the king agrees, taking a seat, half-intrigued, as though he's about to witness a peculiar play that could, in fact, turn out to be very dull.

Papari rolls over the brazier, takes some sticks of aromatic grape wood from the shelf below, and tosses them onto the glowing embers. Soon flames lick them, and a sweet-scented smoke drifts up. He opens the shutters wide and cold air whistles in, swirling the grape wood smoke. The low moon, almost full, hangs like the golden apple of Aphrodite over the stone harbor, dimpling the sighing black water with silver. And it is reflected in the bowl of warm water, as Papari knew it would be.

Amyntas, however, doesn't notice. He's staring at the moon in the night sky, muttering something to himself.

"Sire!" Papari cries, pointing to the bowl. "Look!"

Amyntas leans over the bowl, his mouth gaping in amazement. "It's… We…" He looks up at Papari, his handsome face suffused with a pure joy.

"We have become the Man in the Moon," he says, his eyes filling with tears. "We have done it, Papari." The most disturbing thing is not that he is playing along, but that, to him, it is the truth. His voice is full of unmistakably real emotion. "And it's all because of you," he whispers.

The king turns again to his reflection in the bowl, fused with that of the moon, and touches his cheeks, his forehead, his throat.

"We do feel different," he says. "Brighter, somehow. My dear, dear friend, Papari, how we love you! When you die, we will be sure a planet is named for you. Even if it's a planet that closely resembles the testicles of a horse." At this Amyntas laughs uncontrollably.

"I'm delighted to hear it," Papari says, picking up the

straight razor. "And what planet shall I name after *you* when *you* die?" he inquires.

Amyntas looks at him in the darkness, his eyes strangely moonlit. "When we die? That will never be. The Man in the Moon cannot die. Unless we die from too many boring questions from men with the balls of a horse." He laughs at his own joke.

"Or by the hands of such a man," Papari, ever the fool, responds. But though he jests, his voice is serious. So serious, that the king is completely startled…

…as Papari, in one swift move, cuts the king's throat.

Amyntas gags and splutters, trying to staunch the lethal flow with his hands. Blood pumps out between his fingers, spurting over his robe. His gray eyes are open in surprise as he looks at Papari, and then the light in them fades and vanishes. He tips over and lands heavily on the floor.

As Papari kneels and washes his hands in the dead king's blood, he feels power—hot and vibrant—pooling in his fingertips. It is a delicious feeling, as if he had the strength of an entire army inside him. It slides through the veins of his hands and up his arms… Now it pricks him from the inside, like a thousand red-hot needles. He opens his mouth to scream but a gust of wind pushes smoke down his throat. He cannot scream; he is choking. He feels the smoke slide into his lungs, charring them, and searing his heart, his liver, and stomach. It slips into his heart, filling it with glowing cinders. More wind pummels the smoke. It twists around him, crushing him, squeezing the life out of him.

He falls to his knees, then onto his hands. He didn't do this right. Perhaps there was some spell to say, some ritual to perform. He had patched this together from observing the queen and learning the old Illyrian tales of men of smoke. Now it will cost him his life.

With a gurgling, choking sound, he collapses.

He hears a drip, drip, and opens his eyes.

Next to him lies Amyntas, dead eyes open in surprise. Blood drips from the ghastly wound in his neck. Papari doesn't want that to be the last thing he ever sees.

Wind whips in through the window, disbursing the smoke. The hot coals in his blood cool. The pain lessens. Slowly, he sits up, touching his arms, his face.

He is all right, but he is different.

And just in time, as he hears something in the hallway. Footsteps. They are here. He grabs the chair to pull himself up.

The door bursts open and horned soldiers bearing torches tromp into the room. The Aesarian Lords have come, just as Papari asked.

High Lord Gideon enters, and takes in the scene. "Well done, Lord Timaeus."

And Papari—*Tim*—feels a rush of rightness at hearing his own name, his real name, uttered aloud after so long.

"Now, where," High Lord Gideon asks, "is Queen Cynane?"

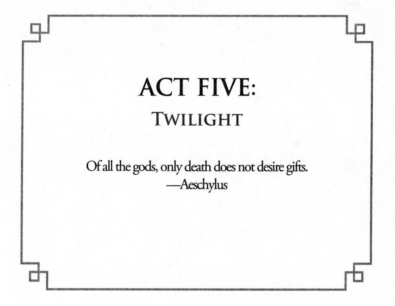

ACT FIVE:

TWILIGHT

Of all the gods, only death does not desire gifts.
—Aeschylus

CHAPTER THIRTY: CYNANE

CYNANE IS OUT OF TIME.

She glances out her window and sees horned helmets gleaming by the light of torches on the parapets overlooking the beach. The palace has been taken by the Aesarian Lords, who have just killed Amyntas, according to her handmaiden, Rachel. They are now coming for her.

She would rather kill herself than let them capture her again. She will never forget their daily torture sessions in the Pyrrhian Fortress, how they smashed her with iron bars as she spun on a wheel, how they put her in a horse trough of water with a millstone on her chest. Taulus's protective spell healed her wounds and kept her alive.

With Taulus dead, the protective spell has vanished. It would take years—maybe even centuries—for her to develop Taulus's powers. Even as she feels power unspooling with within her, she also feels oddly vulnerable. Since Taulus's death, Priam has been her protector, stalking the royal hallways at night, and now his absence worries her. Is he fighting the Lords? A prisoner? Dead?

"Go, Rachel," she tells the terrified handmaiden. "I will escape. I have a plan."

The girl nods, blows out her lamp, and darts into the dark hallway.

Luckily, Cyn is ready. She removes her sleeping tunic and puts on a man's robe, cloak, and boots. From her belt, she removes the old family hunting dagger her mother took to Pella when she married Philip, with the Dardanian royal crest incised on its hilt. Cyn could practically kiss Olympias for giving it to the guards on the ship in Crete. It fits in perfectly with her plan.

She slices the white, delicate skin on the inside of her forearm, and blood bursts from the seam. Pain throbs through her, and she channels it to push every particle of thought, every beat of her heart, into another form. Even as she hears heavy booted footsteps tromping upstairs and men's voices growing closer, her energy lingers lovingly on her jaw, envisioning it stronger. Power tingles along its curved edges, reshaping it. She moves on to her delicate arched eyebrows, imagining them thicker. Her shoulders: wider. Her chest: flatter. Her hips: slimmer. Her skin: rougher. Her hands: larger, stronger.

The transformative smoke in her blood pumps through her with ecstasy. She doesn't want to stop, but she hears the military marching of men's boots nearby. A rich deep voice—Lord Gideon's, her torturer-in-chief—issues a booming command ending with "…take the queen alive."

The door slams open and men with torches spill into the room like floodwaters. Gideon strides toward her, his hand on his sword hilt, and studies her. Cyn's heart skips a beat. Did she have enough time? Will he recognize her? Imprison her and torture her again?

She folds her arms across her chest in the way men often stand, leans back against the cosmetics table, and stares calmly back at him.

Gideon's dark gaze flits around the room. "Where is Queen Cynane?" he asks in a deep rich voice.

Cyn spreads her arms wide, gesturing to the empty room. "Gone. I don't know where."

The High Lord fixes her with his stare once more. "And who are you?" he asks.

"Her cousin, just arrived from the north," Cyn replies casually. "I am General Pyrolithos."

CHAPTER THIRTY-ONE: ALEXANDER

PAIN BURNS IN HIS NECK, SPREADING PULSATing talons of fire. Has he been injured in battle? He smells sweet herbs burning nearby, and feels heat. Could he be on a funeral pyre?

Opening his eyes a tiny crack, he sees blurry faces hover over him. He can tell they are moving their lips, but he cannot hear them, at least not clearly. He only has a vague sense that they are grieving an insuperable loss, that their hearts are breaking.

As his vision clears, he can make out Heph, his forehead creased in concern. But Heph… Didn't he go away?

"I didn't have him very long," says a girl. There's such a deep sorrow twisting through her voice that Alexander wonders what tragedy has struck her. She speaks again. "And yet I have never loved anyone as much as I loved Alexander."

Alexander. His name.

And that voice, Alex knows that voice. *Loves* that voice. It floods him with a healing warmth, dulling the throbbing pain. Wherever he is, *Kat* is here. His sister. His twin. They are together again, with Heph. Everything will be all right.

"This is all my fault," Heph says, his voice a scrape of his usual baritone.

"How is it your fault? I'm the one who—the hairpin…" She breaks off, the anguish in her voice a gushing wound, painful to hear. Alexander wants to comfort her, raise his hand and pat her shoulder, but everything remains both hazy and heavy, as if he were waking from a slumber induced by a physician's brew of poppy juice.

"There's something I should have told you long ago, Kat," Heph says. "Before we left for Egypt, I discovered a scroll that Leonidas kept hidden. It was another one of the Cassandra Prophecies."

Alexander's right hand twitches, feeling a layer of soft combed wool. His fingers push into what must be a feather mattress. He is in bed.

"What did it say?" Kat's voice is high, taut like the littlest string of a lyre.

"It said that you…you were destined to kill your twin—Alex."

Alexander hears a muffled sob, and then Kat must have whispered something, because Heph croaks out:

"In the womb of the night
Twin stars struggle to shine their light.
The moon with great joy will blot out the sun
When the girl kills the boy and the world comes undone."

"Don't you see?" Heph pushes out. "You and Alex were twins in the darkness of your mother's womb. The moon, ruled by Artemis, is the feminine, while the sun is masculine, ruled by Helios. And now—" Heph's voice breaks "—Alex is dead. All the greatness the soothsayers said he would bring into the world is gone. *Undone*. If I had just told you—"

"But I'm not," Alex tries to say. He manages to push the

words over his lips, but as puffs of air only, unheard over Kat's sobs. "I murdered my own brother," she moans. "My twin." Alex can't let her believe that, not for one moment longer.

"I'm not dead," he rasps out.

There's a beat of silence, and then a scream. Suddenly Kat's face is above him, and in the next second, she's flung her body over him, hugging him so hard that he can barely breathe.

"Kat, get back!" Heph snaps. Alex can sense Kat's confusion, but she still scrambles away.

Alex turns his head to see the sharp tip of Heph's sword inches from his nose. "How do we know you are Alex?" Heph practically snarls. "How do we know you're not Riel?"

"Heph," Kat says quietly. "Look at his eyes. Before, they were glowing green, but now...one is brown and the other blue. Exactly as they've always been. I think... I think that is *Alex*."

"My eyes..." Alex repeats. He remembers someone else telling him something about his eyes. But the details dance tantalizingly just beyond his reach.

"Do you...do you remember?" Kat asks. "Riel said he'd taken over your body, pushed you back into the void of your mind..."

Her words buzz around him. Alex shakes his head to try to clear it. Then he remembers that voice inside his head: *I am Riel. I am a god. I am your father.*

He remembers the powerful force pushing him down, squeezing him into a tiny place in his own mind, blowing out the lamp, and locking the door. Then he recalls staying there intentionally, not allowing the door to open, holding it tightly shut from the inside to protect others. Now Alex searches himself and realizes no one is there silently watching him. He is alone. He feels only his own power rushing through his body now. The dark, overpowering presence— *Riel*—is gone, truly gone this time.

Alexander is wholly Alexander again.

Alex coughs long and hard. His throat feels as if he has swallowed fistfuls of sawdust. When he looks up, Kat holds a cup of wine out to him.

"Drink," she says, scooting onto the bed next to him. Behind her, Alex sees Heph silently sheath his sword.

Gratefully, he accepts, and takes long gulps of the cool sweet liquid, which revives him a bit. He looks at Kat and Heph, how close they stand to each other, the comfort and ease they have being together. There is something between his sister and his friend that was not there when he sent them away.

"Where am I?" he asks, looking at the richly decorated room. "This is not Pella."

"Byzantium," Heph replies. "For your father's wedding to Cleopatra Attalida."

Alex remembers…vaguely. Not his memories, but Riel's. A wedding, yes. He hands Kat the cup and notices her gold fingertip. He takes her hand and touches it. The gold is fused to her flesh.

"What is this?" he asks in amazement.

"There's so much to tell you," Kat says, sounding overwhelmed. "But I don't want to tire you with it all right now. When we were in Egypt, Olympias sent Cynane to kill me, but she ended up only cutting off my fingertip."

"*What?*" Alex yelps, sitting up.

Kat rushes to comfort him. "It's all right! Princess Laila of Sharuna gave me this so that I would not be maimed," she says, flicking her golden fingertip on her thumb. "Sharuna is destroyed, though. Alex… I'm afraid we've failed in our mission. Laila will not be your bride."

"But then we went to Meninx," Heph jumps in, "an island off Carthage, to investigate the Lotus-eaters, who Kat suspected were Earth Blood. That's where we found Aristotle and where Ada of Caria fell from the sky."

Alex's head swims, but he's fairly certain it's not from loss of blood. "You have many stories to tell me indeed," he says.

Heph has drawn close to them now. He reaches out his hand, and Alex clasps it. As they grip each other, Heph stares into Alex's eyes. Alex stares back, and senses within his closest friend the wonder, the gratefulness, and the love, all directed toward him. He is humbled by Heph's devotion, and he knows, at last, that he can trust him again.

"I see now," Heph says, voice hushed. "The prophecy. It turns out she had to *kill you to save you*."

"But I'm not an Earth Blood," Kat says. "And Ada said that only an Earth Blood could kill Riel."

At her words, something stirs within Alex. Memories, but not *his* memories. They are memories of time before time, of the beginning and of wars long ago settled, the bones from both sides long ago turned to dust. He remembers a large-eyed oracle telling him—telling Riel—that Earth Blood would kill him.

He struggles to swing his legs over the bed, but they are heavy, uncooperative. His throat is raw, and the room spins around him for a few seconds before it steadies. Taking in the room, he sees that a fight has occurred in it recently. The floor is covered with blood. Alex runs his finger over the wound on his neck and feels only a slight wetness. He wonders how something so small can hurt so much. But the blood on the floor, at least, isn't his.

"Where did all the blood come from?" Alexander asks.

Kat shakes her head. "It was like this before I entered."

"How did I get this wound?"

Looking slightly embarrassed, Kat says, "I scratched you—*Riel*, please keep in mind—with a hairpin."

Alex's mind still feels fuzzy, as though it was wrapped in one of his mother's gossamer scarves, but he can sense he's close to figuring it out. "And was the hairpin covered in blood before you scratched me with it?"

Kat's eyes widen, and he can tell his sister has caught on. "Heph," she says, "the mechanism!"

Alex watches as Heph retrieves something from across the room and hands it to Kat. It is made of a marvelous metal, something between gold and bronze, which radiates an inner light. Almost as long as a man's hand, it has gears, knobs, and an arrow that wobbles and spins. Yet another story, he's sure, that Heph and Kat will have to tell him. When the arrow finally stops, it points directly at an ivory hairpin on the table.

"Our Earth Blood was here," Kat says, awe in her voice. "That must be his—or her—blood that was spilled…" She trails off and looks at Heph, wide-eyed.

"So," Heph breathes, eyes wide in astonishment. "The prophecy was fulfilled, but not in the way we expected. We thought the Earth Blood would slay Riel with a weapon. But the drops of the Earth Blood itself on this hairpin acted like a fatal poison on the Last God."

He slides his glance from the table to meet her eyes. "And, Kat, I think only you could have killed him with Earth Blood. Don't you see? What you did brought the two different prophecies together, fusing them into one. You were fated to kill Alexander. And Earth Blood was destined to kill Riel."

Kat exhales sharply and bows her head in reverence. "The voices of the gods work in mysterious ways," she says quietly.

Indeed, they do, Alex thinks. He quotes Aristotle, "'The highest training of the mind is to see fate's strings.'" His teacher does not believe in coincidences, and only a fool would doubt the wisdom of Aristotle.

"But who was the Earth Blood and where did he or she go?" Kat asks. "The mechanism also pointed toward the courtyard…"

Heph shakes his head. "It doesn't matter. We don't need

the Earth Blood anymore. We accomplished what we set out
to do. Riel is dead, and the evil he planned to bring into the
world has come undone. The Age of Man can begin. The
Age of Monsters will never be."

"But...there still are monsters," Kat says, her voice quiet.
"The Spirit Eaters. Have we freed the world of *their* evil?"

At her words, something within Alex seizes. He breathes in
sharply. That name—it's woken something in him. A memory
of foul creatures. Of devastation. Destruction.

A cool hand cups his cheek, and Alex sees Kat's worried
face. "What happened, Alex, while we were gone? What
happened to you?"

Heph sits on the bed, and slowly, Alex sorts through his
thoughts, his memories. It is an uncomfortable feeling to
know someone has been there and seen all, but he hopes,
within time, the traces of Riel in his mind will fade, like
shadows in a rising sun.

"My memories are now mixed with *his*," Alex says, rubbing his eyes. "But I think one night I went to bed, and when
I woke up it was a month later. Kadmus..."

Sadness twists inside him. Riel stabbed Kadmus. Did he
get the wound stitched in time? Did he heal? Where is he
now? "Kadmus told me I hadn't been acting myself for a
month. That I had reversed my own commands and didn't
seem to care about what used to be important to me. That I
had been to Delphi three times, though I couldn't remember
going there at all since I was twelve. And then I saw the water
swirling around my feet, dragging me down..."

And as Alex remembers, more of Riel's memories come
back to him. Yes, this prophecy that frightened Riel still
swirls in Alex's confused memories of shining gods and rushing waters. And so does the memory of the Spirit Eaters and
how they came to be through the Fountain of Youth. They
are *things* that crave, desire...and devour. Riel was not al-

ways a god of vengeance and evil. Once he, too, longed to do what was right. To become a hero. And so he'd destroyed the fountain that humanity had thought was a gift but had only cursed them with terror.

A horror clutches Alexander's insides with icy hands, as suddenly he knows. He remembers that Riel tossed aside news of the new rise of the Spirit Eaters with cold indifference. It hadn't mattered to Riel, as he planned to rejoin the gods long before the loathsome creatures ever got near him.

"The Spirit Eaters," Alex says. "They still roam, and they will destroy our world if they are not stopped." The truth feels more certain with every word.

Silence hovers over them. The angry bray of a donkey floats in through the window, followed by the loud curses of a man, and for a moment, Alex marvels at the strangeness that life seems to go on, despite everything that has just happened. That all men, all mortals, are going about their ways without ever sensing that the world as they know it was just in danger—and still very much might be.

But as he looks at Kat's and Heph's faces, twin expressions of concern on them, Alex no longer feels afraid. Instead, a surge of love for both of them rushes through him. Even with Riel truly dead, the Age of Man or the Age of Monsters has yet to be determined. They must battle, and the victor will decide the fate of the world, both known and unknown.

He looks between his closest friend and his sister, a new understanding of what they must do dawning on him.

"The gods are gone," Alexander tells them. "It's up to us now."

★ ★ ★ ★ ★

ACKNOWLEDGMENTS

ALL AUTHORS HAVE THEIR DAILY WRITING ROU-
tine. Mine is to sit in an absolutely silent office, soaking in the
energy of ancient statues and antique paintings, with several
cats in baskets on my desk. The cats look out the wide window at birds pecking away at the bird feeder while I look at
my keyboard as I peck away at my writing.

While I revel in the solitude, it's a great comfort to know
that I am supported by an incredibly talented team of people.
Thanks once again to Paper Lantern Lit, whose cofounders,
Lauren Oliver and Lexa Hillyer, and editor, Kamilla Benko,
have helped me so greatly in bringing Alexander and his
friends (and enemies!) to life. It's a joy to work with you!

Thanks also to Adam Silvera, marketing guru, and Diana
Sousa for helping me with social media. I am grateful to my
courtly agent, Stephen Barbara of Inkwell Management, for
his continued support, and to Jess Regel of the Foundry Lit-
erary Agency for all those foreign sales, which make it possible for the Pegasus to fly in several languages.

At Harlequin TEEN, thanks go to my eagle-eyed editor Natashya Wilson, who catches *everything* and asks all the
right questions. A heartfelt thanks to assistant editor Lauren

Smulski, to marketing manager Bryn Collier and to my delightfully fun publicists, Siena Koncsol and Shara Alexander, as well as Evan Brown and Amy Jones.

AUTHOR'S NOTE

ANCIENT GREECE WAS A WORLD ALIVE WITH myths, gods, and magic. There might be a nymph in that tree, a sprite in the pond, and a monster on the mountain. Many of these beliefs were rooted at least partially in facts that—without modern science—were misinterpreted.

The legend of the hydra—a serpentine water monster with multiple heads—goes back to the dawn of ancient Greek myth. In one well-known tale, the Greek goddess Hera, jealous of Heracles, her husband's bastard son, sent a hydra to kill him, but the hero succeeded in slaying the monster. In some myths, each time one of the hydra's heads was cut off, two sprouted from the stump, unless someone was standing by with a torch handy to cauterize the wound.

It is likely that ancient myths of multiple-headed creatures like the hydra and Cerberus—the three-headed dog guarding the gates of Hades—as well as griffins, dragons, and giants, come from fossils the ancients unearthed. They were always quarrying stone for all those temples and palaces and often came across fossilized remains. When several creatures died together, sometimes the heads and necks are visible, but there appears to be only one body. Sometimes the head of one creature appears to be on the body of a different species entirely.

Ancient people had no idea the bones were millions of years old. They believed they were fairly recent and, therefore, it was only logical to suppose that such creatures still existed. Birth defects, too, must have fueled these myths. If a goat can be born with one eye in the middle of its head, or with two heads, or extra limbs, why couldn't other creatures? Or humans?

As for hybrid human-animal creatures such as mermaids, centaurs, sphinxes, and harpies, these stories were probably based on prehistoric shamanistic traditions in which priests and priestesses would enter the minds and bodies of animals and take on their powerful energy. Snake Blood Magic, if you will.

Another myth—that of Atlantis—was much more recent, only a generation before Alexander's time. The Greek philosopher Plato (circa 428–347 BC)—Aristotle's teacher—first wrote of the island's cataclysmic destruction in his dialog, *Critias*:

> But afterwards there occurred violent earthquakes and floods; and in a single day and night of misfortune all your warlike men in a body sank into the earth, and the island of Atlantis in like manner disappeared in the depths of the sea.

From Plato's time on, people were divided as to whether he was referring to a real island or speaking metaphorically. Plato had studied for many years in Egypt with priests who reputedly knew more of civilization's history than any other people on earth.

I personally believe the myth of Atlantis, like the legend of Troy, could be a dim memory of the end of the dazzling, sophisticated Bronze Age in about 1200 BC, and the coming of the Dark Age when technology, trade, lifestyle, and literacy all took a nosedive. Archaeologists have confirmed that earthquakes, fire, tsunamis, warfare, starvation, mass migration, and epidemics caused the downfall of all the Eastern Mediterranean civilizations—Hittite, Minoan, Mycenaean, Cypriot, Syrian—except for Egypt. The Biblical stories of Jews leaving Egypt, the nine plagues of Moses, and the conquest of the Promised Land are all part of the environmental and societal upheavals that remained, a thousand years later, a dull ache in the soul of man for the loss of a golden age.

I have based Kat and Heph's Atlantean Mechanism on the Antikythera mechanism, an ancient analog computer found by Greek sponge divers in a shipwreck in 148 feet of water off the island of Antikythera in April 1900. Hauled up as a lump of corroded bronze and rotten wood, archaeologists set it aside while they glued together the chunks of ancient statues found in the same shipwreck.

Two years later, when they finally got around to studying the lump, they got the shock of their lives. Originally housed in a protective wooden box, the intricate clockwork mechanism featured at least thirty interconnecting bronze gears and a hand crank. The largest gear was almost six inches in diameter and had 223 teeth. The 1902 researchers were so amazed they decided it hadn't come from the shipwreck at all, but was something far more recent that had been dropped on top of it by a passing boat. It wasn't until the 1950s that anyone took it out of storage and dusted it off for a new look.

As far as scientists can tell today, the mechanism was used to predict eclipses and the positions of the sun, moon, and stars to set the calendar, including the proper timing of the Olympic Games. Scientists have dated the mechanism to about 200 BC, and the instructions inscribed on the bronze are in the common ancient Greek dialect of the time. Though it is unique in the world now, experts believe there were many such mechanisms at the time—this clearly wasn't a prototype—and at some point the technology was lost.

Unfortunately, bronze—because of its usefulness in

weapons—was often the first thing melted down when trouble loomed on the horizon. Visit any ancient Greek or Roman city still standing and you will see long rows of empty stone pedestals on main thoroughfares, but all the bronze statues that once graced them have been hauled off and melted down. Those few remaining bronze statues in museums today were found either in shipwrecks or in the buried cities of Pompeii and Herculaneum.

The land of the Lotus-eaters, where Odysseus landed with his men on the way home from Troy, is called Djerba now, and sits off the coast of Tunisia. In antiquity, it was called Meninx. Lotus plants reportedly covered the island, causing those who ate them to fall into a dazed stupor. We can only wonder if, for a time, the island served as a kind of crack house where addicts indulged their dirty habits away from the eyes of decent folk.

Alexander's half sister, Cynane, did marry Amyntas, her cousin, though on her father's side, a member of the Macedonian—not Dardanian—royal family. We don't know if Amyntas was mad, but whatever he was, Cyn was delighted to find herself a young and merry widow, and never remarried, no matter how glittering the offers that came her way.

The second-century AD Macedonian historian Polyaenus wrote:

> Cynane, the daughter of Philip, was famous for her military knowledge: she conducted armies, and in the field charged at the head of them. In an engagement with the Illyrians, she with her own hand slew Caeria their queen; and with great slaughter defeated the Illyrian army.

The wedding of King Philip and Cleopatra Eurydice of the House of Attalid did occur, much as I have written it. The Greek historian Plutarch (45–120 AD) wrote that Olympias, "a woman of a jealous and implacable temper," was behind much of the family discord, and "exasperated Alexander against his father." Plutarch explained:

> At the wedding of Cleopatra, whom Philip fell in love with and married, she being much too young for him, her uncle Attalus in his drink desired the Macedonians would implore the gods to give them a lawful successor to the kingdom by his niece. This so irritated Alexander, that throwing one of the cups at his head, "You villain," said he, "what, am I then a bastard?"
>
> Then Philip, taking Attalus's part, rose up and would have run his son through, but by good fortune for them both, either his over-hasty rage or the wine he had drunk, made his foot slip, so that he fell down on the floor. At which Alexander reproachfully insulted over him: "See there," said he, "the man who makes preparations to pass out of Europe and into Asia, overturned in passing from one seat to another." After this debauch, he and his mother Olympias withdrew from Philip's company...

We can only imagine that during the debauch there was a good old-fashioned ancient Greek food fight, as I have portrayed.

Delphi was a place of awe-inspiring religious veneration, just as Jerusalem, Rome, and Mecca are today, drawing pilgrims from all over the world. The city was as I have described it: one of the most magnificent sights of the ancient world. Even today, its ruins, surrounded by rugged mountains and dramatically sloping hills, pulsate with a kind of divine energy, as if it is the one spot on earth the ancient Greek gods have not utterly abandoned.

The tale of the oracle begins with a flock of playful goats, who liked to frolic over a chasm in the rock. One day the goatherd stuck his head into the cleft, breathed in strange fumes, and fell into a trance. To his surprise, he could predict the future. In about 1600 BC, a shrine was built on the site sacred to Gaia, goddess of the Earth, served by priestesses, but in a sign of things to come, the god Apollo took it from her around 800 BC. The conqueror kept the women, however, to serve him, as male conquerors always do. I believe this story echoes the ancients' path from worshipping the fertile female energy of the earth to the warrior gods of the sky, a slide from a matriarchal to a patriarchal society.

Confirming the goatherd's experience, recent excavations have found two major fault lines that crossed each other below the temple of Apollo, probably right below the oracular chamber. (Scientists are not certain, because the chamber was obliterated when the two faults rubbed against each other, but they have a good idea.) They also found that the area below the temple was crisscrossed with passages, caves, and pools of gaseous spring water, just as Jacob himself discovered. It is likely that the oracle inhaled gases that made her hallucinate and chatter uncontrollably.

Modern researchers debate what kind of gas it may have been. The site of Apollo's temple is, perhaps, the most geologically active in the world, and the gas vents of the ancient era have been rerouted deep in the earth. Some scientists speculate that the hallucinogenic fumes came not from gas but from toxic oleander plants burned in a brazier in a chamber below the oracle's prophecy room that floated up through a grate in the floor. And, indeed, archaeologists have found an area below what they think was the location of the oracular chamber that would have served this purpose perfectly.

Plutarch, who spent the last thirty years of his life serving as a priest in the temple, reported a sweet smell when the "deity" was present, but whether it was from ethylene gas or oleander plants is impossible to say.

The first Pythias, according to the Greek historian Diodorus (90 BC–30 BC), were young virgins—much like our Pythia—as Apollo wanted only pure vessels to speak through. But then:

> Echecrates the Thessalian, having arrived at the shrine and beheld the virgin who uttered the oracle, became enamored of her because of her beauty, carried her away and violated her; and that the Delphians because of this deplorable occurrence passed a law that in the future a virgin should no longer prophesy but that an elderly woman of fifty would declare the Oracles and that she would be dressed in the costume of a virgin, as a sort of reminder of the prophetess of olden times.

There is debate, too, on how the Pythia gave her prophecies. Some ancient sources relate that she babbled incoherently, while priests "translated" and wrote down the predictions. Other ancient writers state that she spoke clearly or even in the pure poetry of dactylic hexameters. Given that hundreds of priestesses prophesied over a period of two thousand years, it is safe to say the manner of delivery varied.

Before prophesying, the Pythia would bathe naked in the Castalian Spring, which was just as Jacob found it. It is still there, but depressingly, most of the sacred water has been siphoned off to provide for the inhabitants of modern Delphi just outside the ruins, whose bars, hotels, and souvenir shops cater to tourists.

The oracle of Delphi prophesied until 390 AD, when the Roman emperor Theodosius I destroyed the temple to stamp out the dangers of paganism. Interestingly, early Christians didn't doubt the existence of gods and goddesses, oracles and centaurs, but saw them all as powerful demons leading people away from the straight and narrow path of Christ.

One thing all sources, ancient and modern, agree on is that you couldn't trust a Delphic prophecy. Even though it might come true in the end, it won't occur in the way you thought it would. This fact is best illustrated by the story of King Croesus of Lydia (595-547 BC), who sent a messenger to Delphi asking if he should go to war against the Persian Empire. The messenger brought back the following prophecy: "If Croesus goes to war, he will destroy a great empire."

Delighted that he would finally bring down his dangerously ambitious neighbors, Croesus beefed up his army, declared war, and lost. The oracle was right. A great empire was destroyed, but it was Croesus's empire, not the Persians'.

Perhaps the most important aspect of the Delphic Temple of Apollo was the inscription "Know Thyself" chiseled in large letters on its pediment, which is, after all, the best way of truly predicting your future.

Thank you for reading REIGN OF SERPENTS!
What will happen next to Prince Alex and his friends
and enemies as the Spirit Eaters rise and war looms ever closer?
Don't miss the final magical and exhilarating adventure in
THE BLOOD OF GODS AND ROYALS *series,*
DAWN OF LEGENDS,
only from Eleanor Herman and Harlequin TEEN!